SCENT OF JUSTICE  CHRISTIAN ROMANTIC SUSPENSE

DEADLY TRACKS

JENNIFER CHASTAIN
LISA PHILLIPS
KARI TRUMBO

Do you love anthologies?

Sign up for the Two Dogs Newsletter to stay up-to-date on upcoming collections and releases, as well as news from our partner authors that have been included in previous releases! Scan or tap the QR code below.

FATAL ENCORE

JENNIFER CHASTAIN

CHAPTER ONE

The late September Georgia night air shimmered in the twilight, humming with laughter and carnival lights. An undercurrent of excitement rippled through the crowd—or maybe it was danger humming beneath the strung bulbs and the distant mechanical whir of gears from the carnival rides. Caleb Hunter felt all of it too...he just never trusted it completely. Six years in the Army, patrolling the open deserts of Iraq, had wired his instincts tight. Open-air venues meant exposure. No cover. Too many variables. Too many ways for a peaceful night to fracture.

Now, as a K-9 officer with the Willow Creek Sheriff's Department, Caleb usually appreciated the quieter rhythm of small-town life. It was steady, familiar, predictable. But fairs were a different animal. Even if he couldn't remember the last time he'd come to one just for fun. Willow Creek was the only home he'd ever known outside of those years in uniform. Beside him, Rider worked the midway with effortless focus, sweeping arcs through drifting red-clay dust, nose low, ears sharp, every inch the dog Caleb trusted more than himself some days.

A warm breeze, with a hint of rain, ruffled his K-9 partner's fur. A bead of sweat rolled down his back and he couldn't wait to remove the heavy police vest. September in Georgia offered no relief from the sweltering humidity.

The savory-sweet aromas of hot, buttered popcorn, corn dogs and funnel cake teased his senses. Happier times when he and his high school best friend would eat all the deep-fried foods and cotton candy. Now, he watched his diet. No sugar, no excessive carbs. He stuck to his food plan. If the military taught him anything, it was discipline. In his work life and personal life. As a K-9 officer, he prided himself on being in top shape.

His stomach growled and Rider looked up at him with large brown eyes.

Rider whimpered and Caleb patted his head. "Sorry boy, no snacks today. We're on duty."

The German Shepherd tilted his head to the side as if he understood. They'd been a team for over three years now, ever since Caleb was discharged from the military.

A few clouds scuttled across the clear sky as the sun sank beneath the horizon. The breeze stirred the Edison lights strung across the midway, their warm glow flickering to life one by one.

He blinked against the glow of the ferris wheel, but his mind flickered back to that late September day ten years ago when he and Shelby were dating, of simpler times. Excited to head to the fair, he drove his dad's pick-up truck, a pocket full of cash from his summer job ready to spend on his girlfriend. A man's heart never forgets his first love or his first kiss. Her lips tasting of yellow mustard and the hot pretzel they shared.

"Hunter! Wait up!" Caleb tugged lightly on Rider's leash and the dog obeyed, slowing his trot to a slow walk, keeping close to Caleb's right leg, tongue lolling. It almost looked like his K-9 was enjoying the fair more than he was. They had a job to do, not lose themselves in corn dogs and cotton candy.

"You're a hard one to catch up to. What's the rush?" Micah

Bristow jogged to a stop beside him, red clay dust curling around their boots.

Caleb stopped in front of the ferris wheel, a crowd queueing up to ride. The tinny sounds of piped in calliope music competed with the garish flashing lights arching over the entry. He and Rider scanned the bustling midway. "Just doing a perimeter check," he said, voice steady even as his gaze swept the crowd. Rider sat beside him, nose twitching as the aroma of hamburgers and donuts wafted on the breeze.

Micah snorted. "Perimeter check, my foot. You're looking for the funnel cake stand." Caleb gave him a flat look. "Not exactly part of my nutrition plan."

"Man, live a little," Micah said, brushing a streak of red clay dust off his sleeve. "It's one donut and you're not in basic training."

"Just doing my job," Caleb said, scanning the crowded midway. "Keeping Willow Creek safe from funnel-cake crimes."

"Real menace, that powdered sugar." Micah grinned, shoving his hands into his vest pockets. "You could at least pretend you're having fun. It's the county fair, not a funeral."

Caleb's lips twitched, almost a smile. "Yeah, tell that to my former commanding officer. He'd rise from the grave if he saw me with fried Oreos."

"We live in the South, dude. Fried food is a way of life." Micah waved at a little girl with a bright red balloon stringing along behind her, her parents pushing a stroller.

"We're on duty," Caleb reminded him.

"You sound like my granddad. Lighten up before your face cracks."

Caleb exhaled a short laugh despite himself. Rider's tail thumped once, as if seconding the motion. "I know, buddy, that funnel cake does smell good." Rider's tongue hung out of the side of his mouth. In this Georgia heat, they both needed water before a sugar rush.

Rider's ears pricked, nose working the air as they moved toward the grandstand. A cacophony of sounds collided with the carousel music, the barkers hawking the carnival games and the happy shouts of children riding the tilt-a-whirl. The dog's muscles rippled beneath his dark brown coat, alert but calm, the picture of control. The pair blended in easily among fairgoers, just two officers keeping an eye on things.

Then Caleb heard it, music drifting over the crowd, low at first, then swelling into a melody he knew by heart. He froze mid-step.

A voice, husky and smooth, laced with a hint of sorrow and sunlight. Shelby Lane.

He hadn't heard that voice live in nearly ten years, but time hadn't dulled the way it hit him. The song was new, something about coming home and finding forgiveness, but her tone carried the same warmth that used to undo him.

Micah followed his line of sight toward the stage. "Well, what do you know? Didn't know Willow Creek's own star was back in town. Did you?"

Caleb's jaw tightened. "Nope." Which was a lie and why he tried to get out of this duty. But that was the hazard of being on a small-town force. Two K-9s and limited manpower. He forced the one word out. He would've asked to trade patrols with another officer if he'd known she'd be here.

Although he couldn't keep running away.

Under the string of Edison bulbs, Shelby stood center stage, guitar slung low, golden hair catching the lights like fire. The crowd pressed in close, swaying, singing along. She looked confident, every inch the country star she'd become, but something in her eyes tugged at him. The same quiet sadness he remembered.

Rider gave a soft chuff, sensing his tension. Caleb crouched, resting a hand on the dog's neck. "Easy, boy."

Micah leaned closer. "You okay, man?"

"Yeah." Caleb straightened, but his voice came out rougher than intended. "Let's finish the sweep."

He turned away from the stage, but the lyrics chased him, every note pulling him back to what they'd lost. Back then, he'd left town for the military, thinking distance would protect them both. Instead, it had wrecked them.

Rider suddenly stiffened, ears forward. Caleb's hand tightened instinctively around the leash. The dog's low growl vibrated through his arm.

"What is it, buddy?"

Rider's nose tracked toward the side of the stage, muscles coiled. Caleb's instincts kicked in. The crowd was dense, so dense that he couldn't discern where one shadow started and another ended. Shelby's popularity had grown from small-town girl to popular country music artist. Midway lights cast their garish glow over the entire area. A maintenance worker moved behind the bleachers, carrying a bulky black duffel—nothing unusual. Still, the dog didn't relax.

Micah caught his eye. "You thinking what I'm thinking?"

"Probably." Caleb unclipped his radio. "Unit Two to Command. Possible suspicious package near the north stage entrance. Requesting secondary sweep."

Static crackled in his ear. "Copy that, Unit Two. Keep eyes on it until backup arrives."

Caleb's pulse steadied into the familiar rhythm of focus. Duty before emotion. He didn't let himself look back toward Shelby again. Not yet.

But as Rider sat alert at his side, the faint echo of her voice floated over the midway. For the first time in a long while, Caleb wondered if coming home would cost him more than he'd ever expected.

❖

A lone microphone on a stand and a wooden stool sat in the middle of the stage. Just the way she liked it. Shelby loved playing her guitar for others. Always had. Grandpa said she had a gift from God, although she really wasn't using that gift for Him now, was she?

She inserted the inner ear device in her right ear and plugged in her guitar to the amplifier. She gave her guitar a last-minute tune and then strummed a few chords of her latest chart-topper, *Here's to our love.* It was a soulful, country ballad, written with a certain man in mind.

A gentle wind blew a few leaves across the lip of the stage and she shivered.

"Ready when you are, Ms. Lane." Her sound technician's voice startled her.

"Right." She glanced over her shoulder and looked at her band as her drummer, Jade, tapped out the beat. They sang through the first verse and chorus, the note in her pocket almost searing her skin. Making her distracted.

She should've told Misty, her assistant, about the note. She would, as soon as she completed her set.

The spotlight burned hot against Shelby's skin, but the chill in her chest wouldn't ease. From the stage, the fairgrounds stretched into a blur of faces, smiling, singing, swaying beneath strings of Edison bulbs. Laughter rolled over the crowd like music layered on music, yet beneath it pulsed something else. Unease. Or maybe that was just her heartbeat.

She steadied the microphone. "Thank you, Willow Creek," she said, voice smooth even as her hands trembled around the neck of her guitar. "It's good to be home."

Home. The word caught in her throat. Bittersweet memories burned through her mind. Of happier times. Of laughter as they rode their bikes and swam in the creek. She hadn't stood on this stage since before she left for Nashville, before the music and the heartbreak and all the miles in between. Before all the regrets of the way she left the one boy who captured her heart.

Her gaze swept the crowd and snagged. Near the ferris wheel stood a familiar silhouette. Broad shoulders. Ball cap pulled low. K-9 at his side.

Caleb Hunter.

Her fingers faltered on the chord. Ten years, and she could still pick him out of a hundred faces. The soldier-turned-officer who'd once promised forever with a lopsided grin and a pocket full of dreams. The man who'd left to serve and never really came back. Only he wasn't a boy anymore but a man.

Shelby forced a breath, let it settle into the next lyric. *Coming home means learning to forgive what broke you.* She'd written that line in a motel room at two in the morning, never imagining she'd sing it with him listening.

The crowd cheered as she hit the chorus, but the roar only blurred the edges of her focus. Movement near the stage caught her eye, a man in a dark jacket weaving through the shadows behind the grandstand, where security wasn't stationed. Her pulse spiked. Probably nothing. County fairs were full of harmless chaos. Still, the same prickling at the base of her neck she used to get before a storm returned.

A low bark drifted through the noise, sharp, controlled. Must be Caleb's K-9.

Shelby's strumming hand froze mid-air. The song ended, the final note fading into uneasy silence. For the first time all night, she couldn't tell if the tremor running through her came from the music or from fear. Performing at the fair as a last-minute replacement was a bad idea. And she'd had plenty of those over the years.

She shook off those thoughts. She needed to stay focused. Stay engaged with her audience. That's what they came here to see. Shelby Lane. She'd been crowned the Country Music Artist of the Year.

Applause swelled, then faltered as a murmur rippled through the front rows. People turned, whispering, pointing toward the side of the stage. Shelby blinked against the glare, her vision adjusting just enough to see movement in the wings—security converging near the equipment ramp.

"Everything okay?" she asked into the mic, her voice light, practiced. The crowd laughed nervously, thinking it was part of the show. But something in her gut twisted tight.

The man in the dark jacket vanished behind the speakers.

She set her guitar on the stand, pulse drumming in her ears. "Y'all give a big hand to our local deputies keeping us safe tonight." Her smile was forced.

Then she saw him.

Caleb cut through the crowd, his K-9 pacing perfectly at his side, scanning every shadow. The fair lights painted him in motion, focused, steady, all business. The years had carved strength into his frame, command into his movements. Yet when his gaze lifted, just for a heartbeat, and locked with hers across the venue... time stuttered.

The noise, the lights, the music, it all fell away until it was just Caleb, and the echo of what they'd once been. His radio crackled, loud, overpowering the other sounds.

Shelby flinched at the sound. A uniformed officer waved him toward the north end of the stage. Caleb's jaw tightened as he issued a quiet command to his K-9, then turned away, disappearing into the throng.

The moment shattered, leaving her with nothing but the hum of the amplifiers and the bitter taste of fear.

Someone touched her arm, a stagehand, eyes wide. "Ms. Lane, we need to get you backstage. Now."

Her heart stumbled. "What's going on?"

"Possible threat. They're checking it out, but..."

A low boom cracked the night. Not loud, but enough to send a pulse of panic through the crowd, the metal stage shaking with the impact. Screams rose, echoing off the ferris wheel's flashing lights.

Shelby's breath hitched.

Somewhere beyond the floodlights, the K-9 barked once, sharp and warning.

The crowd rushed the exits, tripping over each other while the deputies tried to keep order. Her stomach churned with the protein shake she'd had before her performance. *This was a dumb idea, Shelby.*

Lights, trusses, and cables littered the backstage area of the portable stage. "Right this way, Ms. Lane." One of the stagehands grabbed her arm and rushed her off the platform and down the steps.

"What's going on?" She glanced around at the chaos. "I need my guitar case!" She ran over and grabbed the case, staring at the ensuing chaos.

"Come on, Shelby, we need to leave." Misty tugged on her arm, but she stood frozen in place.

Shelby nodded, hugging the guitar case against her chest. They slipped past the ropes and headed toward the back gate. The cool breeze kissed her damp skin, a welcome relief from the heat of the stage lights. She took a long breath, the night air thick with popcorn, fried dough, and motor oil from the nearby tractor pull and for a moment, she could almost believe she was seventeen again.

That night came rushing back, vivid as a photograph: Caleb's old pickup parked under the midway lights. His laugh when she got powdered sugar on his shirt. The way he'd kissed her with the taste of mustard and pretzels on her lips, promising her forever.

Forever hadn't lasted long.

The Army had called him away; fame had called her elsewhere. They'd both answered and neither of them had come back the same.

Her throat tightened. She whispered a small prayer. *Lord, I'm grateful for where You've brought me. Please keep everyone safe.*

The fair's cheerful music stuttered to silence, replaced by static over the loudspeakers.

"Everyone stay calm and move toward the exits," a voice commanded.

Caleb was already moving, hand on the dog's harness, weaving through the throng with precise, urgent strides. The German Shepherd barked once, sharp and focused, guiding him toward the commotion.

Shelby's breath hitched. The professional in him, the soldier, the protector, was still there. She wanted to call out, to tell him to be careful, to tell him *she was here*, but her voice stuck in her throat.

Every inch of him looked controlled, disciplined... except for the flicker of recognition that passed between them when their eyes met.

She paused mid-step. The world narrowed until it was just them, the noise of the fair fading into a distant hum.

Shelby's pulse tripped, her breath catching. *After all this time...* Misty gripped her arm. "Shel, we need to keep moving. Now."

Security propelled through the barricade surrounding the midway and away from the danger. A large white tent was staked at the edge of the parking lot.

Shelby took one last look toward the crowd, toward Caleb disappearing into the chaos.

After a decade of silence, fate had thrown them back into each other's orbit.

And deep in her gut, Shelby knew it wasn't chance.

But what was worse? Knowing that coming home wasn't going to be simple. Or that it might not even be safe.

CHAPTER TWO

The blast wasn't loud, but it was wrong. Too heavy, too close, too deliberate.

Caleb's instincts kicked in before the crowd even started screaming. "Rider, heel!"

He pushed through the crush of people, heart pounding, scanning for the source. The sharp tang of burnt fuel mixed with sugar and smoke. Someone knocked into him, a spilled soda soaking his boot, but he didn't slow.

"Hunter to Command," he said into the radio clipped to his vest. "Possible detonation near the main stage. Initiate lock down and get Fire and Rescue on standby."

Static crackled, then the dispatcher's voice came through, tight and controlled. "Copy, Hunter. Containment teams en route."

Rider lunged against the leash, nose to the ground, barking once, deep, focused. Caleb followed the pull. The dog's hackles rose, muscles bunching under the short brown coat. "Micah!" Caleb shouted.

"Here!" His partner's voice answered over the chaos. Micah was already at the north ramp, crouched beside a bulky black duffel half-hidden behind a stack of sound equipment. "Tell me that's just a stagehand's gear," Caleb said, moving in low.

"Wish I could." Micah pointed. A few inches of wire poked from the zipper. "Smells like fuel."

Caleb's stomach dropped. "Back everyone up. Now."

Micah lifted his radio. "Command, we've got a suspicious device, at the north stage ramp. Request bomb squad and EOD techs, immediate."

Caleb scanned the crowd, families ducked behind game booths, a teenager cried as she held on to her boyfriend's hand, popcorn trampled into red clay. The lights still flashed, grotesquely cheerful against the fear rising like smoke. He tracked the edges, watching for secondary devices or movement.

"Secure the performer," Command said through his earpiece. Shelby.

He turned. Through the glare, he saw her near the stage exit, framed by the curtain, wide-eyed, gripping her guitar like a shield. For one second, the years peeled away, and she was eighteen again, sitting on the tailgate of his pickup with mustard on her lips and forever in her smile.

"Not now," he muttered under his breath, pushing through the crowd. Rider paced beside him, matching his urgency.

"Stay back!" he called to a stagehand. "Evacuate this section. Slow, steady, no running!"

When he reached Shelby, she looked pale under the lights, her hand pressed against her collarbone.

"Caleb, what happened?" Her voice trembled, soft and familiar as a song he couldn't stop hearing.

"Could be a device. We're not sure yet." His tone stayed even, all business. He scanned her quickly, no blood, no visible injuries. Relief eased some of the pressure behind his ribs. "I need you to move to the command tent with Deputy Bristow."

Her wide eyes searched his face. "You think someone did this on purpose?"

"I think you need to get clear of the stage."

"Caleb—"

"Shelby." He lowered his voice, the weight in it enough to still her words. "Please."

That one word carried years of silence and everything he hadn't said the night he left.

She paused a moment, as if she wanted to say something else, but then nodded.

"Go on."

She spun on her booted heel, and heaven help him, his eyes never left her as she crossed the lot with Bristow. Only when she vanished inside the command tent did the tension in his chest release, letting him breathe again.

Rider growled low, nose tilting toward the ramp again. Caleb's pulse jumped. He unclipped the dog's harness. "Find it," he ordered, and Rider shot forward, tail stiff, body tense.

Micah's voice came through the radio: "Hunter, EOD's five minutes out. I'm coming back to help with crowd control."

The crowd noise swelled again, shouts, questions, the distant wail of sirens. Caleb dropped to one knee beside the duffel, heart steady now, everything narrowing to focus.

"Everyone stay back!" Micah held out his arms to create a perimeter.

The wire poking from the zipper wasn't attached to anything. A decoy. A distraction. "Micah," he said quietly, "this isn't live."

"You sure?"

He exhaled through his nose. "Yeah. Somebody wanted attention, not casualties."

"Or they're testing response time," Micah said.

Caleb's gut tightened. He zipped the bag closed and stood, scanning the perimeter again. The fairgrounds were chaos, but his mind had already shifted into pattern. Who had access? Who knew Shelby would be here tonight?

He turned just in time to catch the tent flap shifting as Shelby peeked out, her gaze searching from the edge of the crowd. Their eyes met, hers filled with questions, his with answers he wasn't ready to give.

For a heartbeat, the noise dimmed, and it was just her and him. The years between them collapsing into silence.

Then the radio hissed. "All units, perimeter sweep complete. No secondary devices found."

"Hey man, I'm going to check on Shelby." Micah gripped his shoulder. "You okay?"

Caleb nodded once. "Yeah. Make sure she stays in the command center before another round of chaos hits." He swallowed past the ball of dread in his throat. "Shelby's tour bus is probably the safest place for her. I need to clear this first." He looked toward the dark beyond the midway, where shadows gathered near the tree line. Somewhere out there, someone was watching. Waiting.

"I'll let you know when I get there."

He watched as Micah disappeared into the crowd. He brushed a hand absentmindedly down Rider's neck. "Good work, partner."

The dog's tail thumped once, steady and alert.

"What do we have here?" Sheriff Brent Metcalf broke through Caleb's haze.

"Sheriff." He shook Metcalf's hand while Rider nudged his leg. Caleb reached down and gave the dog a treat. "Good boy." Rider inhaled the treat and sat by Caleb's leg. "Small explosive device near the stage. No injuries that we know of."

The sheriff scanned the midway. "Any signs? Notes? Anyone suspicious?"

"Nothing concrete," Caleb said. "Could be a hoax device meant to draw attention or test security response. But Rider alerted and there was residue consistent with accelerant."

Metcalf grunted. "Fire Marshal's team can confirm. We'll treat it like a dry run until proven otherwise." He keyed his shoulder mic. "Dispatch, set a hard perimeter. No one in or out without clearance.

Get Explosives Ordnance to sweep every vendor truck, generator, and stage compartment. Copy?"

"Copy, Sheriff," the dispatcher replied.

Metcalf turned back to Caleb. "Where's the performer now?"

"I had Shelby moved to the command center. Bristow's following up."

"Good." The sheriff removed his ball cap and scratched his head. "Shelby Lane. I've heard of her. She's good."

Just saying her name conjured all sorts of emotions Caleb thought he'd stuffed away, never to resurface.

"Yeah." Caleb dug his toe into the hard packed dirt. When would her memory stop haunting him?

"Anyone else with her?" The sheriff pulled out a small notepad from his shirt pocket.

"I think I saw her with some of her security." Caleb kept his tone neutral, but the sheriff caught the flicker in his eyes.

"You two have history, right?"

"Yes, sir. Grew up here together."

Metcalf nodded slowly. "Good. You'll know her tells if she's hiding something or downplaying a threat. Get her back to her bus and I'll have Detective Barnes come talk to her." He flipped open his notepad, jotting a few notes. "If this was a test run, she might be the target or she might've been the bait. Either way, we're not taking chances." Metcalf raised his voice toward the cluster of deputies nearby. "I want cameras from every booth and ride pulled within the hour. Check for anyone loitering before the show. Get the media cordoned off, no statements until we verify what we're dealing with."

Metcalf turned to Caleb. "Hunter, you and your K-9 are now on personal-protection detail for Ms. Lane. Shadow her until further notice--home, rehearsals, anywhere she goes. I'll get you a rotation partner after the EOD clears the area."

Caleb straightened. "Understood, Sheriff."

Metcalf gave him a hard look. "Keep it professional, son. I know how small towns work and how gossip travels."

"Yes, sir."

Metcalf's expression softened just a fraction. "You've got good instincts, Hunter. Use 'em. Whoever did this wanted to rattle her, maybe draw her out. Let's make sure they don't get another chance."

"Absolutely." Even though he and Shelby had history, he'd make sure this didn't happen again.

"I'm calling the State Bureau of Investigation. If it turns out this wasn't just a firework gone wrong, SBI's taking lead. Until then, we hold the scene."

"Got it."

Metcalf looked like he wanted to say more but simply shook his head. "Bag and tag the evidence. Stay here until CSU arrives." He handed Caleb a roll of evidence bags before heading off toward the command tent.

Caleb snapped on a pair of disposable gloves and crouched beside the duffel. He sealed it inside an evidence bag, careful not to disturb the wiring. A few minutes later, a crime scene tech trudged up, toolbox in hand. "What've we got?" the tech asked. Caleb glanced at his name tag—Hanover.

"Decoy." Caleb passed him the bag. "EOD confirmed it's not live."

Hanover nodded. "Copy that. I'll tag it, shoot a few photos, and log the coordinates." He raised his camera; the shutter clicks echoed in the heavy, emptied air.

Caleb pointed toward a dented trash can about fifty yards away. "You might want to check that, too. Small blast went off near the stage."

"Could've been a firecracker," Hanover muttered, snapping another photo.

"Maybe." Caleb's gaze swept the deserted midway, the trampled popcorn, the toppled barricades, the flickering lights that refused to die. "Or a warning."

Hanover said nothing. Just kept working.

"Rider, heel." The German Shepherd rose immediately, muscles coiled, alert as always. Caleb exhaled, scanning the fairground one last time before heading toward the command center. He turned, the glow of Shelby's tour bus illuminated by streetlights. Her name was scrawled in large letters across the side of the slick, black bus. The air smelled like burnt sugar and smoke, and heavy with questions.

Would she even want talk to him after all these years?

Didn't matter. They'd both have to put their past behind them. Because if someone wanted her scared, or worse, tonight was just the opening act.

🐾

Flashbulbs strobed against the night, painting the fairgrounds in harsh bursts of white. The laughter and music were gone, replaced by shouts, sirens, and the shrill hum of camera drones hovering overhead.

Shelby blinked against the glare as she stepped out from the command center tent. Her boots stirred up the packed red clay dirt and she sneezed. The air still smelled like smoke.

"Ms. Lane! Shelby!" Reporters pressed forward, voices overlapping—sharp and hungry.

"Were you the target?"

"Did you know about the bomb?"

"Is this connected to your benefit concert next week?"

She froze, every muscle tight. Someone's mic nearly hit her in the chin. The crowd noise swelled, closing in, and suddenly it felt like she was back under those lights again, trapped onstage, nowhere to run.

"Back up!" Deputy Bristow barked, stepping between her and the reporters. "Give her space!"

The line barely held. Flashes kept exploding. Shelby held a hand up to her eyes, trying to shield them.

And then—"Sheriff's office. Step back."

That voice.

Low, steady, commanding. It cut through the chaos like a blade.

She turned, heartbeat slamming into her ribs.

Caleb Hunter strode toward her, K-9 pacing perfectly at his side, eyes scanning the crowd like he could see every threat before it happened. His vest still bore traces of dust from the explosion site, and under the harsh lights, he looked carved from the same steel as the badge on his chest.

Her pulse tripped. "Caleb?"

"Ms. Lane," he said evenly, professional. "We need to move you to a secure location."

Before she could answer, Sheriff Metcalf appeared beside him, barking orders to a cluster of deputies. "Lock down the perimeter. Pull every camera feed from the fairgrounds. Nobody leaves without a statement." Then his attention swung to her. "Ms. Lane, you'll be escorted off-site under protective detail."

Her gaze snapped to Caleb. "Protective detail?"

"Hunter's your lead," Metcalf said. "He and his K-9 will stay with you until we know who planted that device."

For a second, she thought she'd misheard. "You're assigning *him*?"

Metcalf didn't flinch. "He's the best handler we've got. You'll be safe with him."

Safe. The word twisted in her chest. Caleb Hunter was a lot of things, steady, disciplined, infuriatingly composed, but *safe* had never been one of them. Not when it came to her heart. "Sheriff, I have a security detail. I don't need—"

"Yes, you do," Metcalf cut in, voice hard. "Until my office clears this as a prank, you follow his lead. That's not up for debate."

Shelby's jaw tightened. The cameras were still flashing, and she could feel her control slipping, her image, her calm, her carefully curated distance. All of it unraveling in front of half the county.

Caleb met her eyes, dark, unreadable, a thousand unsaid things simmering beneath the surface. "We'll get you out of here quietly," he said.

Quietly. Like the past ten years hadn't just detonated in front of them.

Reporters shouted more questions, but they blurred together as Caleb guided her toward the patrol SUV. His hand brushed her elbow, impersonal, but it sent heat spiraling up her arm all the same. The K-9 trotted close, tail low, a silent shadow between them and the chaos. "Sheriff," Caleb called over his shoulder. "We'll radio once we're secure."

Metcalf nodded. "Stay with her, Hunter. Eyes open."

Shelby exhaled shakily as Caleb opened the passenger door. "Guess I don't get a say in this?"

His tone was quiet, almost gentle. "Not tonight."

Her pulse stuttered. He helped her inside, closed the door, and the noise outside dimmed to a distant roar. "Where's my guitar case?"

"I stowed it in the cargo area. It's fine."

As the SUV pulled away, she caught a final glimpse of the flashing lights in the rearview mirror. The dark outline of Caleb beside her, eyes on the service road, jaw tight, the weight of ten lost years hanging thick between them.

"Where are we going?" She watched a muscle twitch in his jaw.

"Your bus."

"You're kidding, right?"

He parked the SUV behind the bus, away from prying eyes of the press, and cut the engine. "Afraid not. At least, we'll have a contained space."

Her heart beat out an unsteady rhythm and she swallowed against the panic rising. *Contained space.*

Caleb stood at the open bus door, a sympathetic smile on his face. "Coming?" She slowly opened the patrol car's door and stuffed back all her fear. She could do this. The door to the tour bus closed with a dull, final thud.

Instantly, the chaos outside muffled, the hum of generators, the wail of sirens, all pressed into a faint, distorted roar behind the glass. Inside, it smelled faintly of coffee, hairspray, and the lingering sweetness of her last performance.

Shelby sank onto the built-in sofa, arms wrapped around herself. The sequins on her top scratched her skin as she exhaled. "I can't believe this is happening," she whispered.

Caleb stood just inside the doorway and removed his ball cap, his vest still streaked with red clay. The K-9, Rider, sat obediently at his heel, eyes scanning the interior like it was another crime scene.

She looked up at him, still trying to process the words she'd heard outside. "You're seriously staying with me?"

"Until further notice," he said, his tone measured. "Sheriff's orders."

Her laugh came out tight, humorless. "Of course. Sheriff's orders. You always were good at following the rules."

He didn't rise to the bait. He just scanned the space, every movement efficient, checking exits, curtains, corners. She remembered that same focus from before, when they were just kids and he'd volunteered for the Army because he'd needed to *do something right.*

"Caleb." Her voice softened, unwilling but honest. "You can't be serious about this. I've got a team, security, drivers—"

"Who weren't trained to handle explosives or crowd panic," he said quietly. "I was."

She flinched, turned away. Through the tinted window, she could still see the reflection of camera lights flaring like heat lightning in the distance. "They're out there, expecting me to say something. When they find out where I am, they'll surround this bus. And I..." she swallowed back the rest of what she really wanted to say. *I'm terrified.*

"Let them wait. You don't have to give a statement tonight. Or even tomorrow." She looked back at him sharply. "That's easy for you to say."

His gaze met hers, dark and steady. "Nothing about this is easy."

The silence stretched before them like an endless night. Only Rider's soft panting filled the space.

"I, uh, need to call in." He walked to the back of the bus. She heard his voice low and urgent. "Yeah, we're at her bus. Can you send a couple of other officers, just in case?" He paused, his voice receding the further he moved toward the back of the bus. "But I don't think she needs to talk to the press." His voice faded as he entered her bedroom, the door closing with a soft click.

Just in case... what? Another bomb threat, only this time the person who targeted her wouldn't miss. She shuddered and pressed her face into her bent knees. Maybe this was all a bad dream. Rider tilted his head as if trying to get a read on her.

Caleb returned. "All set."

She pushed a hand through her hair, dislodging a few stubborn curls. "You shouldn't be here, Caleb. Not after everything that happened back then..." She trailed off, unable to finish.

Caleb leaned against the counter, shoulders tense, gaze fixed somewhere past her. "I know," he said. "But walking away felt worse."

Her breath caught. "You don't have to act like this is just protocol."

"I'm not."

"Then what are you doing here, Caleb?"

He looked at her then, really looked at her, and something raw flickered across his face. "Trying to do the one thing I failed at before."

The silence pressed in and Shelby swallowed. "You promised you'd keep us safe," she said softly. "Both of us." Her voice didn't accuse. It remembered.

"And I've been living with what happened ever since."

That landed like a body blow. He didn't move, didn't speak, but his eyes flickered with guilt, pain, and something raw he didn't want her to see.

Rider shifted, sensing the change in energy. Caleb crouched to calm him, running a steady hand down the dog's back. "Easy, boy." Then, quieter, almost to himself: "We both made choices back then. Tonight isn't about that."

She watched him, throat tightening. "Maybe not for you."

He straightened, the air between them heavy with everything they hadn't said.

Outside, someone banged on the bus door. "Ms. Lane! There's a detective that needs to talk to you."

Caleb's gaze didn't waver. "The detective will take your statement in here. For now, stay put."

"Since when do you get to tell me what to do?"

"Since someone decided to plant a bomb less than fifty feet from where you were standing."

The sharpness in his tone silenced her. For a long second, neither of them moved.

Then Rider gave a soft, low whine, breaking the spell. Caleb reached for the leash clipped to his vest. "I'll sweep the perimeter. Lock this door behind me. No one comes in unless I clear them."

Her throat was dry as a piece of sandpaper. "And if I say no?"

His expression softened, just barely. "Then I'll still do it."

He opened the door and stepped out, and for a moment, the light from the flood lamps caught the edge of his uniform before it shut again, sealing her inside. Shelby leaned back against the seat cushion, pulse hammering.

She'd spent ten years building a life that didn't include him. And in one night, he'd walked back in, uniform, badge, and all, just like she'd never really let him go.

CHAPTER THREE

The night air felt heavier now. Too quiet after the chaos. Or maybe it was simply the humidity of the hot day pressing down. But that didn't explain why the echo of Shelby's shaken voice still clung to him, even though she was safe inside, giving her statement to the detective.

The noise had thinned to a low mechanical hum, generators, distant radios, the pop of camera flashes still bleeding through the fairground fence. Caleb's pulse finally slowed, but his mind hadn't stopped running since the blast. Caleb adjusted the tactical vest and scanned the fairground's shadowed perimeter. He swept his flashlight in an arch along the fence line behind the stage. Candy wrappers and empty paper cups tumbled across the cracked asphalt. Rider padded a few feet ahead, nose low, tail rigid, following a scent trail—alert mode. Searching for clues that only he could sniff out. The K-9 lived for this kind of activity.

Rider paused, a low growl emanating from him and then sat beside Caleb and whined.

"Easy, boy," Caleb murmured, lightly fisting the leash. He glanced over his shoulder, a familiar unease zipping through him.

"You felt it too." The dog sneezed once, and Caleb stifled a laugh. "Okay, I get it. One more sweep, then we call it."

He couldn't shake the memory of Shelby's wide eyes when he'd told her to stay inside. He'd seen that look before, on her sister's face the night the ice gave way. A soundless scream, the rush of freezing water, his own hands going numb as he tried to pull her out.

He swallowed hard. Not now. Focus.

He could still see Shelby's face—the way she tried to look steady, arms wrapped tight around herself, refusing to let fear show. He knew that expression all too well. It was the same brave, brittle mask she wore the night he tried to save her little sister and the ice gave way beneath them.

That memory was burned into his mind. All these years later and her sister's death still haunted him. Made him physically sick to think that he failed his best friend. His throat tightened. He'd tried. He'd been too far, too slow, his frozen fingers unable to pull Ava to safety. Her brother had never forgiven him. Maybe she never would either.

He exhaled once. A soft night breeze swept across his heated skin, and he shivered. The last remnants of gunpowder from the fireworks hung in the air. A couple of roadies began loading equipment onto a dolly.

Rider stopped suddenly near the back curtain, head lifting, ears pricked. A low rumble vibrated through his chest. Moonlight reflected off the metal stage. Lights and microphones lay in an abandoned heap off to the side. Fur stood at attention along Rider's back.

Caleb halted mid-step. "What is it, boy?" Caleb followed Rider's line of sight. The German Shepherd pawed at a folded piece of paper wedged beneath a sandbag by the amplifier stand.

Caleb's pulse kicked. "Rider, sit." The dog obediently sat as he crouched, tugged on a glove, pulled out an evidence bag from his vest, and slid the note free. The card stock was thick but cheap. Edges bent like someone had gripped it too tightly. He unfolded it and angled his flashlight on the writing. Cheap ink. Block letters scrawled across the front:

SHELBY LANE — READ THIS BEFORE YOU SING AGAIN.

He eased it open, the words inside punching through the quiet.

You can't steal someone's music, their story, and expect a happy ending. The real musician always finishes his composition.

No signature, just a flourish of pen strokes that cut deep into the paper. Caleb stared at the handwriting and frowned. Slanted, aggressive.

He studied the message. The letters were sharp, slanted right, the pen digging deep into the fibers. A memory tugged of an evidence photo he'd seen earlier in the briefing folder from this afternoon.

"Rider," he said softly, setting the note down. "Check." The German Shepherd sniffed, circled once, then sat, tail flicking once, a solid alert.

Caleb's stomach dropped. "You smell something familiar?" Rider huffed, nose pressed against the paper again.

Before he could radio in, footsteps crunched across the dirt. Sheriff Metcalf approached, Deputy Bristow at his side, both still carrying the weight of too many long nights.

"What've you got?" Metcalf asked, voice brimming with tension.

Caleb handed over the evidence bag. "Found under the stage. Addressed to Shelby."

Metcalf shined his flashlight on the message, jaw tightening. "Same tone as the others." Caleb frowned. "Others?"

Bristow flipped open a slim file folder, pulling out several printed photos sealed in plastic sleeves. "Three reports filed over the past six months. Anonymous letters sent to her production company, each signed *The Musician*. We ran them through state databases, nothing solid. No prints, no traceable paper stock. Paper you could buy at any big box store."

He held one next to the note in Caleb's hand. The scrawl was identical, the same long slashes on the *t*, the same furious pressure marks.

"She never mentioned this," Caleb said, more to himself than anyone. Why not? What was she hiding?

Bristow's expression tightened. "Her manager filed the reports, not her. Said they didn't want to spook the fans before the tour."

"Does Shelby know about the threats?" Caleb asked.

Metcalf nodded. "She does."

"Then why…?" Caleb removed his ball cap and ran his hands through his hair.

"From what her manager said, she's not afraid. She thinks these," Metcalf waved the papers, "are the result of jealousy. A prank."

Caleb shook his head. "This is not a prank."

Bristow snorted. "Yeah, well, someone needs to talk to her. She needs to take this threat seriously."

"Any leads as to who might have done this?" Caleb asked.

Metcalf grunted. "Nashville PD didn't have enough to charge anyone. But one name kept showing up."

Caleb looked up. "Who?"

Metcalf flipped the page. "Tyler Meadows. Shelby's ex-songwriting partner. Got tossed from her label after an altercation two years ago."

"He helped her write her first number one hit," Bristow said.

Caleb's pulse kicked.

Bristow continued reading. "They cut him loose and according to Shelby's statement, he wasn't too happy."

Caleb's nerves felt as taut as a guitar string. "And now he's back."

"Maybe," Bristow said. "Or maybe it's someone trying to frame him. But the handwriting…"

"Matches," Caleb finished, glancing at the side-by-side samples. "Same downward stroke pattern. Same pressure on the descenders."

Rider gave a quiet whine beside him, as if sensing his tension. Caleb reached down, resting a steady hand on the dog's neck. "He picked up the same scent on this note that he tracked earlier near the amp cords. If Meadows has been anywhere near that stage, we'll know."

Metcalf nodded once. "Good work. We'll send this to CSU for confirmation, but it's a solid lead. Keep her inside. No leaks to the press."

Caleb's jaw flexed. "Yes, sir."

"Make sure she understands that she is not to go anywhere without you and the dog," Metcalf said.

Even with their history, he'd protect Shelby with his last breath.

As they turned away, he looked back at the stage, the moonlight washing it in sterile white. The note still burned in his mind, every word aimed like a bullet at Shelby.

He rubbed the back of his neck, the weight of old guilt pressing in again. He'd failed once before to save a girl who slipped through the ice while Shelby screamed his name from the bank. He wasn't about to fail again.

He looked down at Rider. "Not this time, partner."

Rider's ears pricked, eyes sharp in the dark. Caleb took one last look toward the tour bus, the glow from its windows steady in the distance.

"Let's finish the sweep," he murmured. "She's counting on us."

Caleb straightened, adrenaline threading through his guilt. Maybe he hadn't been able to save her sister all those years ago, but he'd be danged if he let Shelby down now.

Caleb looked toward the tour bus, its windows dark and reflective, giving nothing away. Still, he knew she was inside. Knew her movements. Knew the weight she carried.

He let out a slow breath and set his hand on Rider's head.

"Not this time, partner," he said quietly. "We're not losing her."

Rider's tail thumped once, as if in agreement.

❧

The air inside the bus felt too still, too close. Shelby wanted to escape from this confined space and run across the Georgia farmland and jump into her mother's arms like she was ten years old. They were only a couple of miles from her family home. But that couldn't happen. Maybe the police would allow her to slide open the windows, inhale fresh air, and not the stale recirculated air.

The hum of the overhead lights was the only sound between her and the detective sitting across the narrow table. She'd introduced herself as Detective Olivia Hanlon, soft-spoken, kind hazel eyes, the type who had probably seen more trauma than she'd ever admit. She'd already asked her the same question three times in three different ways.

"Did you notice anyone unusual before the explosion?" Hanlon quirked one eyebrow, studying Shelby.

This was getting old. How many times could she explain what she didn't see? "Half the county was out there, Detective." Shelby rubbed her temples. "Cameras, fans, vendors, people everywhere. I couldn't even see beyond the front lip of the stage."

"I see." Hanlon's pen paused over her notebook. "Any threats before tonight? Messages? Letters? Emails?"

She shook her head automatically, then hesitated. "Well... there were a few strange things, I guess. Packages that turned out to be nothing. Notes from someone claiming to 'know the truth' about one of my songs. My manager said it was just spam. A hoax."

Hanlon straightened in her seat. "When did this all start?"

Shelby shrugged. "I think my manager mentioned something about a prank six months ago. That he took care of it. Why?"

"You didn't file reports?" The detective didn't look convinced and leaned her forearms on the table.

"How could I if I didn't know?" Hanlon was way too close for Shelby and she settled against the chair back. "I assume my manager handled it. That's why I hired him." Her throat tightened. "I didn't think it mattered, since he told me it was a prank. He said he didn't want any perceived trouble with my concert tour leaked to the press."

The protein shake she chugged earlier before her set churned in her stomach. Her entire career hinged on the success of these tours.

If her sponsors or fans discovered the danger surrounding her concerts, she might as well hang up her guitar and move back home.

Hanlon's expression softened. "I understand. But those notes might matter now."

A soft knock sounded at the door before she could respond, and Detective Hanlon opened the bus door. Humid night air, tinged with a hint of rain swept through the bus. Bristow stepped inside, ball cap held in both hands, and what she assumed was his usual grin was replaced by something grim. "Detective. Ms. Lane." He nodded at Shelby. "You'll want to see this."

He handed Hanlon a plastic evidence sleeve. Inside was a folded card, smudged with red clay. Shelby's breath hitched.

Hanlon unfolded it carefully and read aloud.

You can't steal someone's music, their story, and expect a happy ending. The real musician always finishes his composition. The Real Composer

The words blurred for a second before snapping into focus. The Real Composer.

Her breath hitched and a cold dread shivered through her body. "That was addressed to me?" She pushed out the words through clenched teeth.

Bristow nodded. "Found it under the stage. Sheriff Metcalf's comparing it to previous notes that were found. Sending it off for analysis. It appears to be the same handwriting."

Hanlon's brows furrowed. "Previous?" The detective's eyes darted between the two of them.

Bristow exhaled, weariness in every movement. "Yeah. Three incidents, from the last six months. All notes mailed to Ms. Lane's management office. Her manager, Eric Lane, thought that he should handle the notes quietly. Not let Ms. Lane see them because it might upset her. He said, and I quote, 'she would've canceled the tour'. Not telling Ms. Lane worked for a while, until tonight."

Shelby stared at him, the air punching from her lungs. "Eric knew? What about the Nashville police?" She stood and paced the narrow bus aisle, hands clenched. How could her brother keep this information from her?

Bristow nodded once. "Yeah, they were made aware of the notes. Your manager filed through the label's security firm. Said you didn't need to be involved." He hesitated, lowering his voice. "We contacted Nashville PD and they told us that they didn't have enough to charge anyone, but one name kept showing up. Tyler Meadows."

She abruptly stopped. For a second, the world tilted and she grabbed the edge of the table. *No.* The name was a ghost from another lifetime, whiskey-stained notebook pages, late nights in Nashville, promises that turned to poison.

She sank back against the sofa. "That's impossible. Tyler's gone. He hasn't tried to contact me since…" She stopped herself before the word *lawsuit* could escape. She cradled her head in her hands and massaged her temples. *This couldn't be happening.*

Hanlon set the evidence sleeve on the table. "The handwriting matches his old lyric drafts, Ms. Lane. It's a solid lead, but we'll verify."

A dull ringing filled her ears. She could almost hear Caleb's voice outside the door, low and steady, giving orders, the sound of safety and danger at the same time. "Is Caleb…Deputy Hunter…does he know?" she asked quietly.

"Yeah," Bristow said. "He's the one who found the note. His K-9 caught the same scent we lifted off the abandoned backpack found near the stage. It's the same scent from the old evidence bag."

Something inside her cracked. "So he's been here," she whispered. "Watching."

Hanlon exchanged a look with Bristow but didn't answer. "We'll post deputies around the perimeter for the night. You should stay inside. Tomorrow, we'll review security footage from the fairgrounds."

She nodded, though she barely heard him. Her gaze drifted to the window. Through the blinds, she could make out the silhouette of Caleb and his dog moving through the floodlight glare. Two shadows methodically circling her world, keeping the monsters out. "Detective?" she said softly, when Hanlon started to rise. "Can you leave the light on?"

She paused, understanding in her eyes. "Of course." Detective Hanlon held out a business card. "My cell number is on the back. Call me if you see or hear anything."

Shelby slowly reached for the card and tucked it into the pocket of her jeans. "Thank you." After the door clicked shut, Shelby sank to her knees beside the couch. *God, what am I going to do now?* She hadn't prayed in so long, would He even hear her?

The silence closed in on her, suffocating and warm, until she felt something warm nudge her arm. Rider sat next her, those large brown eyes of his seeming to understand. "Hey boy."

He licked the side of her face and she grimaced. "You should know, I don't let just any old boy kiss me." She smiled and pressed her forehead against Rider's warm fur. After the evening's excitement and Rider's warmth, a wave of sleepiness rolled over her. "Where's Caleb?"

The dog gave a quiet whine, as if in answer.

"Oh, I see, Caleb sent you inside to watch me."

Rider let out a soft bark and she ruffled his fur.

"What do you know that I don't?" Her pulse slowed just enough to breathe. "Caleb's still outside, isn't he?" she whispered.

Outside, Caleb's voice carried faintly through the night, infusing her with warmth and a sense of protection.

For the first time in ten years, she wasn't running.

But she couldn't shake the thought that someone else still was, and this time, they were running straight toward her.

CHAPTER FOUR

The night air pressed thick and heavy, humid with the odor of dry clay, diesel engines, and the unmistakable mixture found at county fairs. The smells were comforting, wrapping him in warm thoughts of simpler times. Times when life moved slow and his favorite girl held his hand. A lone owl hooted from the trees, probably looking for a nighttime snack. A full moon disappeared behind a bank of clouds, bringing with it a gentle breeze and a hint of rain.

Floodlights bleached the fairground into stark contrast, where every shadow was too sharp, every noise magnified. Caleb's radio buzzed with clipped updates from deputies securing the outer fence, but his focus stayed locked on the black tour bus parked in the center of the cordoned lot.

The bus door hissed open. Rider appeared first, alert and ready, then Shelby stepped down behind him. She handed Caleb the leash without a word—like they'd done this a hundred times before.

Her fingers lingered for half a heartbeat. Shelby glanced back at the darkened fairgrounds, then at Caleb, her expression unreadable but careful, as if she were memorizing where he stood.

Caleb closed his fingers around the smooth, leather leash. Solid. Familiar.

"Come on, boy," he said quietly. "Time to work."

Rider shifted instantly, ears high, body aligning with Caleb's. The routine steadied him after the chaos. They moved into patrol mode, Rider's steps measured and silent. Every few feet he paused, nose lifting to sample the air, tail flicking once before pressing on.

Caleb trusted that instinct more than any surveillance feed. He had reason to, his four-legged partner sensed danger he couldn't see.

They swept the radius twice, checked the entry points, watched the detectives come and go. Still, something in his gut refused to settle. Maybe it was seeing that card, the threat written in looping, angry script. Or maybe it was knowing how pale Shelby looked under the floodlights, eyes hollow with shock but still trying to hold herself together for everyone else.

He reached the edge of the bus again and touched the side mirror, cold metal grounding him. "Stay sharp, buddy," he murmured. Rider gave a low whuff in response.

A voice crackled through his earpiece. "Hunter, forensic team confirmed it. Prints and ink match. Meadows."

Caleb froze. He'd seen the social media posts, how Tyler was the one man she once trusted with every lyric, every secret. The one she'd been engaged to but then she abruptly broke off the engagement.

He'd read the reports, the unhinged late-night messages, veiled threats, the kind that never quite met the threshold for charges. The kind that festered quietly until they turned lethal.

"Copy that," he said, though the words tasted like ash.

Tyler Meadows. The idea of that man back in Shelby's orbit twisted something deep in

Caleb's chest. He clenched his jaw and scanned the perimeter again. She'd been through enough tonight. He'd seen it in the tremor of her hands when Bristow passed her that evidence sleeve. The way her body curled in, trying to protect herself. Fear she tried to hide but couldn't quite cage.

He couldn't let that happen again.

"Perimeter clear," he reported, moving toward the bus steps. Rider reached them first, sitting automatically at the door like a sentry carved from muscle and discipline.

A young deputy was stationed in front of the door. "All good? No problems?" Caleb asked.

"None." The deputy shifted his stance. "She's inside, sir. Been quiet."

Caleb rapped twice, waited. When her voice came, soft but steady, it loosened the metal band wrapped tightly around his chest. He straightened, then opened the door and stepped in, instinctively ducking under the low frame.

He paused at the top of the steps and scanned the interior. He'd never been inside a music star's tour bus before. The space smelled faintly of coffee and hairspray and nerves. Loose sheets of music with scratched out lyrics lay scattered over the built-in couch. A half-full water bottle sat on the table. Shelby stood near the window, one hand braced on the glass. Her eyes found him like a lifeline.

"Perimeter's secure," he said. "You're safe for now."

"For now," she echoed, voice thin but controlled.

He hesitated, weighing how much to tell her but she deserved the truth. Caleb studied her for a long beat.

"There's something I didn't want you hearing from anyone else," he murmured.

Shelby nodded once, but her gaze drifted past him, past the bus, as if she were staring at something only she could see.

"Forensics rushed the comparison," he said. "The note. The device. It's not speculation anymore," he said quietly. "It's Tyler."

Her breath hitched. "No." She shook her head, threading her fingers through her tangled hair. "He knew my songs. My notebooks. He sat on that bus and helped me tear verses apart until they bled." Her voice thinned. "He knew how to get inside my head."

Caleb's chest tightened.

"I trusted him with melodies I hadn't even sung yet," she whispered. "With pieces of me I didn't know how to protect." She dragged in a breath that trembled. "This isn't just about the bomb. It's like he rewrote something that was supposed to be ours."

Caleb stepped closer, not touching, but close enough she'd feel him if she swayed. "I won't let him use that against you," he said. "Not again."

"He already did," she whispered. "He—he sent me a message last week. I didn't even open it. I thought he was just being dramatic again."

Caleb wanted to reach for her but stopped himself. This was strictly professional. "You couldn't have known," he said softly. "But from now on, you don't answer anything that comes from him or anyone connected to him. You call me first, understood?" He held out his hand. "Can I see your phone?"

She tugged her phone out of the back pocket of her jeans. "Why?"

He felt her gaze on him. "I'm adding my cell number to your contacts." What he didn't say was, just in case Meadows escalated his threats.

Her eyes flicked up to his. "You're really staying?"

"Yeah," he said, voice low. "I'm not going anywhere."

He watched as she sank onto the couch, hugging a throw pillow with the words "I live for music" across the front.

Rider padded forward and pressed his head against her leg. His dog had never done that before. Rider had a dual purpose, protective duty and detection, but not once in three years had he ever offered comfort to anyone but Caleb.

She dropped to her knees, fingers curling into his fur, whispering something Caleb couldn't quite hear.

He looked away, giving her the illusion of privacy in this confined space, and swept the interior again. He checked the bunks, the small bedroom in the back, the tiny bathroom. He had to stay focused on his job, not allow buried feelings for the girl who got away to muddy his thoughts.

When he turned back, she was watching him.

"Thank you," she said quietly.

He wanted to tell her she didn't have to thank him. That this was his job. That he'd die before letting anything happen to her. But none of those words made it past the lump in his throat.

Instead, he said the only thing that felt safe. "Get some rest, Shelby. We've got a long night ahead."

"I think I'll just rest on the couch out here, if that's okay with you."

It was *very* okay with him. He preferred her staying where he and Rider could see her and alert her if danger arose.

Caleb holstered his sidearm and took a seat near the door, one hand resting on the dog's collar, the leash kept short. Rider settled at Caleb's feet, vigilant eyes tracking every sound outside.

The bus ticked softly as its metal cooled, the faint, uneven pops echoing through the narrow space.

Rider shifted, glanced toward Shelby, and let out a low whine.

Caleb followed the look. Shelby lay on the built-in couch only a few feet away, too still, her hands folded tight. The familiar ache tightened in his chest.

After a beat, he unlatched the leash.

Rider rose and repositioned himself, angling across the narrow aisle until he was close to the couch, his flank nearly brushing Shelby's boots. He lowered his head between his paws and sighed. Caleb let him settle there. Some protection didn't require distance, just vigilance.

He'd stand guard until dawn if he had to. They both would. Because tonight wasn't about procedure anymore.

It was personal.

❖

The world had finally gone still. Shelby sat up and ran her hands through her messy hair. The dim running lights along the bus aisle were the only illumination. A soft snore coming from under her feet pulled her attention to the floor. She smiled down at the dog as he dozed, one ear twitching.

Most of the law enforcement vehicles had cleared out, leaving only the hum of a lone generator and the soft hiss of rain beginning to fall. The fairgrounds would be a slippery mess tomorrow if the rain didn't let up. And she wouldn't be able to perform either. She shivered and rubbed her arms to generate some warmth.

"Here you go. You might want to wear this." Caleb held out a hoodie with the Willow Creek PD symbol scrawled across the middle. She quickly pulled it over her head.

"Thanks." She buried her nose in the soft fleece, inhaling the warm, woodsy scent. It smelled like Caleb. "What time is it?"

"After one." Caleb handed her a ceramic mug and she wrapped her hands around the warmth. The scent of strong coffee cut through the tired fog in her head.

A tense silence settled between them. As teenagers, they never ran out of topics to talk about. Now, too many years had passed, too many unspoken longings that were never shared. She glanced at him over the rim of her mug and sipped.

His lips formed a crooked smile. "Cream? Sugar?" Caleb held up a small carton of heavy cream and pushed a few packets of raw sugar across the table.

"Cream and sugar, please," she said, voice low. He poured the cream and she added one packet of sugar. "Didn't realize how cold it got."

"You were out cold. I didn't want to wake you." Caleb shrugged, leaning against the counter opposite her. "Adrenaline wears off. Body crashes after." He took a sip from his own cup, eyes flicking toward the dark window, then back to her. "You should try to get some more sleep."

She huffed out a quiet laugh. "Yeah, because that's going to happen." She stared into the mug, watching the swirl of cream dissolve. "You really think he did it? Tyler?"

Caleb's jaw flexed. "The evidence points that way. But until we have him in custody, we stay alert."

She nodded, fingers tightening around the cup. "He used to write me songs about the moon, about our love," she said softly. "Guess he finally found a way to blow up my stage instead."

He didn't respond, but the muscle in his cheek jumped. "He's not getting near you again."

Rider yawned and adjusted his position, stretched out at her feet, chin resting on his paws. Every few seconds his ears twitched, tracking sounds only he could hear. When she shifted, his tail thumped once. He sat up, placed one paw on her lap. That earned the faintest ghost of a smile, one of those rare, unguarded ones that pulled a dimple from hiding. For the first time all night, the air between them didn't feel so heavy.

She glanced up at Caleb and he shrugged. "Guess he wants to be your friend."

"It's okay if I pet him?"

"Sure. When we're on duty, I don't let him get pets from anyone. But tonight," Caleb exhaled, his gaze unfocused, "he seems to want to reassure you."

She ran her fingers through Rider's soft fur, giving his ears a good scratch. "He likes it." She held her hand out, palm up and the dog placed his large paw in her hand. She shook his hand and Rider leaned over and planted a sloppy kiss on her cheek.

Caleb kneeled next to his partner. "Seems you made a friend for life." Caleb's profile was almost unrecognizable in the dim light. "And you, you little traitor," he gave the dog a good rub and then stood. "He's been a good partner."

"He really doesn't stop working, does he?" she asked.

Caleb looked down at the dog, affection softening the hard lines of his face. "He knows when something's off. Don't you, partner?"

Rider lifted his head, eyes bright, as if he understood every word.

Shelby smiled. "You trust him that much?"

"With my life," Caleb said simply. Then, after a pause. "He's never been wrong. I trust his nose."

The way he said it made her chest tighten. *Trust the nose.* It wasn't just about scent, it was about instinct. About faith when the evidence hadn't caught up yet.

She reached down, fingers brushing the top of Rider's head. The dog leaned into her touch, warm and solid, grounding her in a way nothing else had all night.

"I think I get it," she murmured. "He trusts what he's made for. No hesitation, no doubt. Just... certainty."

Caleb's gaze held hers, steady and unreadable. "You'd be surprised how many people could use a little of that."

For a moment, while the storm outside deepened, rain pattered against the roof like soft percussion. It was times like this, when she wished, sometimes, that her life had taken a different path. But this was her choice. The lights flickered once, and they both laughed quietly, like they were afraid to break the fragile peace they'd found.

Shelby set her cup down and glanced at him. "You always this calm after nights like this?"

He tipped his head, half-smiling. "No. But he is." He nodded toward Rider. "Guess I take my cues from the smarter partner."

"Smart, loyal, protective," she said, looking at the dog but her words hung between her and Caleb. "I never did thank both of you for protecting me tonight."

"It's our job."

She hoped she was more than just an assignment or part of the job for Caleb. Because sitting here in the early morning hours, it didn't feel like it was just a job for him.

"Remember when we snuck out to go look at the meteor shower that summer before our senior year?"

"Yeah," Caleb smirked. "And fell asleep. When we had to sneak you back into your house, and your mom saw us, I thought for sure we were toast."

Shelby laughed. "You should've seen the look on your face."

"What was it? This?" Caleb made a silly face and they both laughed. Their gazes locked and their laughter faded. She held her breath for a moment, the air sparking with old emotion before she cleared her throat and looked down at her mug. Caleb cleared his throat. "Good times," he whispered.

It was the best of times, times she wished she could go back and do over.

Caleb looked away first. "Metcalf said he didn't want anyone talking to the press."

"I want to. I need to reassure my fans that I'm okay." She had to make him understand, she needed to do this for the fans. Show them she wasn't going to let one past relationship derail her future. "I don't want to give Tyler the satisfaction that he scared me." She crossed her arms and waited. "That he was the reason I stopped touring."

His brows furrowed as if he wanted to say something else. "All right then."

Rider yawned and settled closer to her boots, as if standing guard. Caleb watched the motion, then met her eyes again.

"I guess we disturbed your partner."

A gentle smile curved his lips. "Get some rest," he said softly. "You have a big day tomorrow. We'll keep watch." Caleb gave a soft whistle and Rider stretched and rose to his feet.

We. Not *I.* Not *the department. We.* The word settled deep, steady as a heartbeat. Steady as his resolve.

"We're going to check the perimeter one more time."

Caleb put the leash on Rider, then paused long enough to pull a blanket from the storage area and drape it over her.

"Get some rest," he said softly.

"Night, Caleb."

Shelby leaned back against the couch, eyes tracing the silhouette of man and dog as they exited the bus, framed in the dim glow of the security light outside. Two shadows—one human, one hound—keeping vigil over her. Protecting her no matter what.

The rain continued to beat against the metal side of the bus, creating a rhythmic tune. Soothing.

She pillowed her hands under her cheek and closed her eyes. As she drifted off, thoughts of tours, fans, and explosions were pushed to the back of her mind.

For the first time since the explosion, she let herself believe she might really be safe.

CHAPTER FIVE

A few rays of early morning sun slipped through the blinds. Caleb squinted against the brightness and stretched out his long legs into the aisle. Rider gave him a look that said *somebody stayed awake.*

Caleb scratched under Rider's chin. "I know, boy. Thanks for watching my back."

Rider swiped his tongue across Caleb's hand. He glanced over at Shelby, still asleep on the couch, curled beneath a blanket.

He glanced out the front windshield where the fairgrounds had been transformed from crime scene to media circus. At least they had a little bit of time before Shelby needed to face the crowd. Three Willow Creek sheriff's cruisers formed a protective barricade around the front of the bus. He scraped his hands down his face, the bristles rough against his palms.

Rider cocked his head to the side. "I know. I got a whiff of myself. I need a shower and a shave."

Rider placed one paw over his nose.

Caleb smirked. "Yeah, thanks for that. I know what I smell like."

Rider turned around once and sat at the door, his signal that it was "business time." Caleb looped the leash around his hand and clipped it in place.

Opening the door, he had to shield his eyes against the camera flashes masquerading as sunlight. He paused on the bottom step and inhaled. No trace of gunpowder. Just fresh, clean, country air.

Reporters clustered like crows along the perimeter tape, camera lenses glinting in the pale light. A temporary podium stood near the ruined stage backdrop, the sheriff's department seal taped haphazardly to the front.

Rider scanned the crowd, nose in the air, and then chuffed. He finished his perimeter check, completed his business, and began sniffing around the bus. They circled it twice, Rider's tail swishing the entire time.

As they came up the stairs, Shelby's bleary-eyed guitarist, Wyatt, slipped past a deputy, clutching a padded instrument case to his chest. He tried for a small smile, but his skin was pale beneath yesterday's stage makeup.

"Morning," Wyatt mumbled, voice rough. "I just...needed my guitar." His gaze darted to the fairground's wreckage. "She okay?"

"She will be." Caleb's response was crisp, controlled.

Wyatt nodded once, eyes haunted. "Tell her the band's here. We're not going anywhere." He hurried past the crowd, disappearing behind a cruiser. Bristow stood at the door.

"When did you get here?" Caleb opened the door and Rider climbed inside.

"About five minutes ago. I relieved Spencer." Bristow studied him a moment and then clapped a hand on his shoulder. "You okay? You look a little tense."

Caleb nodded, his gaze following Wyatt as he scurried across the parking lot. Entering the bus, he scanned the interior, but Shelby wasn't on the couch. He tamped down the tightness in his chest. His gaze landed on the blanket neatly folded over the back of the couch.

A flash of color caught his eye. A glossy concert poster was taped to the side of a cabinet near the kitchenette. Not just any poster. This one was slashed down the middle, the tear jagged and violent, cutting straight through Shelby's smiling face. A black Sharpie scrawl bled over the ripped edges.

DON'T SING AGAIN.

His pulse slammed into his throat. This wasn't left by accident. Whoever planted the bomb had been inside the bus. Inside her sanctuary. Someone she trusted had access. Band. Crew. Family.

He gloved up in muscle memory and snapped a quick photo before signaling CSU on his radio.

"Shelby?" His nerves spiked and Rider bumped his leg. "Find her." He held out the blanket. Rider sniffed and then trotted to the back of the bus and sat in front of her bedroom. "I'm in here. Just finishing up." Her voice was muffled through the door.

Caleb exhaled. High alert was his default but this assignment wasn't just another job. It was her. And someone out there had already tried to take her away.

She opened the door, and a soft cloud of hairspray and perfume drifted out. Glamour as armor. Her gaze caught immediately on the torn poster taped to the cabinet.

"What's that?" she asked, the faintest tremor in her voice.

"Nothing." He stepped in front of it. Too quick.

"Caleb." She tugged his arm, gentle but insistent.

He didn't want her to see. Rider moved closer, tail stiff, nose hovering near the glossy paper. The dog's muscles bunched, a low growl raking from his throat as if the ink itself carried malice.

Shelby's breath stuttered as she saw the jagged tear slashing through her own smiling face. The thick black letters screamed across the page:

DON'T SING AGAIN.

All the color washed from her cheeks. "Where... when did you find that?"

"After we came back from our patrol," he said, voice tight. "CSU's on the way to collect it. Could be some coward's idea of a joke, but we're treating it as a threat."

Rider pressed against Shelby's leg, protective, sensing her fear as clearly as any scent.

Caleb's jaw locked. Fury surged hot and bright, sharp enough he had to curl his fist to keep from ripping the poster down and shredding it to nothing.

Someone had been inside her space. Close enough to touch her things. Close enough to imagine harming her.

He wouldn't let them get close again.

Shelby swallowed hard, lifting her chin despite the tremble she didn't quite hide. "Please... don't tell Eric yet," she whispered. "My brother will pull the plug on everything. He already thinks touring's too dangerous."

Brother. Manager. Gatekeeper to every corner of her life. And someone who could've opened that door to anyone. He forced calm back into his tone. "Ready?"

Her lashes flickered with fear, courage, and something fierce he'd always admired. Fight welding into resolve. She bit her lower lip, pushed her shoulders back. Strength over fear.

"Yeah," she whispered. "Let's do this."

Caleb placed himself between her and the violated space behind him. His hand brushed Rider's back, a silent pact.

Whoever wanted to silence Shelby Lane, well, they'd have to go through the two of them first.

They followed her to the front and he held out a hand. "Any time you feel unsafe, use the word 'dog' and I'll be there. Got it?"

"Dog? That's the best you can do?"

He shrugged. "Hard to forget."

She smiled at him and patted his chest. "Whatever you say, deputy."

Heat shot up his spine. He shoved it down. He'd analyze that emotion later. Or never.

They stepped off the bus into a wall of sunlight and flashes. Camera shutters snapped like insects. Willow Creek deputies had their cruisers angled nose-out, forming a barrier. Reporters leaned forward like vultures, hungry for any hint of blood.

Eric Lane stormed through the cluster of deputies, badge-lanyard swinging, jaw tight enough to crack.

"Shelby! This is insanity." He placed an arm around his sister's shoulders. "We should be in a hotel, not a war zone."

Caleb stepped in to maintain space. "We have protocols. She's safe here."

Eric shot him a glare sharp enough to cut skin. "Safe? There was a bomb."

Shelby put a hand over her brother's. "Eric, please. I can do this."

The conflict in Eric's eyes flickered. All the emotions warring. Big brother vs. manager vs. fear. Finally, he let her go but stayed close, protectiveness radiating off him.

Caleb positioned himself so that their shadows nearly merged. Rider paced slow, tight circles. Caleb stood beside Bristow. "We need to talk."

"About what?"

Caleb pulled out his phone and showed him the picture of the poster. "This." His voice was tight, accusing.

Bristow leaned in, eyes narrowing. "That wasn't there earlier."

"No." Caleb pocketed the phone. "Found it after perimeter." He squared his shoulders. "Which means someone breached security—or already had access."

Bristow shoved his hands through his hair. "Band members came through for equipment. All IDs checked."

Caleb nodded once. "That protocol ends now. I'll coordinate with Shelby and issue an approved-access list with names and photos. Anyone outside that list doesn't cross the line."

Sheriff Metcalf glared at Caleb and Micah.

"Sorry," Caleb mouthed.

Bristow turned on his heel and crossed to the far side of the press briefing, placing the press line squarely between himself and law enforcement.

The sheriff's department PR rep approached the makeshift podium and tapped the microphone. "We'll begin shortly," she announced into microphones.

Caleb scanned the crowd. Phones up. Hands too close. A cameraman shifting just outside the tape too close.

Metcalf appeared at his side, coffee in hand. "She sure about this?"

"She thinks canceling gives the threat power," Caleb said. The bitterness crept into his tone before he could stop it.

Metcalf studied him. "You two go way back."

"High school." Caleb swallowed. "We were close. Then I left for the Army, and she... didn't."

"And now?"

Caleb didn't answer. Couldn't.

Rider froze, hackles rising like brush bristling in a storm. His low growl vibrated through the leash.

Caleb's instincts snapped tight. "Easy," he murmured, palm steadying Rider's shoulder. "What do you smell, partner?"

Rider's gaze locked on the press line. One man with a camera stepping too far forward, attention not on the stage but on Shelby. Caleb keyed his radio. "Bristow, tighten the front."

"Already moving," came the quick reply.

Shelby stepped to the microphones. She was beautiful, composed, yet brittle around the edges. No one would know she was barely hanging on except for him. The tightness around her mouth was a dead giveaway. The sun caught in her hair, turning the gold strands into a crown she didn't want.

Reporters surged.

Rider barked—a sharp, chest-deep command.

Caleb was there instantly, one hand on his holster, the other shielding Shelby's side. Deputies closed ranks. The line staggered, then retreated.

"Back up!" Metcalf boomed.

For one suspended heartbeat, everything held still. Caleb's pulse pounded in his ears. He waited for the explosion that never came.

No threat. Not this time. Just too many people and too little distance.

Shelby turned to face him, pushing the sunglasses on top of her head, wide-eyed gaze questioning. "You okay?" she whispered.

Should've been his line.

"Yeah." He forced a breath. "Rider just made sure nobody forgets boundaries."

Instead of returning to Caleb's heel, Rider leaned into Shelby's boots and pressed his nose to her ankle. Protective, claiming.

Caleb felt the ache of it. The truth of it.

Rider already knew who needed guarding most.

Far beyond the cameras, past the tape line, movement flickered. Someone slipped into a white van parked just out of view. Watching. Leaving.

Caleb's jaw locked. Whoever had stepped into Shelby's private world left proof in Sharpie. He would find them.

Shelby lifted her chin and turned back to the podium. Brave. Determined. Terrified. Caleb tightened the leash in his hand, never taking his eyes off the crowd.

Metcalf's voice rumbled low beside him. "This isn't about the cameras," he said. "It's about keeping her safe. Everything else is noise."

Caleb didn't trust himself to answer.

Because with the world pressing too close, cameras flashing, and Rider braced at Shelby's side, he wanted that more than he'd ever admit.

And wanting Shelby's love was dangerous—because it made him forget, for half a heartbeat, that his job was to keep her alive, not hold her close.

🐾

Caleb hustled Shelby back to the tour bus. He and Rider were at the front of the bus, waiting for the crime scene unit. And her? Well, all she wanted to do was curl up into a ball and disappear. This nightmare continued to escalate and she wanted to wake up.

Shelby collapsed onto the narrow couch and stared at the ceiling.

Her stomach churned as the last of the coffee turned bitter, her emotions tangling tight beneath her ribs. The faint ringing in her ears—leftover from the blast—made the silence feel wrong. Unnatural.

The night had stayed quiet, and now the morning had followed suit. No sirens. No shouted orders. No calliope music pretending everything was fine. Just the low hum of the air conditioner and the steady scrape of Caleb's boots pacing near the front.

Her voice surprised her when it slipped out. "Caleb?"

His footsteps stopped. "Yeah?"

She swallowed. The words felt too big for the small space. "Would you... would you take me to church?"

There was a pause. Not long, but enough for doubt to creep in. Then his answer came, simple and solid. "Sure thing, Shelbs."

No one had called her *Shelbs* since, well, Caleb.

Maybe God was trying to get her attention. If He was, He was doing a good job.

Before she could breathe through the swirl of emotions, the bus door slammed open. Eric jumped aboard, protective fury radiating from every line of his posture.

"What were you thinking letting her go out there alone? Cameras everywhere. A bomb. Caleb, this ends now. We're leaving town, today."

She moved toward her brother. "Eric..."

"No." He planted himself between her and Caleb like a shield. "Shelby, you're my responsibility."

Caleb didn't step back. His voice stayed calm, controlled, but edged with steel. "She's under my protection, per Sheriff Metcalf. We'll move her when it's secure, not before."

Eric's glare could've cut steel. "And who gave you the right to make decisions for my sister?"

Shelby's heart squeezed. Two men, both trying to protect her. One from the world. One from fear.

Wyatt appeared behind Eric, backpack slung over a shoulder, his guitar almost hidden behind him. His gaze darted to Shelby, then flicked away, shame tightening his jaw.

"Hey," Wyatt said softly, voice ragged. "Just wanted to grab my stuff. And—uh—sorry about earlier. Should've been closer." His fingers worried the frayed strap of the bag, restless. Guilty?

Eric snapped. "You shouldn't have left the bus unattended."

Wyatt swallowed hard, looking wounded. "I was only gone a minute. I had to call my mom. She watches the news and was freaking out." His eyes locked briefly with Shelby's. It was a look heavy with something unsaid.

Caleb stepped closer, asserting the boundary. "We'll handle statements later. Shelby needs space."

Eric muttered something under his breath but didn't leave. His protectiveness hovered like a storm front.

Shelby managed a thin breath. "Give me a minute." She paced the narrow aisle.

Caleb's somber eyes studied her from the tips of her cowboy boots to the deep blue V-neck sweater and black jeans. Heat rose up her neck and the force of his gaze rooted her in place. No man had ever looked at her as if she was the center of his universe. Caleb hadn't changed at all. Oh sure, he might be older, filled out, gotten a little taller, but he was the same. Caring, compassionate, always looking out for the needs of others.

He cleared his throat. "I'll wait up front." He scurried to the front of the bus, Rider on his heels.

Eric watched him go, arms crossed like he didn't trust Caleb any more than the stranger in the van. Wyatt lingered in the doorway, shifting his weight. "Shelby... if you need anything.

Anything. You call me first." The way he said it tightened something in her chest.

"Thanks, Wyatt," she said gently.

His smile never reached his eyes as he backed out of the bus, his gaze lingering a beat too long on the empty space where the torn poster had hung before CSU bagged it. A shiver rippled across his shoulders before the door thudded shut behind him.

What *was* that about?

She checked her hair and makeup in the mirror and smiled at her reflection and shrugged. No amount of concealer could cover the dark circles under her eyes. But the woman staring back at her looked at peace.

Shelby didn't look back as she left the bus. She couldn't. She'd have to trust Caleb to keep her safe. Whatever Caleb was shielding her from she wasn't ready to face it. Not yet.

Press lights strobed. Cameras buzzed. Caleb's hand hovered near her back. Always close, never touching without need. Rider kept pace at her side, taut as a drawn wire.

They maneuvered through the questions and the elbows and the greed disguised as concern.

"Ms. Lane? Are you canceling your tour?"

"What did the police find?"

"Whatever happened to your songwriting partner?"

Questions were hurled at her at a frenetic pace, all jumbled together into one loud, dissonant jumble of sound.

Caleb quickly guided her into the SUV, his movements controlled but razor-edged. As they pulled away, Shelby glanced in the side mirror. The white van was back.

Parked near the fence. Engine running. Window cracked. A shape behind the wheel, still and patient.

A hand lifted. A phone glinted. Recording her.

Watching.

Her pulse tripped. "Press?" she whispered, though she knew.

"No." Caleb's voice was as sharp as splintered glass. "Not press."

The van peeled away as if it had simply finished errands. But as the sun broke through a passing cloud, she caught a glimpse of a faded bumper sticker: **Shelby Lane — First Tour**

Her own face, smiling bigger than life, stared back at her.

Someone had kept that sticker for years.

Someone had followed her home.

Her skin went cold and she dropped into the passenger seat, hugging her arms around her middle. Rider must've sensed the tension because he stuck his nose through the panel and rested his head on her shoulder. She reached back and absentmindedly patted his head.

"Hey boy." She glanced over at Caleb, eyes focused on the road, and the gathering crowd. "Is he always this sensitive?"

"Yeah, pretty much. Hang on." Caleb hit the gas a little harder than necessary and she lurched forward against the seatbelt. They rode in silence until they arrived at the little red-brick church. She exhaled and it felt like stepping into a memory she'd locked away.

He parked the SUV at a side entrance. Away from the crowds. Away from the crush of parishioners once the service ended. The sanctuary was warm with stained-glass light and old wood polish. It smelled like hymnals and nostalgia.

She slid into a back pew, head bowed. Caleb sat at the aisle, Rider curled protectively at her feet. She could feel Caleb scanning every corner. She could feel Rider's vigilance like static in the air. But what she felt most was an ache. Heavy and sharp. Music swelled. Not polished, not professional. Just honest.

Amazing Grace.

Her throat constricted.

She used to sing that hymn at the top of her lungs, certain God heard every off-key note and loved her anyway. Before record deals and bright lights. Before strangers felt entitled to her life. Before fear. Tears slipped down her cheeks unchecked.

...that saved a wretch like me...

Her fingers still shook, no matter how tightly she clasped them.

She pressed a trembling hand to her chest as an old memory struck her hard:

She was backstage at the state fair. She'd auditioned and won the chance to sing. Nerves churned and she shifted her converse-clad feet. She was thirteen years old and it was the first time she wore lipstick. Her mama kneeled with her, holding her hands, praying with her, before she went on.

"Remember, baby — you sing because God gave you a voice. Don't ever let the world make you forget why." Somewhere between then and now, she had.

Caleb's hand covered hers—warm, steady. A silent *I'm here*. The song ended. Her heart felt cracked open and a lone tear escaped. Caleb shifted in his seat and placed a tissue in her hand. Her eyes were cloudy with tears as she glanced over at his handsome profile. She'd carelessly tossed aside the one man who cared deeply for her. Why did she think she would ever find contentment outside of God's will?

The congregation stood as the pastor began to pray. Caleb gave her a choice with just a look: leave through the crowded foyer or slip out the side door. She nodded toward the exit closest to the parking lot.

They stepped into bright sunlight and she paused outside the door. The gravel crunched underfoot like brittle bones. There. At the edge of the parking lot, the same white van was parked.

Engine rumbling. Windshield too dark. Still and patient. A cracked headlight.

Caleb's hand brushed his holster. "Don't look. Get in." He held open the door for her, voice low and lethal. She stared anyway, trying to memorize the angle of that cracked headlight. The shape of a decal she couldn't make out. A license plate blurred by sun-glare.

The van backed out fast, tires spitting gravel, and disappeared around the corner. Caleb's jaw flexed, a tiny tell, but she caught it. He wasn't calm. He was barely holding the panic back.

Caleb radioed the dispatch. "K-9 Two. Do you read?"

"Go ahead K-9 Two."

"I'm at Willow Creek Bible Church off Hwy 38. White van, last seen speeding south on Hwy 38. Need back-up." Caleb's short, clipped commands sliced at her tenuous calm.

"Copy that."

Rider paced in the back, unsettled, and whined.

"Easy boy," Caleb murmured.

Shelby leaned against the SUV door, breaths shaking loose all her resolve. Her sanctuary wasn't safe either.

Lord, I'm scared.

And for the first time in an extremely long time, she whispered a prayer.

God, please don't let me be alone in this.

CHAPTER SIX

Caleb's grip on the steering wheel tightened with every mile of cracked pavement between them and the church. His pulse still jackhammered from the sight of the van. Too close. Too bold. And the way Shelby had looked at him with a mix of trust and terror braided together, nearly undid him.

"You okay?" His voice came out rougher than intended.

"Yeah." Her voice was small, a little broken around the edges.

He didn't believe a word of it.

Her phone chimed in the cup holder and Shelby frowned. "Probably my tour manager…" She unlocked her screen and he heard her inhale.

Caleb knew that sound. Pure fear.

"What is it?" he asked, already braced.

Her screen shook in her trembling hand. An email. Just one line. No signature.

The next song will end in silence.

Heat speared through his chest. Fury, fast, molten, uncontrollable, surged up his spine. "That's it." He snatched the phone from her grasp and tossed it into the center console. "We're done playing nice."

"Caleb…"

"No." His voice cracked like a snapped cable. "Shelby, someone wants you dead. I'm not giving them another chance."

He hit the call icon. "Metcalf."

"What's going on, Hunter?"

"We spotted the van at church. He's following us."

"Where are you?" The sheriff's tone sharpened.

"North on Hwy 38. Planning to circle back to the fairgrounds."

Sirens bled through the line. "Negative. Too many cameras and reporters waiting there. I've got a different idea."

"I'm listening." Rider placed a paw on Caleb's shoulder, a low whine rumbling in his throat.

"My cousin has a cabin about five miles from you. Security lights, cameras. Take Ms. Lane there."

Caleb hesitated. He glanced at Shelby. She sat huddled against the door, her frame small. The faint scent of her perfume filled the cab but it was her eyes staring at nothing that bothered him most.

"Okay. Send the location." His phone pinged with the text.

"And Hunter? Call me when you get there. I'll send patrols when I can, but we're stretched thin."

"I've got it under control."

"Well, accept the help anyway."

Rider nudged his ear. "I know, boy. We're almost there." Caleb removed Rider's paw from his shoulder and eased the SUV back onto the road.

Shelby didn't speak for a long moment. Then quietly, "So… we're not going back to the bus."

"No," he said. "Not tonight."

Her jaw tightened, but she nodded. Tired. Resigned.

"I'll have Bristow grab essentials and bring them out," Caleb added. "Clothes. Your guitar. Anything you need for a couple days."

That got her attention. She looked at him then. "Okay."

Leaves skittered over the asphalt, red and gold swirling in the headlights as the two-lane highway narrowed. The silence thickened between them, heavy with things neither of them knew how to say. Ten years of unspoken words pressing close. The pavement gave way to gravel.

The SUV bounced lightly as pine trees crowded in, their trunks flashing past like sentries. Shelby stiffened, recognizing the turn even though she'd already heard the plan.

"This is the safe house," she said.

"Yeah. Off-grid and secluded."

"You can't lock me away like I'm fragile—"

His laugh was humorless. "Fragile? You survived a bomb last night. That doesn't make you fragile." He glanced at her, then back to the road. "It makes you a target."

The cabin appeared in a small clearing, weather-beaten and tucked deep into the trees. Quiet. Too quiet.

Shelby turned toward the window, jaw tight. "I can't stop my whole life because someone hates me."

Caleb killed the engine and faced her fully. "They don't hate you. They're fixated on you." His voice dropped. "That's different. That's worse."

Her eyes glimmered with hurt and anger in equal measure. "You think I don't know that?"

Rider let out a low growl from the back seat, hackles lifting.

"Easy, boy." Caleb inhaled, choosing his next words carefully. "Shelby... please. Let me do my job. Let me keep you breathing."

Her chin trembled. "I want to trust you," she said softly. "But it doesn't come easy."

He felt the weight of the years between them settle, heavy and earned.

He stepped out first, scanning the tree line, then opened her door. An owl hooted somewhere above them. Pine needles whispered as the wind picked up, carrying the damp scent of earth and leaves.

Rider bounded ahead, nose sharp, body tense, tail stiff as he checked the perimeter before skidding back to Shelby's side.

She gestured at the cabin, frustration sharp in her clipped tone. "This—" she spread her arms wide, "—feels like a little much. I need my band. I need to rehearse. I still have deadlines. This tour—" Her shoulders sagged. "People depend on me."

He saw the moment reality hit, how her world wouldn't stop just because danger had found her.

Caleb grasped her shoulders, steady but gentle, forcing her to meet his eyes. "I know. But there are protocols we need to follow. Just for now. Hold on."

He keyed the door. "Rider...search."

The dog swept the interior, quick and efficient, then returned and sat, barking once.

"That's our signal," Caleb said softly. "All clear."

The tree limbs made a soft swishing noise as the breeze picked up. A hint of something else in the air besides rain. Sunlight illuminated the clearing, but it was the shadows that bothered him. The earthy scents of pine and molding leaves drifted on the late afternoon breeze.

He carried his gear inside and turned on the lights. The cabin was modest but safe-ish: fireplace, couches, small kitchen, single bedroom, one bathroom. It was clean but cozy with a few colorful throw pillows tossed on the couches. A cream-colored crocheted blanket was draped over the arm of a chair. Looked like he and Rider were bunking in front of the fireplace.

A few minutes later, Bristow arrived. Caleb met him outside, Shelby and Rider following closely.

"I grabbed what I thought you might need," Bristow said, unloading a small suitcase and Shelby's guitar case. "Clothes for a couple days. Toiletries. Instruments and work stuff."

Shelby stared at the guitar case as if seeing it for the first time, her shoulders sagging in relief.

"Thank you," she said softly.

Bristow nodded once, his gaze flicking briefly between her and Caleb before he stepped back. "I'll let you know if CSU finds anything else."

Caleb carried the guitar inside himself, careful with it in a way that had nothing to do with its weight. Rider followed Shelby up the steps, never leaving her side.

Only once the door shut behind them did the quiet settle again—deep, unnatural, and waiting.

Caleb cleared his throat. "If rehearsing calms you," he said, placing the guitar on the couch, "do it." He checked the cabinets. Basic supplies, coffee, canned goods. They'd make do. He dug around in his duffel and handed her a tiny transmitter. "This links your mic to my comms. If anything happens, I'll hear it."

Her fingers brushed his, memory sparking under her touch. Of happier times, times when they were carefree teenagers. When the world outside their small town held endless possibilities.

He attached the small device to her shirt collar. "Leave this on."

"Even when I'm sleeping?"

He nodded once, assessing her mood. If he still knew her, which he was pretty sure he did, then she wanted out.

She looked away quickly and sat on the edge of the loveseat. Head bowed in prayer or defeat, he couldn't tell. Or was she plotting her escape?

He unloaded the duffel and filled Rider's bowl with water, the dog slurping up most of the liquid. Caleb pushed the black and red plaid curtains back from the multi-paned picture window and scanned the woods again. Every shadow a possible threat. His chest tightened with the thought of losing her again.

Rider positioned himself by the door, coiled tight.

He checked the fridge and removed a couple bottles of water and held one out to Shelby. They needed a break from the tension. "Here. Drink this, then I'll make dinner."

She began to the peel the label off the bottle, her gaze never meeting his. "You think this place will hold him off?" Shelby asked.

"Not for a second," he answered. "But it slows him down. And that's all I need."

"For what?" she whispered.

He stepped closer, breath stirring her hair. Oh, how he wanted to grab her and hold on. His younger self was a fool for letting her go. He wanted to promise her that nothing was going to happen as long as she was in his arms.

But that was a promise he couldn't make.

He sat next to her. He had to keep her close. "To end this. Before he ends you."

Rider's growl deepened, hackles sharp as wire.

Shelby's hand clamped around Caleb's forearm and her eyes widened in fear.

"Caleb... he's still out there."

He stood, his free hand found his holster.

"No," he murmured, gaze slicing through the tree line.

"He's here."

🐾

Her gaze drifted to the guitar case leaning against the river-rock fireplace. The cabin looked like something out of a postcard with its hand-cut logs, stone fireplace, and a soft glow from a single lamp. Caleb puttered in the small kitchen, stirring something on the stove. The entire situation felt domestic and cozy. But beneath the warmth, Shelby felt the truth like a bruise: she wasn't here for peace. She was here to hide.

The isolation stripped away her stage armor.

No fans.

No spotlight.

Just her. And Caleb. The one man she couldn't hide from no matter how hard she tried.

The one man who knew her, even after ten years. And a stalker who was intent on hurting her or worse.

Caleb lightly touched her guitar leaning against the hearth as if it were fragile. Sacred.

"Food's ready," he murmured.

Shelby wrapped her arms around herself, her hands shaking. She was barely hanging on to her sanity. "Do you really think he'll find us out here?"

Caleb's jaw flexed. "He already has. Twice."

Her stomach dropped, a sinking feeling that felt like she was falling into an abyss. "What? How?"

Her phone lit up on the coffee table with a sudden, accusing glow from her oldest brother.

> Dylan: WHERE ARE YOU?? Answer
> me. Now.

Another message popped up immediately.

> Dylan: If I don't hear back, I'm calling the
> sheriff and the state police. This isn't a
> game, Shel.

Her throat tightened. Dylan was scared. And angry. And she understood both.

But answering... meant opening a door she couldn't close.

"How did he find out?"

"It's a small town, remember? Word gets around. Shoot, you're the biggest thing to happen since the Golden Arches opened a store twenty years ago," Caleb said. He gave her a gentle smile and glanced over at Rider by the door.

"So what you're saying is, I'm hotter than McDonald's fries? I'll take it."

"That's not..."

"I'm teasing." She watched the color rise up his neck.

Her phone buzzed again. This time, a banner slid across the screen:

Band Fam 🎸🔥

Misty, Wyatt, and Jade, all of them had been with her from the start of her career.

Her people.

She shouldn't look. She looked anyway.

> Misty: Update. Now. Are you with law enforcement? Label's blowing up my phone.

> Jade: I just saw that van clip on the news. Was that the SAME one from the fairgrounds??

> Wyatt: Please tell us you're okay. Don't ghost us, Shelby.

> Misty: We need to know if we should cancel the next three shows. I can't make that call without you.

> Jade: Yeah, and maybe tell us if someone's trying to actually KILL you?? That feels like a detail we should know.

A hysterical laugh bubbled in her chest and died there. They weren't being dramatic. They were scared. For her. For themselves. For their livelihoods.

Her phone buzzed again, another text stacking over the thread.

> Eric: You didn't tell me you were going to that church. Reporters said they saw you leave. Where did he take you?

Going dark felt like betrayal. To her brother. To her band. To her crew.

But turning that screen on and typing back felt like lighting a beacon.

Caleb cleared his throat and crouched by the table, striking a match. The candle caught fast, flame blooming in the heavy Georgia humidity. Outside, the night pressed close and damp, cicadas buzzing their late-summer pulse. The amber glow climbed his face, revealing his exhaustion… and the quiet ferocity of someone still standing guard in the storm's silence. He went to the kitchen and ladled soup into two bowls.

"You never used to be so intense," she joked softly.

He didn't smile. "You were never in danger before."

Her phone shivered across the wood again.

Band Fam

Misty: Security wants to know if they should stay on your parents' street or stand down. I'm not guessing on this, Shel.

Wyatt: Eric says he doesn't know where you are either. That's not like you.

Jade: If this is some PR stunt, I'm out. But if it's real, we've got your back. Just TELL us.

A fresh knot of guilt tightened in her chest.

"Maybe I should just text them I'm okay," she murmured, mostly to herself.

Caleb's head snapped toward her. He'd heard the vibration. He'd seen her glance at the phone. His voice dropped, low and firm. "Don't. Not from here. Not until we know how he's tracking you."

"They're worried," she whispered. "Eric's going to come looking for me."

"He won't find you," Caleb said quietly. "That's the point."

Her fingers twitched toward the phone again. Another buzz.

> Wyatt (DM): Shelby… if this is about the
> notes before the tour… we can fix it. Just
> call me. Don't shut us out.

Notes before the tour. The ones she'd brushed off as overzealous fan mail. The ones she hadn't told Caleb about. Shame burned sharp and hot.

Why would Wyatt bring those up now? How much did he know? Or… had he sent them?

She sat on the rug near the fire, knees pulled up. A shiver raced up her spine and she rubbed her hands up and down her arms. The warmth seeped into her chilled skin, loosening something tight inside. She wasn't Shelby Lane, superstar. She was a girl from Willow Creek who used to sing at potlucks and church camp.

Caleb handed her a bowl of soup, savory chicken and thyme, and set his bowl on the coffee table. He lowered himself onto the floor across from her, elbows resting on his knees. The firelight glinted in his eyes. This moment seemed frozen and she simply wanted to be Shelby Lane, girl in love.

"Talk to me, Shelbs. Tell me what's really going on inside."

Oh, how she wanted to tell him what her heart wanted. How she wanted a second chance. The logical side of her heart listed all the reasons she needed to run away from this danger. She grabbed a pillow from the couch and propped it behind her. She wanted to lie, give him a half-truth. But the quiet here demanded honesty.

"I'm scared," she whispered. "And angry. And I hate that needing help makes me feel weak." A shaky laugh. "There's the truth." Well, most of the truth.

He leaned closer. "Being scared doesn't make you weak. It makes you human. And anger?" His voice lowered. "That means you're still fighting. Been there, done that. Got the T-shirt and hat."

Her breath lodged in her throat. He'd always done that, stripped her excuses clean. She saw the weight he carried too. The guilt from years ago. The regret that still lived under his ribs. She had to tell him it wasn't all his fault. That she had a part in what happened too.

Her phone vibrated once more, then finally went still as if everyone on the other end of those threads had run out of words.

For now.

"Caleb," she said gently, "you're not responsible for everything that's gone wrong in my life. Or for my sister's death."

He flinched, as if her words hit him dead-center.

Caleb's gaze dropped, like the weight of the past physically dragged his eyes downward. "You and I stepped on that ice thinking it was solid. We didn't know it was thin. But *she* saw us from the far bank and came out anyway."

His jaw tightened, pain flickering behind his eyes.

"We waved at her. We yelled for her to go back." His voice hitched. "But she thought we were calling her forward. Ava trusted us."

He raked a hand through his damp hair.

"The ice cracked like a rifle shot. She went under before the echo died." He swallowed, throat working. "I dove in. I crawled across the shards. I *tried*. But that lake..." His voice broke. "It took her faster than I could move."

Silence thrummed between them, thick and unbearable.

"That's why I left," he said, the confession finally splitting open. "Not because I didn't care. But because I couldn't stand in front of the people I loved knowing I walked onto a lake that killed your sister."

His hands trembled—not violently, just truthfully.

"I blamed myself every second since." His eyes lifted to hers, fractured and pleading. "And the worst part? You still think you have to comfort *me* for it."

He shook his head once, ashamed and certain.

"I didn't leave because I was strong, Shelby." His voice cracked with regret. "I left because I thought if I disappeared, the world would stop breaking around you. I was reminder of what you lost."

Rider stretched and let out a slow sigh and nudged Caleb's boot with his nose.

Caleb didn't look away this time.

"But I was wrong." His voice was rough, quiet, real. "Me leaving didn't save you from the cold. It just made you stand in it alone."

His voice cracked with emotion or regret. Or both. He cradled his head between his hands.

"You didn't let us down," she said, voice soft but anchored in conviction. "You showed up. You dove in. You tried until the lake stole the choice from you. That's not failure. That's love arriving too late."

She held his face gently between her hands, guiding his gaze to hers, refusing to let him disappear into the memory again.

"We both carry pieces of that night," she murmured. "When I saw Ava following us, I should've walked her back home. But I didn't. I wanted more time with you." She caressed his cheek. "But God is a forgiving God, Caleb. Mercy is bigger than one moment." Her thumb brushed once at his shoulder. "It *was* an accident. Not a sentence. Not the end."

She swallowed hard, eyes cloudy with tears, her own fatigue-threaded honesty slipping through. "Grace doesn't erase what happened," she whispered, "but it meets us in it. And mercy is strong enough to hold the both of us."

Before he could answer, Rider's guttural growl shattered the moment. The K-9 jumped up, staring at the door, his movement startling her and she placed a hand on her chest. Rider was a flash of snarling teeth silhouetted against the window.

Shelby jerked back. "Someone's out there?"

Caleb was already moving, gun drawn, stance rigid. He flicked off the lamp. Darkness swallowed the room, almost suffocating. She struggled to breathe.

Rider trotted in front of the door, head low, growling like he'd found a ghost.

Caleb watched the window for a full thirty seconds, barely breathing, before he exhaled.

"He backed off."

That didn't calm her. Not even a little.

To fill the stifling quiet, Shelby reached for her guitar.

Caleb frowned. "Shelby..."

"Please?" She adjusted the guitar on her lap, pick in hand. "Just for a little while." Her voice wavered, but she strummed anyway.

The first notes of "Amazing Grace" floated into the room. The song was raw, stripped of polish, held together only by faith. A faith that she'd strayed from ten years ago but one she wanted so desperately to embrace again.

This was a private kind of worship. One that she needed to return to.

The mic at her collar hummed, the one he'd attached when they first arrived at the cabin. She'd almost forgotten it was there.

Caleb's comm in his ear picked up her voice and she heard the echo. It was a live line connecting them. If she couldn't be with him here in Willow Creek, then maybe they could have this one last time.

Rider eased down beside her, head resting on her thigh as if the music soothed his instincts too. Verse by verse, she remembered how to breathe again.

When the song faded, the only sound in the room was the low rumble of the distant thunderstorm. Silence pressed in. This time, it didn't crush her.

Caleb eased down beside her on the couch, close enough she could feel his heat. His hands, strong and scarred, hovered near hers.

"I think God heard that," he said quietly. He reached over and squeezed her hand. How she missed his touch. No other man set her heart on fire like Caleb.

A tear slipped free and he caught it with his thumb. "Maybe He never stopped listening."

Something inside her unclenched. Hope... flickering back to life.

His touch and voice were tender. Tracing an old ache with new promise. Healing an old wound that never healed for either of them.

"Shelby, I—" He leaned in, the heat from the candle warming her, or was it simply Caleb's presence?

She leaned closer, the flame from the candle illuminating one side of his angular jaw.

Rider's bark exploded with a snarl, snapping them both back into the present. Rider lunged at the window. Glass rattled and a shadow flinched outside.

Caleb's fury surfaced with no restraint this time. He grabbed his gun and flashlight. His voice edged with violence. "No one threatens her. Not again." The veins in his neck stood out as he shouted at the intruder.

Shelby's heart hammered as Rider growled louder, the hairs along his back rising like warning spikes.

Not her imagination.

Not paranoia.

Someone was out there.

Watching. Waiting.

And somewhere miles away, her family sat in the dark; 2 brothers, a tour manager, and a band still staring at unanswered messages, wondering why the girl they loved had gone silent.

CHAPTER SEVEN

Rider's snarl still vibrated in the air, low and feral, a warning that cut through the cabin's thick quiet. The candle guttered on the table, wax popping softly in the damp, storm-swollen air, its small flame waging a losing war against the dark beyond the windows.

Rain hammered the glass, a heavy, rhythmic claim for dominance, but it was the silence between the strikes, the pauses where the woods held their breath, that set Caleb's teeth on edge.

He pressed close to the window, one hand braced on the frame, scanning. The woods swallowed everything past the porch: thick pines, wet earth, and shadows layered in unbroken hush. No movement. No shape. Just the sense of something watching back.

Rider stood behind him, shoulders coiled, a rumbling growl ticking like a second heartbeat in the room.

His military instincts kicked in. This silence was wrong. As if the forest were waiting for a strike.

He checked every lock and window again until he was satisfied the intruder had retreated. But satisfaction didn't mean the threat was gone.

"Clear," he murmured.

Shelby remained frozen near the cold fireplace, her guitar limp in her hands, breath shaking her frame. Fear flickered raw in her eyes, unguarded. It punched him straight in the chest. He hated that she'd learned to live with fear. Hated that danger shadowed every stage she stepped on.

He holstered his weapon and crouched in front of her, covering her trembling hands with his steady ones. "You're okay," he said quietly, though adrenaline still rattled his pulse. "He's gone."

Shelby nodded, but her fingers shook against the strings. Rider pressed his head into her thigh, a living anchor. *Lord, I need Your eyes in the dark.*

As much as Caleb thrived on control, this was one battle he couldn't dictate the outcome of.

A sudden buzz lit Shelby's phone on the coffee table. Eric's name flashing bright and loud in the dark.

Caleb's gaze hardened. "Don't answer that," he said. "One message and he'll find us."

She didn't argue. That scared him more than if she had argued with him.

He stood and grabbed the flashlight. "Stay with Rider," he instructed. "He won't let anyone near you."

Her voice was small. "Be careful."

He almost smiled. Because if she knew what careful meant for him, she'd never sleep. "Always."

He stepped outside. Rain slapped against his cheek, sharp as a warning, dragging him fully alert. He swept the beam in slow arcs across the yard, gravel drive, fence line. Nothing obvious. No footprints. No tire tracks. No broken brush. Whoever had crept up on them knew how to vanish without leaving a trace.

His jaw ticked. The stalker wasn't watching from afar anymore. He was escalating. Testing the perimeter. Learning their responses.

A vow carved itself into Caleb's ribs like scripture: *This man will never touch her. Not now. Not again.*

After a perimeter sweep, he returned inside. He secured every lock, checked alarm batteries twice, then let Rider do another sniff of the cabin's edges. Only when Shelby had changed into sweats and curled beneath a blanket did Caleb finally sit down.

She curled in on herself, the same way she had the night her sister died, too brave for tears, too shaken to sleep. He'd carry that memory to his grave, a weight he refused to drop again. "You should sleep," he said softly.

"You too."

"Not a chance."

Not while danger coiled outside these walls.

Her eyes lingered on him like she wanted to argue, but instead her lips eased into a line of quiet gratitude.

"Wake me if... you know," she whispered, fingertips brushing his wrist.

"I will." He lifted an energy drink in a silent toast. "Promise."

It would be over his dead body before anything touched Shelby.

He already lived with one failure. He wouldn't survive a second.

He settled into the armchair nearest the door, weapon resting ready on his thigh. Rider curled at his boots, vibrating tension in every muscle. The fire sank low, but Caleb's focus stayed razor sharp.

Somewhere in the night, Shelby hummed the final bars of *Amazing Grace.*

A prayer.

A shield.

Caleb bowed his head. *God... guard her. Give me strength to do the rest.*

Listening to her voice grounded him. Reminded him why he would stay awake and unbroken.

Sunlight slanted soft and gold through the curtains like nothing had happened. Caleb's body ached with the aftermath of vigilance. His knee throbbed with old injury, the damp morning air sharpening the pain.

The cold candle wax reminded him that peace here was an illusion.

Rider stretched, shook his fur, then shot upright, ears pricked, entire body focused on the door.

Caleb's chest locked tight. "Easy, boy." He joined Rider's position, checking the peephole.

Empty porch. Nothing but his cruiser.

The quiet wasn't comforting. It was calculated.

He opened the door and Rider lunged forward, teeth bared, stopping just short of the porch edge.

A manila envelope sat centered on the welcome mat like a dare.

No postage.

No fingerprints he could see.

Just Shelby's initials scrawled in the same looping letters he'd stared at on the ripped

poster. Caleb's blood chilled.

He retrieved gloves from his cruiser and lifted the envelope with care. Rider stayed pressed against him, growl low and constant.

He carried it inside and opened the flap to reveal a brick-thick bundle of papers. Page after page of screenshot images of Shelby's social media accounts. Dozens of fake posts she never made.

CONFESSION: I LIED ABOUT EVERYTHING

I DID THIS FOR ATTENTION

I'M NOT WHO YOU THINK I AM

Below each twisted lie were venomous comments:

She faked the threats for publicity.

Always knew she was trouble.

Cancel her for good.

Caleb's jaw locked until pain flared. It was hard to pray for enemies when all you wanted was to drag them into the light and let justice burn.

He snapped photos for evidence and alerted Sheriff Metcalf.

Then he heard soft steps behind him.

Shelby stood at the kitchen entrance, rubbing sleep from her eyes, unaware her world was under attack again.

He hid the envelope behind his leg, hating the secrecy but refusing to let this crush her first breath of morning peace.

"Caleb?" she asked, voice still rough with sleep. "What is it?"

Lord... give me the right words.

"Social media is waking up ugly," he said quietly, pulse refusing to slow. *Don't let me fail her again.*

Her face fell. "You think it was Tyler?"

He shrugged. "Possibly. All the evidence points to him. But just in case, I'm calling Metcalf. We don't want to take any chances."

He watched as fear rippled through her but so did fire. "I won't let him take everything from me."

He'd always loved that blaze in her. Now he'd die to protect it.

"That's right." His voice deepened with conviction. "He doesn't get the power."

Rider nudged her hand with his nose, agreement in canine form: *Not while we're here.* Caleb offered his palms. Shelby laid her hands inside his.

He tightened his hold, letting his promise bleed through skin and bone.

"He wants to isolate you," he said. "But you're not alone. Not anymore."

Not ever again if he had anything to say about it.

❧

Rain hammered the tin roof overhead, steady and merciless, each metallic strike echoing through her skull like ticking seconds on a clock she couldn't shut off. The blast still lived in her ears, a faint phantom ring that made the storm sound closer than it was, louder than it should've been.

A smear of gray daylight leaked through the curtains, stirring dust motes in the humid air—spiraling, restless, like the thoughts twisting low in her gut. Thunder rolled somewhere beyond the pines, deep and territorial. Not a soundtrack. A warning. The quiet between the strikes should've comforted her.

It didn't.

Because silence now felt like a breath held too long. Like a storm inhaling before it chose what to break next. And she was still counting down, bracing, waiting for impact that hadn't come... yet.

Her body still thrummed with aftershocks, her nerves trembling, thoughts sparking sharp and fast. She wanted to curl up with Rider and pretend none of this was real, but reality was pounding on the roof.

Caleb stood at the kitchen counter, shoulders rigid beneath his black T-shirt. The overhead light glinted off the tension in his jaw as he poured coffee into a chipped ceramic mug. No vest, but still armed. Even the way he breathed looked tactical.

This wasn't the Caleb she used to know, the boy who snuck her out after curfew so they could chase fireflies by the river. That boy laughed easily. Trusted the world.

This Caleb scanned every window like the glass might shatter inward.

Rider paced a slow line between the door and Caleb's heel, nails clicking on the worn wooden floor. Protective. Restless.

No one spoke, the silence in the cabin becoming increasingly heavy. Her lungs refused to expand.

Shelby sat at the small table, hands wrapped around her own mug, its heat doing nothing for the chill under her skin. Her guitar case leaned against the far wall, still unopened. Still hiding the thing she feared most. Her eyes kept drifting to it. *Don't look. Don't think about it. You'll unravel.*

Caleb finally broke the silence. "Sheriff'll radio check-in in twenty." His voice was low, even. Controlled. Too controlled.

She nodded but said nothing. Words felt dangerous.

He took a seat across from her but kept a slight angle. Always watching the door, the windows. The world pressed closer and she rubbed her hand across her heart to ease the ache.

Rider slumped beside him with a huff, chin on Caleb's boot. The dog's ears twitched every time the wind hit the cabin just right.

Shelby swallowed hard. "Do you think... they're coming here?"

"I don't think anything until I have facts." His tone was steady, not sharp—final, but fair. He wasn't shutting her out. He was anchoring the moment, laying the first stones of protection.

She stared into her coffee, wishing she could crawl inside the mug and vanish between the steam and porcelain.

"Did you sleep at all?" she asked quietly.

He exhaled once, a tired sound. "A little," he admitted. "More than I expected to." His gaze flicked toward Rider, then back to her. "But you're right. I'd have said the same thing last night. Sleep isn't the point." A faint edge roughened his voice, weary but fair. "Staying ready is." The answer caught in her throat, thick and warm and painful, not because he was cold, but because he was carrying the same storm she was trying not to name. Storm light flashed, silvery and cold. The thunder rolled closer.

Shelby rubbed her thumb along the edge of the table, the grain splintering slightly beneath her skin. Anything to keep her mind off the guitar case. Off the secret crouched inside like a snake waiting to strike.

Tell him. The voice had whispered all night. *Tell him before he finds out and hates you for it.* She opened her mouth to speak, but the radio on the counter crackled to life, the sudden burst of sound making her flinch.

Caleb was already moving in one smooth motion. "Hunter."

Sheriff Metcalf's voice pushed through the static. "Any activity on your end?"

"Affirmative," Caleb said, eyes never leaving the window. "Movement near the tree line overnight. Rider alerted. No visual confirmation."

A beat of silence filled the small space and then the radio

crackled to life. "Be advised, we've got a break-in at the venue. Someone cut through a locked access panel near the stage equipment. Nothing taken."

Shelby's stomach dropped hard. Nothing taken meant they weren't looking for money.

They were looking for her.

"And the van?" Caleb's glance landed on her.

"Still no leads. State police are expanding the search radius." Static hissed, thick and uneasy. "We're not operating under the assumption they've backed off."

Shelby's pulse slammed in her ears. Caleb's gaze flicked to her, just long enough to register her fear before his expression locked down again.

"Copy," he said evenly. "Keep me updated."

When he set the radio back on the counter, he didn't sit. He stayed where he was, shoulders squared, staring out at the pines as they swayed under sheets of rain—watching the world as if daring it to make the next move.

Shelby forced her breathing to slow. She could do grateful. She could do calm. She would not make this harder.

"Caleb?" Her voice barely made it past the knots in her chest. "Thank you for keeping me safe."

He didn't turn. "It's my job."

His job. Not his choice.

A tremor went through her. She pushed back from the table, needing movement, air... something.

She crossed to where her guitar case leaned. The leather handle pressed against her palm, grounding. Familiar. Safe.

Except it wasn't safe. Not anymore.

She crouched and unlatched the case, careful not to draw attention. She only meant to check her strings. That's what she told herself. But her heart knew the truth.

The letter peeked out from beneath a stack of lyric sheets like it had been waiting for this moment. Taunting her.

Her pulse roared in her ears. She hesitated then gently lifted the pages.

Her breath caught.

The paper was colder than she remembered. She traced the looping handwriting... too similar to the Sharpie scrawl on the bus poster.

The next song will end in silence.

A chill slid beneath her skin.

Shelby folded it and tucked it deeper beneath spare picks. Hide your fear. Hide the evidence of it. She snapped the case shut, heartbeat frantic.

She stood too quickly, dizzy for a second as the room tilted.

Caleb was watching. Eyes sharp. Cop-alert. Reading everything.

"What was that?" he asked.

"Just...strings," she lied too fast.

His eyebrow twitched. Knowing. "You don't need strings. Your gear's locked at the evidence tent."

Heat flooded her face. "Old habit."

He stepped toward her. She backed up until the wall pressed into her shoulders.

"Shelby." He lowered his voice. "I know you're scared. But you can't keep things from me right now."

She opened her mouth. Closed it again. Her throat tightened around all the words she couldn't say.

She couldn't tell him because he'd break.

She couldn't tell him because he'd blame himself.

She couldn't tell him because she needed him to be strong.

He took another step and Rider suddenly stood, nose pointed at the case. Whining. Caleb's eyes cut to the dog. "What is it, boy?"

Panic coiled tight in Shelby's chest. "No. Rider..."

Too late.

Caleb reached past her and unlatched the guitar case. The lid creaked open. The letter slid out like a confession.

Caleb froze and his expression went blank. It was the kind of blank that meant a storm was pacing behind his eyes.

He lifted the paper with two fingers. Read it once, fast. Then again, slower.

Shelby's lungs tightened painfully. She couldn't swallow. Couldn't think past the ringing still lodged in her ears.

When he looked up, something sharp flared in his gaze, not fury, but the sting of impact.

"You've had this." Not a question.

"Yes," she whispered.

"How long?"

Her voice cracked. "Three months."

A suffocating silence filled the cabin.

"You get a threat like this," he said, each word quiet, precise, edged in disbelief, "and you don't tell anyone?"

Anyone. Not *me*.

Tears scorched her lashes. "I didn't want my family living on red-alert," she said, the truth surfacing small but sharp. "Reporters already think I manufacture drama. My tour sponsors bolt at the first sign of 'unstable.' And I just gave a statement saying the night was calm." Her breath hitched. "If I admit someone is hunting me, everything I still get to choose, my music, my band, my schedule, goes up in smoke."

His jaw tightened, not at her, but at the impossible math of threat versus control.

"This isn't about theories," he said, voice low, controlled, lethal only in its certainty. "This is about the person hunting you."

She shook her head once, pain-tired honesty rough in her throat. "You weren't part of my world when it started, Caleb. I don't know who carries what now. I only know I can't lose the people depending on me."

Thunder cracked overhead, a storm-sharp period.

Rider stepped between them, sensing fracture, a soft rumble ticking low in his chest.

Caleb set the paper back down with careful precision. He didn't shout. Didn't explode. That alone told her this was bigger than anger.

"I need air," he said, and it sounded like *I need space from you.*

The door opened with a groan. Rain and wind rushed in. Rider hesitated, then followed him out.

Shelby slid down the wall to the floor, breath hitching as the last illusion of control finally slipped from her hands. The storm outside raged loud, but the one inside the room had struck deeper.

It wasn't a foolish thing she'd done to protect *him.*

It was a human thing she'd done to protect the parts of her life she still got to steer. And the burn of silence now felt like a held breath before impact.

The cabin felt too small. Too dark. Too silent.

And the storm outside wasn't nearly as dangerous as the one she'd just unleashed inside.

CHAPTER EIGHT

The storm swallowed him the second he stepped outside.

Warm rain snapped across his face, a sharp, grounding sting that chased away the last cling of sleep. His shirt soaked through fast, the fabric dragging heavy against his shoulders as pines whipped and bent in the wind beyond the porch. Thunder rolled low overhead, deep and restless, syncing with the dull, stubborn thrum still lodged in his chest.

He admired her fight. He always had.

But the wound the silence had woken was older, quieter, harder to name. It didn't roar like thunder.

It *pressed*. A jagged reminder beneath his ribs that whispered of missed moments and fragile assumptions. It was the uncomfortable, familiar burn of caring about someone in a world that gave no warnings twice.

He dragged in a steady breath, letting the rain do what it did best —shock, sharpen, *wake*—while his instinct cataloged the quiet beyond the storm. A stillness that never promised safety, only a pause before the next strike.

Rider pushed out behind him, staying close, his fur plastered to his sides. The dog's instincts were on high alert, ears forward, head low, a low growl rumbling like distant thunder in his throat.

Caleb strode toward the SUV parked under sagging pine boughs, phone already in hand.

He needed privacy for the call, but he needed *authority* for the update.

He opened the driver's door, leaned in, and grabbed the radio mic anyway. One tool for quiet. One for command.

The storm beat down around him as he keyed the mic, voice low, steady, awake. "Hunter to Metcalf."

Static hissed before Metcalf answered. "Hunter. Go ahead."

Rain needled Caleb's face as he stared past the windshield toward the cabin. "We have a significant security breach."

"How bad?"

"She received a threat," he said. "Three months ago." The truth sat heavy, but his voice stayed level, controlled. "She kept it quiet."

A beat of silence, charged and tactical.

"She didn't want cameras feeding a panic," Caleb continued, jaw tightening not at *her*, but at the escalating threat. "Didn't want her staff drowning in chaos. Didn't want the media painting a bigger target. Didn't want sponsors torching her tour." The words came clipped, low. "So she sat on it."

Metcalf swore under his breath. "Why would she—"

Caleb scrubbed a hand down his rain-soaked face. "Because she thought control was safer than alarm."

Another crack of thunder hammered the SUV roof, metal vibrating under the storm's impatience.

"She realizes she was wrong to shoulder the threat alone."

"She okay?" Metcalf asked.

"Not really," Caleb admitted.

The pines swayed under thick rain beyond the cabin's roof, the thick clouds hovering low over the landscape. No shapes. No movement. Just silence between strikes.

But inside his head, he couldn't shake the image of her pressed against the wall—eyes bright with guilt and fear. Not fear of the stalker.

Fear of repeating the past.

Fear of helplessness.

Fear of the moment someone finally sees how high the cost of protection can climb.

And the worst part? For a moment, he'd let that fear sound like it was about him at all.

Another crack of thunder. Rain battered the cruiser roof so hard it seemed the metal would cave.

Metcalf's tone shifted, steel replacing understanding. "We found something else."

Caleb straightened, cold spreading deeper than the rain. "What?"

"Photos. New ones. Surveillance from the fair. Shelby backstage. Shelby walking to the bus. That killer was right there in the crowd."

Caleb's pulse hammered. "How close?"

"Close enough we identified the camera angle from the second level of the lighting scaffold."

Caleb's stomach turned. That was less than thirty yards.

"And Caleb," Metcalf hesitated, that alone enough to spike Caleb's blood pressure. "They found a GPS tag under her bus."

A punch to the gut. "He knows everywhere she goes," Caleb rasped.

The sheriff didn't deny it. "We need to move."

Caleb's gaze slid back toward the cabin clearing, rain already fogging the edges of the morning. "Not again tonight," he said, voice rough but controlled. "This storm's bad math. I'm not putting her on the road blind."

"Agreed. We'll send a unit to sweep the tree line," Metcalf answered. "Reinforce your perimeter until daylight. I'll update when we've got something solid."

"Copy," Caleb said, the word clipped, tactical, reluctant but not reckless. "Hunter out."

He snapped the mic back into place and leaned both palms

against the SUV's roof, letting the warm September rain strike him again and again, rhythmic as old memory and new fear.

Sleep wasn't the point.

Control wasn't the point.

Presence hadn't been the point either. Not ten years ago, not now.

The point was this: he'd assumed he'd never miss the signs again.

Another crack of thunder rattled the morning like punctuation.

He pushed off the vehicle and turned back toward the cabin. Rider glued himself to his heel, every step fast, deliberate, head down against the storm's roar. He slammed the deadbolt behind them, not in anger, just urgency, a sound meant to secure, not to wound.

Shelby jerked on the couch, knees pulled close, trying to fold small into space she still didn't believe was safe.

"Shelby," he said. Not steady yet, but honest in the trying.

He knelt in front of her. Rain dripped off his hair, pooling on the floorboards, but he stayed where he was, gaze lifted, apology spoken in quiet cadence, not performance.

"I can replace roads, cameras, sponsors, tour miles," he said, thumb brushing her cheek once, gentle, permission-seeking, sure. "But I can't replace the moment you stop telling me you're scared."

A faint edge lived in the words, firm, protective, wounded only by the truth. "I can't protect you in the dark if I don't know the storm you're hearing."

She didn't shrink from the words this time. That mattered.

Outside, lightning split the sky, white-hot behind the curtains, fire tearing dark in half.

The storm wasn't done.

Whoever planted fear in her world wasn't done either.

But here, in this small circle of rain-washed breath, something finally shifted. They were bracing for impact together now.

Not healed. Not safe. Not yet.

Just awake.

Just aligned.

Just no longer alone.

And for the first time since the explosion, Caleb exhaled a full breath that didn't feel stolen by panic or the past. It felt claimed by duty and shared, impossibly, by the woman whose fire he still recognized even when the world tried to dim it.

Behind them, Rider thumped his tail once against the floor, entirely uninterested in the storm outside.

Caleb almost smiled at that.

"Yeah, boy," he murmured. "Perimeter stays tight. But we don't hide from the quiet anymore."

Not ever again if he had anything to say about it.

❅

All day long the wind howled around the cabin unrelenting until the storm and night melded together. Almost as if the storm itself wanted to claw its way inside. The roof creaked with each gust of wind. Thunder rattled the windows, and each flash of lightning stuttered across the walls, briefly illuminating the room in stark white.

Shelby stayed pressed to Caleb's side, listening to the heavy rhythm of the rain and the slower, steadier rhythm of his breathing. His shirt clung cold and damp to his skin from being outside, but his arms were warm and solid around her, an anchor she hadn't realized she was so desperate for.

Rider curled at their feet, watchful eyes half-open, head resting on Caleb's boot. Even resting, he had one ear ticked toward the door

"You're shaking," Caleb murmured against her hair.

"I'm cold," she lied.

He shifted just enough to drape the quilt from the couch over both of them. "Better?"

She nodded, even though the chill running through her had nothing to do with the temperature.

He wasn't angry anymore. But that didn't erase the sharp edges of doubt she felt about herself. About the choices that had dragged them here.

She tipped her head up until her gaze met his. Rain shimmered on his lashes. He looked tired. More than tired. Haunted. The fire popped. Rain hammered. Still he said nothing.

"Caleb?"

"Mmm?"

"You didn't fail me." The words cracked, fragile. "You never failed me."

He inhaled slowly, chest rising beneath her cheek. For several long seconds, he didn't speak, he just stared into the dark cabin as if he were trying to absorb it.

Finally, he exhaled. "I'll try to believe that someday."

The honesty in those seven words made her eyes sting.

She lifted her hand to touch his jaw. Rough stubble brushed her fingertips, a tether to real, breathing Caleb, not the guilt-ridden warrior his nightmares wanted him to be.

He leaned into her palm, just barely. But it was enough.

"Shelby..." he whispered, his voice lower, rougher, softened by exhaustion and something warmer. "I'm not letting you go through this alone again."

Her heart squeezed so tight she almost didn't hear the faint buzz from Caleb's phone.

He pulled away just enough to reach for it. When he saw the caller, his shoulders went rigid.

"Sheriff Metcalf." He answered. "Hunter."

The calm in his tone was a taut wire.

Shelby sat up, dread pooling low and heavy as Rider stirred, ears pricking.

Caleb listened, not interrupting, not breathing, then stood abruptly.

"When?" Caleb's voice sharpened blade-thin.

Static. Then Metcalf's tense reply crackled loud enough Shelby heard the sheriff's response.

"We've got him on camera outside your perimeter."

Shelby's blood iced over.

Caleb's eyes locked to the window like the killer might materialize that very second. "Send the image."

Seconds stretched, excruciating in their slowness. A buzz and then the incoming file.

Caleb tapped the screen. The glow lit his face. His jaw clenched so hard she thought his teeth might crack.

It was a grainy still image, but unmistakable. A figure in a hooded rain jacket, camera in hand...standing less than fifty yards from the cabin.

Watching them.

Watching *her*.

She hated that Caleb still blamed himself for her foolish actions. Shelby gasped, hand flying to her mouth. Rider sprang up, low growl vibrating in her bones.

"He was right there," Caleb ground out. "Watching me when I stepped out."

Her skin crawled. That quick glimpse Caleb thought he saw, that wasn't paranoia. That was real.

He was close. He was bold. He was hunting.

"We're moving now," Caleb told the sheriff, already grabbing his gear. "Prep a location and send coordinates."

He hung up, shoved the phone into his pocket, and turned back to her all the fury gone. Only fierce, focused resolve remained.

"Get your boots on. Don't stop for anything else."

Shelby's throat tightened around a nod. Her limbs were cold, heavy, slow to obey. She fumbled with the laces, her fingers missing the loops.

Her guitar case caught her eye.

The letter.

Her mistake.

She wouldn't let Caleb carry that alone ever again.

She grabbed the case by the handle. Caleb gave a curt nod of approval. There was no sign of resentment now, just partnership.

He grabbed her jacket off the couch and helped her into it, his touch gentle and efficient at once. "Stay right beside me," he said. "One hand on me if you have to. Do not fall behind."

The command didn't sting. It steadied her.

Lightning split the sky, illuminating Caleb's face. Angular, determined, unwavering.

"Caleb?" Her voice wavered.

He paused. And for a heartbeat, he dropped the handler, the officer, the soldier and became the man she remembered. He brushed his knuckles down her cheek. "I'm here. I'm not going anywhere."

Rider pawed impatiently at the door.

"It's time," Caleb said, and swung it open.

The storm swallowed them whole. Rain pelted them sideways, the wind and rain slicing like a knife. They sprinted toward the cruiser, mud sucking at their boots, branches whipping past.

Every shadow felt like a figure waiting to strike.

Just as Caleb opened the passenger door for her, he froze.

His hand shot out, grabbing her waist and pulling her behind him. "What—?"

He pointed to the opposite side of the clearing.

Shelby squinted through the sheets of rain.

A pinprick of red shimmered through the rain.

Not lightning.

Not a reflection.

A laser—steady—tracking across the cabin door.

Sniper.

Caleb's body went rigid. "Down!"

He shoved her into the cruiser, slammed the door, and dove in behind her as Rider scrambled into the back. Caleb threw the car into gear, tires spinning, sliding, kicking up gravel and then caught traction and shot down the dirt road.

Branches scraped against the windows like claws as they sped through the storm.

Shelby clutched her guitar case, heart battering her ribcage.

"Caleb..."

His voice was steady, but his breathing wasn't. "I've got you."

Lights flickered behind them. Headlights? Camera flashes? Or imagination born of terror?

The radio blared. "Unit 4 en route to your location..."

Caleb pressed a button. "Maintain distance. Unknown secondary threat."

Shelby stared at him, struggling to keep the panic out of her voice. "He found us. The safe house wasn't safe."

"Yeah." Caleb's grip tightened on the wheel. "He found you before last night. We're playing catch-up."

Rain smacked the windshield in sheets and the wipers waged a losing battle.

Shelby's fingers dug into the case until her knuckles whitened. "I'm sorry."

He shot her a quick look, he wasn't angry. Not anymore.

"Don't apologize for someone else's evil." He squeezed the nape of her neck. "The only one who should be sorry is the person we're going to put in cuffs."

His confidence should have calmed her. Instead, tears stung her eyes again — too many emotions crashing at once.

"I hate that he's doing this to you," she gasped. "I hate that I brought this into your life."

"You didn't bring danger into my life," he said, eyes fixed on the winding road. "You are the reason I walk into danger with purpose."

The words hit deep, deeper than the fear thrumming through her blood.

She wasn't afraid of storms or bullets.

She was afraid of losing him again.

She glanced over her shoulder at the dog, he seemed unfazed, as if he were used to high-speed chases. The glow from town grew fainter with every mile until the lights were obscured by trees and rain.

Before she could respond, Rider snarled, loud and sudden, claws scrabbling on the backseat.

Shelby twisted to look out the back window.

A flash of dark movement in the road behind them. A vehicle. Lights off. Chasing through the storm.

He was coming. He'd never stopped.

Caleb floored it, engine roaring.

Shelby gripped the dash, murmuring the words like a desperate vow. "Don't leave me."

Caleb's reply was swift and certain. "Never again."

The car rammed into the SUV's back bumper and she jolted forward, the seatbelt digging into her chest. Shelby placed a hand over her mouth, suppressing the scream that wanted to escape. The car backed off but Caleb sped through the night, trying to escape their pursuer. The roar of an engine, this time closer.

Rider barked sharp and fierce in warning. Then the next bolt of lightning revealed the truth in blistering clarity. The dark sedan swerved into the driver's side. The clash of metal filled the vehicle.

"Hang on tight." Caleb's face illuminated only by the dim light of the dashboard, his lips a thin line, hands gripping the steering wheel.

Another jolt from their pursuer bounced her into the passenger door and she screamed. Pain knifed up her side as the door's molded armrest edge pressed too hard against her ribs. "Hang on, we're almost to the service road."

The wipers thrashed against the windshield, unable to keep up with the torrential downpour. "There it is!" Caleb wrenched the wheel right, tires screaming as the SUV fishtailed off asphalt and onto a washboard gravel road.

The impact hit like a battering ram with the front end pitching up, suspension bottoming out, the nose of the SUV spiking toward the storm-dark sky before slamming back down in a hail of flying gravel. The vehicle bounced up and down, jarring her teeth. And then, silence, except for the squealing of one of the rear tires as the vehicle sat at an odd angle.

Everything paused.

Even the storm seemed to hold its breath.

"What are we going to do now?" Shelby whispered.

Caleb unbuckled his seatbelt. "We have to make a run for it." He opened his door and motioned for Rider to exit.

She sat there, hands shaking. "No, we can't."

"Shelby." Caleb's voice was stern, yet gentle. "We won't make it. Our only chance is to hike to the ranger's station." He placed his warm hand over hers — a promise and a command. "I've got you."

Numb, she unbuckled her seatbelt and followed Caleb into the darkness of the storm.

They weren't outrunning it anymore.

They were running straight into the heart of it.

CHAPTER NINE

Lightning strobed through the trees as they stumbled away from the disabled cruiser, Rider bolting ahead with a low, urgent growl. Storm wind tore at them like a living thing hungry for fear.

Caleb kept Shelby tucked tight against his side, one hand gripping her wrist like a lifeline, his weapon drawn in the other. He could feel her shaking but she ran anyway. Brave. Terrified. Determined.

He would die before he let her face this alone again.

Mud sucked at their boots. Branches whipped past their faces in chaotic blurs. Thunder drowned their breath.

Behind them, he heard movement. A glance over his shoulder confirmed a shadowy figure slicing through the rain, mimicking their every step, every turn.

"He stayed on us," Caleb muttered, fury coating every syllable.

"He's still coming." Shelby's voice cracked but she didn't slow. They couldn't stop now, no matter how tired they both were.

Good girl. *His* girl. The thought stormed through him, too wild and dangerous to voice. Right now, they needed to survive.

A warning snarl cut through the wind jerking his thoughts back to the present danger. Rider's entire body was frozen, tail rigid, his head angled toward the ridge. Caleb halted, his boots splashing more cold water up his pants. Arm outstretched, Shelby instinctively tucked behind him without being told.

Lightning flashed, and the world sharpened into a threat. Deep, rolling thunder made an ominous background track.

Red pinpricks blinked from the trees.

Cameras. Multiple. Watching.

"He's been here," Caleb rasped. "He planned this route."

Another flash of lightning and a hooded figure appeared farther up trail, a weapon raised and pointed in their direction.

"Down!"

He shoved Shelby as a gunshot cracked the night, tree bark exploding inches from his head. Heat and splinters bit his cheek.

Rider lunged forward with a snarl that shook the ground, but Caleb barked a command. "Stay!"

The shape vanished into the dark, probably flanking them.

Think, Caleb.

"He's trying to push us," Caleb growled. But toward what?

Shelby's hand clamped his arm, cutting off his circulation. "Caleb..." His name was tinged with fear but he had to make her understand what she meant to him.

He turned, the rain streaming off his jaw, heart pounding molten fear and something fiercer. "I won't lose you again." His promise. His sin. His everything wrapped into one breath. This was his time for redemption.

"When I say run..."

"I run," she said. "But not without you." Her chest heaved with the exertion, and he needed a moment to catch his breath, formulate a plan.

God, help.

His chest cinched tight, his breaths coming in short bursts. "Never without me."

Rider's warning rumble deepened. The enemy was close. Caleb mentally counted off a cadence until the one word exploded.

"Go!"

They launched uphill, the ground slick with rain-soaked leaves and mud. Thick mud coated the bottom of their shoes, slowing down what little progress they made. Caleb kept Shelby ahead of him using his own body as shield.

Another flash of lightning showed the lookout tower rising like a skeleton in the storm. His legs burned with the effort but he pushed forward. He had to keep moving.

Hope gave him a last burst of energy. They were almost at the station when a crack from the trees burst beside him. A searing agony ripped across his upper arm. Hot blood. Burning pain. He grabbed his arm and staggered forward.

"Caleb!" Shelby ducked under his arm, bearing more weight than he wanted to give. "Lean on me."

He gritted his teeth. "Keep moving."

Rider skidded to a stop, snarling at the trail, his fur standing on end.

That's when Caleb smelled it. Chemicals. Explosives.

"Back!" he yanked Shelby with his good arm just as lightning revealed a buried device. Multiple wires snarled through the wet leaves.

A trap. Carefully placed. Waiting for him and Shelby to stumble. His breath locked and his lungs burned from lack of oxygen.

Turning toward Shelby, he cupped her face in both hands, his blood smearing her cold cheeks. "This is all my fault." Her lower lip quivered and she tried to pull away from his touch.

"You did nothing wrong," he growled. The storm could've ripped the words from his throat but he forced them out. "This? This is on him."

Her eyes glistened. "I trust you."

He pressed his forehead against hers, their jagged breaths mingling. He closed his eyes and the dream of "if only" briefly flitted through his mind. This one moment was a stolen grace. Rider's frantic bark jerked them back.

Caleb pulled her close for a fleeting moment and then cupped her shoulders. "Hold on. We finish this together." He bent to look at her, infuse a new strength in her. One he didn't feel, one he needed right now.

Another flash of lightning showed an alternate path, one littered with jagged rocks on a steep incline. He didn't know which direction the threat was coming from next. All he knew was that he needed to get them to shelter. Between the intermittent flashes, blood marked their path. Rider led them upward, always looking for danger.

And somewhere out in the forest, the stalker hunted.

And with every breath, every hammering heartbeat one mantra repeated on a loop—*Never again*. He would walk into hell for Shelby. Tonight, he already had.

The lookout tower emerged through the storm like a skeletal refuge, its steel legs rising into lightning flashes and swirling wind and rain, a shape that promised cover if not safety. Caleb forced his legs to move faster, every heartbeat driving pain across his injured arm. Shelby stayed tight against him, shoulder pressed to his ribs, carrying more of his weight than he'd ever admit.

He wasn't supposed to lean on her.

He was supposed to protect her.

Rider reached the tower first, circling once with a low, uncertain whine. Not clear. Not safe. But safer than the open trail.

Caleb holstered his weapon long enough to grip the slick railing with his good hand. "Up," he urged, motioning Shelby ahead of him.

She hesitated. "You first."

A stupid, beautiful thing to say.

Lightning cast her face in pale silver, her blonde hair soaked and plastered to her cheeks, fear trembling in her eyes... but resolve stronger than both.

He swallowed hard. "I'll cover our backs. Go."

She nodded and climbed, boots slipping once. His palm lingered against her waist, maybe too long, but letting go felt worse than the storm raging around them.

Rider scrambled up next, claws clanging against metal stairs. Caleb went last, every step sending pain knifing up his arm.

The tower platform creaked beneath their weight as they reached the top. It was a rattling metal box, with half-walls offering minimal shelter, roof shielding the platform from some of the rain. Better than nothing.

Caleb swept the perimeter quickly, his body screaming against movement. He wanted to close his eyes and sleep, just for a few minutes. He sank to the floor and rested his back against the half-wall facing the steps.

Trees thrashed in the wind. Dark shapes shifted with the storm. The headlights from the other vehicle were gone. For now.

Rider sniffed every corner, then settled, but not relaxed, against Caleb's legs. Rider's gaze stayed locked on the woods.

Shelby dropped to her knees beside Caleb. "Let me see."

"I'm fine," he lied through clenched teeth.

"You're bleeding," she whispered.

"That's new?" he muttered, trying for humor. It came out more like a grimace.

Shelby slid closer and took his injured arm with careful hands. Her fingers were cold but her touch was warm, although shaky. There wasn't time for proper first aid. She tore fabric from the hem of her shirt and wrapped the graze with quick, focused movements.

He watched her, unable to look away. Mud streaked her legs. Rain glittered in her hair. She was terrified and breathtaking all at once.

But she wasn't breaking under the danger.

She tied the makeshift bandage tight and looked up, right into him. "You can't protect me if you fall."

Her voice fractured on the last word. His heart did too.

He reached up, thumb brushing a raindrop from her cheek, or a tear. Hard to tell. "Shel... you're not my responsibility."

Her breath hitched. "Don't say that."

"It's the truth," he rasped. "You're not my job. You're not my assignment. You're..." Lightning lit her face, her eyes shining with something fierce.

"What am I?" she whispered.

He should have let the storm answer for him. Should have kept the words buried where they couldn't get him killed. Where they couldn't get her killed.

But she was here, clutching him like a lifeline.

She was braver than he deserved.

"My purpose," he breathed.

Her lips parted. Shock. Hope. Something more dangerous flickering there.

"You are the reason I step into danger," he continued, voice low, rough truth tearing free. "Not because I have to. Because I would choose you every time."

He didn't realize how close she'd leaned until he felt her breath on his mouth, warm despite the cold around them. For a second, one impossible second, he almost closed the distance. Almost tasted what he lost years ago.

Shelby's gaze dipped to his lips. Just once. She was so close, he could regain what he lost ten years ago.

A howl of wind slammed the tower, snapping the moment in two.

Rider shot to his feet, ears forward, hackles raised. A deep growl rumbled through his chest like thunder's warning.

Caleb's pulse spiked. The woods below moved different, not wind, not shadow but evil intent shifting through the dark. He gripped Shelby's wrist again, pulling her next to him, the half-wall offering a modicum of shelter. "It's not over."

She nodded as he watched fear shaking through her but resolve steady as steel.

The storm howled back at them as Caleb raised his weapon, scanning the tree line.

This wasn't shelter. It was the eye of the hurricane.

And the worst was closing in.

❧

The metal platform shuddered beneath Shelby's boots as the storm slammed into the lookout tower with a force that felt personal. Rain sheeted sideways, stinging every inch of exposed skin like a thousand tiny needles. Wind screamed through the rafters, turning the whole structure into a shaking, groaning skeleton. Lightning splintered the sky, so close the air hummed in her teeth.

Shelby wrapped her arms around her middle, trying to hold herself together against cold, against terror, against memories that wouldn't stop rising no matter how hard she pushed them down.

They were higher now. They should have felt safer. Caleb had said the lookout station gave them a vantage point. Better visibility. He'd meant to keep her safe up here.

But the higher they climbed, the more wrong everything felt.

Caleb's back stayed fixed in front of her, a rigid wall of muscle and focus. He was reading the darkness, listening with that soldier's instinct that had kept him alive in deserts half a world away. His shoulders were coiled tight, tension radiating from him in a way she felt down to her bones.

Rider pressed against her leg, warm and solid, but vibrating with his own warning. His growl rolled low, steady, and constant like distant thunder promising something worse was coming.

Shelby swallowed hard. The guitar case strap dug into her shoulder, the weight of it heavier than it had ever felt. The letter buried inside, the one she'd kept hidden from Caleb, the one that had followed her from city to city felt like it was burning through the lining.

If she had told him sooner...

If she had trusted him with the truth then perhaps her mistake wouldn't have hunted them into these woods.

Caleb lifted his chin slightly. "He's been here."

She didn't ask how he knew. She felt it too, the way the air felt oily, violated. Like they hadn't walked into a space so much as stepped into a stranger's breath.

A cold prickle wound up her spine. Then the wind shifted.

And there it was.

A scent she hadn't smelled in years, metal and sweat and something sharp, synthetic. The scent of backstage corridors and stolen notebooks. Of obsession.

She choked as a flash of memory sliced quick through her mind.

A dim pub in Nashville. Her former songwriting partner leaning over her lyric sheet. His hand brushing hers just a beat too long. His smile wide but wrong. The way he called her "sweetheart." The way he stared a second too long.

The night she cut him loose.

Her blood ran cold. She knew that smell. Knew that presence.

Caleb froze beside the railing.

Rider's growl snapped into a warning bark.

"Shelby—down!" Caleb lunged, shoving her behind the center post of the tower.

A click sliced through the storm, small, precise, unmistakable. Then the world exploded in a white-hot burst of light. Whatever it was, it detonated at the top of the tower, brighter than any flash bang she'd ever seen on stage, louder than a speaker stack blowing out mid-show. Her guitar case strap was ripped from her shoulder and an invisible fist slammed into her chest. The platform lurched violently under her boots as the blast rocked the structure. Shelby hit the deck hard, the metal grating biting through her soaked jeans. A shrill ringing filled her ears, drowning out the storm, drowning out everything.

For a few agonizing heartbeats, she couldn't see. Couldn't hear. Couldn't breathe.

Her vision flickered back in jagged pieces as Rider skidded across the slick metal, claws scrambling.

The sky strobed with lightning.

The tower swayed like it might rip from its foundation.

Caleb's voice cut faintly through the ringing, muffled, desperate. "Shelby!"

She tried to push herself up, but her palms slid. Rain and blood slicked the surface. She blinked hard as her sight steadied just long enough to see Caleb stagger sideways, his hand pressed to his shoulder.

No, pressed to a wound.

Bright red washed down his arm, mixing with rain. He'd been shot.

"Caleb!" Shelby crawled toward him, dragging herself across the slanted deck, but another burst of light detonated behind her eyes, stealing her vision again.

Then footsteps. Heavy. Controlled.

Someone approached. Not running. Not afraid.

Her sight cleared just as a shadow materialized through the haze. A dark figure with a mask. Gloved hands. Rain sliding off a hooded jacket.

But it wasn't the mask that made her stomach drop. It was the posture. The tilt of the head.

The confident slant of his shoulders, like a man stepping onto a stage and receiving the adoration of his fans.

Her heart lurched.

No.

Please, God. No.

But the recognition was instant. Unmistakable.

Her former songwriting partner. The one who had turned admiration into fixation. The one who had crossed boundaries she didn't acknowledge until it was too late.

The one who kept sending letters, unhinged and cryptic, even after she left town, changed her number, changed her life.

He had found her.

He stepped closer, his head cocked, voice curling through the storm in a dangerous purr. "I knew you'd come back to me, sweetheart."

Her veins iced.

She scrambled backward, spine colliding with the railing, stealing her breath. Pain shot up her back. Rain blurred her sight, but she couldn't look away from him.

"Shelby, stay down!" Caleb tried to raise his weapon again, but his arm shook violently. Blood ran in rivulets through his fingers.

She surged toward him but a gloved hand clamped over her mouth. Another arm locked around her waist, jerking her off her feet so violently the world spun.

Hot breath hit her ear. "We're overdue for our encore."

Shelby thrashed with everything she had. She clawed at his wrist, felt skin split beneath her nails. She bit down hard, tasting blood and sweat.

He grunted but didn't loosen his grip.

Caleb roared, dragging himself upright. "Let her go!"

The stalker hauled her toward the stairs, dragging her across wet metal. Rider launched himself forward but the stalker swung a baton in a precise, brutal arc.

The crack echoed through the storm.

Rider yelped, fell and skidded. He lay motionless on the floor.

"No!" Shelby screamed, her voice breaking open.

Caleb pushed toward them when a gunshot seared the air. Sparks flew off the railing inches from his head.

Caleb stumbled, nearly falling off the platform as he dropped to one knee.

Shelby kicked harder, but her feet slid uselessly on wet metal as the stalker dragged her down the steps.

Then there was more smoke, thick, chemical, scorching billowing upward, turning her lungs to fire. Her vision sputtered into static. Tears streamed uncontrollably.

She coughed until she gagged.

Caleb's silhouette reappeared through the haze, swaying, arms raised, then falling again as the gas hit him too.

"Caleb!" she choked out.

He tried to reach her. Tried to push past the smoke, blind and bleeding, weapon dropped on the deck.

Her heart cracked at the sight of him fighting his own body just to get to her. The stalker kicked her guitar case, sending it spinning across the platform. She reached for it instinctively but it vanished in the storm. He jerked her down the steps, her boots slipping, her knees slamming against metal.

Not the letter.

Not now. Caleb. He was all that mattered.

"Shelby!" Caleb's voice tore through the storm again, guttural, raw with terror. "Hold on! I'm coming!"

Her captor snarled and squeezed her so hard her ribs bowed inward. "He won't get far. He's blind. Bleeding. Useless."

She bit his wrist again, harder this time. He cursed and slammed the butt of his knife into the side of her head. Stars exploded behind her eyes.

Cold metal pressed to her ribs. "Cooperate," he whispered, disturbingly calm. "Or I go back up there and finish him. And you'll hear him die."

Shelby's breath hitched. Her vision pulsed. Terror rose sharp and hot in her throat but then something steadier burned beneath it.

Love. A fierce, relentless, anchor-strong love. "No," she rasped. "You don't get to kill him because of me."

He laughed softly. "Oh, sweetheart... you wrote the lyrics. You know how this song ends."

Lightning flashed, illuminating the cruel curve of his smile. His eyes behind the mask were wild, ecstatic, drowning in delusion.

He dragged her deeper into the woods. Branches tore at her arms. Rocks bit her feet. Her breaths came in ragged bursts.

But she kept fighting. Kept thinking.

Stay awake. Stay alive.

Make him talk.

Buy Caleb time.

"What do you want?" she forced out.

"You," he said simply. "Like before. Before he ruined everything."

Before Caleb. Before she left Nashville. Before the letters turned venomous.

Her legs nearly crumpled, but she pushed forward, dragging her fingers across tree bark, leaving splintered scratches. A trail for Caleb and Rider.

Her stalker wanted her terrified. But Shelby knew she wasn't alone. Fear could live in her bones. Pain could shake her voice.

Her body could tremble, bleed, scream.

But she would survive. Not because she was strong.

But because God was.

And because Caleb Hunter would burn this forest to ash before he let her disappear. She clenched her jaw. She would survive long enough to be found. Long enough to fight back. Long enough to end this.

Even if she had to do it trembling.

Even if she had to do it afraid.

With God's help—she would survive.

CHAPTER TEN

The world was a white smear of agony.

Caleb clawed at his eyes, coughing hard enough that the metallic taste of blood coated his tongue. Smoke and rain filled his lungs with every ragged drag of air. The storm battered him from all sides, lightning flashing so bright it stabbed instead of guided. But none of it compared to the terror ripping through him.

"Shelby!"

His voice was unrecognizable, shredded and raw as if ripped from his chest.

No response. Only wind. Thunder. And a silence that sounded like failure.

Rider pressed against his leg, shaking violently, whining brokenly. The dog's fur bristled along his spine, instinct screaming that something precious had been stolen from them both.

Caleb's knees buckled, slamming into the grated metal. Pain shot up his thigh, the pain grounding him to reality. But the pain was better than the hollowness closing in on his ribs.

He'd let her be taken.

He slammed his fist into the tower railing so hard he heard bone pop. He swore under his breath as pain shot up his arm.

A bolt of lightning flashed too bright. But like him, it was too slow. Too late.

His radio crackled to life with Metcalf's voice, sharp through static. "Unit Two do you copy? Status!"

Caleb groped for his shoulder mic, fingers numb. "Officer..." coughs tore through him, "Officer... down. Shelby Lane abducted. K-9 injured. Coordinates transmitting now. Officer in pursuit."

"Stay put!" Metcalf barked. "Backup is en route..."

"No!" Caleb roared, adrenaline drowning out pain. "I'm going after her."

He was a failure. Failed to protect Shelby now. Failed to protect ten years ago. He stumbled to his feet, Rider circling anxiously, bumping his leg, whining mournfully. The dog wanted to charge into the woods, but he wouldn't leave his handler. Not unless Caleb gave the command.

Caleb blinked hard, once, twice, smears of trees forming vague shapes. He wiped at his eyes and hissed when the sting tore fresh tears loose.

"Hunter," Metcalf's voice cut back in, low but fierce. "Don't rush blind. You'll get yourself killed."

Caleb bit back a snarl. "Better me than her."

Rider's bark was sharp, insistent, as the K-9 stared into the dark where Shelby had vanished. He knew. He felt the bond severed. "She trusted me," Caleb rasped. "I promised her..." His voice broke entirely.

He'd broken his promise when he said never again.

He lied to Shelby. To himself.

The shrill sound of sirens cut through the rain as squad trucks fishtailed into the clearing. Red and blue flashing lights projected eerily against the dark forest. Deputies leapt out, flashlights slicing into the night.

Rider lunged when a deputy tried to leash him. Not attacking, simply directing the officer to where they needed to search. Rider's entire body pointed down the slope after Shelby. A living compass of devotion.

Caleb grabbed the dog's collar, establishing their bond, their position. "We go together, buddy," he whispered. "I'm not losing you too."

One EMT rushed him, medical kit already unzipped. "Your eyes, we need to flush the irritant immediately or..."

"Later," Caleb snapped, pulling away. "Flush them when she's safe."

"You're risking permanent damage..."

"I don't care!" It ripped from his throat like gunfire. "I can't help her standing here!"

A heavy hand clamped Caleb's shoulder. Sheriff Metcalf. The sheriff was close enough that Caleb could see the storm reflected in his eyes.

"Son..." Metcalf's voice came low, pained. "You're in no shape to run after anyone."

Caleb shrugged off his grip. "She's out there terrified, thinking I'm not coming for her, but I am."

Metcalf stepped in front of him, blocking the path. "Look at me."

"Move." His voice was a low snarl.

"Look. At. Me!"

Caleb finally lifted his gaze, wet eyelashes burning, vision doubling Metcalf into two.

"You are not God," Metcalf said, voice steady as a foundation stone. "You are not the one holding her life."

Caleb's breath fractured. "I was supposed to protect her."

"And you still will," the sheriff said firmly. "But not by tearing through the woods blind and alone."

Rider whined, pacing, tugging at his leash, nose dragging the ground since Shelby's scent was still fresh.

Caleb pressed the heel of his palm to his forehead. He couldn't stop shaking. His fingers fumbled with the latch on Rider's leash.

The dog shook his head, nose twitching. Waiting for his command from Caleb.

Metcalf softened just a fraction as he led him over to the back of the ambulance. "Do you remember Who she belongs to?"

Caleb froze. The dog followed him and sat by his leg.

"Shelby doesn't belong to fear," Metcalf continued. "Or fate. Or that twisted man who thinks he owns her story."

He set his hand on Caleb's shoulder again and he winced at the touch. This wasn't to restrain Caleb, but to steady. "Shelby Lane belongs to God." He gently pushed Caleb to sit on the top step of the bus.

The sheriff waved over the paramedic. "Check that shoulder wound. And his eyes."

The medic nodded and cleaned the wound and then bandaged it. "Get to the urgent care tomorrow. This bandage will hold you tonight."

Caleb nodded and his throat closed. Hope scraped beneath the rising panic, demanding to be heard.

"You love her," Metcalf said quietly. "I can see that clear as day. But God loves her more. He always has."

Lightning cracked overhead, loud enough to rattle the tower.

The medic tilted Caleb's head back with a gloved hand and began to irrigate his eyes. He exhaled as the solution flowed down his face. Blessed relief from the sting of the chemicals.

"And since she trusts God," Metcalf continued as the medic administered first aid. "You need to do the same."

The medic patted his shoulder and handed him a wad of gauze. "All finished. You might want to have your eyes checked out by a doctor." The medic snapped closed his toolbox and stowed it in one of the compartments.

"Thanks." Caleb nodded and squeezed his eyes shut, the tears slipping out unhidden. He stood and paced a few steps away from the ambulance. He whirled around, hands fisted. "I can't lose her. Not again."

"And you won't," Metcalf said. "But before you go, we're going to do the smartest thing you've done all night."

Caleb's breath shuddered. "What's that?"

"We're going to pray."

Caleb hesitated. The fear, pain, and rage all fighting for dominance.

But Metcalf bowed his head anyway.

Rider sat, eyes forward, perfectly still, as if standing guard during the prayer.

As Metcalf began to pray, the storm abated. The only sound now was the gentle plops of a few raindrops drumming against the leaves in the trees and Metcalf's deep baritone as he lifted their petition.

"Father, You love Shelby more than we ever could. Keep her safe under Your wings. Give Caleb the strength and clarity to find her. Blind the eyes of the wicked. Guide every step he takes. And remind him that he does not walk this path alone. Amen."

Even though he was cracked and desperate, a sense of peace settled across him as the sheriff prayed.

Metcalf looked him dead in the eyes. "Now go find your girl."

The words snapped something back into place inside Caleb. Not the soldier. Not the officer.

The man who refused to let fear speak louder than faith.

"This is your investigation, son. What do you want to do?" Metcalf leaned against his patrol car.

Caleb turned to the deputies. "I need drones in the air. Roadblocks at every exit of this forest. Pull every file on known obsessive fans and stalkers associated with Shelby. Anyone who bought backstage passes, sent threatening letters, or used multiple aliases to contact her, we need to prioritize those. And she's still wearing a mic that's linked to my comm."

A deputy took notes at lightning speed.

Caleb continued, voice strengthening with the added confidence. "He's injured. Right leg dragging. You can see a shallow footprint pattern. He's using smoke as cover which means tactical training or military background. He's familiar with the terrain and may have stashed supplies."

Another bolt of lightning cracked, illuminating a glint in the mud near a tree root.

Caleb moved fast, heart punching. He knelt, scooping the object up carefully. He turned it over in his hands. Shelby's cell phone case. The cracked one with the faded guitar decal.

His fingers shook around it.

"She dropped this on purpose," he whispered. "Breadcrumbs."

Rider barked once. He shoved his snout beneath low branches, tail slicing the air like a blade. He looked over his shoulder, as if to say, "got it." Rider had the scent again.

Caleb straightened, eyes still burning, yet fixed forward.

He whispered a promise breathed into the storm. "Hold on, Shel. I'm on my way."

Metcalf signaled two deputies. "You heard him. Stay on formation. We're moving."

Caleb placed his hand on Rider's vest. His command was a vow. "Track."

Rider launched into the forest, Caleb on his heels. Deputies flanked them, flashlights cutting white beams into the dark.

Every breath hurt. Every step jarred his injured arm. Tears continued carving tracks down his face.

But he ran anyway. For her. For the life he wanted.

The rain returned, only this time it was a wall. Branches slapped at his face and arms. Mud sucked at his boots.

Ahead, Rider's bark echoed like a battle cry.

Caleb didn't feel blind anymore. Didn't feel hopeless.

He felt driven by something greater than fear. This wasn't adrenaline anymore. This wasn't desperation.

It was faith in motion. With every stride he vowed, *I'm coming, Shel. You're not fighting this alone.*

Not anymore. Whatever hell that man dragged her into, Caleb would walk straight through the fire.

And he would not stop until she was home.

❧

Darkness swallowed the forest whole.

This wasn't the soft dark of night but a hungry dark, the kind that wanted to consume her. Erase her very existence.

Shelby's captor hauled her through dripping underbrush, his grip bruising bone. Mud sucked at her boots. Roots clawed her shins. Every stumble earned a wrench backward so violent her teeth rattled. She couldn't process fear fast enough to feel it.

"Stop," she begged around a sob she hated. "Please, I need to rest." She didn't want to show weakness to this monster but she had no choice.

His laugh was a low hum against her ear. "Begging already? Sweetheart, we haven't even begun."

Rain slid down her spine like icy fingers. She tried digging her heels into the earth. Her resistance lasted all of one second before he yanked her forward again.

Lightning illuminated a shack through the trees. It was a dark structure raised above the forest floor. A hunting blind. Elevated. Boxed-in.

A prison.

Her breath snapped short. "No, please don't make me…"

Cold steel pressed harder to her ribs. "Climb."

She shook her head instinctively. His blade scored her skin as she lurched forward, fire erupting along her side. She had no option but to climb.

The wooden steps glistened with rain, treacherous beneath her boots. She slipped once, hard, her free hand snapping to the railing to steady herself. The knife dragged with her momentum, biting shallow, enough to mark her, enough to burn. His grip clamped her shoulder, yanking her upright before she could fall.

When she reached the top, he flung her into the blind. Inside, it smelled like damp canvas and sweat. A combination of human fear baked stale into the walls. The putrid stench made her stomach churn. A single lantern flickered on a crate, spitting weak light that twisted shadows into monsters.

Riley would hate this place.

No. Not Riley. Rider. The dog's name was Rider. Her mind was unraveling from lack of sleep and terror.

Her captor followed her inside, closing the hatch. The click of the latch echoed like a coffin sealing shut. She closed her eyes, tried to breathe through her mouth, and sent up a silent prayer for protection.

She stood rooted, throat locked. If she screamed, the walls would swallow the sound.

"Sit." His tone wasn't raised which only made it worse. A man didn't need volume when he believed he owned the room.

She lowered herself onto a rickety bench, the rough splinters biting through her soaked jeans.

He crouched before her, inches away. Too close. Every muscle in her body begged to recoil. However, her instinct told her he fed on that reaction. Her fingers gripped the edge of the bench, and she forced all her fear into keeping herself grounded.

"Do you know why I picked you?" he asked, head tilted, voice soft enough she almost leaned in just to hear better.

"You're sick," she whispered.

He smiled like she'd told him something sweet. "No. Because you saw me. My work."

Her heart lurched. What in the world did he mean?

"You looked into the crowd of potential songwriters. And your eyes..." He lifted gloved fingers, touched the point between her ribs and collarbone and she flinched. "...found mine."

"I wasn't looking at you," she said, her voice breaking on the denial.

He leaned closer. The faint scent of rain mixed with something metallic clung to him. Was it blood? Oil? Gun solvent?

"You noticed me before anyone else did," he murmured. "Before the world cared."

His thumb ghosted over her lower lip. She turned her head away from his touch. She was trapped. Stuck in this small box with a madman.

"Before he cared." His voice hissed, snake-quiet, and shivers rocketed through her body.

Caleb.

The bottom dropped out of her stomach. Bile swirled and she had to force back the nausea. This was simply a game to him. A trap for Caleb.

He saw that his remark hit its mark, and his delight sharpened. "Oh yes. Him. The soldier. The hero. The one who let you burn alone for ten long years."

She sucked in a shaking breath. "He went to war."

"He left you," he corrected. "I was the one who stayed by your side through the tough years. I watched every show. I was there for every interview. Every late-night livestream. We were a team." He pulled something from his pocket. It was a paper, creased. He unfolded it slowly, savoring the motion.

It was a photograph. Of her.

Asleep in a hotel bed. Her hair spilled over her pillow... the window behind her slightly cracked.

Her spine iced over.

"You never lock the latch," he murmured. "You should be more careful."

She gagged on a cry.

He tucked the photo away like it was something precious. "I loved you when you were nothing but a girl with a guitar who couldn't fill a bar. We wrote the songs that made you a star. And I will love you long after the crowds forget your name."

Shelby forced a breath into lungs that didn't want to work.

She needed a strategy. She needed control.

Even if she had to fake it.

"Take the mask off," she demanded, voice hoarse. "Look me in the eyes if you're telling the truth."

He paused, then laughed softly, delighted. "You want to see the face that loves you most?"

She shook her head. "I want to see the coward hiding behind the lies."

His hand shot out, gripping her jaw, forcing her gaze forward. His eyes behind the black fabric burned, not with romance. With obsession.

"I'm your audience," he breathed. "Your muse. Your destiny." His thumb pressed into her cheek, bruising. "And when our final chorus hits? The whole world will know it was always us."

Her stomach churned. Every headline. Every performance. Every moment she thought she was alone...

He was there. Watching.

Claiming.

"No," she rasped. "I choose who I sing for."

He flinched, it was just a fraction, but enough. "You chose wrong," he snapped. "He is blind. Weak. A distraction."

"He's coming," she said, with a strength she didn't feel. "For me."

"Then he can watch the encore live," the stalker murmured.

He stood and reached for a rope. Her pulse screeched warning, but it was too late. Metal shutters slammed over the windows, a violent symphony of locks and darkness. The flickering lantern became the only glow left, trapping heat and terror with nowhere to escape.

He walked to a tarp-covered object and pulled the sheet away.

A mounted camera. Pointed directly at her.

Not an audience of thousands. An audience of one.

Her chest crushed inward.

He stepped behind the lens, adjusting the focus. "We never finished our song," he said softly. "Let's rehearse."

A tremor shook her bones.

He lifted a remote and a small red light blinked to life on the camera.

"Smile for me, Shelby."

Her breath fractured. *No.*

No. No. NO.

"I want Caleb," she said, the truth ringing like a weapon in her mouth. "Not you."

The stalker stilled and then his voice changed. It was soft and charred with hatred. "He will be the first to hear you scream."

He lunged, grabbing the rope hanging from a rafter, snapping it taut above her wrists. Before she could move, he yanked and her arms jerked overhead, body pinned upright.

Pain tore through her shoulders. Panic exploded in her chest.

"No—please—" she gasped, kicking at the bench for leverage as it slid away.

He leaned in, whispering against her cheek. "It's okay to be afraid before the applause."

Her fingers tingled, the blood struggling to reach her hands. Her vision speckled black-silver.

She forced air into her lungs. She had to remind herself to breathe one breath at a time.

Think. Don't panic.

Caleb is coming.

Her stalker noticed and stood in front of her. "You're trying to be brave," he crooned. "I like that."

He stepped back and pulled a knife from his belt as the steel gleam caught the lantern's flame. Every sound in the blind seemed too loud, the rope creaking, her heart pounding, his breath steady.

She tasted fear like acid, burning her tongue. But beneath it... Anger.

"You think you know how our story ends," she whispered, voice shaking but sharp. "But you're not the one who gets to write it."

He laughed again because he didn't understand. Couldn't understand.

Shelby wasn't the girl he used to follow through dive bars. She wasn't that scared, small version of herself anymore. She had survived worse storms.

She had faced silence longer than any darkness he could throw at her. "You're right," she murmured as she lifted her chin, meeting the black eye holes of his mask. "I did write the lyrics."

She let him see the steel behind her fear. "And I know exactly who the villain is."

His body jerked with her statement, his body coiled as the truth struck. Fury tightened the shadows where his expression hid. Her stalker stepped toward her, his blade hovering over her.

Shelby's heart pounded the promises Caleb made to her. The darkness wouldn't defeat their love.

Caleb will come.

He will tear this place apart to find me. She just needed to stay alive long enough to let him.

Even if she had to bleed.

Even if she had to scream. Even if she had to do it terrified, she would make it to the encore.

She would make it home.

CHAPTER ELEVEN

The forest pressed in around him like a living thing, breathing, shifting, swallowing light whole.

Caleb stumbled through slick underbrush, one hand clamped over the wound in his shoulder. Every step matched the pounding of his heartbeat. His other hand kept his pistol trained forward, though every muscle trembled with exhaustion.

The storm had fractured into a relentless drizzle, the raindrops colder now, needle-sharp as they spilled down his neck. His ears still rang from the flash-bang. His vision pulsed at the edges.

But none of it mattered.

All he heard over the wind, over the rain, over the hiss of the woods, was her voice echoing through his memory. The comm he attached to her shirt earlier had malfunctioned.

"Caleb—hold on!"

He bit back a curse and forced his legs to keep moving.

Rider limped ahead, his left flank bruised and his gait uneven from the baton strike, but his eyes were fierce, his nose locked on the trail like a laser. Every few steps, the dog would glance back, not for permission, but to make sure Caleb was still conscious.

"I'm right here," Caleb rasped, though he wasn't sure how true it was. His voice sounded foreign, shredded and thin. "Keep her trail."

Rider huffed once, a determined sound, and surged forward, nose pressed to the ground. He followed splintered bark, smeared mud, drags in the earth where Shelby's boots had skidded.

She'd left him a trail, even while fighting.

Caleb's throat constricted. "Good girl, Shel." His voice cracked. "Keep leaving me signs."

A wave of dizziness hit him hard enough he staggered sideways into a pine trunk. Bark scraped his cheek. The forest tilted, and he forced his eyes to steady, blinking until the double-vision narrowed to one agonizingly clear image.

He wasn't allowed to fall.

He wasn't allowed to fail.

Not again. Not with her.

A branch cracked to his right—sharp, instantaneous.

Caleb spun, pistol up, light and muzzle aligned, finger riding discipline on the trigger.

The woods answered with silence. Darkness devoured everything beyond the reach of their flashlights.

Two deputies fanned out on either side of him, boots grinding into wet earth as they swept their sectors.

Rider surged forward a half step, ears pitched, low growl vibrating in his throat in warning.

Caleb's heart battered his ribs like it wanted out. He waved the deputies over. "Bates, north tree line. Carver, take the creek bed," he ordered, voice edged steel. The deputies nodded, breaking apart to hunt the sound, leaving Caleb and Rider braced in the trembling quiet. The forest held its breath. Somewhere out there, Shelby was bleeding. And they were running out of trees to hide the devil behind.

He moved again, sucking in air that tasted of wet soil and rain. The storm had softened, but every now and then, a distant roll of thunder vibrated through the ground, echoing in his bones.

Rider stopped abruptly, head lifting. He sniffed hard, fur bristling.

"What is it?"

The dog stepped left, weaving between two thick oaks before darting down a narrow, shadowed trail. Caleb followed, the ground sloping sharply downward. His boots skidded in slick mud, nearly sending him tumbling, but he caught himself with his good arm, cursing as pain shot across his chest.

The air changed. It was colder, staler. The trees parted and Caleb froze as they stood in small clearing.

An elevated hunting blind stood ahead, dark, square, and perched on splintering stilts. The shutters were sealed tight. Lantern light flickered through narrow cracks like a dying heartbeat.

His pulse stopped, then slammed forward. "Shelby," he whispered, the word tearing out of him.

Rider gave a low, savage growl and trotted toward the stilts, circling like a predator assessing its prey. His tail was stiff, his movements sharp.

Caleb scanned the perimeter, eyes sweeping the ground and found two sets of tracks leading straight to a set of rickety stairs. Shelby's lighter steps first, then deeper boot prints behind her where the mud was disturbed. A small smear of something dark was on a rung. Blood.

Not fresh. But not old.

His stomach twisted and he reached for his radio. "Bristow, Metcalf, Carver—anyone—come in. I've got a confirmed structure. Possible hostage location." His breath released in a stagger. "Coordinates—thirty-six point two-one-four by zero-eight point three-three-three. Need immediate backup. Suspect is armed. Danger high."

Static crackled. Then, then the faint response, breaking up. "—copy—Hunter—hold posi—backup en—route—"

The radio died in a hiss. Of course. He tilted his head back and exhaled as he studied the structure. The canopy overhead was too dense. The blind was metal and the storm killed signals.

He shoved the radio into his vest and drew a steady breath, willing his body to hold together for just a little longer. He reached down, giving Rider a quick hand signal. "Guard the base. Do not enter until I call."

Rider lowered into a crouch, muscles vibrating with focus.

Caleb grabbed the railing, pain ripping across his shoulder. His breath shuttered and he clenched his teeth. Still, he climbed.

One step. Then another. And another.

Halfway up, he paused, forehead pressed to the cold wood. He prayed, not with words, but with desperation, his forehead braced to the rain-soaked structure. This was a prayer filled with a raw, reckless need. *God, don't let me be too late.*

Behind him, Rider's claws clicked a deliberate cadence on the steps as the dog climbed in his wake, focused, silent, tracking his handler's every micro-shift.

Caleb lifted two fingers without looking back—follow, close, quiet. The dog answered instantly, shortening his body line, climbing tighter to Caleb's boots.

Caleb forced himself higher. Rain sluiced off the blind's overhang, needling his skin. The ladder jolted under him when his boot skidded, the SUV crash earlier still living in his nerves. His numb fingers cinched around the rung, refusing to let go.

He reached the hatch, angled his flashlight through the seam, and saw movement. A shape towering over Shelby.

He kicked the hatch. Wood spider-cracked but held.

He kicked again. The hatch exploded inward.

Caleb launched into the blind, pistol raised, his breath gone, heartbeat drumming out of his chest.

Rider cleared the hatch behind him, a controlled surge of power… then hit the floor and held, muscles coiled, awaiting the release command. His ears flicked once toward Caleb, seeking the signal.

Caleb gave the smallest downward dip of his hand—wait. The stalker turned toward Caleb, startled, and froze, just long enough for the moment to shift.

Caleb seized it. "Rider," he growled, flicking his hand forward, "go."

Rider surged from his crouch, low and lethal, a snarling blur of teeth and vengeance, aimed at the threat. He slammed the stalker to the floor. A fight erupted. Violent, chaotic. The blind shook with the struggle, and the lantern tipped, rolling dangerously close to Rider.

Caleb charged forward, grabbed Shelby's waist with one arm, and sliced through the rope with a quick snap of his tactical knife. She collapsed into him, her sobs tearing at every frayed inch of his soul.

"I've got you," he whispered, pulling her close despite the agony ripping down his shoulder. "I've got you, Shel. I swear, I've got you."

Her fingers clutched his uniform, desperate and shaking, and she buried her face into his chest. For a brief second, he relished her safe in his arms. He led her over to the hatch. "Can you get down by yourself."

Shelby's broken sob tore down his defenses.

"Yeah."

Behind him, Rider and the stalker thrashed against crates, metal, walls. The cries of the stalker mixed with Rider's snarls. Caleb whirled to help, but a strange sound cut through the struggle that made Caleb's blood run like ice in his veins.

A soft, chilling *click*.

He looked at the stalker, now pinned under Rider. He held his uninjured hand away from the dog, a device clutched between his fingers.

It was a small, blinking detonator. A timer lit up and a shrill beep began.

Fast. Rhythmic.

"No..." Caleb breathed. "No...NO..."

The stalker's voice rasped in triumph. "Encore."

The timer escalated. Rider barked, frantic.

"Rider... release!" The dog backed away, teeth bared.

Caleb grabbed Rider's harness, pulling him toward the hatch. "Move. Out!"

Caleb and Rider were halfway down the makeshift steps when the floor vibrated. The woods outside lit with a blinding burst. Caleb and Rider rolled to the ground, stunned. He stood, unsure where Shelby was.

"Shelby!"

She ran toward him but he waved her off. "Stay back!"

And then the blind exploded.

🐾

The hospital waiting room felt like a cage made of fluorescent light and cold tile. Shelby paced the length of the hallway until the scuffed linoleum memorized the rhythm of her boots. Her hands balled at her sides, nails digging crescents into her palms as she stared at the double doors that had swallowed both Caleb and Rider hours ago.

A nurse had offered her a blanket, which was still wrapped around her shoulders. She shivered. Why couldn't she get warm?

Metcalf had offered her a chair, which she refused.

Bristow offered her water and half a prayer.

The man she loved was back in one of those rooms and she felt like she was going out of her mind for lack of an update.

Sitting and breathing felt impossible.

Hope hurt as much as fear.

Her throat was raw from smoke and screaming, her clothes stiff with dried blood, and not all of it her own. Rope burns banded her wrists like dark bracelets. Her hair was still tangled with ash. She must've looked like something dragged out of a nightmare.

But none of it mattered.

All she saw was Caleb, pale and bleeding on that stretcher.

All she heard was Rider's heartbreaking whine as they loaded him into the second ambulance.

"Lord," she whispered, hands trembling, "please... please don't take them. I don't..." Her voice cracked into a sob. "I don't know how to bear that, just when I found him again."

Her voice echoed softly, swallowed by the antiseptic air. The doors swung open, and her heart seized. Not Caleb. Not Rider.

Just the young nurse again.

"Ms. Lane?" she asked gently. "Do you want an update?"

Shelby stepped forward so quickly the room tilted. "Rider? Caleb? Please, just tell me something."

The nurse softened. "Your K-9... they're working on him now. Internal bleeding. Broken ribs. But he's strong."

Shelby swallowed a sob. "He's... alive?"

"For now, yes."

For now. Two words sharp as knives. Carving up what little hope she had for Rider's recovery.

She closed her eyes, didn't dare hope. "And Caleb?" she whispered.

"He's coming out of recovery now and they're moving him to a room." The nurse checked the tablet. "He'll be in room 427. I'll meet you there."

Shelby's heart stuttered a beat. "He's awake?" she asked, voice shaking.

"Barely. He keeps slipping in and out. He's in a lot of pain, Ms. Lane. He lost a lot of blood."

Shelby's knees buckled and she held out a hand to steady herself. Only the wall kept her upright.

Shelby didn't walk. She ran. She shoved through the double doors, sprinting down the muted hallway. Every smell hit her at once, the sterile alcohol, latex, metal, and something scorched still clinging to her clothes. The beep of machines accelerated, echoing down the hall like frantic heartbeats.

She paused outside his room. Her breath caught. Her hand hovered inches from the handle. Then she pushed it open.

The sight inside tore her soul in half.

"Oh, Caleb," she breathed. She stood rooted to the floor, unsure if she should even touch him.

Caleb lay unmoving in the hospital bed, washed in the fog of anesthesia. The world around him was muffled, distant, like sound traveling through water.

Shelby pulled a chair close to his bed and sat, cradling one of scarred hands in hers, the earlier terror finally catching up to her. Gravel still seemed to rattle in her bones from when the SUV had been forced off the road. The sting of the shallow knife wound at her side throbbed with a persistent, hot, burning every time she drew breath.

She didn't dare reach for hope. Not yet.

Machines hummed a low, steady mechanical hymn. The monitors blinked a quiet rhythm.

And beneath it, soft, fragile, stubborn, was his pulse.

A nurse slipped in, quiet shoes on quieter tile. She checked the IV flow, the chart, the bandage blooming faint red beneath the medical tape. She adjusted a dial, watching the numbers climb toward stability.

"He's holding," she said to no one in particular, half a prayer herself.

Shelby nodded, voice gone.

When the nurse stepped out, Shelby stayed exactly where she was, because leaving wasn't an option she could survive again.

Her voice, hoarse and worn, was the only weapon love had left her.

She closed her eyes, braced her hand near his forearm without touching the medical lines, and began to sing. It wasn't loud enough to disturb Caleb's sleep, but strong enough to disturb the dark:

"When the night falls hard
And the world goes quiet,

When the storms you fear
Are louder than the silence..."

Another nurse entered then, scanning vitals, shining a small penlight at Caleb's eyes. He didn't wake. He didn't move.

But the monitors answered to her presence, the numbers leveling under practiced hands.

I'll stay right here.
I won't walk away.
If you lose your light,
I'll give you mine
Until dawn finds its way..."

The nurse checked his blood pressure cuff and oxygen sensor, the gentle beep of the pulse-ox keeping time with Shelby's melody. She adjusted a sensor pad, watching the waveform strengthen in small, rising mountains.

"He's stable," she whispered, exiting again.

Shelby kept singing.

"Hold on, love—
Just breathe again.
You don't have to fight this
On your own.
You're not alone..."

Caleb's head shifted the slightest fraction against the pillow, a faint exhale escaping like wind finding a crack beneath a door.

And then, barely there, barely a fraction of an inch, his lips parted. "Shelby..." Rough. Groggy. A ghost of a whisper. But alive.

Her breath detonated into a gasp she didn't let turn into a sob. He needed quiet.

Another nurse returned, tablet in hand, scanning his chart. "We're checking incision sites and vitals every fifteen. He should sleep awhile."

Shelby swallowed, nodded again.

The nurse glanced at Caleb's lax, pale stillness, then back at her. "Sing to him if you want," she said gently. "It can't hurt."

Shelby's laugh was sharp, cracked, but it tangled into a tear instead.

So she did the only thing she could do. She sang him back to life.

And every time a nurse returned to check his vitals, she never stopped.

Because love wasn't loud. It was loyal.

And loyalty was louder than the storm.

CHAPTER TWELVE

The first thing Caleb became aware of was pain. A deep, dragging ache in his shoulder that pulsed in time with the sluggish monitor beeping somewhere above him.

The second thing he noticed was warmth wrapped around his right hand. Soft. Small. Familiar.

Shelby.

He didn't open his eyes all at once. He rose to consciousness slowly, like surfacing from deep water, the world thick and muffled. Voices drifted through the fog. Nurses moving somewhere down the hall, a soft conversation, shoes squeaking on polished floors. The rattle of carts. Muffled announcements over the intercom.

But the warmth around his hand pulled him the rest of the way up. He cracked his eyes open and saw her.

Shelby sat slumped forward in a chair pulled close to the bed, her head resting on his arm, her hair a halo of tangled honey-blonde waves around her face. A blanket had been draped around her shoulders, probably by a nurse she'd ignored. White bandages circled her wrists like ghostly bracelets to cover the rope burns. She had fallen asleep clutching his hand in both of hers, cheek pressed lightly against his forearm. One thumb rested over the pulse point at his wrist, as though she'd been monitoring it.

His breath caught.

Her eyelashes fluttered just a little, as if she dreamed something fragile. Her lips were parted, soft. She looked exhausted, battered, bruised...and was the most beautiful thing he had seen since the woods swallowed her.

"Shelby..." The word came out a hoarse whisper.

Her head shot up. She blinked rapidly, disoriented for a moment until her gaze locked on his.

"Caleb." Her voice broke on his name. She surged up, leaning over him, hands shaking as she cupped his face. "Oh thank God, you're awake." She dropped a light kiss on his cheek. "Oh thank God."

Emotion slammed into him so hard his throat tightened. He wanted to reach for her, stroke her hair, kiss her properly. He yearned to say everything he'd meant to say before slipping under but only his fingers moved, curling weakly into her blanket.

She caught the movement instantly, slipping her hand into his again.

"You scared me to death," she whispered, her forehead dropping gently to his. Her breath trembled against his cheek. "Don't you ever do that again."

He swallowed, voice raw. "Didn't... mean to."

A wet laugh escaped her. She brushed her thumb across his cheekbone. "You're warm," she said, relief softening her voice. "You were cold earlier. Unresponsive. I thought..." Her voice faltered, and she shook her head, then smiled through her tears. "It doesn't matter now. You're here."

He exhaled slowly, grounding himself in her nearness.

"How long... was I out?" he managed. Every word was a struggle, but he needed to see her, to fight for her.

"Almost twenty-four hours," she said softly. "You came in and out a couple times, but not like this. Not awake."

He absorbed that. An entire day.

He had lost twenty-four hours. His fingers tightened around hers and she leaned closer.

"You need water," she murmured, already reaching for the cup on the tray.

She lifted a straw to his lips. He sipped slowly, the ice-cold water refreshing and painful against his dry throat.

His voice returned enough to rasp, "Shelby… Rider?"

Her breath caught. She placed the cup back on the tray, turning to look at him again.

"He's alive," she said, and the relief in her eyes was unmistakable. "He's still in the K-9 unit's medical wing. Surgery went well. They said his ribs are fractured and he has internal bruising, but… Caleb, he's going to make it."

Caleb closed his eyes for a moment. A breath shuddered out of him. *Thank you, God.*

"He's a good boy," he whispered.

"He is." Shelby moved her hand to his hair, brushing it back gently. "He won't leave us."

A small, weak smile formed on Caleb's lips. "Think… he can visit?"

Shelby nodded, voice softening. "I asked the vet tech the same thing. They said once you're more stable, they'll bring him in. He's been whining and pacing whenever anyone walks by. He's looking for you."

His eyes stung. He didn't bother hiding it. "Yeah," he whispered, voice cracking. "I'm looking for him too."

Shelby leaned closer, pressing a soft kiss to his forehead. "You'll see him soon. I promise."

Caleb absorbed that promise, letting it settle like warmth beneath his ribs.

The door cracked open and Sheriff Metcalf stepped inside, his hat in his hands, face lined with worry and something else. Guilt, maybe.

Behind him stood Bristow, who gave Caleb a small nod, relief flickering across his features.

"Caleb," Metcalf said quietly. "Good to see you awake, son."

"You had us worried there for a moment." Bristow moved into the room and gave Shelby a one-armed hug.

"Hey, that's my girl." Caleb cracked a smile but everything hurt.

Bristow grinned and raised his hands. "Hey man, just happy to see everyone."

"I'll uh, leave you all alone." Shelby's glance bounced between the three men, looking torn between staying and giving them privacy.

Caleb lifted his fingers weakly. It was just a small gesture, but she understood instantly.

"Stay," he murmured.

She sank back into her chair, her hand resting in his again.

Metcalf stepped closer to the bed. Bristow remained near the door, arms crossed, eyes sharp and alert. Reverting back to protective mode.

"Hunter," Metcalf said gently, "we've got some updates on the investigation, but before we go into any of that, how are you feeling?"

"Like somebody... ran me over," Caleb said hoarsely. "Then backed up... to make sure they finished the job."

Metcalf's lips twitched. "Sounds about right."

Shelby brushed a soothing thumb across the back of Caleb's hand.

Caleb's gaze sharpened slightly. "The stalker...?"

Metcalf exhaled slowly. "We found what was left of the blind after the explosion. The suspect is missing."

Caleb stiffened. Tried to sit up. "Missing?"

"Blood on-site," Bristow added. "A lot of it. Enough that no man should be able to walk away, according to the doc we consulted." Bristow clenched his teeth.

"But he did," Metcalf finished. "He vanished into those woods before we arrived."

Shelby's breath hitched. Her fingers tightened around Caleb's, cutting off the circulation in his fingers.

"He must've jumped out of that blind before the explosion," Metcalf said.

Caleb fought a surge of anger that shot through him like lightning. "He's still out there."

Metcalf nodded once. "We're not stopping the search. We've got a grid sweep covering six square miles. Drones, dogs, thermal imaging. Everything. But the storm messed with our equipment. The terrain's thick. It's going to take time."

Caleb lifted his head slightly. Pain lanced through him, but he ignored it. "He's not done," he said. "He's fixated. He'll come back for her."

Shelby flinched, but she didn't release his hand.

A muscle in Metcalf's jaw twitched. "We know. Which is why we're doubling protection detail. Jesse Thompson from the Marshals is flying in. You're off duty until you're cleared by medical, Caleb."

Caleb's eyes flashed. "I'm not sitting on the sidelines while he's out there."

"You don't have a choice," Metcalf said firmly. "You nearly died. If that blind had blown five seconds earlier, we'd be having a very different conversation."

Shelby's nails dug into his skin and Caleb let his head fall back against the pillow, breath shaking.

"Caleb, please." Shelby leaned close, voice low and steady. "For once... let someone protect you."

He swallowed hard. He was used to being the protector, not the protected. He shifted in the hospital bed, unable to get comfortable.

Metcalf cleared his throat. "Listen, I know this is difficult. Security is being increased around Shelby. She won't be alone for a second."

"I'm not leaving him," Shelby said, voice trembling but fierce.

Metcalf nodded. "And he's not being left alone either. He'll be guarded as well."

Caleb closed his eyes briefly, overwhelmed. He'd always been self-sufficient. Taken care of everyone under his care. Perhaps God was trying to get his attention. Make him realize that he'd been walking in his own power.

Then something tugged at him. It was urgent, emotional, primal even. He turned his head slightly to Shelby. "You... sang," he said. "I heard you."

Shelby's expression froze, as if she'd been caught.

Metcalf and Bristow exchanged a glance. "We'll be in the cafeteria. Seems like you two need some space to talk." The men stepped out of the room, their footsteps fading down the hallway.

Caleb brushed her cheek with his hand. "Your singing kept me here."

Her eyes flooded instantly. "I didn't know if you could hear me."

"I did."

She leaned forward, resting her forehead against his. "I thought I was going to lose you."

"I'm right here." His voice was ragged, weak. But like Scripture said in his weakness, God's power is made known.

"You better stay that way," she whispered fiercely.

He smiled faintly. "Wasn't going anywhere."

The door opened softly again. The vet tech from the K-9 unit stepped in, holding his hat in his hands.

"Ms. Lane? Deputy Hunter?" he said.

Shelby jerked upright. "Rider?"

The tech nodded. "He's awake."

Caleb's breath hitched. His dog. His partner. The one who risked his life for both him and Shelby. "Can I see him?"

"If you're up for it," the tech said, eyes softening, "we can bring him in for a short visit."

Shelby turned back to Caleb, eyes shining.

Caleb swallowed hard. "Yes. Please."

The vet tech nodded and slipped back out.

Shelby squeezed his hand, tears trembling on her lashes.

Caleb closed his eyes for a moment, letting the weight of everything settle. He was alive. Shelby was safe. Rider was alive. The man who hunted them was still out there.

Caleb felt something stronger than fear. He felt hope as Shelby leaned into him, warm and steady, his dog being brought down the halls, nails ticking softly against the tile.

🐾

The hallway outside Caleb's room hummed with the low throb of fluorescent lights and the steady beep of medical equipment in rooms up and down the corridor. Shelby paced that narrow stretch of tile for what felt like hours, blanket trailing behind her like a ghost of the night before.

Inside the room, Caleb slept while Rider lay curled vigilantly at the foot of his bed, ears twitching every time a shoe squeaked in the hallway, every time a nurse passed.

Shelby sank to the ground beside the dog, feeling the burn in her knees as she settled onto the cold linoleum. Rider shifted, pressing his warm body against her hip.

"Hey, buddy," she whispered, threading her fingers behind his ears. "You scared me half to death."

Rider nudged her hand with a soft grunt. It meant *don't fuss; I'm fine.*

But he wasn't fine. Neither was she.

"You kept him alive," she whispered. "You kept *me* alive. You're the reason I'm sitting here right now."

Rider thumped his tail once in a tired, loyal beat.

She leaned her forehead against his, eyes slipping closed as her breathing slowly found his rhythm. His presence, steady, warm, and irreplaceably *there,* was the only thing keeping her from unraveling.

A knock snapped her upright. She rose fast, smoothing her shirt, brushing hair from her cheeks. "Come in."

The door opened in a controlled click, followed immediately by the quiet presence of two additional deputies stationed outside, uniforms crisp, posture alert, one posted on either side of the frame like silent guardians. They scanned the room, verified the scene, then stepped back to resume their watch beyond the door.

And then, like a tidal wave breaching a dam, her mother rushed past them and flew across the room.

"Shelby Lynn Lane!" she cried, voice fracturing on the final syllable.

Before Shelby could brace herself, her mother leaned down, wrapping her up in an embrace fierce enough to compress ribs and crack Shelby's heart wide open. Lavender lotion, laundry soap, and *home* wrapped around her like a lifeline.

Shelby clung back, breath shaking loose. "Mama..."

Her family poured in like a gust of summer concert applause. There were too many voices at once, too much relief crashing into the sterile quiet Caleb needed to heal in.

She turned, pulse skipping at the sight of them: her father slower behind the rest, ball cap clutched tight in one hand, eyes wet but steady. Hannah, her baby sister, anchored to his hip, and watchful, like she feared another door might swallow someone she loved.

Her heart twisted painfully. Her family. They'd always been there for her. Why did it take her so long to see that she needed them as much as they needed her?

"Shel," came the deep, tight voice of her oldest brother, Dylan. He reached her in three strides, hands bracing her shoulders, pulling her into a hug fierce enough to steal air. "You okay?" he demanded, scanning her wrists, her bruises. "Whoever did this—I swear—"

She lifted both hands, voice scraped raw from fear and forests and sleepless miles.

"Shh. Stop. All of you, please," she said, stepping back, shoulders rising with the effort to steady herself. "He's only just woken up. He needs *quiet*."

Her mother's gasp froze in her throat. Eric nearly knocked over a chair behind them, brother-and-manager-panic written all over him.

Caleb stirred behind them, the monitors flaring a startled leap with the sudden noise he'd been dragged into. Everyone's attention focused on him.

His eyes cracked open, unfocused, heavy, pain-clouded...then found her. "Shel..." he exhaled.

Only her name. Nothing more. But it landed like a vow he hadn't meant to speak aloud.

Her mother's hand flew to her mouth. Dylan froze mid-threat. Eric sagged into the nearest chair. Hannah hugged herself tighter to their dad's side.

One nurse appeared in the doorway, eyes widening at the crowd surrounding her patient. "Everything okay in here?"

Shelby straightened, already moving her family toward the hall.

"Yes, ma'am," she said. "We're stepping out."

She guided them into the empty room beside Caleb's. They stood looking at each other, no one breaking the tense silence.

"Shelby Lynn Lane," Eric blurted, voice cracking, "do you have any idea what you put me through? I've been calling every law enforcement office in the tri-state area!"

"But Shellybean—he saved you?" Hannah asked, eyes filling, voice small now, cracking over the truth.

Shelby nodded once, breath burning where the knife had marked her.

"Yes. He did. But he paid the price for it."

Despite everything, despite bruises and blood and nightmares, Shelby almost laughed.

Eric dropped all pretense the moment he reached her, pulling her into a clumsy, desperate hug. His breath hitched. "You scared me, kid."

"I'm sorry," she whispered. "I'm so sorry. I didn't... I couldn't..."

"You don't have to explain," Eric murmured, pulling back. "Just don't do that again. Ever."

Her family, her world, surrounded her in a tight circle.

Her mother's hands shook as they cupped Shelby's face. "Look at you, sweetheart, you're hurt..."

"I'm fine," Shelby said softly. "I promise. Caleb saved me."

Her mom swiped at tears. "God bless that boy."

Her dad stepped forward, voice thick. "We've been praying nonstop, Shellybean."

Hannah flung her arms around Shelby's waist. "I kept your picture on my pillow."

Shelby's throat tightened painfully. "Thank you," she whispered. "Y'all being here... it means everything."

The hallway outside carried the measured cadence of boots from the vigilant law enforcement officers. Then the door opened again, slower this time, controlled.

Sheriff Metcalf stepped inside, Detective Bristow at his back. Both men lifted their hats off in the same motion to indicate respect first, news second.

Shelby moved to stand in front of the sheriff, heart bracing, breath steadying. The room quieted instinctively under the shift in air, in authority, in stakes.

Metcalf gave a single nod to the group, voice low and anchored, like he understood storms and survival. "Morning, Lane family. Eric."

Eric nodded tightly. "Sheriff."

Bristow cleared his throat. "Shelby. We have updates for you."

Metcalf softened. "First, we found the stalker's blood trail. A good one."

Shelby's pulse kicked. "Did he die?"

"No," Bristow said. "But I don't think he'll make it far."

Her mother drew in a sharp breath.

Shelby steadied her voice. "Did you find... where he was staying? Where he planned everything?"

Metcalf nodded grimly. "We did. His staging ground. And Shelby..." He hesitated. "You need to know something. He's been planning this a long time."

Shelby's stomach twisted. "How long?"

"Years," Bristow said. "Since before your first album hit radio."

Eric blanched. "Dear Lord..."

Metcalf continued, "We found maps, surveillance notes, rehearsed scripts he planned to use on you. Cameras, burner phones, clothing fibers, bomb making supplies, fingerprints."

Shelby felt bile rise.

"He had recording equipment too," Bristow added quietly. "Audio journals."

Shelby froze. "Of what?"

"Talking to you," Metcalf said. "Practicing conversations. Rehearsing how he'd approach you. Some of it... was recorded in the mask."

Shelby clamped a hand over her mouth. Dylan swore under his breath. Her mother grabbed her hand and squeezed.

Eric sat heavily in the chair nearest the wall, face drained of color. "I could've stopped this when the first letter came. I thought it was just a prank."

"I can see why you would think that. I'm sure you get a lot of crazy fan mail," Sheriff said. "It's no one's fault."

Shelby wanted to disagree. She didn't hand over everything that the stalker sent her. She was partly to blame. She'd been too focused on her career. As a result, the people closest to her had been put in danger.

The sheriff placed his hand on her shoulder and gave a gentle squeeze. "You're not to blame, Shelby. This guy needs help."

His words were meant to comfort but regret still lingered, cold and bitter.

"But," Bristow said firmly as he looked at Shelby, "he made mistakes. We've got enough forensic evidence to issue a warrant."

Shelby's voice shook. "So, you're close."

Metcalf nodded. "We're hours away from an arrest once the lab confirms the DNA panel we submitted overnight."

Her father exhaled heavily. Her mother whispered a prayer. Dylan's fists clenched as if he wished the stalker was in the room with him.

Eric let out a shaky sigh. "Thank God."

Shelby swallowed, her heart hammering. "This nightmare is almost over?"

Metcalf looked at Caleb, then back at her. "It's close, Shelby. We're closing in."

Her breath wavered. "Thank you."

Metcalf tipped his hat. "We'll need to talk about security once Hunter leaves the hospital."

When the officers stepped out and her family left, Shelby returned to Caleb's side and sank onto the edge of his bed.

Rider dragged his tired body closer and rested his head on her knee. She stroked the soft fur between his ears, feeling his warmth seep into her trembling hands.

"I need both of you," she whispered. "Please... don't leave me."

Rider huffed softly.

Caleb stirred and Shelby's heart leapt. His lashes fluttered open, unfocused at first until they found her.

A faint smile ghosted his lips.

"You're... both still here," he murmured. "I thought it was a dream."

"We're not a dream. We're reality." Shelby leaned close, brushing her fingers along his jaw. "We're not going anywhere."

And for the first time since the woods went dark, Shelby believed it.

CHAPTER THIRTEEN

Caleb had been shot before.

But he had never felt as useless as he did sitting on the edge of a hospital bed, one arm braced across his bandaged shoulder, a nurse rattling off discharge instructions he barely processed. His head throbbed. His ribs ached. His legs felt like sandbags. And he couldn't wait to leave this small room behind.

But Shelby was standing beside him again, and that alone was enough fuel to make him grit his teeth and force his boots to the floor.

"Take it slow, Deputy Hunter," the nurse said, catching his elbow as he swayed. "Your body's still adjusting from blood loss."

"I'm good," he muttered.

She gave him a look that said *liar,* but she didn't argue further.

Shelby stepped into his line of sight, the bruise on her cheek had faded to a sickly yellow. Her brows pulled tight, hands hovering near his ribs like she expected him to collapse at any second.

"You don't have to act tough," she said with a soft smile. She *knew* him even though they'd been separated for years. She still knew him and his stubborn self.

He exhaled through his nose. "Not acting."

She arched a brow. "Sure."

Before he could respond, Rider let out a low chuff, trotting carefully toward him. Rider was still bandaged, moving stiffly, but determined to stay glued to Caleb's side.

Caleb reached down, fingers brushing Rider's ear. "You ready to get out of here, buddy?"

Rider's tail wagged.

The nurse handed Caleb a folder. "Follow-up in forty-eight hours. No strenuous activity. No lifting more than ten pounds. Keep the wound dry. Pain meds every six hours, use sparingly, given the dizziness."

Shelby took the folder before Caleb could reach for it. "Thank you. I'll make sure he follows the instructions."

Caleb shot her a narrowed look. "I don't need a babysitter."

Shelby stepped closer, voice low. "You almost died twice. You need several."

Rider barked as if seconding the motion.

Caleb sighed. "Traitor," he muttered.

Shelby gave a light laugh as the nurse wheeled in a chair. "Hospital policy. You can't walk out unassisted."

"I'm not sitting..."

Shelby pointed at the chair. "Sit."

Caleb blinked, his eyes narrowed to slits. "You giving orders now?"

"Absolutely. Somebody has to."

Rider nudged the chair with his nose.

Turncoat.

So now his dog was siding with his girlfriend. *Girlfriend.* He liked the sound of that more than he should admit while half-dizzy on pain meds. Once he wasn't falling apart at the seams, he was gonna make sure they both knew exactly what they were to each other.

Caleb lowered himself slowly, careful of his shoulder, and the nurse began pushing him toward the elevator.

Sheriff Metcalf and Detective Bristow waited near the hospital entrance, tactical vests fitted, radios clipped and ready, as if the war hadn't ended, it just changed location.

Metcalf stepped forward. "Hunter. Shelby. You both ready?"

Caleb straightened, jaw tight, every instinct in him already scanning exits and threat lines. *Ready was a dangerous word.* But it was the job. It was always the job.

Beside him, Shelby exhaled. "Yes, sir," she said.

And then she voiced the question smoldering beneath the surface of his discharge from the hospital. Because beneath the memories he knew she carried this fear, too.

"Where are we going?"

Caleb didn't look away from Metcalf, but he felt the shift in the air, the way her words tugged at something old and unresolved inside him. *Yeah, sweetheart... that makes two of us.*

"Back to your tour bus," Metcalf said. "It's being moved to a secured location at the fairgrounds' east lot. Controlled access. Single exit. Cameras already live."

Shelby blinked. "My *bus*?"

"Most consistent environment for you," Bristow answered. "No new layouts for him to exploit. And frankly?" His jaw flexed once. "It's the bait he won't resist."

Caleb stiffened beside her. "Bait," he echoed.

The word should've rattled her. Maybe it did but she never flinched. But fury, fear, and being hunted forged something harder in a person.

Metcalf's voice dropped low. "We do this on our terms. We draw him out. We end this."

Shelby inhaled and he watched as Metcalf's words changed her demeanor. Not fearless. Just focused.

"Lab confirmed the warrant," Bristow added. "You walk out of here protected, and he walks into our perimeter."

She swallowed, nodding once, jaw tightening like a soldier she'd never been trained to be. "Then let's go."

A deputy stepped in from the hall behind them, followed by another, then two more, forming a practiced, protective exit corridor around Caleb's discharge chair. Tactical. Quiet. Official.

"Escort detail's yours," the lead deputy said to Shelby. "We clear the route. We ride front and rear. No press, no public, no interference."

Shelby turned toward Caleb, voice dropping to a whisper meant only for him: "Is that okay?"

He nodded once. "As long as I'm with you."

Her mouth trembled, not in disagreement, no hesitation, but the effort of believing. "Okay," she breathed. "Then let's end this."

Metcalf cleared his throat. "Before we move, your family wants to speak with you both in Conference Room B."

Caleb sighed. Brave as he could be against gunfire Shelby's family was another arena entirely.

Shelby squeezed his good shoulder. "You won't face them alone."

He nodded, already bracing himself for whirlwind that was the Lane family .

The conference room buzzed with voices, Shelby's parents, her brothers and sister, and bandmates gathered around a long table, tension thick as smoke.

But the moment Shelby walked in, silence fell.

Eric stood first. "Shelby, the label wants to know about..."

"No." Her voice was steel.

Eric blinked. "We need a decision about the tour, the social media posts..."

"I'm not stepping on a stage until the man trying to kill me is in handcuffs." She crossed her arms. "Besides, my real fans know me, that I would never post that type of content on social media."

Eric opened his mouth to respond but she held up her hand. "Not now. The truth will come out when all this is over."

Jade, her drummer, crossed her arms. "We back you. Period."

Wyatt offered Caleb a grateful nod before turning to Shelby. "Just stay alive. That's the only schedule that matters."

Shelby moved to stand beside Caleb. "Exactly."

Dylan muttered, "Dang right."

Her father stepped forward. "We know what the sheriff said. But you should be home with us. Not on a bus."

"I'll be with her," Caleb said, straightening despite the pain stabbing his shoulder. "Round-the-clock protection, along with the extra security."

Eric tried again. "A statement, then..."

"No," Shelby said, firmer. "I'll speak when this is over."

Her mother cupped Shelby's cheek. "We want you safe. We want you home."

Shelby swallowed. "It's not safe for you if I'm home."

Her father's jaw ticked. "We're not afraid of him."

"But I am," Shelby whispered. "I can't risk losing any of you."

Silence took over.

Finally, Dylan leaned down to Caleb's level. "You saved my sister once. But if you get yourself killed, I'm dragging you back from the afterlife myself."

Caleb huffed a laugh. "Noted."

A knock on the door ended the discussion and Bristow poked his head inside. "Ready?"

Shelby stiffened her spine. "Ready as I'll ever be."

The deputies moved them forward, chair rolling toward the exit, boots clicking a quiet cadence of protection instead of pursuit this time.

A cruiser idled, engine humming. Armed deputies scanned every direction.

Rider trotted ahead, tail high, ready for duty.

Caleb gritted through the pain climbing into the backseat. Shelby slid in beside him. Rider laid his head on Caleb's good knee.

As the cruiser pulled away from the hospital, pine trees blended into long shadows, the world shrinking to the space they shared.

"You okay?" she asked, voice hushed.

He nodded. "You?"

She let her shoulder brush his. "Ask me when this nightmare ends."

He wanted to take her hand. Wanted to say *more*.

"We'll stop him," he said instead. Quiet but absolute.

She met his gaze. "Together."

The cruiser turned into the fairgrounds. Floodlights bathed the east lot in stark white. Her tour bus sat alone inside a temporary barricade. A lone fortress.

Bristow opened Shelby's door. "We'll have plainclothes mixed in the crowd tomorrow. We made the announcement about the rescheduled concert tomorrow evening. If he's watching, he'll think you're returning to normal."

Metcalf added, "Thermal scans every fifteen minutes. Perimeter patrols every five. We'll monitor comms from inside the bus."

Caleb narrowed his eyes at the empty dark beyond the fence. "You sure the area's clear?"

"Triple-checked." Bristow's tone left no room for doubt.

Shelby hesitated on the first step until Rider nudged her leg.

Inside, the dim overhead lights cast a warm glow over familiar chaos of guitars, pillows, and photos taped to the bunk walls. Her home.

Safe. And yet a trap.

Shelby trailed her fingers across her dressing table. Caleb watched her, heart aching.

"We're safe here," he said quietly.

Shelby turned, tears shining, fear and fierce love mingled in her gaze. "I know."

He swallowed. "Shelby... I won't let anything..."

She stepped into his space, one hand rising to cup his jaw, silencing him. "You don't have to protect me alone," she whispered. "Not anymore. There are some things out of our control that only God can determine the outcome."

His breath caught. Letting people in had always felt like weakness. Vulnerability.

But this? This felt holy.

Her thumb brushed his cheek. The world shrank to that touch.

"We do this together," she breathed.

He nodded, leaning into her hand. "I'm not going anywhere."

Her breath trembled. "Good. Because I'm not letting go."

And Caleb knew the stalker wouldn't take one more thing from them.

Not tonight. Not ever again.

🐾

Rider snored softly beneath the small dining table, paws twitching as if chasing something in his dreams. The hum of the generator outside was steady, comforting in a strange way. A reminder that they were surrounded by protection, even though danger pulsed right beyond the fence line.

The fairgrounds looked eerie through the bus window. Deserted vendor tents cast long, skeletal shadows under the floodlights. The September air outside was warm, but a quiet chill lingered inside her chest.

Caleb sat on the short sofa, head tilted back against the cushion, eyes closed. His breathing was even, but the tension in his shoulders never eased. Not really. Pain and exhaustion tugged on him, but he refused to let his guard down.

She watched him for a long moment, memorizing the scrape of stubble across his jaw, the way his lashes brushed his cheek, the rise and fall of his chest. She wished he'd sleep for real. He needed it more than air.

But even in the dim stillness, he was listening. Always listening.

"You're staring," he murmured without opening his eyes.

She jumped a little, then smiled. "You caught me."

His lips twitched. "You think I don't feel when you're looking at me?"

"Oh, so you're psychic now?"

"No. You just breathe differently." He opened his eyes, pinning her gently. "Like you're worried."

Her breath stuttered. Caught. She tried to play it off with a shrug. "Well… you did get shot less than four days ago. And there was that whole almost bleeding out in the woods thing before that. And that little mishap on the lookout tower. And…"

"Alright," he cut in, brow raised. "Point made."

She crossed to him, kneeling on the floor in front of him so they were eye level. "I'm allowed to worry about you. You worry about me every second."

"That's different."

"How?" she challenged softly.

He hesitated. "Because the idea of losing you…" He swallowed, voice roughening. "It terrifies me."

Her heart squeezed hard. She reached up, fingers brushing the side of his cheek. "You think I'm not equally terrified of losing you?"

He exhaled slowly, like he'd been bracing for that truth. He reached out and tugged lightly on the sleeve of her hoodie. "Come here."

She stood and sank down beside him, settling into the space beneath his arm. He kept his touch gentle, mindful of his shoulder, but the warmth of him curled around her like a shield.

For a moment, the world felt steady.

She leaned her head on his uninjured shoulder. His scent of cedar soap, clean cotton, and something uniquely Caleb filled her lungs.

"You prayed earlier," she whispered.

"I always pray," he said quietly. "But tonight… yeah."

"What did you pray for?"

He didn't answer right away.

She thought he might dodge it. He didn't. "For peace," he said finally. "For the kind that doesn't make sense unless you believe God still fights for you."

Her chest tightened. "Do you feel it?"

"A little," he said, thumb brushing the back of her hand. "Especially when you're close."

Warmth spread through her ribs like sunrise spilling slow across Georgia fields. She turned her hand, lacing their fingers together. "Can I be honest?"

"You saying you *haven't* been?" he teased, gentle grin tugging at his mouth.

She bumped him lightly with her shoulder. "Smart aleck."

His laugh came low, warm, and brief. It was medicine disguised as sound. Then his expression gentled. "Tell me."

She turned toward him fully, inhaling once like she was about to step up to a mic, only this time, there was no crowd, no stage, no performance armor.

"I used to think applause was proof I mattered," she admitted, searching his eyes, letting the truth come slow but solid. "That if enough people yelled my name, the world would stay bright and safe."

She shook her head, almost smiling at her own past foolishness. "I spent so many years craving the praise of strangers... the cheers of critics... the *applause of men*."

His frown flickered, hurt on her behalf.

"But you?" she continued, palm flattening gently against his chest before he could argue, her voice lowering into something steadier, wiser. "You don't run *for* the cheers. You run *toward* the danger that scares everyone else."

She swallowed once, pulse thrashing quiet rebellion in her wrists where rope bruises still lived.

"And somewhere between the fear, the blood, and you charging into the dark..." Her breath trembled, but her voice didn't bow to it. "I realized I didn't need applause to be seen. Didn't need the praise of men to be *loud*."

Her thumb brushed his heartbeat now, gentle but certain.

"I needed a life worth singin' about when the stadium goes silent."

His eyes flicked open to argue, but she shook her head again. No spotlight, no uncertainty.

"God didn't wire my heart to shrink," she whispered, conviction rising like a quiet crescendo. "I was makin' myself small for an audience that never had the power to save me."

Caleb froze behind the words, breath held like the hush before a final note.

"And suddenly," she added, leaning in so close her voice was a vow, not a performance, "I'm not afraid to exist out loud anymore, not for the applause..." Her pulse beat against his palm, steady now. "But for the One who never needed me small in the first place."

His gaze locked to hers. It was fierce, tender, and reverent all at the same time, like he saw the same thing she did now.

"You're not supposed to hide," he murmured. "The world needs your voice."

She smiled then, eyes shining with something deeper than stage lights ever gave her. "Turns out," she said softly, "I didn't need the world to clap."

She angled her face toward his, letting his hand rest over her heartbeat like a promise returned. "I just needed a song worth singing when they don't. You make me believe that."

His gaze flicked to her lips for a second before he closed them and exhaled shakily.

"This is dangerous," he said.

"Me sitting here?" she teased.

"No," he whispered, forehead resting lightly against hers. "Wanting you this much."

Her heart cartwheeled with the joy of his confession. "But good dangerous?" she breathed.

His voice was warmth and fire. "The best kind."

They stayed like that, breath mingling, barely touching and yet entirely wrapped around each other.

Rider lifted his head suddenly, nose sniffing, ears perked. Alert.

Caleb's body shifted beneath her, protector instincts immediately awake. But after a moment, Rider's ears relaxed. He huffed, curled back up, asleep again.

Shelby released all the air in her lungs. She pointed her chin toward Rider. "He's on edge too."

Caleb nodded, gaze still fixed toward the door. "He'll know long before we do."

She tangled her fingers back with his, grounding them both. "Tomorrow?"

"Tomorrow," he echoed.

"We're still here."

"We are."

"We're still together."

A faint smile tipped his lips. "We are."

"And God hasn't forgotten us," she added with a quiet assurance.

He squeezed her hand in silent agreement.

A different silence settled again in the bus. Not suffocating this time, but sweet and sacred.

Caleb kissed the top of her head and whispered into her hair, "Rest. I've got you."

She closed her eyes, letting her body melt against him. Letting herself believe him. For a few precious minutes, the world stopped spinning. The comforting sounds of Rider's steady breathing and Caleb's heartbeat beneath her ear were like a whispered prayer.

She didn't know if she fell asleep but she drifted into a half-dream where the darkness couldn't reach them, where love wrapped around her like armor.

And she clung tightly to that stillness...

...not knowing the next knock on the door would bring the storm.

CHAPTER FOURTEEN

Night draped over the fairgrounds like a dark threat waiting to pounce.

The tour bus should've been home turf for Shelby with its familiar layouts, predictable exits, and controlled angles. For Caleb, it was just another box to defend. Even surrounded by live surveillance feeding quiet eyes from darker corners, something felt off.

The air was too still. Too breakable. Like a storm pausing mid-breath, deciding where to land its teeth.

Radios were silent. Engines cooling. No crowds. No threats in motion.

That was the problem.

Danger didn't always announce itself with tires or taunts or knives. Sometimes it crouched. Listened. Waited for arrogance or exhaustion to speak first.

He'd walked into those ambushes before thinking noise meant risk, thinking silence meant safety.

The dog's ears angled forward, reading the same static in the air his handler did.

Not home. Not safe. Just staged.

And staged meant the game wasn't over. It meant the pieces were finally on the board.

Now he just had to make sure the next move belonged to them.

Caleb sat on the edge of the sofa, shoulder throbbing with every heartbeat. The hum of the bus generator vibrated through the floor, a constant reminder of the artificial security they were clinging to. Outside, the perimeter stayed invisible by design—no badges, no flashlights, no patterns to track.

Rider lay near the front step, alert even as he pretended to rest, his ears reacting to every shift in the night air.

Shelby stood at the tiny kitchen counter gripping a mug of untouched tea. Her gaze flicked from window to window, as if expecting danger to manifest through the glass.

Too quiet.

Caleb knew this kind of tension. The way your own heartbeat became the loudest threat in the room. The way silence could strangle. "Shelby?" he asked gently.

No response.

Her eyes had latched onto the bus door like it was about to explode inward. Her fingers tightened around the ceramic mug until her knuckles bleached white.

He stood slowly, ignoring the stabbing pain lancing through ribs and shoulder. "Hey," he murmured. "Talk to me."

She startled as if she hadn't even known he was there.

"I'm fine," she said, breath uneven.

He shook his head. "You're not."

Her chest rose too fast. Her gaze darted, wild and trapped. The mug clattered to the counter, tea splashing onto the laminate. She backed into the cabinets as panic surged.

Caleb grabbed a towel, but she pressed both hands against her temples like she could quiet the trauma clawing at her mind.

"I can still feel the rope," she whispered hoarsely. "The camera light, it's still there. Like I'm still in that room."

Rider let out a soft whine, creeping closer.

"Shelby," Caleb said softly, lifting his hands in surrender. "Look at me."

She shook her head violently. "Don't... don't touch me."

He stepped closer anyway, ignoring the sting in her words because fear was talking, not her. He cupped her face carefully, grounding her.

"You're safe," he whispered, resting his forehead against hers. "I swear it."

Her breath hitched. Tears spilled. "You can't promise that," she choked.

"Yes," he said, voice unwavering. "I can."

He lowered his voice into a gentle command. "Breathe with me. In... and out..."

She tried. Her breath stuttered and her eyes widened.

"You're here," he told her. "Not there. He's not here. I am and you're safe."

Her fists curled into his shirt as she sagged against him, trembling.

"I was so scared," she sobbed.

He brushed a hand over her hair, jaw clenched with rage, not at her, at the monster who had done this. "He's never getting near you again."

She shuddered, her shoulders curving in. "Please don't leave me."

"Not a chance." His voice cracked with the vow. He'd make this promise over and over if it helped her feel safe.

Slowly, her breathing steadied. Her body softened against his.

"You got out," he whispered. "He didn't win."

She looked up, eyes swollen with unshed tears. "But he's still out there."

He framed her face with his palm. "Not for long."

Rider's ears pricked. A deep growl started in his chest and Caleb stilled at the alert.

Shelby's lips parted. "Caleb?"

He pressed a finger to her lips. "Shhh."

Rider stood at attention facing the bus door, muscles rigid, posture shifting into protection mode, his gaze fixed on whatever, or whoever, was outside.

Caleb eased Shelby down behind the kitchen island. His shoulder screamed as he reached for the pistol Metcalf had returned earlier. He flicked the safety off with a quiet click. His heart hammered but his hands were steady. "Stay low," he breathed.

Shelby crouched behind the built-in table, phone already trembling in her hand.

Caleb crept to the small window by the door, lifting the edge of the shade just enough to glimpse outside. A shadow. Tall. Dark.

His pulse spiked hard enough he tasted metal. He flicked his gaze to Shelby and tapped two fingers toward his ear—*comms live.*

Then he pointed once to her screen. *Call Metcalf.*

She nodded, already dialing, thumbs flying, breath thin but determined.

The figure limped toward the bus door, steps slow, deliberate. Black clothing. Gloves. A glint of metal catching a sliver of moon.

Caleb adjusted his stance, pistol raised, not reacting to shadowy movement, but to the voice encrypted in his ear.

Bates and Diaz holding rear angles. Booker and Carver, plainclothes, blind corners. Perimeter set.

He slowly chambered a round, every movement deliberate. "Come on," he whispered, "show yourself."

Rider dropped into a crouch at his heel, a low growl rolling like thunder under glass. Caleb's hand rested briefly on the dog's harness in connection, not comfort.

He lifted his hand in a tight arc, two fingers forward, palm flat: *go on my mark.* Rider answered with a low chuff, teeth showing, body coiled, waiting for release.

Five yards.

Four.

Three.

The lock clicked, a quiet, deliberate sound. The stalker picked it.

Caleb inhaled, chest tightening, not from injury this time, but instinct sparking into anticipation.

Now. He snapped his hand forward—*go.*

Rider surged up from his crouch, a blur of muscle and fury given purpose. He hit the attacker's blind angle, teeth sinking into the man's forearm, momentum dragging him down before the blade could arc.

The stalker screamed but kept fighting, hand clawing for the gun at his waist.

Glass detonated behind them as a round thundered out, Shelby's scream cutting the air like shrapnel. "Caleb!"

"Freeze, police!"

The stalker continued to fight but Caleb was already moving, already firing. One controlled shot clipped the attacker's leg, dropping him fully to the floor.

Rider held tight on the weapon arm, snarling low, unrelenting, a living barricade between the threat and the man he'd been trained to protect.

Caleb kicked the gun away from the attacker's reach, and it skidded to a stop under one of the seats. Caleb kept the muzzle locked on the threat, breath controlled but razor-focused. Beside him, Rider held his stance too, teeth locked on the stalker's arm, a low growl rolling like a warning not to move.

Not done until the cavalry arrives.

The stalker writhed, bleeding and furious, unable to escape Rider's grip. The bus shifted as deputies swarmed in, Bristow leading the way. "Weapons down! Show hands!" Caleb holstered his weapon and stepped back.

Rider stopped only when Caleb commanded, "Rider...release." He clipped Rider's leash back on his harness.

Pinned to the floor, the attacker's mask slipped sideways revealing his face. Caleb's blood boiled as he finally looked on the face of evil.

Tyler Meadows. Shelby's once brilliant former songwriting partner, now diseased with obsession.

Tyler's eyes flicked to Shelby in a wicked glare. Possessive. "You were mine," he rasped. "You ruined everything…"

Caleb lunged forward, fury strangling his breath. Bristow blocked him with a firm grip to the chest.

"Not worth the trouble," Bristow hissed. "Medic's waiting at the jail for him."

"Fix him up so he can rot in jail," Caleb said, his voice terse.

Deputies swarmed Tyler, cuffing and dragging him toward the exit.

Tyler snarled, spitting out madness. "She's nothing without me!"

Caleb leaned in close enough that the stalker saw absolute promise in his eyes. "You will never speak her name again."

Tyler's laugh was hysterical, maniacal even, until the cruiser door slammed shut and his voice vanished in the night. And silence descended.

Every muscle trembled as adrenaline drained too fast. His shoulder throbbed like fire. His knees threatened to buckle.

Shelby rushed into him placing her arms around his waist and holding him up as much as he held her.

"You're okay," she breathed against his chest, her voice shaking. "You're okay."

He didn't trust his voice. Instead, he cupped the back of her head and pressed a kiss to her temple.

Rider pushed himself against Caleb's side, tail wagging shakily, desperate for reassurance.

Caleb knelt, ignoring the agony that simple movement caused and wrapped his good arm around Rider's neck. "Good boy," he said, voice cracking. "You saved her. You saved us."

Rider licked his cheek, whining.

Shelby dropped beside them, wiping her tears with the back of her hand. "Thank you," she whispered to Rider. "My hero."

Metcalf and additional deputies flooded the bus, clearing every corner, voices low and purposeful. The bright assault of fear finally eased, replaced by exhaustion and dizzying relief.

Shelby pressed her forehead to Caleb's. "Is it really over?"

He brushed a tear from her cheek, his thumb trembling. "Yeah," he whispered. "It's over."

She let out a sob that sounded like a prayer answered.

Rider rested his head against her thigh with a satisfied sigh, eyes saying exactly what Caleb felt: *Told you I had this.*

Caleb drew Shelby close, holding her tight against his chest.

"We made it," she breathed.

He kissed her hair. "He was never going to win."

Metcalf approached, lowering his radio. "Meadows is in custody. He's being booked as we speak. Two counts of attempted murder."

Caleb nodded, and he sagged against the cabinet. Relief loosening every knot inside his muscles. "Thanks, Sheriff."

Metcalf glanced at the three of them, disheveled, shaking, alive and a rare softness flickered in his eyes. "Get some rest. You all deserve it."

As the deputies cleared away and the night finally felt like night again, Shelby cupped Caleb's face, eyes shining. "What happens now?"

"That depends," he said, voice low. His hands encompassed her waist. "On you."

She swallowed, voice trembling with hope. "On me?"

"Yeah." He gathered her closer. "Stay. With us. Me and Rider."

Her heart hammered under his hand. "Is that... a proposal?"

He gave a crooked smile. "It's honesty."

"And what does honesty sound like?" she whispered, her arms looping around his neck.

His thumb brushed her lower lip. "It sounds like I've been in love with you since sixth grade."

Her breath hitched. "Good," she said softly. "Same."

He rested his forehead against hers and sighed. He could die a happy man just holding her like this.

"You gonna kiss me?" she asked, voice hardly a breath.

He leaned back and gently cradled her face in his hands. The face he'd loved since he was twelve. His kiss was slow and sweet and certain and full of every hope he thought he'd buried long ago.

The kind of kiss that meant more than survival.

The kind that meant *forever*.

Rider huffed at their knees, exhausted, proud, slightly jealous.

Caleb didn't let her go. Not for a second.

He pulled back and brushed the moisture off her face. "We did it." His voice sounded like rough gravel but full of promise.

Wrapped in moonlight and relief, Caleb finally believed what his heart had been screaming for years.

He would spend the rest of his life protecting this woman and he wasn't running from that truth ever again.

EPILOGUE

...nine months later...

Summer twilight draped Willow Creek in soft gold as the final notes of the orchestral intro faded into a hush. Edison bulbs twinkled like captured stars strung from the pavilion rafters, casting a warm glow over thousands gathered on the open-air lawn. Tonight wasn't just a concert. It was a homecoming threaded with victory.

Shelby stepped toward center stage.

She'd stood beneath brighter lights, arenas packed with strangers roaring her name, but nothing compared to this. Here were the people who raised her on hymns and hope, who prayed her through life's storms. Family, the kind bound by blood and the kind bound by love.

Home.

A warm Georgia breeze curled through her hair as she adjusted the microphone. Her fingers brushed the princess-cut diamond resting on her left hand. It was simple, stunning and a reminder that love didn't have to be flawless to be faithful. It just had to stay.

Her heart fluttered, but not with fear. With joy so big she didn't quite know how to hold it.

In the wings, Caleb stood tall in his deputy uniform, boots planted steady, a quiet, reverent awe in his eyes, as if he still couldn't believe he'd been granted the right to stand guard beside her again.

At his heel, Rider sat alert and proud, tail thumping the rubber-lined stage mat in eager rhythm, his harness-mounted badge catching the glow of the arena lights like it had claimed its own private spotlight.

The crowd hummed with excitement, energy swelling, expectant.

Shelby lifted her guitar, letting its strap settle against her shoulder like an old friend. "Good evening, Willow Creek!"

The roar that answered made her eyes sting with sudden emotion. Rows of lawn chairs and patchwork quilts covered the grass. Kids waving posters with "WE 🤍 YOU SHELBY!" in glitter glue, church ladies already teary-eyed behind their fans, and sheriff's deputies standing a little taller, pride shining in their eyes.

The mingled scents of funnel cakes, kettle corn, and freshly cut grass wrapped around everything like summer itself.

Her stomach rumbled loud enough she winced. "Well, I was gonna pretend I'm all about that high-protein, low-sugar life these days but that funnel cake smells like holiness right now."

The laughter that rippled through the crowd felt like balm.

Then, as if pulled by an invisible thread, her gaze found Caleb.

He smiled at her. That small, private smile, that was only for her and everything she had waited for.

She pressed her palm lightly over the guitar strings, quieting them. "Tonight is about grace... and finding your way back. Back to the people who stay. To the love God never stopped writing. And to the heroes who fight for us. Even the four-legged ones."

A fresh wave of applause surged that included loud whistles and a few "Preach, girl!" shouts from the back row.

Her eyes sparkled. "And speaking of heroes… Willow Creek, I'd like to introduce the two who saved my life."

She held out her hand and motioned toward the wings. "Deputy Caleb Hunter and his K-9 partner, the one and only Rider!"

Caleb stepped into the light first, broad shoulders straight, jaw strong, heart visible in his eyes. The crowd erupted. He tipped his hat, cheeks reddening at the sudden celebrity.

Then Rider trotted out.

The applause doubled. Louder, higher, unstoppable.

Shelby bark-laughed into the mic, a joyous sound that echoed across each member of the audience. "Looks like we all know who they came to see!"

Rider gave a proud woo-woo bark, then because he was always the center of gravity, he wedged himself between his humans, staking claim to the middle of the stage. Flashbulbs exploded as cameras captured the trio.

Shelby knelt, fingers sliding into Rider's fur. "You saved my life," she whispered.

Rider licked her chin in response in a sloppy, shameless show of affection. And she loved it.

Caleb stepped closer, hand brushing her back, voice low so only she heard, "You saved mine right back."

The stadium lights flickered over his face, catching the glint of the ring he had slid onto her finger during a quiet moment far from spotlights.

He looked at her like she was his answered prayer. "You ready for forever?" he asked.

Shelby's heart squeezed tight, like every good memory and every nearly-lost moment collided in her chest.

She leaned her forehead to his. "I already said yes."

The crowd felt the shift, the intimacy of the moment unfolding, and cheered like they were witnessing a fairy tale in real time.

Caleb didn't back away. He gripped her hands and helped her stand. Slipping his hand to her waist, he tugged her closer and kissed her. He tasted like funnel cake and peppermint candy. He was her everything her heart desired. This kiss, not unlike the others they shared, was tender but certain and confirmed every vow their fear had tried to break.

The crowd's reaction was seismic.

Then Rider, unwilling to be upstaged, headbutted between them, barking indignantly.

The laughter was a tidal wave.

Shelby wiped tears from her cheeks. "Okay Rider, you get the first verse. You earned it."

Caleb laughed behind her. "Not gonna argue with the hero."

Music swelled as the band slid into a gentle opening riff, soft percussion like a heartbeat.

Shelby rose smoothly, guitar poised, her voice pouring out like a prayer finally answered:

I was lost in the dark, breath too afraid to find,
But love kicked down the door and quieted my mind.
I found home when you called my name,
I found my heart when you stayed...

The audience swayed together beneath the lights in a sea of love and relief and gratitude.

Lantern lights glimmered among the trees like oversized fireflies. The fairgrounds smelled of sugar and cut hay. Her mom cried openly now, wiping tears with the corner of a handkerchief. Her dad stood behind her, one arm protectively around her shoulders, jaw unashamedly trembling.

Dylan whooped and waved a ridiculous "Welcome Home, Sis!" sign. Her bandmates swayed along with her. Wyatt, with his guitar, Jade keeping a gentle rhythm with her drumsticks, her eyes shining with pride.

Even unmovable, steel-spined Sheriff Metcalf blinked harder than usual and offered a tight nod as if to say, *good job and thank God.*

Caleb stepped beside her, arm draped across her shoulders, thumb tracing comfort at her collarbone. Rider leaned into her legs, tail thumping in time.

We made it. We survived.

We are *never* going back.

Shelby let her voice lift higher, steadier:

Grace found the cracks where fear had grown,

Turned the broken pieces into something known.

Here with you — I belong,

Your love rewrote my song...

The final chord rang out, echoing against the historic brick buildings across the street. Summer night air held the last note aloft like a blessing. Shelby lowered her guitar and closed her eyes.

Thank You. Thank You for saving us. Thank You for bringing us home.

When she opened them again, Caleb was watching her with that open, vulnerable expression meant only for her when the world faded.

She swallowed around the lump in her throat and raised the mic again. "One last thing before we wrap tonight," she said, fiddling with the ring on her finger as the crowd leaned in. "This guy asked me a pretty important question..."

She held up her hand, the diamond sparkling like a promise caught in starlight and the crowd roared.

Caleb's ears reddened adorably.

Shelby laughed, bashful but bursting. "Don't worry, I said yes."

Someone in the front row hollered, "When's the wedding?"

Caleb leaned into the mic, deadpan. "Soon as we convince the Sheriff to give me a week off."

Metcalf crossed his arms and shouted, "You get three days!"

The crowd lost it.

Shelby grinned, heart light. "We're thinking... early fall. Maybe right here under these lights." She leaned into Caleb's side. "Y'all better save the date, Willow Creek."

Another swell of cheers warmer than summer heat rolled over her and Shelby felt something click into place.

Peace. Belonging. Future.

As the audience's applause rolled on, Caleb reached for her hand and brought it to his lips, eyes soft.

Rider pushed himself proudly forward, chest puffed out, the picture of canine triumph.

Shelby laughed and kissed Rider's head. "Don't worry, bud. You're the Best Dog of Honor."

Rider barked once like he'd known it all along.

Families waved glow sticks. Kids danced. The band drifted into a reprise. Stars pressed extra close, curious witnesses.

God had written a better story than fear ever dared to tell. And here she was at center stage, singing from the healed places.

She turned toward Caleb, their fingers tangling. "I love you," she said, no mic, just truth.

He brushed her cheek. "Forever."

The crowd didn't need to hear it to understand. Because love was already singing loud enough for everyone. As fireworks cracked above the fairgrounds and Rider howled in joyful approval, Shelby knew this eternal truth: hope had the final word.

And tomorrow was theirs to build.

Together.

ABOUT JENNIFER CHASTAIN

Ever since she was a little girl, living in her small town at the foot of the Catskills Mountains in New York State, Jennifer has been a voracious reader and has dreamed of epic adventures. A northern transplant, she has grown to love the grace and the charm of the South. In fact, she even married a Southerner.

Jennifer is a member of ACFW, ACFW-Charlotte chapter, Blue Ridge Reader Connections, and My Book Therapy/Novel Academy. Several of her early stories were finalists in the Blue Ridge Mountains Christian Writer's Conference Foundations Contest and she was a finalist in the Touched by Love contest sponsored by the Faith, Hope, and Love Christian Writers. During the day, she works for a research center on the campus of the University of North Carolina Charlotte and at nights and weekends, she's a writing ninja, cramming in as many words as possible.

A hopeful romantic, Jennifer loves dark chocolate, Diet Coke, and a good rom-com. She and her husband have been married for over thirty years and have been "cat parents" to several rescue cats over the years.

www.jenniferchastain.com

Newsletter signup – receive a free short story with signup

Scan or tap the QR code below to learn more.

instagram.com/jenniferchastain.author

facebook.com/JenniferChastain.writer

bookbub.com/authors/jennifer-chastain

amazon.com/stores/author/B08N5SHV78?

FAMILY

LISA PHILLIPS

CHAPTER ONE

"You're early."

Durango James—known by his friends as Jay—glanced over at the guy who slid onto the barstool beside him. "It's what I do."

He hadn't drunk much of the beer in front of him. The thing could sit there untouched for all he cared. A whole lot of alcohol never did him any favors. But "when in Rome…" and all that.

Or in this case, Breckenrow.

The place was total Montana small-town ranching community. Right now, it was a chilly spring, which meant it was basically still winter. After spending far too long in the Middle East, the shock of cold was a blast to his nervous system he needed. So long as he could keep from getting frustrated by it.

Caleb Rourke, the guy sitting beside him, was a former DEA agent. Now he ranched every day with his grandpa and worked on his computer from the main house, coordinating with his twin brother, Noah. The two of them had partnered up recently, and the team had welcomed Caleb as part of the group. All of them worked in the international private security business, but everyone on Jay's team knew that Noah and Caleb working together officially was a cover for them to search for their parents. To finally find out why they'd disappeared so many years ago.

Jay wished them good luck, but his only interest was in the assignments he was given.

Caleb thanked the bartender for the bottle of beer and turned to Jay. "Just because your job is forward recon doesn't mean you need to be early everywhere. This is just your average hometown bar in nowhere, Montana."

"That's why the two guys playing pool are packing weapons under their jackets and the woman flirting with the truckers in the corner is an undercover fed."

Caleb tensed, as though he wanted to turn around and look—see if he knew the woman. But he didn't, probably because he was still every bit the fed he'd been before things with his team went sideways. Caleb had uncovered corruption, reunited with his twin, and found a better life here at home. With the girl next door, Tessa. The two of them were set to get married this summer.

That was not why Jay was here.

So yeah, everyone on the team called him Jay. He liked it better than Durango James, so he'd never argued with the moniker.

"How long have you been here, anyway?" Caleb asked, like he didn't know whether to laugh or call the sheriff with intel. Instead of waiting for Jay to answer that he'd clocked all that in mere seconds after walking in, Caleb said, "This is supposed to be about recuperating. Getting some perspective...and healing."

"I'm not injured."

"Taking time *off*. Not working. You know what I mean." Caleb shot him a look like he was unimpressed. "Is Cass in your truck?"

Jay nodded, sipping his drink. It tasted like it wasn't going to fix his problems.

Nothing would.

Except that still small voice he conversed with when he was all alone, usually in a tense situation, told him that there was something that *would* fix his problems. And that he already knew exactly what it was.

"Folks wouldn't care if you brought your dog in," Caleb added. "After all, she's a war hero."

"They don't need to know. And she doesn't like being bothered."

Caleb chuckled. "You two make a good match."

"The love of my life is a seventy-two-pound German shepherd with a weakness for kettle corn who prefers her long walks at night and not during the day."

She was currently curled up in her crate in the back of his truck, probably warmer out there than he was in here.

"For now," Caleb said.

Jay frowned at the guy. Noah had pretty much ordered him to stay here in Montana until he and Cass were "recovered"—whatever that meant.

Caleb nudged him. "I'm just saying."

Jay eyed him. "I have no idea what you're saying."

"You being here isn't about doing your job in my town. It's about healing. That won't come with you ignoring everything and everyone and pretending you're fine. We all have to face who we are, and the brokenness in us, and realize we have a long way to go."

"Sure," Jay said. "One sec." He slid off the barstool and headed for the back hall.

The two guys from the pool table had gone that direction just a moment ago, moving almost in sync. Walking like two predators. Wolves on the prowl. They'd followed a younger guy back here.

The exit door at the end was closed. No sign they'd gone out that route.

Bathroom?

Jay pushed the door open like he had to hit the head in a hurry and swayed against the door. He righted himself and grunted rather than speaking as he took in the bathroom layout.

The only indication of what he was looking for was a sharp intake of breath. The last stall would be his guess.

Jay kicked the door open.

The two guys had the younger man up against the wall, a knife to his throat. So this was about intimidation, and maybe making him bleed a little. Otherwise, they'd have their guns out.

"Whoops." Jay pulled up short. "My bad. Don't mind me, you guys. 'Whatever floats your boat' and all that."

The guy closest to him had the young man's wallet in his hands.

This was a shakedown. Or a way to make some extra cash on the side.

"You...robbin' this guy?" Jay asked, slurring his words so he sounded drunk.

Wallet Guy rounded on Jay. "Walk away."

"Nah, that's not really what I do."

Problem was, stipulations of this "recovery" time staying with the Rourke family at the ranch included the caveat that if he so much as threw a punch, he'd be out of the team. No exceptions.

Jay wanted to be annoyed about that, but Noah had a point. Jay had always run hot—with anger. It seemed to burn in him, and no matter how he tried to channel it into productive career choices, nothing calmed him.

Except Cass.

Hence the less-than-honorable discharge from the army.

If he got kicked off the team, no one would be surprised. Least of all him. But part of him respected Noah too much not to at least try to keep his word.

"How about you let the kid go?" Jay suggested. "And we'll forget I ever saw you."

Wallet Guy shook his head, shoving the billfold in his jacket. "Doesn't work for me."

Jay spotted the intention in his movements and braced. He turned his shoulder and met the guy that way, shoving off the attack.

Punching was out, but Noah didn't say anything about a well-placed elbow.

The guy stumbled.

His buddy held the kid against the wall with his knife, blood on the guy's neck. He might be midtwenties, but that didn't mean he wasn't in danger of peeing himself by accident.

Wallet Guy drew his weapon and lifted it, one-handed.

Jay clocked the make and model just before he grabbed it. The weapon clicked under the press of his hand, and the magazine slid away, clanged on the ground, and skittered across tile.

Wallet Guy started in shock that he'd been summarily disarmed. But he still had a bullet chambered.

Jay kicked out at the guy's knee, and he crumpled to the floor. The weapon clattered onto the tile, and Jay kicked that as well.

Knife Guy flinched. "We don't want no trouble."

"Then let the guy go, and I won't call the sheriff."

Knife Guy shoved back from the young man, lowering the blade. He looked like he was backing down, but Jay's instincts told him otherwise.

Jay stepped to the side so he'd be closer to cover the victim as he left.

Knife Guy took a step toward the stall door—this was going to get tricky with the lack of space, even if this was the disabled accessible stall.

Jay braced.

The guy feinted and came at him, knife first.

Jay blocked the swing and punched the guy in the flank without thinking it through.

Shoot. He'd be in serious trouble with Noah, but now that he'd broken the seal, he was going to finish this.

Jay grabbed the side of Knife Guy's head and slammed it into the wall of the stall, making a major dent in the metal.

Knife Guy slumped to the ground.

Jay looked at the young man. "Good time to get out of here."

The kid nodded.

"You good?"

"Yeah." He sniffed. "Thanks."

"You know these guys?" Jay stepped back.

The young man stepped over Wallet Guy and grabbed his billfold. "I've seen 'em around. They do this to people sometimes. Guess I was due."

"If you want some tips on how you can protect yourself, come by the Rourke ranch. I'll show you some defense moves."

"Right." The kid headed for the bathroom door. Probably embarrassed that Jay had to step in and save him.

Jay gave the guy a second of clearance, then used one of the men's phones to call 911 before he left the bathroom. He used the triangle bit of wood by the exit door to jimmy the bathroom door shut so those two wouldn't be able to get out.

Back over at the bar, Caleb said, "Everything okay?"

"Sure." Jay didn't sit. He told the bartender, "If a cop comes in, tell them the guys in the bathroom are armed." Then he dropped a twenty on the bar and walked out.

Being here was one thing, but it wasn't going to change who he was.

No matter where Jay went, trouble always seemed to find him.

❖

Veterinarian Morgan Lawson snipped the thread on the stitches and stepped back. She checked the monitors on the retriever's vital signs. "Okay, she looks good." Morgan peeled off the protective gloves she was wearing. "Hopefully, Sunny won't be eating any more squeakers from toys in the near future."

The nurse assisting her chuckled, smearing the sutured wound with a gel that would help it heal and prevent infection. "I wouldn't count on it."

Morgan grinned. "We can hope. And so can the Sullivans, given I think they'd rather not have to regularly pay for the surgery."

"I'll finish up here if you want to do your rounds." The nurse, Bethany, glanced at the clock.

Morgan tugged on a fresh pair of gloves. "How about I finish up, you head home, and then I'll do my rounds of our patients before I head home?"

Bethany shook her head. "That doesn't seem fair."

Life wasn't fair. But if Bethany believed it was, or should be, Morgan didn't plan to burst her bubble.

"Still, it's fine if you want to get home," the vet insisted. "You have farther to drive than I do." She had to bandage this lady, get her transferred back to her crate, and turn things over to the night attendant. She didn't usually hire overnight help—just when there had been an emergency surgery that day and one of her patients needed observation.

Half an hour later, Bethany pulled her coat on and grabbed the small lunch cooler she always brought from under the front desk. "See you Thursday!"

Morgan waved at her from the reception chair. "Have a good day off!"

Bethany waved back, then locked the front door of the veterinary office behind her as she went out.

Morgan let out a sigh. The clock said it was after nine, but she usually didn't feel the exhaustion of a long day until she slid into the driver's seat of her car to head home.

By the lamplight, she filled out her paperwork with only the orange glow for company. That, and the tiny scratching sounds of the hamster that lived in a cage on the reception desk. Just not where customers could see her.

Morgan signed her name at the bottom of the page and leaned over. "You gonna have those babies yet, mama?"

What she was going to do with a passel of hamsters, Morgan had no idea. But that was a problem for Ava to figure out. She still had fifteen minutes until the vet tech showed up, so she lifted the handset on the phone and dialed her mom's number.

A chirpy eight-year-old voice answered as if she'd been expecting the call. "Hi, Mommy."

"Hi there, Sweetness. What are you and Grandma up to?" Morgan leaned back in the chair and closed her eyes.

"We're making garlic knot rolls. I like twisting them up, but I don't think I like garlic."

"It's better in things than on them."

"Huh." Ava paused. "Maybe that's how I like it, too."

"Did you do your homework?"

"Yes, Mommy. I did two whole paragraphs about the story, and I ate all my cucumber with dinner."

Morgan smiled. "What are the garlic knots for if you already had dinner?"

"Grandma is taking them to a pots luck at lunch tomorrow with the ladies. She's going to let them rise overnight and cook them tomorrow when I'm at school. Did you remember I have that choir assembly at ten?"

"Yes, ma'am. I'll be there." Morgan had rearranged her schedule so she was open during that hour. And thankfully, the elementary school wasn't too far from her office. "What's Grandpa doing?"

"He's reading a sturgeon book."

Morgan smiled to herself. "Do you mean Spurgeon?"

"Grandma, do I mean *Spurgeon*, not *sturgeon*?"

Morgan didn't hear her mother's answer.

Ava came back on. "I mean the man, not the fish."

"Got it." Morgan smiled. She'd bought her father that book for his birthday, trying to find tangible ways to thank them for everything they did for her.

But given how much they helped her, and the fact she couldn't do any of this without them, there really was nothing she could do that was even adequate. She was still going to send them on a cruise for their anniversary this summer.

There was absolutely no way she'd have been able to do any of this without them. Her life as she knew it had crashed and burned hard, halfway through med school, when she'd discovered she was pregnant.

She didn't want to think about Jared and his insistence that she give up her career and stay home to raise their child single-handedly while he climbed to the lofty heights of cardiac medicine. Or how the people at her church had agreed with him.

She'd rather feel the warmth of acceptance she'd always felt from her parents. Insisting she follow her dreams. Reminding her that with their help, she could do what she believed God had called her to do and raise a child.

The fact her attorney father had represented her during the divorce, convincing Jared to sign away his parental rights, only gave her so much more to be thankful for.

But if she thought about that, she'd only start crying.

Thank You, Lord.

She couldn't do much else but be grateful—and be the best mom and veterinarian she could be.

Ava said, "Grandma wants to know if you're working late."

"Not too much longer, I don't think. Then I'll be there."

"Grandma said I could sleep over and she'll take me to school tomorrow."

"I wouldn't see you until the assembly."

"But I could have Grandma's cream cheese French toast before I go to school."

Morgan smiled to herself. The allure of her mother's stuffed French toast was a powerful thing, but she'd reached her weight loss goal a few months ago and it wasn't the season for eating sugar and enjoying life right now. She needed to tighten up her diet before the summer barbecue season started.

Thankfully, just thinking about it didn't pack on the pounds.

But this whole conversation was making her melancholic.

Thinking about seasons, and how life ebbed and flowed through the year. Eventually, Ava would need braces, then she'd be driving.

"Mommy, can I sleep over?" her very teenage-sounding child asked, jogging Morgan from her musings.

"Yeah, honey. It's fine."

"You'll have to feed Mr. Pickles in the morning. And can I come over and see the animals after school?"

"Sure, you can."

"Okay, byeee. Byeee. Grandma says bye, too." The call dropped, and Morgan stared at the phone with what was probably a goofy grin on her face.

Going home to an empty house would actually be a sweet treat at the end of a long day. The chance to take a bath in peace?

Bliss.

A car pulled up out front, shining headlights through the glass doors.

Morgan recognized the night vet tech's car and went to her office to grab her iPad for the last round through the patients on site, a spring now in her step.

She updated charts for two cats that had both been spayed, one of which would go home tomorrow.

The retriever she'd done the surgery on earlier wouldn't wake up for a while, so she wrote instructions for medication when he did. Just in case. Though dogs like this tended to bounce back fast even after major surgery. She'd had an Airedale here a few months ago who'd been trying to bound around with pent-up energy just a day after surgery. It would have been amusing if the animal hadn't been in danger of injuring himself.

"Hey, Betha—" the tech began. "Doc, I wasn't expecting you."

She straightened out of the cage of a husky who'd been hit by a car a few days ago and broken his hip as well as two ribs. The old dog needed a lot of care but would be going home soon. "I'll be out of your hair in a second."

Her night vet tech was twenty-four with red hair and freckles. He flushed easily, which he did right now. "I didn't mean..."

"I know." She chuckled, patting his shoulder as she passed. "But I'm more than ready to go home."

She was going to eat a girl dinner of meats, cheeses, and crackers and for a while not think about any of her responsibilities.

It would be glorious.

All she had to do was get home.

CHAPTER TWO

Jay leaned into the crate and clipped the leash on Cass. He ran his fingers along her warm fur. She shook off, panting. "Ready to go, girl?"

He didn't use her name. Not yet.

Cass had been originally trained with German dog commands by the military, but after being retired he took her on. Together they had forged a path with some work in the field, but mostly Cass got to take it easy these days.

Jay moved to the side of his open rear door, holding the leash loose in his hand. "Come."

Cass hopped out, shaking off again.

He watched her move. The scar along her side was barely visible with the way her fur had grown out. "Let's go for a walk."

The dog trotted beside him, eager to stretch her limbs.

Jay had parked over by the elementary school, hoping the folks who lived around here would be all tucked in for the night. It wasn't as late as he usually walked, so he'd chosen this place specifically.

But mostly so he could make a phone call without being overheard.

Jay put his earbuds in and called Noah, tucking the phone in his pocket. He rubbed the top of Cass's head and listened to it ring.

"Jay, how's it going?"

He didn't even know what to say. "Caleb probably already told you." He'd broken the one stipulation of his downtime at the Rourke ranch. He'd thrown a punch. Which was why he had to just quit. Much better idea than suffering through Noah trying to be nice about it.

"Told me what?" Noah said. "Kind of in the middle of something here, bro. Let me get outside so I can hear you better."

Great. He didn't even know.

Jay turned the corner onto a residential street, Cass trotting along at his side. Stopping to sniff bushes and enjoy the scenery.

"Okay," Noah continued, "what did you wanna tell me?"

Jay winced. The stars overhead offered little comfort, even though he usually wanted to be where he could see as many as possible. Being out on location scouting an area, doing recon, or even in the middle of nowhere Montana. As long as there were stars, he wasn't alone, as if the whole scope of humanity across history was with him.

"Spit it out, bud. Or I'll call Caleb. I'm guessing you'd rather tell me yourself."

Jay cleared his throat and told his boss about the two guys in the bathroom and how he left them locked in for the police to pick up.

"Sounds like you did the right thing, helping out that guy."

"I guess I'm done, then." Jay shrugged a shoulder. "You said no punches, and I threw one without thinking."

"In defense of an innocent person."

"Doesn't usually make a difference." A few streets over from where he'd parked, he found the edge of an industrial complex. "At least not for me. You said—"

"How is Cass?"

Jay flinched. "Why?"

"I'm just curious."

"She's doing fine. We're out walking."

"Good. That's good," Noah said. "I really am in the middle of something, so maybe we can pick this up tomorrow. That okay?"

Jay didn't think there was anything to pick up, but he said, "Sure."

What else could he do? Tomorrow's conversation would probably be about ending his retirement contributions and cancelling his medical coverage.

Jay would have to find a whole new line of work.

Maybe start a dog training business.

Somewhere.

"Thanks. Don't worry, okay?" Noah hung up.

Caleb had totally called him and told him about the bathroom incident. Or he was calling right now to explain how badly Jay had screwed up. Noah probably was in the middle of a job and didn't have time to let Jay down easy.

Jay sighed, long and loud, and pulled out his earbuds. He tucked the case in his jacket pocket.

Cass slowed, her attention drawn by something.

"Come on, Cass." He'd tell her to heel if he needed to, but usually the gentler invitation worked.

She slowed even more and stopped completely.

Jay heard a cry. Male, and from a distance. He crouched by her and whispered, "Want to check it out?"

She gave him a little woof of agreement.

"All right." He scratched her chin. "Heel."

The cry sounded again, giving him a direction. They rounded the construction company's single-story office building and found a forecourt behind it ringed with chain-link fence. Floodlights shone among the stacks of construction equipment, rows of diggers and back hoes, and several white trucks.

He followed the fence line, looking between pallets and even a shipping container inside the fence.

The cry sounded again, followed by a male voice speaking.

Jay found them and stopped.

A tall man in a suit faced off with another man on his knees, heavy-built goons surrounding him. The man on his knees had blood running down the side of his face onto his bare chest, which was peppered with abrasions and red marks.

Jay muttered, "Worked him over good, didn't they?"

Cass let out a low growl.

The man on his knees said, "I can get it for you! I can!"

"You owe me fifty thousand dollars, Whitman." The man in the suit pulled out a pistol and pointed it at him.

Jay hissed in a breath. "Are you kidding me?"

What had he been thinking not too long ago? For the second time tonight, he was going to voluntarily walk into trouble. *Unbelievable.*

Jay wasn't going to let a man, innocent or not, get killed while he stood around watching. He crept to a break in the fence, then reached down and unclipped Cass's leash, a move she understood because they'd done it a hundred times before.

Jay crawled through first, Cass right behind him. She lowered into a "down" but kept moving along beside him. As long as she didn't scratch her belly on something sharp, they would both be fine.

"I'm telling you, Marco! I can get it. If you kill me, you'll never get paid."

"No?" Marco held the gun aimed at Whitman. "You have two daughters. I can get my money out of them."

Whitman cried out.

Which told Jay enough about the character of the two men. He didn't believe that only innocent people deserved to be rescued, but in the heat of things, it helped him to know he was doing the right thing.

Like calling the sheriff.

He pulled out his phone and dialed 911 but left the cell in the dirt. He didn't need to be caught up in a police investigation but wasn't about to get in a sticky situation that no one knew about. He probably should've called Caleb, but the guy had a fiancée and an elderly grandpa and, after all, said the cops in this town were solid enough.

"You, on the other hand, I'm done with." Marco lowered the gun and shot Whitman in the leg. "No one will ever find the pieces that are left of you when we're done."

Jay gave Cass the command "Break," and she sprinted forward. He raced out from behind cover, firing as he went. Cass jumped and slammed into one of the goons, sending him flying into the man beside him.

Whitman fell to the side, crying out.

Jay fired his gun but missed Marco. A split second later, he was staring up at the stars, blinking.

What had knocked him off his feet?

A massive Rottweiler stepped onto his chest, breathing hot dog breath into his face.

Cass barked, crying out.

Jay started to push up, but the weight of the dog held him down. "Cass!" He added the command to back down, knowing she wouldn't give up when he was down. Not even if it pushed them to hurt her.

She had enough injuries. He couldn't let her get hurt.

"Rex, come!"

The Rottweiler backed off and went to stand by Marco.

Jay lifted his shoulders and saw one of the men had Cass by the collar. Whitman was still alive, so he hadn't failed yet.

Marco wandered over, looking down at him. "A regular hero. What do you think you are, some kind of vigilante?" He laughed.

Jay brushed dog paw prints off his shirt front but couldn't get up yet. He would look too imposing. "You were gonna kill that guy."

Marco leaned down. "Now I'm gonna kill both of you."

Jay bent his knees and kicked Marco in the shins.

The guy yelped and nearly went down but called out to his guys, "Get him up."

Two men in jeans and jackets stomped over. Bigger looking from down on the ground as they towered over him, but Jay refused to go down without a fight. They hauled him to his feet, and he used the momentum to launch his attack.

Hook. Uppercut. Roundhouse.

The classics were classics for a reason. He fought like a wild dog against the two of them, trying to do as much damage as possible.

He heard Cass yelp, and saw her run for the gate, chased by the Rottweiler.

"No!" Jay channeled all his frustration into renewing the fight.

Finally able to break away, he raced in the direction his dog had gone.

A gunshot rang out. He ducked his head and kept going. Running harder.

A block or so later, another shot rang out. He could hardly see Cass now. Could hardly...

His knees buckled. White pain exploded in his chest.

Jay hit the ground and fought to stay conscious.

🐾

Morgan hit the brakes and narrowly missed hitting the dark blur that darted across the street.

Another dark blur followed it, and her front end clipped the animal.

She screeched the car to a halt and threw it in Park. Shoved the door open and nearly fell trying to scramble out.

A Rottweiler she'd seen around town limped away from her car, back in the direction it had come.

"No! Wait!"

The dog didn't stop. It broke into a run, with nothing but a slight indication the animal was hurt.

A second later, she couldn't see it in the dark.

Morgan turned back the other way to try to find the first animal, the one she hadn't hit. If it wasn't for the fact that she had slowed upon seeing the first dog, she would have hit the other a lot harder than she had.

"Hey, puppy. Where'd you go?" She kept a crooning tone, moving to the opposite sidewalk. Scanning the bushes.

There.

"Hi, how are you?" She moved slowly, then crouched. "Hey there, gorgeous."

The dog stood up, looking nervous.

"It's okay."

The German shepherd really was gorgeous, staring at her with those big brown eyes.

"It's going to be just fine. That big mean dog ran off. You're safe now." She ran her hand under the dog's chin and scratched.

The animal stepped toward her, and she found a collar. So this wasn't a stray, but she had no tag or name. Halfway down the dog's left side she had a raised area, scar tissue that was in the process of healing. Probably a few weeks old.

"Who hurt you, baby?"

She needed to take the dog with her and ensure she was returned to her owner—if the owner proved responsible.

"Let's go somewhere warm and safe. I'm sure I have some dog biscuits in the car. What do you say?"

The dog followed her to the edge of the curb and stood staring at the sidewalk across the street, where that Rottweiler had gone.

"Come on."

The animal walked with an awareness that she didn't see in a lot of dogs. But there weren't any military dogs, or ex-military dogs, in this town. She was the only vet, so she would know. Well, apart from the old guy across town who treated farm animals.

Morgan stared down at the animal. "Who are you?"

The dog trotted off, going in the direction the other had gone. Turning the tables? Chasing the animal who chased her?

Morgan grabbed her keys and slammed her door.

She spotted red and blue flashing lights a few streets away but didn't hear sirens. They probably didn't want to wake local residents.

Morgan raced after the dog. "Hey! Puppy! Come!" She frowned, rushing along the sidewalk. "Heel!"

The dog ignored her.

Morgan didn't know how long she was going to follow the animal before going back to her life, and her plan for a restful evening. It had taken a bit to get out of the office, but now that she had, it was so tempting to abandon this dog.

But she couldn't, could she?

Thankfully, Ava and her parents weren't waiting for her to show up.

Morgan followed the dog across Baker Street until she stopped on the side of the street by the entrance to the park. A place where she regularly brought Ava to play in the summer.

The dog rushed over to a dark shadow, a man lying on the ground, and sniffed around his face.

"Oh my goodness." Morgan fell to her knees, easing the animal away so she could roll the man to his back.

He groaned.

"Yeah, I bet." She patted his cheeks. "What happened to you, dude?"

People medicine wasn't her thing, but he'd clearly been injured. His shoulder was covered in blood.

Morgan reached back for her phone...

Which was in the car.

The animal whined and licked the man's face.

"Okay, if he's your person, then I guess he's not some kind of sicko serial killer or something crazy like that."

Morgan had never seen this guy before. Not that she'd met everyone in town. But this guy? Oh yeah. She'd have remembered him. Not just because of his size and the heavy set of his brow, but those full lips and...

Okay, Morgan.

He was nothing like her ex-husband, Jared, but this was about injuries, not ogling.

The dog whined again.

"Right, let's check him for a phone. We can get an ambulance or something."

The dog paced around but didn't indicate in any way to Morgan that the mean dog or anyone else was around.

She patted down the man's pockets and found earbuds in a case before she found a phone. Morgan hit the power button and the screen illuminated. "Okay, emergency call. Here we—"

A huge weight rolled her to her back, and suddenly she was looking up at a dark face completely in shadow.

Morgan tried to breath, but he was crushing her chest. "Um." She coughed and patted his shoulders trying to push him away. "Get off."

He shifted a little, and she could breathe.

"Thanks." She sucked in a full breath. "You okay? I think you need a hospital."

"No." The word was so short and sharp it might have been a bark.

She dealt with dogs every day, and the most standoffish ones eventually came around. She just had to figure out how to reach them.

And yes, she knew he wasn't really a dog. But most of God's creatures, including the ones made in His image, could be reached with the basics. Respect. Affection. Treats.

She wondered which would get him to tell her what had happened.

His head dipped. She wondered what was happening for a second but realized quickly he was passing out.

"Whoa, buddy." Morgan rolled him to his back. "Let's figure this out."

He blinked up at the sky and seemed to stare at it. But with the dark out here, she couldn't tell exactly. "No doctors. No hospital." He reached out, and the dog came close, lying down by his side and putting her head on his uninjured shoulder.

"Unlock your phone." She held it out. "I'm not going to call emergency services."

"Already did." He grunted. "Left my phone..." He looked around, almost confused. Maybe he'd hit his head?

"It's right here."

He unlocked his phone with his thumbprint, and she turned on the flashlight. He hissed.

"Sorry." She moved the light away from his face and shined it on his shoulder. The bullet hole was an exit wound, which meant he'd been shot in the back. "Maybe I should call and ask for the police instead of EMTs. Someone put a bullet through you."

"Not the first time," he said. "And it's fine."

And he didn't seem bothered by her suggesting the police. Why didn't that actually reassure her? "You need help."

"Then help me," he grunted, running his fingers over the dog's fur. Almost like he needed the connection to reassure himself.

"Who shot you? Are they still around here?"

"Hopefully, the police in this town already arrested them."

"Well, you can't just lie here forever, and I need to go home. It's late, and while this has been fun..."

He chuckled, then groaned like it hurt.

"Sorry. What are we going to do?"

He lifted his head. "You have a car?"

"Yes, of course. I nearly hit your dog, then another dog, and then followed her to you."

"Help me up."

She grabbed his elbow, and as he got his feet under him, she put an arm around his back.

He hissed out a breath. "Let's do this."

Morgan wasn't so sure about it, but said, "Up we go."

The guy stumbled, but she got under his good arm, and between the two of them he remained upright. He was even bigger standing!

Morgan bit her lip. "Are you sure you don't want an ambulance?"

"I just need a ride. I'm fine."

"Sure, buddy. Listen, you should probably tell me your name." She chuckled. "Since I'm giving you a ride and all."

They set off, and she steered him toward her car. His dog walked in front of them, periodically looking back at them.

"Durango James," he finally said. "Call me Jay."

"Nice to meet you, Jay. I'm Morgan Lawson."

He grunted as Morgan guided him to the passenger door, and he leaned against her car while she opened it.

The dog jumped in before he could, hopping through to the back.

Morgan got him into the seat, with a lot of heavy breathing, then tucked his booted feet in and shut the door. "Okay, then. Not the resting plan, but I guess it'll do. No one can say I don't know how to have a good time."

She rounded the trunk and got in on the driver's side. Turned the car on. Lowered the volume on the radio.

"Okay, if not the hospital, then where are we going?" she asked, glancing over.

His head lolled to the side.

Unconscious.

CHAPTER THREE

J ay blinked, shifting in the seat. Suddenly awake. Which hurt considerably, but not as much as previous injuries. His surroundings came into focus. He let out an undignified sound from his mouth and tried to figure out what had just happened. Not his car.

This was also not his garage door in front of the parked car—because he didn't have one.

Not his house, either. Though he had to appreciate the hominess of it. Because he didn't have a home either.

Growing up the only child of older parents who worked full-time, he'd done daycare before and after school. Later it was sports, because the folks paid for whatever he wanted. Church on Sunday because life was about appearances. A nice car—nicer than he'd deserved—because all their friends bought cars for their sixteen-year-olds. The flashier the better, all to show each other up.

He'd realized eventually that what their friends thought of them meant far more than his opinions, or what he might choose for himself. Or showing each other affection.

Going into the army had been a massive middle finger to them both when they'd been applying for colleges for him, determined that he go to Harvard and be a lawyer. They'd probably donated enough money that the school had no choice but to let him in.

And it turned out the army had been the best place he could've landed. Discovering a brotherhood in his squad, and a bunkmate who'd explained what the gospel actually was. What redemption meant, and how grace made it so there was nothing Durango James could do to earn his salvation. All he had to do was believe.

Help my unbelief.

These days, he was a little more aware of his shortcomings in that department. Things were becoming harder to ignore.

He needed to get a handle on the anger, once and for all, but had no idea how to do it.

Jay heard something to his right and looked out the side window. He was in the passenger seat of...her car?

She had his dog on a leash. The woman he remembered standing over him.

Dark hair falling around her face. Concern in her features. She cared about the injured. Cared about his dog.

Jay managed to grab the door handle and open it, then realized he was still buckled in and hit the latch. His right shoulder screamed, but he ignored it—a skill he'd developed over the years.

He set his feet on the ground and heard her.

"No more sniffing. Just go pee, doggy. We need to get him inside."

Jay couldn't see her that well, but what he could make out appealed to him. Probably more than it should. Still, he had to respect a woman who understood the value of teaching a dog to pee on command.

"Cass," Jay called out. "Go pee."

The dog immediately squatted and took care of business. If only the rest of his life could be that simple.

"You're awake." She came over, Cass bounding in front of her so she was forced to drop the leash or be pulled over.

His dog stopped in front of him, sniffing and craning her neck toward him. He scratched her with his good hand. "You didn't drive to a hospital and shove me out of the car?"

"Do people often do that to you?"

He almost smiled. "You'd be surprised."

"You said no doctors and no EMTs. Or something like that. It seemed important, anyway. I wasn't sure of the protocol."

"No protocol." He shook his head. "I just don't like needles."

She shook her head at him like she was surprised. "You're bleeding all over my car. Maybe I should have dropped you at the hospital. Or taken you back to my office and dosed you with a tranquilizer first. I've got some real powerful stuff. The kind that works on stubborn large breed dogs."

Jay covered Cass's ears. "Pretend you didn't hear her say that."

"She led me to you."

"And you're a vet?"

She nodded. "Your dog seems concerned, but uninjured. Except for what she's healing from."

"If you're a vet, you know how to stitch."

"And why would that possibly be relevant right now? There's literally a twenty-four-hour clinic half an hour from here."

"I don't want my name on any paperwork."

"Are you a criminal?"

"No. Just the guy bleeding all over your car." He grabbed the top of the open door with his good arm and hauled himself up. "I'll get out of your hair."

He'd need a ride back to his car. Or he could call Caleb and get picked up, maybe? Either way, being here wasn't all that helpful. But he didn't fault her for coming home.

"Thanks for your help." Jay turned to the street, commanding Cass to heel, but took only two steps before he had to lean against the car.

"Yeah, good luck walking...wherever it is you're going." She sounded amused by his feeble attempt. "How about you come inside and let me at least take a look at your wound? I can clean you up and tell you again how you need a doctor."

He looked back at her. "You're sure? I could be a killer for all you know."

"So could I." She folded her arms.

He huffed, amused. Another point in her favor—the woman could handle herself. People were more than the sum of their physical features. He much preferred knowing the whole person before he decided if he wanted them in his life. Or he could just follow Cass's lead and trust based on instinct.

But then, it wasn't as if he would see her again after tonight. So what did it matter?

She unlocked her front door, and he bit back the comment he wanted to make about her needing a security alarm. None of his business.

Jay nearly tripped over a pair of purple child-sized rubber boots. "You have kids?"

"She's with my parents tonight. It's just us."

Jay wasn't sure he felt better knowing that.

"Her name is Ava, and she's an eight-year-old tornado."

Whatever that meant. "Cool."

"You have kids?"

"Nope. Just me and Cass."

"That's an odd name for a dog. It's a girl name. I mean, people give their dogs people names all the time, and that's fine. I just..." She shrugged and didn't say more.

"It starts with a hard consonant. When you give dog commands, it has to be sharp, and brief. A hard consonant gives it an edge. You can put authority into their name in a way they respect. Rather than it being soft, like Lucy or Ella."

"Huh. I didn't know that."

Jay shrugged, using the move to shuck off his jacket. It fell to the floor before he could grab it. "Sorry."

"Don't worry." She flipped on the entry light and winced. "That looks bad. You should take off your shirt."

Considering she was looking at him with the assessing gaze of a medic, he didn't think it was a come-on. Then again, a woman with a family had no business flirting with a strange man she'd found on the side of the road anyway.

He reached behind his head with his good hand, grabbed a fistful of his T-shirt, and pulled it forward over his head.

Which felt great.

"Let's sit at the dining table." She motioned with her head.

Jay pressed the material against the front of his shoulder, where blood ran down his chest, and she held his elbow as they walked through the house. The dining table had four chairs—an inviting place where a family would gather, even host dinners.

He'd never sat at a table like this in his life.

"You gonna pass out again?" She dumped a first aid kit on the table.

He shook his head, drawing his attention from the nicks and scratches in the table back to her. Big mistake.

Now that he could see her up close in the light? Oh boy.

She has a kid, and probably a husband.

Thankfully, that put a stop to the attraction that flared to life. Sure, he put a whole lot of stock in a person's personality being the reason he respected them, or connected with them, but...

Oh boy.

The woman was straight-up gorgeous.

🐾

Morgan tried not to stare, but the guy was seriously built. And had a serious wound on his shoulder—which actually tempered the attraction that wanted to steal the words from her mouth and leave her tongue-tied.

She should be scared, but she wasn't. All she could think was how utterly different he was to Jared. Morgan didn't want to be the kind of woman who always compared a man to the last relationship she had. Or the only. But being so close to a guy with no shirt on?

It had been a long time.

"I'd like to say at this juncture," she began, needing to be reasonable and rational right now, "that I am not a people doctor. I treat animals."

"I'm not asking you to do surgery. It's a scratch."

"That's the dumbest thing you could've said. This is a gunshot wound, and the only reason it's not surgery is because the bullet went in your back and came out the front." She was still going to clean it, though. Which was why she opened a bunch of packets and got to work. "You should see a doctor. You probably *should* have surgery to fix all the damage."

"I will. I'll see a doctor, I promise."

She looked at him, one eyebrow raised. "Am I supposed to believe that?"

"There were a lot of things you were 'supposed' to do the last couple of hours. That's on the list now."

She got up and moved around behind him to address the entry wound on his back. She knew that's what it was because Jared had explained the difference after a police shooting, and for some reason the details stuck with her. "Maybe you could tell me about that."

"You come across a bleeding man in the street, and you don't call the cops?"

"You ordered me not to." She swiped a cleansing wipe across the dirt and blood on his shoulder.

"And you complied?"

"You didn't give me much choice." She frowned. "There were already police in the area. Maybe I figured they'd sort it all out."

"I'm the one who called them. I left a phone for them to pinpoint the location."

A phone. Not *my phone.* Interesting distinction.

"You decided to help me," he added.

Morgan pressed the bandage down and ran her finger along the edges. "Yes, I decided to help you."

"Why?"

"Your dog."

He twisted in the seat and looked at her. Dark eyes, deep set, and dark brows. A scruff of late-day shadow on his jaw. Lines of stress and experience around his eyes and mouth.

"Is that supposed to be some kind of dog whisperer thing? Do the animals talk to you?"

She sat back down facing him, a smile tugging at her lips. The weight of the long day dragging her down. "A dog doesn't show someone the kind of respect and affection your dog shows you to a garbage human being that doesn't give a crap about them." She looked over at the German shepherd lying on the kitchen tile, head on her paws, watching them.

"So you judge people based on how their pets feel about them?"

Morgan shrugged. "It's my job." After a second she said, "Is Cass your pet?"

"We're a team at work and at home." He hesitated for a second, then said, "This is where I joke that she's the love of my life." He glanced at the dog, his face immediately softening.

"It's easy to feel that way about dogs." And children, though given his reaction when they entered her house, she wasn't sure he'd agree with that. "Maybe I should have been more cautious helping you, but I just didn't feel like I was in any danger."

Morgan sat back in the chair and handed him back his T-shirt.

"A few months ago..." Did she really want to share this? Morgan decided it didn't matter. It seemed right to explain. "There was a police officer. A deputy with the sheriff's department. He kept calling, coming by the vet office when I was working late. Showing up here when Ava was with my parents for the night."

She brushed some fibers off her pant leg, still dressed in her work clothes, even though it was late. So much for her night-alone plans.

"One time, he even pulled me over, flashing lights and everything. Just to tell me that I should go out with him." She rolled her eyes. "And I don't mean ask. I mean he told me like it was an order."

"Is he still on the force here in town?"

Morgan shook her head. "He was fired a month ago and left town. At least, that's what I heard." Her cell phone started to vibrate across the table. She glanced at the clock on the oven. 10:08. Then lifted the phone to her ear. "Everything okay?"

"Did you take care of the gerbils?"

Ava. Morgan chuckled quietly. "No, but I will. You should go to sleep. It's a school night."

"I know." The eight-year-old dragged the words out, sounding like she was actually sixteen. "Grandma and I just got done reading *The Hobbit*. We're on chapter four now."

"Awesome. Listen, I'll see you tomorrow at that assembly, okay?"

"Okay, Mommy." Ava yawned, sounding tired. "Love you."

"Love you, too, kiddo. Sleep well."

Morgan hung up.

Jay was staring at her now. "I'm thinking the pet rule applies to kids as well. Not that I met her first, like you did with Cass."

Morgan got up, needing to move around so she didn't fall asleep as well. She grabbed the wrappers and took them to the trash, then filled two glasses with water. "What do you mean?"

"How people treat their pets. How people treat their children? Shades of the same thing. Who we invite into our lives. Who chooses to stick with us, and love us, and trust us to look out for them."

She handed him one of the glasses of water, wondering if Jared had ever said anything like that to her. "See why I couldn't have believed you might hurt me?" Though definitely capable, Jay seemed more like the guy who defended those who needed it.

"I could still be a bad guy," he pointed out. "Life isn't usually black-and-white. Good people do bad things, and bad people can do good."

"I don't think you aren't dangerous. I just don't think you're dangerous to me."

But he should be going now, because this was starting to drift into an intimate conversation. She might be comfortable giving him a ride and helping patch him up, but him staying at her house overnight? That was something different entirely.

"Do you need a ride somewhere?" She didn't want to leave her house, but letting him walk off on his own didn't seem right.

Jay shook his head and stood, surprising her with his size again. Standing over her, he seemed imposing. But once again, she wasn't sacred. Even if he thought she should be. Morgan had been a terrible judge of character with Jared, but having Ava in her life more than made up for what he'd put her through.

She wouldn't be able to read this guy so well if this was a relationship, so she figured the fact she could meant otherwise. She'd probably never see him again.

"Thanks for your help."

She frowned. "Are you going to call a rideshare, or what? You might not get one at this time of night."

"I'm good." He grabbed Cass's leash. "Seriously, thanks for all your help."

"You're welcome." What else was she supposed to say? "I really could give you a ride or take you to your car."

"I'm good."

She followed him to the door, knowing it was for the best. But still, what if he collapsed on the street? "At least call someone to pick you up."

He almost smiled. "Not sure anyone has ever cared about me this much."

Why did that make her infinitely sad? Morgan tried to ignore the feeling and opened the door for him, holding it wide. "I guess...take care?" She wasn't going to see him again.

"You, too." He nodded.

For a second, it seemed as if he wanted to say something, but instead he just walked away down her drive. Like he didn't have a bullet hole in his shoulder. Like he'd taken some pain pills—which he hadn't.

Who was this guy?

Morgan watched him walk his dog down the sidewalk until she couldn't see him anymore.

And then she shut the door.

Whatever tonight had been didn't matter. Morgan had a good life—actually, it was a great life. She had the best kid in the world, her parents were amazing, and her ex left her alone most of the time. She loved her job, and business was good.

Being alone wasn't lonely, it was peaceful. She had everything else she needed in the Lord. What more could she wish for?

And yet, for some reason, part of her wanted to dream for things she didn't have. That she'd almost convinced herself she didn't need.

Almost.

Maybe it was time to rethink.

CHAPTER FOUR

Jay insisted on driving himself to the hardware store. Two days after he'd met Morgan and made his way back to his truck. Got all the way back to the ranch—after sleeping a few hours in the front seat. Now he was still pretty stiff, but life didn't stop long enough for you to heal. People with chronic pain had to still go about their lives, so he was going to stick with the same plan.

Besides, the sun was shining. It was Saturday, as good a day as any to get supplies and help the Rourke men fix the roof on the barn.

Added bonus—he'd be too sore and tired to think about Morgan.

Cass whined from her crate in the back.

He stuck his head in the open door. "Stay."

She quit whining and he shut the door, leaving the windows cracked since it was fifty-five and she liked the breeze. Sure, he could've brought her into the hardware store. It wasn't that he didn't trust her. It was everyone else in the world and their untrained dogs on a Saturday, thinking a trip to the hardware store was a good idea.

Caleb's grandpa, Ian Rourke, climbed out of the passenger side of Caleb's truck. Jay hesitated a second, just in case the old man needed a steady hand, but he settled on the ground well enough and heaved the door shut.

"Sleep all right?" The old man sipped from a hot cup.

"Yes, sir. Just fine." They'd given him a cot in the back of the barn, which suited him and Cass well enough.

"Hear those wolves again?"

He wasn't asking out of concern for Jay, more that he was worried about his cattle getting dragged off by predators. And Cass, to an extent.

Jay shook his head as they walked through the parking lot of the hardware store. "No, sir. I didn't hear them last night." He would know, since he'd woken up from dreams about Morgan plenty of times throughout the night. "If you want, I could install some motion-sensor cameras. Or heat-sensing ones that can tell the difference between a cow or elk, and a wolf or coyote?"

Caleb moved to the other side of his "Pops," who was pushing eighty but didn't seem to ever slow down. Until it was naptime midafternoon, and he'd always disappear for an hour before coming out of his room with sleep lines on his face.

Now the older man shook his head, sipping his coffee.

"If you change your mind, just let me know. I won't be around much longer." Not after Noah got around to officially firing him.

The guy was supposed to have called, but apparently things kept "coming up" on the case the rest of the team was working.

It was starting to feel like some kind of *Princess Bride*, Dread Pirate Roberts kind of thing.

Sleep tight. I'll most likely kill you in the morning.

Jay grabbed the handle on a flatbed cart and shoved it forward. Living in limbo was not his thing.

"Whoa, Tiger." Sounded like the old man was amused.

Jay slowed.

Caleb was grinning like an idiot as if he knew what Jay was thinking. He probably thought it was about Noah firing him. Which it was, but it was also a lot more about the woman he couldn't get out of his head.

"Wanna talk about it?" Caleb walked beside them while the old man veered off to look at whatever.

Jay figured out where roof tiles were and headed that way. "I already told you about those guys in the construction company forecourt. The dog, the victim the cops found dead, the"—he lowered his voice—"gunshots. So there's nothing left to tell."

Caleb nodded. "Sure."

Jay didn't roll his eyes, because he was a grown man.

"Sheriff Cartwright called me on the way over." Ah, so that's why he'd agreed so readily to his pops walking off.

"And?"

"Autopsy is complete. Thomas Whitman, the victim, was definitely murdered."

"I said he was." Jay just hadn't stuck around to take everyone's pulse. He'd been too busy running—and getting shot in the back. Whitman had been alive when he left the forecourt.

So much for ideas of regrouping.

"Right," Caleb said. "So they'd like your official statement, even though I explained your job is one of a sensitive nature as assigned to you by Uncle Sam. But the sheriff isn't as inclined to bend rules as others might be. He wants full transparency."

"No-go."

Caleb tilted his head. "I explained the sensitive nature of your work. He said, 'Bring an ID.' He doesn't care if it says John Doe on it. He wants to hear what you know, what you saw, and he wants to hear it from your own mouth."

Jay pushed out a hard breath. "Of course, he does. I'll head over there later."

"Thanks."

"What about the shooter, his thug friends, or the dog?" Jay said. Given the police had already been there Thursday night after Morgan patched him up, he'd given the street a wide berth on the way back to the car.

"Animal control took the dog, the thugs are in the wind, and the shooter got away. That's why they need your description. So they can be certain who it was."

"You'd think in a town like this the police would know who was going around acting like mafia thugs, squeezing people to pay their debts. That Whitman guy called him Marco."

Caleb chuckled. "Yeah, this isn't the big city. I'm used to crime on a bigger scale than Breckenrow."

"I bet. Coming from the DEA, you probably see cartels around every corner."

Caleb's chuckle switched to a laugh, and he scratched the side of his head, above his ear. He'd certainly mellowed out from the guy Noah told stories about. Now he was planning a wedding and living a small-town Montana life.

Jay loaded supplies from their list onto the cart. He was happy for the guy. Didn't mean Jay wanted the same for himself. But he could appreciate the finer parts of marriage.

"It's a different life here, but it's not a bad one." Caleb hauled a pack of roof tiles off the stack and flipped it onto the cart. "Between Tessa and Jesus." He shook his head. "It's a different life all around."

"Trouble followed you back here, though. Didn't it?"

Caleb nodded. "Sure did. Kessler sent a dirty FBI agent to take us out. The agent is dead, and Kessler is in custody. It's only a matter of time before Noah figures out working his way up the chain to find the boss Kessler was working for."

"I'm glad it worked out for you and Tessa."

"Now I know what peace really is." Caleb paused. "Sounds hokey, maybe. But it's true. I'm just...settled in a way I've never been before. Noah and I still don't know where our parents are, but my peace isn't dependent on me having answers."

"I could probably use a little of that peace."

"I'm glad you're coming to church with us tomorrow. It's important."

Jay figured stuff like that was about as life-or-death—eternally speaking—as it could get, but he just nodded. "It'll be nice to get back to it actually. I've been putting that off for too long."

A little kid's voice entered the periphery of his awareness. "...then Jesse said we should do an escape room for her birthday, when I just said we should do it for mine."

"That wasn't very nice."

They turned the corner at the end of the aisle.

Morgan, and a younger version of her. Ava.

The kid didn't notice them.

"I know!" Ava continued. "I told her that to her face, even though you told me I should be respectful. She needed to know that wasn't nice to steal my idea and use it for her party." She looked up at her mom. All gangly knees and long hair in two dark braids. She had a couple of wonky teeth and a little button nose. "Mommy?"

Morgan's steps faltered. "Jay."

Ava looked at him, then at her mom, then at him again. Then she noticed the man beside him. "Uncle Caleb!" She bounded forward and launched herself at him.

Caleb caught her and swung her up onto his hip, even though she was arguably too big for that. "Hey, Pickle. How's things?"

"Good!" When he set her down, she said, "But Grandpa's faucet is leaking, so we're buying a washer."

Morgan just stared at Jay, and he stared back. And no one said anything.

Caleb cleared his throat. "Jay, this is Tessa's cousin. Morgan Lawson. She's a vet. And this princess is Ava."

Jay said nothing.

"You guys know each other?"

Morgan looked at Caleb. "We've met."

"Right. Cass," Caleb said. "Of course."

If he wanted to think that, Jay wasn't going to explain otherwise.

"Caleb!" Pops called out from down the aisle. "Need to show you something, Son."

"I'm going with Caleb, Mommy." The little girl took his hand, and the two of them left Jay alone with Morgan.

But not without Caleb glancing back over his shoulder with a quizzical look on his face.

Better than him noticing Jay wasn't using his right arm to lift anything or talking about him having to visit the sheriff's department.

He smiled at Morgan. "Hey."

Definitely better.

🐾

"Hey?" She stared at him. "That's what you're going to say to me?"

He scratched at the side of his nose, hiding a smile. "You really are Tessa's cousin, aren't you?"

Morgan put her hands on her hips. "What is *that* supposed to mean?"

He grinned full-out at her, which she had to admit made him look a whole lot more handsome. Or at least more approachable than the dark and broody good guy she'd found bleeding in a bush.

Not that she had been thinking about him the past two days or anything. No, ma'am.

Sunday couldn't come soon enough. Morgan was feeling the need to confess a few things, so to speak.

Jay stepped closer and held out his hand. "Durango James. Nice to meet you in the daylight."

She took his hand. "Morgan Lawson. Nice to meet you when you're not bleeding."

Weren't sparks supposed to arc between their fingers. She was meant to feel the sizzle of his touch, right?

At least that was how it happened in the movies she watched.

Then again, with Jay there was something a whole lot more...

earthy about him. He didn't seem like the sizzle kind of guy. More like the kind who tossed a woman over his shoulder and carried her off. A thousand years ago, maybe.

He drew his hand away. "Your dad has a leaky faucet?"

She nodded. "Right. He told me about it this morning. He can fix it, but he prefers to stick to the house as much as he can. He had surgery on his foot a few weeks ago."

Jay nodded.

"You have older parents?"

"I guess." He shrugged. "They live in Miami. I haven't seen them in a while."

She sensed that was a line of questioning she didn't need to follow to its end. He didn't seem the kind of person who wanted someone else's empathy. He'd see it as pity, most likely.

She peered at his cart. "Tessa said something about the Rourkes fixing the roof this weekend. She didn't mention they had a house guest, though."

"It's classified, I'm afraid."

"Ah." She grinned. "Of course."

She had no idea what Caleb or his twin did for a living, but Tessa had given her enough hints that Morgan knew not to ask. It certainly put Jay in a different light. "You work with Caleb and Noah, on their super top secret international crime-fighting team?"

He laughed, and she enjoyed seeing it. "I'm surprised you know even that much."

She shifted her weight from one foot to the other, glad she wore her nicer Saturday jeans today. That way she didn't look completely homeless. "He wanted to tell Ava that Noah is a superhero, but I told him she would tell all her friends, so it wasn't really a good idea."

"For the record," he said, "Noah *is* a superhero."

Morgan smiled. "I remember him from high school. Both of them, actually. They were football players. Heartbreakers. Everyone wanted to go out with them. All the moms wanted to adopt them since their parents were AWOL so much."

"Doesn't seem like it did them much damage." He shrugged. "I don't know why they're set on finding their parents so badly."

Morgan bit her lip so she didn't ask him about it. She wanted to, but it wasn't really a first-daylight-encounter kind of conversation. "Want to walk me over to the washers?"

Jay pushed on the cart. "Sure. Let's go."

"Why is it that you don't seem like you have a bullet hole in your shoulder?"

He looked around.

"Sorry." Morgan winced. "I should've said the B word quieter."

"It's fine. I didn't exactly tell Caleb I got shot. But I will be telling the police later."

"Um, are you going to tell them that I patched you up?" She'd put a bandage on. Stitches would've been problematic, because she didn't have a license to practice medicine on people. Maybe in the movies and on TV people did that all the time, using dental floss and whatnot, but that was just nuts.

"Not if you don't want me to."

She didn't want to ask him to lie, though. Not to the police. "Tell them what you think you should. It'll be fine."

Jay nodded. "All right."

She wasn't used to feeling like she had to carry the conversation with a man. Compared to Jared, who hadn't once quit jabbering about everything that popped into his head, Jay was downright stoic. The quiet that stretched between them was…refreshing.

After she had selected the correct washer, and he'd sent whatever message on his phone and put it away, she said, "I'm actually glad I ran into you. I was wondering how you were."

"Surprised you didn't see if you'd find me in the county jail records they post online. Or maybe in the obituaries."

"I hoped not, but I'd be lying if I said it didn't cross my mind."

He smiled. "I'm not here to cause trouble."

"Shame."

His eyes flashed with attraction.

Eek! She was flirting. She got all nervous, wondering if he'd think she was terrible at it.

Jay touched her elbow. "I also might not be here that long."

She could see the gold flecks in his brown eyes from this close.

"As much as I'd love to ask you out right now, I'm not sure it's such a great idea. My trip here might get cut short any day now."

"Oh." She wanted to step back, but that would mean he'd let go of her. "Right. Yes, of course."

"Morgan—"

She cut him off, her cheeks flaming. "No, no." She waved her hand. "Of course. You're only visiting town for a few days. You're one of those superhero types, after all. Out there saving the world so normal, everyday folks like me can feel safe, not even knowing that you put your life on the line."

He tugged her closer, so close their bodies were almost touching. Near enough she could see the attraction flare in his eyes. "I'd like to kiss you. I'd like to take you out for dinner. Not necessarily in that order." His arm slid around her back. "But it's a bad idea." He shook his head. "I'm not a safe bet. I'm a wild card at best."

She shook her head. "There's no way you'd hurt me."

"It wouldn't be intentional." His breath whispered across her lips, his face was so close.

Above them, an announcement about a sale on kitchen tile played over the speakers.

Morgan found herself staring at Jay once again. This time far too close. Did it feel dangerous? Sure. But aside from feeling more alive than she'd felt in a really long time, she also felt completely safe.

"But it might be worth the risk," she countered. "You can't know unless you take the chance."

A small feminine voice said, "Uh, Mommy, why do you look like Han Solo and Princess Leia right now?"

Morgan pulled back from Jay so fast she nearly tripped over. She saw him reach for her but put an arm around Ava's shoulders instead. "We were just talking about something, honey."

She could see Caleb and his grandpa out the corner of her eye but didn't dare look at him when it felt like her cheeks were on fire.

"Becky and Simon talk to each other like that behind the bike sheds sometimes."

"As long as you're not the one going behind the bike sheds." Morgan waved over her shoulder. "Bye, guys! Good to see you!"

Sure, she sounded delusional, but Morgan was going to cut and run and just not worry about it right now.

She gave Ava a squeeze. "Let's get this washer back to Grandpa."

Ava stopped beside her at the checkout and put a hand on her hip. "Maybe I should tell Grandma about that man you weren't behind the bike sheds with."

Morgan gasped. "Or we could...not mention it."

Ava lifted her chin. "Depends. Are you going to get me that mountain bike for my birthday?"

"Who taught you about extortion?"

"Grandpa."

Morgan pocketed her change. "Good thing he was on the right side of the law. And if you end up in trouble, he can represent you."

"I think I'm gonna go to law school. If they'll let me bring my cat."

Morgan put an arm around Ava's shoulders. "We should watch *Legally Blonde* this afternoon."

Why did that make her wonder what Jay would think of it? He might have even seen it. Did he like *Mean Girls* better?

Ava eyed her. "Mommy."

"Fine, we can watch something else." She looked both ways so they could cross the lane in front of the hardware store.

"No, Mommy." She grabbed Morgan's arm. "Someone's hurting that dog!"

She looked where Ava indicated and saw... "Cass." She spun to Ava. "Run back inside. Scream for Uncle Caleb and Jay as loud as you can. Tell them Cass is in trouble."

Her daughter ran back inside the store, and Morgan heard the screaming yell at the same time she took off running toward Cass.

Two big heavyset guys tried to drag her by her collar. The dog fought, turning her head side to side. Growling.

One of the men tried to grab her back legs and got donkey kicked.

"Cass!" She sprinted toward the men and didn't think about what she was going to do.

Morgan dipped her shoulder and tackled one of the men straight on.

CHAPTER FIVE

The doors didn't slide open nearly fast enough. Jay got enough clearance to angle his body between the doors and ran out, sprinting flat out toward where he'd parked.

The second Ava ran in, screaming for Caleb, he'd known something was wrong with Morgan. But apparently, Cass was the target.

Two men—the goons from the other night—were trying to take his dog. He'd figured it would be the guys from the bar's bathroom coming back around to get back at him for the fact they got arrested. Nope. These were Marco's guys. Which meant someone had looked him up...and found Cass's military service record.

His dog had a mouthful of one guy's arm, whipping her head back and forth.

Morgan rolled around on the asphalt with the other guy, and she was getting overpowered fast. She wasn't going to last much longer before she got seriously hurt.

Jay yelled, "Aus!"

Cass spit the guy's arm out.

He gave the command, "Gib Laut."

She barked at the attacker, keeping him back with the force of her presence. The volume of her incessant barking.

Morgan cried out.

Jay grabbed the guy off her and tossed him toward his buddy. The guy landed on the ground nearby, up against the right side of Jay's SUV.

Cass kept barking. But the deterrent wasn't going to work for much longer.

He scooped up Morgan next, with no time for a visual assessment. He just wanted her on her feet.

Caleb ran over, and Jay handed Morgan to him, who passed her off to her daughter and Pops, who were coming up behind him.

Way too close to danger.

"Get back!" Jay turned to face the two men and saw the glint of a knife. He grinned. "Let's go."

Police sirens sounded in the distance. The cavalry on the way. It would be much better if Jay and Caleb took care of this situation before they arrived.

"You try to take my dog?" Jay took a step forward, squinting against the sun in his face.

The first guy, the one Cass had a hold on before, shifted the weight of his knife from hand to hand.

Jay gave Cass a command to back up. She would absolutely go for this guy—and likely get stabbed for her efforts. He gave her another command to back up, because he wanted as much clearance as he could get. She didn't want to go far.

The guy he'd tossed lunged at Caleb like this was fun.

Meanwhile Jay's guy swiped the knife from right to left, giving Jay the option to grab the back of his forearm and turn the guy in the way he was moving. Take his momentum and use it against him. With one hand holding the guy's arm—and the knife—away from him, he kicked the man in the back of the knee.

The guy yelped as his leg started to collapse.

Caleb wrestled with the other guy, and a gun clanged on the pavement by his boot.

Cass barked.

Jay punched his guy in the small of his back.

An elbow swung back, catching him off guard. But he didn't let go. The elbow slammed into his shoulder—where he'd been shot.

Jay swallowed back the cry.

Caleb looked at him. A cop car pulled into the parking lot, flashing lights and sirens.

Jay swung the guy onto the ground and put a knee in his back, not letting go of the guy's hand. "Drop the knife."

Cass approached then, snarling and growling at the guy.

A deputy sheriff climbed out the driver's seat of the patrol car and came over. "Gentlemen." He read the situation and tugged plastic ties off his belt. "Here."

Jay took one.

The deputy slid the weapon from his holster. "Sir, let go of the knife. You're under arrest."

As soon as the guy let go of the knife, Jay dragged his hands behind his back.

Caleb did the same with his guy, shifting back on his ankles. "Mills."

"Rourke." The deputy looked at Jay. "We gonna have a problem with your dog?"

Cass, still snarling and growling, looked at the deputy.

"Cass!" He barked her name like it was a command.

Her attention came to him immediately.

"Leash."

The dog trotted off to the open door of the car.

Jay shifted his weight and stood, rolling his shoulders. Cass came back from retrieving her leash, and he clipped it on.

"Huh." The deputy glanced between them. "Durango Jay?"

"Guess I'm famous." Jay looked at Caleb, who lifted his chin. "Morgan needs medical attention." He clicked his tongue, and Cass walked beside him over to where Morgan stood with Ian Rourke and her daughter.

The three of them looked a little stunned. Well, maybe not Pops. Maybe the old man was more used to things like this happening on a regular Saturday.

"You guys okay?" He asked the question to Ava more than the rest of them.

She nodded, hugging Pops around the hips.

"We're good," the old man said.

"Morgan?"

"I'm...okay." She sounded freaked.

Out the corner of his eye, he saw Ava reach a fist toward Cass so his dog could get her scent. It distracted him into turning toward the little girl. Also freaked like Morgan had sounded.

"Ava, you want to hold the leash?"

The girl nodded in answer to his question. "She protected you."

"That's her job. But she does it because she wants to. Not because I ordered her to do it."

Ava ran her fingers over Cass's head, and the dog leaned into it.

"Here." Jay handed over the leash so Ava could feel a little bit safer. He gave Cass the command to guard, and the dog sat with her back to the child. Then he touched Morgan's elbows, about to draw her away from them, when she hissed. "You're hurt."

She winced, tears in her eyes.

"Come on." He put an arm around her and led her toward the deputy, who had one guy in the back of his vehicle already.

There was probably another car on the way here, if this town had enough available. That was always preferable to transporting two prisoners in the same vehicle. He'd learned that the hard way on an op in Somalia years ago.

But that wasn't the point right now. "Morgan needs an EMT."

Caleb looked at him like he'd grown another head.

"I'll be okay. I probably just need a bandage." She lifted her chin. "What just happened?"

He didn't move his arm from around her back, wanting to ask if she had any other injuries for them to treat.

Anything to distract him from the throbbing pain in his shoulder.

She turned to him. "They were trying to steal Cass, weren't they?"

Deputy Mills said, "Whatever it was, they can tell me down at the station. We'll get to the bottom of this."

Jay wanted five minutes alone with them to ask the question himself, given it was his dog in danger, but didn't think the deputy was about to grant him that. Jay turned to her. "Did he attack you?"

She shook her head. "I saw them trying to take Cass and ran to stop them."

He'd figured as much, but hearing her say it was different. "They could've seriously hurt you."

"They were going to take Cass." She lifted her chin.

"No, they weren't," Jay said. "Because she would have died first before she let that happen."

"That's not better!" She rounded on him.

Jay saw Caleb smile. To Morgan he said, "Tell that to her," and motioned toward his dog. "She has her own idea of what is okay and what isn't." Jay glanced over at the deputy. "When you ask them why they were trying to kidnap my dog, ask them about their boss, Marco, who killed that guy the other night."

The deputy lifted his chin. "Maybe you should come in as well."

"Fine." He left Morgan's side and went to the second guy, tied up against Jay's SUV. "Why did your boss order you to take my dog?"

"You cost him an animal. Fair's fair."

"The Rottweiler that chased my dog halfway across town? I did nothing to that dog."

"Fair's fair," the guy repeated.

"Sir, I'll take it from here." The deputy tugged the guy away. "Like I said, see you at the station."

Right. He was going to have to do that. But first things first.

He turned to Morgan. "Let's get out of here."

Two hours later, bandages on both elbows and the palm of one hand, Morgan still didn't know what to make of what happened. How that whole thing had gone down.

"You okay, honey?"

She nodded in answer to her mom's question and realized the kettle had boiled and the button clicked off. She poured the hot water over her tea bag.

Jay had drunk two cups of coffee, one while talking with her father in his study and the other he'd taken to the bathroom where he was currently fixing the sink.

Her daughter had opted to go out back in the yard with Cass, who was lying down, head on her paws, watching Ava's animated chatter. Telling a story that included big gestures and laughter or, more likely, recounting the plot of a musical. Whichever it was, Cass seemed content to enjoy Ava's presence.

Her mom gave her a side hug, then gestured toward the window. "He has a great dog. Says a lot about a man, the way his dog is."

Morgan rolled her eyes. "I told him the same thing."

"Two peas." Her mom squeezed her shoulders.

"Yeah, yeah." Morgan chuckled.

Everyone said that about her and her mother. Morgan and Ava? Thankfully, the girl wasn't too much like Jared. But Morgan would love her regardless if she was her father's daughter through and through, so the limited similarities were a blessing. And the bond she shared with her mother was unique.

She lifted her tea. "I'm going to see if Jay needs anything."

"Interesting man, Durango James."

"Mom." She dragged the word out, sounding more like a teenager than she wanted to. Or like Ava when she was far too embarrassed to talk about something.

She left the room to the sound of her mother chuckling and trailed through the hallways of her childhood home to the bathroom she used as a child. And those few weeks after the divorce. And the weeks after Ava's birth.

Generally, anytime she needed solace, she came back here.

Now Ava was the one finding that same peace in this house.

Morgan stopped in the doorway. "Hey."

Jay sat in front of the bathroom cabinet. One knee cocked to accommodate the length of his leg in the small space, the other curled under it. He looked over. "Cass all right?"

"Seems to be. She's relaxed."

He nodded. "You okay?"

Morgan lifted her elbow and looked at the bandage in the mirror. "Why does it sting so bad I wanna cry, and you're sitting there like you don't have a"—she lowered her voice—"bullet hole in your shoulder?"

"Practice?"

She frowned at him.

"A higher pain tolerance?" He shrugged a shoulder. "Probably just surprise. Once the adrenaline wears off, it feels different."

That didn't really explain it either, but Morgan didn't want to get into a whole conversation about it.

She backed up and sat on the floor in the hall, like she used to do when Ava was younger so she could keep an eye on her in the bathtub. Then sipped her tea, the warm liquid sliding down her throat. "Mmm."

"Need anything?"

"I was making more progress when you weren't distracting me."

"Oh." She shifted to get up.

Jay reached out and squeezed her socked foot. "It's fine, Morgan."

If he wanted to chitchat, she was happy to stick around. After all, she was seriously curious about this man.

"Okay." She pulled her legs in and crossed them. "That looks like more than just switching out the washer."

He smiled, still facing the cupboard. "It is, but don't worry. I've got it."

"I'm not used to having a man around who actually volunteers to help out. Dad would if he could get down onto the floor and back up, but that's impossible. And he's more of an...intellectual."

Hopefully, her father couldn't hear her from his office.

Jay chuckled. "We all have skills. Some are learned, and some are innate. Like you and vet work. I'm guessing...it's a bit of both?"

Morgan shrugged. "I always knew I wanted to take care of animals. Mom and Dad encouraged it, getting me internships in the summer in vet offices, and on working farms. I've helped out all kinds of creatures. But I prefer pets and being closer to home rather than miles out on someone's land, treating an animal while they argue about whether to just shoot it and put it out of its misery."

"Sounds like a story."

She flushed. "More like a bad dream. I was thirteen, and it was my first internship. Baby cow born lame. The rancher shot it right in front of me. I nearly quit right then, but Dad convinced me to give it another try and not go back to that ranch."

The rancher's son had asked her to the middle school dance that next school year and she'd turned him down flat. Told him she wouldn't date the son of a murderer.

That had started some interesting school rumors.

Morgan shook her head.

"So no farms. Just household pets."

"Is Cass a working dog, like with the military?" Morgan had certainly seen indications there was a military bent to their training. Both of them. But she didn't get the impression this was just leave.

"She was a Marine Corps dog. Even protected the president for a while."

"Wow. That's amazing."

Jay used his left hand to tighten the wrench, the only indication she had that using his right arm would give him pain. "She was medically retired. Tumor in her abdomen. But there's nothing wrong with her now."

"Do you work her…as part of your superhero gig? You said you guys were partners in work and off duty."

The corner of his mouth curled up. "She doesn't work much in official capacities anymore. She's more of a partner the rest of the time, because the situations I go into aren't always suited to a dog. We have a computer tech in the office, and Cass stays with her if I think Cass would be in danger in the field with me."

"I'm sure you have teammates to back you up, then." She sipped her tea.

He shook his head. "Just me."

"You go into dangerous situations on your own?"

"Prefer it," he said. "I scout things out before we go in. Get the lay of the land. Or I'll join up with a group until we figure out what we need to know."

"That all sounds suitably vague."

"Let's put it like this." He looked at her. "One day, someone kidnaps a bus full of kids. Or the mayor. Or a popstar. We know who took them, but we don't know where they are. So I join the group, show up like I'm a new recruit. I want to sign on. I stay long enough to ascertain exactly where they're being held and mark the location. I've also managed to get guard rotations, numbers of personnel we'll be facing, and what resources they have. Response times. All that."

"Sounds dangerous."

"It takes time, it's precision. It isn't kicking the door in and losing half the hostages in the process of rescuing them all."

When he put it like that, it did make sense.

"It's risky for you, I mean." She eyed him. "You must feel alone in those situations, knowing you're surrounded by dangerous people. Trying to get them to accept you."

"Sometimes there's minimal risk. Others, it takes some finesse."

"Sounds like you get a lot of satisfaction out of it."

"I don't wanna do anything else," he said. "And I don't want to sound like I'm bragging, but I'm good at what I do. I can sell a story, become part of the group like a chameleon, and I always get my team the info they need."

"That's how I feel about veterinary work." And it was what Jared had never understood. "It's a calling. I'll keep working until I figure out what's wrong, and I never back down."

She smiled. "I bet you could tell a whole lot of crazy stories that no one would ever believe."

He laughed. "I wouldn't want people at school to think Ava is making up fantastic tales."

Morgan joined in with his laughter. "Knowing Ava, she would start a blog or something, and post them online, and wind up going viral."

"Probably not the best idea."

Morgan wasn't worried about them. "Do you think Cass is in danger from more of those guys? Or their boss? Will they try to take her again?"

"I'd love to believe they'll quit now they failed once, but that's probably not going to happen." He shifted back and shut the cupboard. "I'm not going to let anyone hurt Ava, or any of you. We'll get out of your hair once the threat has passed."

In her mind she saw him racing across the parking lot to save Cass—and her.

This man, who risked his life to save others. She wanted to ask him...

Morgan wasn't even sure what. It wasn't like she could ask him to stay. That was crazy. He didn't live in this town. He was just visiting.

One of these days he was going to leave.

And she wasn't enough to convince him to give up his whole life and stay.

CHAPTER SIX

J ay pushed the door to the sheriff's office open and led Cass inside. Going to Morgan's parents' place, meeting them, and fixing the sink had been a nice distraction. A slice of normalcy in his otherwise distinctly not-normal life. But now he had to get back to reality and take care of the threat at hand.

"Hey." The deputy he'd seen earlier at the hardware store stood up and waved him over. Mills. "Glad you're here."

Jay lifted his chin. "Had some things to take care of." He clicked his fingers for Cass to settle into a "down."

She complied but remained alert. Head up, ears pricked. Taking in this new environment.

He slid out his wallet, and the deputy made a copy of his ID. No need to tell him it was a fake, or that Jay Anderson had a few real estate holdings across the country but not much else to speak of.

"I'm Eric Mills. Can you tell me what happened?"

Jay nodded, grateful the deputy hadn't seen Morgan in the mix. Otherwise, she'd be here, too. And right now, Jay needed some breathing space from her proximity and the effect she had on him.

Her and her entire life, her family. The way she seemed to understand things about him that most people didn't.

Once she knew it all, she'd ask him to leave.

He pushed the thoughts of her out of his mind and explained about the other night and the connection to those two men.

Once Jay was done giving mostly the truth, Mills said, "If I show you some photos, you think you might be able to ID him?"

Jay shrugged. "Worth a try."

Cass gave up observing and slid over to lie on her side, mostly on his right boot. He reached down to run his hand along her side, alongside the scar from her surgery. She groaned. He finished it with a chin scratch, thinking how they didn't really need anything else but each other.

It was what life had taught him. The same way Morgan's life had taught her that all animal lives were worth fighting for. Eventually, though, he'd settle back into his routine and she'd be nothing but a memory. Unless Noah went through with his threat and fired Jay. Maybe he was already canned and his boss just hadn't gotten around to making it official.

If that happened, and Jay was cut loose, could he stay in this town? Maybe he could ask out Morgan. Take her and Ava to the fair when it came to town.

The whole idea was crazy. As if Jay could live a domesticated life.

He didn't even know how.

"Here." Mills set a huge binder in front of him. "Let me know if you see the guy. Hey, you want some coffee?"

"Sure. Thanks."

Jay flipped the pages, all photos of wanted men or known criminals. Once he'd exhausted the local county pages, he moved on to federal criminals. Known suspects. Even some with only a short dossier and no photo.

He was halfway through the coffee when he spotted the guy.

Jay checked no one was paying attention to him, then drew his phone out and took a photo. He hit Send, adding it to the More Information channel in the app the team and associates used to communicate.

"Mills." Jay tapped the page. "Found him."

Cass sat up, alert because of the shift in his body language. He scratched the fur on her head. "Who is Anthony Montbatten? I heard the other guy call him 'Marco.'"

Mills settled behind his desk. "Let's find out." He scanned the computer screen as he typed, his gaze roving back and forth. "Wanted by the FBI in connection with the disappearance of two truck drivers," he read aloud. "One in California, the other in Nevada."

"Makes sense then that it's federal, if it's crossing state lines." Jay finished the coffee in one gulp. "That's the guy I saw."

"Sure?" Mills tapped the screen. "Says here he's suspected of being in Texas."

Jay shrugged. "I need to take Cass outside, if you know what I mean. But I'm telling you, that's the guy I saw."

"Hopefully, he skipped town and went back to Texas right after he killed that guy and shot at you."

"What did his buddies in lockup say?"

Mills eyed him. "They're locals."

Jay shifted to the edge of the chair. "Did they say anything about who they work for?"

"Who says they work for anyone?"

"The fact they were acting like bodyguards in the construction forecourt. And they weren't coming after my dog for the novelty. They're working for someone."

Mills shook his head. "That's not what they say."

"Maybe ask them about this Montbatten guy. See if they know him."

Mills didn't like that—probably because Jay had just told him how to do his job.

"Like I said"—Jay stood—"gotta take Cass outside. Let me know how it goes finding this guy and solving your case. What with Cass being potentially in danger."

"Might be better for everyone if you just left town." Mills folded his arms. "Eliminate that variable, and you get to keep your dog safe. Curtail your visit due to the circumstances."

"I'll sure think about that." Jay doffed a nonexistent hat. "Thanks for your time."

He walked Cass to the side exit and let her sniff her way around the building back to his SUV.

The question wasn't what Anthony Montbatten was doing in this town, but why he'd sent those two guys after Cass.

As recompense for Jay costing him his dog? He wasn't sure he bought what that guy had said. But it was possible. After all, the dog might have been lost. Or was hit by a car.

Who knew.

He drove back toward the Rourke ranch, his shoulder growing to a nagging pain so that he lay his hand in his lap and drove with the other arm.

About halfway there, his phone rang.

Jay swiped the screen and hit Speaker. "Yeah."

"What bit your butt?"

"Sorry. Hi, Marina. How are you?"

The company tech guru was ex-NSA. Though not so "ex" depending on who you asked. She was a hacker like no one Jay had ever met, and she ran comms when they were on missions. She wore Converse in either purple or light blue and never anything other than jeans and an oversize blue sweatshirt.

Marina groaned. "Never mind how I am. This is bad."

"Montbatten? How bad?"

"If he's up there in Nowheresville, Montana, I need to alert Caleb. Good thing you're already boots on the ground. Punched anyone lately?"

He gripped the wheel, flexing the fingers of his other hand in his lap. "This afternoon?" What was the point in pretending things were fine?

"Wait. Seriously?"

"Two thugs showed up, sent by Montbatten. They tried to steal Cass."

Marina sucked in a breath. "I'll kill them all."

That at least made Jay feel better. "They're in jail now, and not talking. The sheriff's department isn't going to look for Montbatten. All they have is my word he's even involved, and I'm pretty sure that deputy didn't believe it."

"Good," she said. "They'll be in over their heads anyway."

"Send me everything you've got. I'll go over it with Caleb, and we'll come up with a plan."

"I'm afraid backup might not be an option. Except each other."

"And Cass," he added. "The three of us can take care of this."

"Keep each other safe, Jay. I'll fill in Noah when they're back on radar. It'll probably be eighteen hours, though."

He wanted to ask her what the mission was, but he had no right to know. And discussing it over an open phone line could put lives at risk. The last thing he wanted to do was endanger their friends.

Marina continued, "I can make a couple of calls. Put some people on alert who are a lot closer to you. Just in case?"

"Caleb and I have it." Jay reached toward the phone. "I'll keep you posted." He hung up and drove faster, wondering who on earth this guy was and what put Marina on edge. Usually nothing ruffled the woman—except Noah being captured and out of contact.

It was a big part of what had convinced Jay not to get into a relationship. The last thing he wanted was for a woman to be at home, worrying herself sick about him. Not to mention he'd be on the op, worried about her at home.

Good way to get himself killed because he was distracted.

His life didn't need to change. He just had to convince Noah to let him keep his job. Then he could have it back. He'd be out of this town and away from the temptation of Morgan and everything she had to offer.

Finding Montbatten and bringing him to justice so the feds could prosecute him could go a long way to convincing Noah he was good to go.

Finally, he had a plan to get back in.

❖

"Amen." Morgan stood up and gathered her purse and jacket, trying not to look again at Jay on the other side of Caleb.

Tessa had already caught her looking that way more than once.

"I should go find Ava."

"Yeah." Tessa slid an arm through Morgan's. "She can find you when her class finishes."

Morgan made a face. "Fine."

Technically, she didn't have to go pick up Ava from her Sunday School class, but it was more that she didn't want to ask uncomfortable questions about...

"What do you want?" She eyed Tessa.

"Can't I chat with my favorite cousin?"

Morgan didn't buy that one bit. "Spill it, woman."

Tessa laughed loud enough to draw attention to them, which of course made Morgan's cheeks flame. Her cousin was the best person she knew, a homebody who loved her family and someone who had faced a dangerous situation and been rescued by her now-fiancé. If anyone could make a marriage work, it was Caleb and Tessa.

"Fine." Tessa smiled. "Caleb said it seemed like you and Jay like each other. As in, you *like* each other."

"What is this—middle school all over again?" They'd been in the same grade. Morgan's mom and Tessa's mother had been pregnant in the same year, and there wasn't a Christmas that went by that Morgan's mom didn't go out to the gravesite to see her sister.

Tessa grinned. "Caleb said there were *sparks*."

"This is ridiculous. The man has a job somewhere else."

"So did Caleb."

"Jay has important things to do."

"Caleb does his from the ranch. Full-time."

"I'm not talking about this." Morgan rolled her eyes. "And what is it with people who seem to think everyone who isn't married should get married? You forget I already did that, and it ended in a disaster. Except for Ava."

Caleba and Tessa weren't going to be married until this summer, but that wasn't the point.

Tessa chuckled. "That's why you know that when it's good, it's so worth going for it."

"I guess," Morgan said. She was happy for her cousin, but that didn't mean falling in love and living happily ever after had to be a contagion.

"Come over for lunch." Tessa tugged on her arm as two busybody older women passed them. Once they were out of earshot, she said, "Jay and Caleb won't even be there. They've got some big operation they're planning. It'll just be us. And I need some company other than crusty old men."

"I resemble that remark." Tessa's father eased by them. "Ladies."

Morgan gave him a side hug. "Great sermon, today. Like always."

"Thanks." He hugged her back, then headed off.

Morgan's phone vibrated in her purse. "It's the office."

"I'll go find Ava. You see what they need." Tessa trotted off before Morgan could thank her.

"Doctor Lawson." She held the phone to her ear.

"Doctor, it's Laura. There's been an emergency. A dog with serious lacerations and other wounds."

"How soon until they arrive?" She would need someone to stay with Ava.

"That's the thing. They pulled up in van, with him wrapped in a blanket, and dumped the animal on the back stoop." Laura paused, sounding flustered. "I didn't realize what it was until the blanket flopped open. By the time I got out there, they'd driven off."

"I'll be there in ten. Do as much as you can in the meantime."

"I will. I'll need your help to get the dog inside. It's a large breed."

"I'll be fast."

"Thanks." The call ended.

Morgan stowed her phone and rushed down the aisle, finding Tessa and Ava in the lobby. "An injured dog was brought to the office. I need to go take care of it." She turned to Ava. "Can you go to lunch with Auntie Tessa?"

"I want to come and help the dog."

"Maybe when you're a little older, honey. It might be scary."

"I can help with the other animals."

"How about we make your mom lunch?" Tessa suggested. "When she says it's okay, we can bring it to the office, and you can see the animals."

"Okay."

Morgan leaned down and kissed Ava, giving her a hug. "See you in a bit." To Tessa, she said, "Thanks."

Ten minutes later, she sped into the vet office parking lot and ran inside, just about remembering to lock her car.

Laura was on the back porch, holding pressure on the dog's abdomen with a stack of bandages that were soaked through with blood. "Thank goodness."

"Let's get the patient inside." Morgan lifted the dog with her vet tech's help, grunting with the weight. "I need to work out more."

Laura grinned around clenched teeth.

They set the dog down on the surgical table, and the soothing sounds of animal life in the building around Morgan helped her focus on the task at hand.

The vet blew out a breath. "That's a big laceration." She made a few more observations, and the two of them got to work.

Two hours later, she'd sewn up that deep cut and three others she'd found. During the procedure, she'd discovered that the Pitbull

Terrier had a fracture of the back left leg. There was also some bruising around the left eye. Two missing teeth, one broken.

"Who put you through this?" Morgan wiped her sleeve across her forehead.

"Is she going to be okay?" Laura asked.

"It'll be a painful road, but she'll be all right in a few months. The question is, will she heal from the psychological trauma of whatever happened?"

Dogs who were attacked, or abused, often lived with a form of PTSD, reacting with fear when faced with similar situations or a similar kind of person. It would take a steady owner who had the patience needed to give her the life she needed, where she could heal and come to realize that she was safe and cared for.

Laura ran a hand over the dog's head. "It's gonna be okay, baby. We'll show you how to be at peace."

Morgan exhaled a long breath. It was going to be touch and go for a few hours, but the dog was out of the stressful part of treatment. "Thanks, Laura."

"I'll clean up if you want to go write your notes."

Morgan nodded, moving to the industrial-sized sink. She pulled off the soiled protective gloves and dropped them in medical waste, then washed her hands until they were clean.

Her office phone started ringing before she even opened the door and flipped the light on.

"Doctor Lawson." She shrugged off her lab coat as well, moving around the desk, about to sit down.

"Did you fix my dog?"

She stilled, straightening back to standing. "Excuse me?"

"Her name is Nota. Is she dead or alive?"

Why did that sound like a threat?

Morgan tightened her grip on the phone. "You're the one who dropped a pitbull that was bleeding to death on my back doorstep."

"Is. She. Dead."

"Knock on the front door. You can see her for yourself." Morgan sat behind her desk. "While you're here, you can leave your credit card information and take care of the bill."

"If she's dead, I ain't paying."

"Well then, good for me she's still alive. It'll be touch and go for a few hours."

"As long as she pulls through. I need her."

"And I need to pay my rent. So come in and pay your bill." Of course, that wasn't what she was about, but it was reality. And this guy had zero sentimentality in his voice. "I'll take good care of Nota."

"Better than my usual vet already. I'm impressed, Doctor. Most people don't rush out of church to aid an animal the way you did. Not even people paid to take care of them."

"You were watching me?"

"I protect my investments, and I pay good money. You ought to remember that."

He hung up.

"What on earth was that?" Morgan lowered the phone to the cradle and brushed hair behind her ears.

She had dealt with some irate customers in the years she'd been practicing. And during her ugly divorce case. But none of it had ever been like that. He'd sounded cold and unfeeling, but full of authority. As if he expected to be obeyed without question.

As soon as she'd written out her treatment notes for the surgery, creating a new file for the animal, she texted Tessa and told her that this wasn't the best time for her and Ava to pay a visit. She also added a warning for her reception staff that Nota's owner might be belligerent—or potentially threatening.

She didn't like doing that and wanted to give people the benefit of the doubt. But sometimes the risk wasn't worth it.

Someone could get hurt.

Then she went to the window and closed the blinds. If she was being watched, she didn't want to make it easy for them.

Someone moved in the hallway, creaking the floor.

"Laura?" She rounded the desk and stepped out.

A man in a suit with dark hair and black eyes stared back at her.

CHAPTER SEVEN

J ay adjusted his prone position to try to get the rock to quit jabbing him in the ribs. This was a good spot from which to observe what was happening in the valley below, but every solid position came with its drawbacks.

That, and being elbows to the dirt hurt his shoulder.

Caleb eyed him. "Are you gonna shift around all night...or just lie still?"

Jay pressed his lips together, trying to ignore the pain in his shoulder. "Distract me."

"With what?" Caleb asked. "We spent two hours hiking the long way out here, and now that we've found something, you wanna talk?"

"Fine." Jay grunted. "Marco's company appraised this land, so he might not have bought it yet, but he's likely considering it."

"Either way, there's a connection. And given the activity down in that barn, and around it, something is going on here."

Jay trained his binoculars on the people at the front door. Half a dozen pickups lined the parking lot, as well as cars and motorcycles. Pain whipped through his shoulder, and he hissed out a breath—in lieu of screaming. It didn't help. He lowered the binos and rolled to his back so he could see the stars, and try to pretend everything was fine. Which it very much was not.

"How bad is it?" Caleb's tone was flat.

"Through and through."

"And you saw a doctor?"

"Yeah, Morgan."

"Ah. That's how the two of you met. How'd you get from you bleeding to almost kissing her in the aisle at the hardware store?"

"No comment."

For some reason, he wanted to keep their interactions to himself. To hide them in his heart and think about them when he was alone on an operation, or trapped and in danger. He'd need the reminder that life could be sweet in those moments.

He gritted his teeth and blew out a breath around it.

"Did you take anything?"

"Nope."

"Good thing Pops wore out Cass, making her run all over the ranch while he drove around on his ATV, checking the cattle. Otherwise, you'd be lying on the sidewalk instead of walking her."

"I was fine earlier."

Caleb nodded. "Mmm."

"What?" Jay lifted his legs and twisted to sit up, looking at Caleb. "What does *mmm* mean?"

"You ignored it and carried on like usual, and now it's catching up with you."

"So you're gonna sideline me and send me back to 'recovery.'"

"Pretty sure that's what you were supposed to be doing here in the first place."

Jay didn't want to talk about that. At least with this he had an actual physical reason to rest. The "recovery" was supposed to be about getting a handle on himself after watching...

He forced his thoughts away from what he'd seen. Instead, he focused on the view at the bottom of the valley, where two distinctly familiar men got out of a car and headed for the barn doors.

"The bathroom guys," Jay muttered.

"Simms told me they were out on bail."

Jay sighed. "Do all the bad guys in this town go around in pairs?"

Caleb nudged him. "Good guys, too."

"Let's just do what we came here to do, yeah?"

Jay didn't want to talk about any of it. Not his injury, or what he was recovering from. He only wanted to deal with the issue at hand. He'd spent the afternoon going over intel they had about Marco and what he was into—and why the feds thought he was in Texas.

That, and thinking about what the preacher had been saying this morning. About the flesh versus the spirit, and how everyone had that battle inside them. The war between what their human side wanted to do—the corrupt desires of the heart, and the selfish will—and what God's spirit in the person led them to do. And how each believer had to yield their life to the sovereignty of God every day so He could be in control.

It wasn't something Jay had ever heard preached, and he wanted some time to dig in. Look up all the verses for himself. Contend with the idea and what it meant in his own life.

But they also had to figure out what Marco was doing in Breckenrow, Montana.

"Why do you care so much about going after Marco?" Caleb asked. "This isn't about getting him back for trying to steal your dog still, is it?"

"We know he's connected at least peripherally to Kessler, and Senator Chambers," Jay replied. "But that's a whole other egg we need to crack. Bottom line is, Marco is a bad enough guy in his own right and we need to eliminate the threat. Keep the people of this town safe."

"People like Morgan." Caleb nudged him with his elbow.

Jay got up, brushing himself off. "I'm gonna go check out that building."

"Great. I'll come with you."

Jay turned to him. "This is what I do."

"You get I was DEA, right?"

"And now you're a rancher with a fiancée. This—" he motioned to himself then the barn at the bottom of the hill "—is the world I inhabit. Good folks like you don't belong in it."

Caleb frowned. "Did Noah tell you to keep me safe or something?"

"He didn't have to ask." Jay wanted to cross his arms but that wouldn't feel good at all. "You have a different life now. People like Morgan, and Tessa, they get to live peaceful, safe lives, because of guys like me—and Noah, and the rest of the team—who put our lives on the line."

And they never even knew that his team stood in the gap.

"And I'm not one of you?" Caleb asked.

Jay didn't answer that.

"Or my life is somehow more valuable."

This wasn't a conversation he wanted to have out here.

"This is my town." Caleb slapped his chest. "I get to keep it safe for the people I love."

"Better if I do it."

"You think no one will miss you if you're killed. Well, too bad. Because Cass will." Caleb didn't mention anyone else, though. "Let's go. I'll be your backup, Mr. Hero."

Jay ignored the jab and headed down the hill. If he wanted to put his life in jeopardy, that was fine, and Noah would probably give him a bonus if he saved Caleb's life.

The twins had been practically estranged the past few years but reconnected before Christmas. Now they were close and worked together—which meant the team had both twins feeding them information and telling them what to do.

Most of the guys didn't much care, because little had changed, which was especially true for Jay. Until now.

"Weapons?" Caleb asked from behind him.

"Not yet." Jay kept his holstered under his arm, covered by the sides of his jacket.

They crossed a gravel lot, walking in an arc so it didn't look like they were coming from the woods. Just a far corner of the lot, or somewhere down the lane that led up to this property.

Tucked up in the hills, out of sight. Who knew what happened in this building, or any of the other structures around it.

There was a single guy on the door.

Jay figured there was no point pretending he'd been here before. "There a cover charge?" he called out to the guy.

"Sixty bucks."

He couldn't tell from the guy's expression if that was true, or he was just trying to make some cash off a guy who had no idea this was a free event.

Jay dug out his wallet and covered him and Caleb. "Thanks."

"Thank you." The guy pocketed the cash and let them inside.

Jay held the door a second for Caleb, taking in the expanse of the barn interior.

A crowd of rough-looking guys, a lot like the ones in that bar the other night, crowded around the center and some kind of arena. Fighting? Maybe MMA, or bare-knuckle boxing.

On the left side, there was a bar area. Mostly consisting of two barrels, over which had been laid a plank of wood to make the actual bar. Coolers of beer behind it. A woman in a tiny denim skirt and crop top with knee-high cowgirl boots walked around with a tray.

He spotted a couple of other women, but the place was mostly men.

Caleb broke off and skirted the outside.

Jay went to the arena to see what they were dealing with and saw the far end of the barn had a balcony area. The VIP spot by the look of it, where folks who paid for the experience could watch everything from above.

There were a lot more people up there than down here.

He eased up to the crowd and heard a noise he instantly recognized. One that made him go cold inside.

Jay shoved a couple of people aside.

A guy said, "Hey, if you wanna place a bet, go see Carl."

"Just getting a look." He eased around a woman and peered over someone's shoulder.

"Match is just about to start."

A Doberman prowled around an area sectioned off by hay bales. The ground under him was littered with straw...and a couple of spots of blood. The animal snarled, blood on one corner of his mouth.

"Lucky is gonna put up a good fight," a guy said, a fistful of bills in one hand. "I can just tell."

Jay looked at him with two words in his mind. He kept his mouth shut, or the wrong thing would have come out.

Dog fighting.

He backed out of the crowd and circled around to where he saw Caleb. Set back from the main area, along one wall where the level above shielded him from view of the VIP area. But they had still drawn attention.

They weren't fitting in.

"We need to get out of here," Jay said. "I'm thinking we burn this place to the ground on the way out."

Caleb winced. "We need to stop what's going on now. Before the next matchup."

Jay nodded. "Diversion?"

"I like your fire idea."

Jay eased around the guy and dug out the lighter he kept in his pocket—because who knew when you'd need to set fire to something. He bundled up some straw and a stray flyer, creating a pile of kindling. "We need this to catch, big and fast."

Caleb wandered away, far enough to grab two beer bottles and bring them back. He also had a red plastic cup, which he sniffed. "Here we go. Accelerant."

Jay dragged over a hay bale and doused it with the liquor. "I don't see Marco up in the VIP area, do you?"

"Whatever you're doing, get on with it. They're bringing another dog out."

Jay walked with the beer bottle to another bale of hay and poured the second one over that. "Come on." He went toward a rear door, not the entrance, refusing to acknowledge the distressed sounds he was hearing. "Animal control. And state police, and the sheriff."

"Burning this place to the ground might be satisfying, but it's not justice," Caleb pointed out. "The dogs here need to be cared for—if they can be."

That was Jay's line, but hearing it from his buddy helped.

"You make the call." Jay turned and found the exit door just as the fire whooshed to life behind them. Someone screamed, and people started running. He glanced back and saw a couple of drunk guys fall over each other. Then he spotted a fire alarm on the wall by the door and pulled it.

Nothing happened.

"Let's go save some dogs," Jay said.

"And ruin someone's day." Caleb grinned, the phone already to his ear. "Wait..." His expression shifted, flashing with worry. "What?" After a second, he moved the phone away from his mouth. "Tessa says Morgan isn't answering her phone. No one can get ahold of her. Ava is really worried."

"Let's get this done so we can find her."

✾

Morgan huddled against the car door, trying to be as far from the man on the other end of the back seat as she could.

Only problem was, out the window two men dug their shovels into the ground and tossed dirt onto a growing mound. Disguising the spot where they had rolled the doctor's dead body into a shallow grave.

She had been biting her lip long enough she could taste blood.

But what she wasn't going to do was cry. This guy wasn't the kind of man who would respect a woman that couldn't control her emotions.

The two men burying his body—her thoughts stuttered in her mind and saw the veterinarian she'd trained with so many years ago. High school, junior year. He'd been kind. Firm, but respectful. Now he was dead because they had shot him over his wanting out of "the business"—whatever it was. The dog on her back step at work had been a test, an interview of sorts. This guy beside her in the back seat had decided she was going to be his new veterinarian.

After calling her and getting a feel for her over the phone, he'd shown up in the office.

Morgan shuddered. They'd threatened her technician, forced her into the car, and shown her the dead guy in the trunk.

This guy wasn't wasting any time filling his open position.

Marco.

"Now we can get going," he said, his voice low and lethal. But he probably thought he sounded charming.

He wore a suit, and shoes that were slightly scuffed. Not a total city guy like Jared, this man seemed more like a chameleon. He could dress the part and fit in a lot of places.

The trunk slammed shut.

Morgan flinched. She should be home, taking care of Ava. Getting her daughter in bed because it was a school night.

Two men climbed in the front, and the one in the driver seat glanced at Marco in the rearview mirror. "To the barn, sir?"

She recognized him from the news. He'd been arrested along with another man—not the one beside him—as the crew who'd been robbing customers at bars across town. Mugging men in bathrooms, holding them at knifepoint and stealing from them. Petty crimes, but over and over again. Somehow, he was already back out on the streets.

She'd watched the news the Saturday night before church—which seemed almost like days ago. So much had happened since then. She had no idea about that stuff, but it didn't seem right.

"I need to get home," Morgan told Marco. "It's late."

"I'll show you my setup, and then one of my men will transport you back to town."

"How long is this going to take?" She'd flat out told him no already, but he didn't seem to have noticed. "Because you're really only wasting your time. I have a vet clinic, I'm not looking for supplemental income."

The fact they'd shown her the burial place of the guy who was supposed to be her predecessor wasn't a good sign.

At all.

She could testify against all of these guys. But then, the boss Marco beside her, he hadn't done anything but look scary. Right? No doubt he'd skate out from under whatever charges he faced, and the two in the front—grunts who hurt people for money—would take the fall.

"I have need," Marco said. "You are the most qualified. Aside from moving the business elsewhere, which will cost money, you are my only option."

"And when I continue to refuse?"

Marco leaned over. "You wouldn't want anything to happen to your business, or your family. Like that sweet little daughter of yours."

"Threatening me isn't the way to get me to cooperate." She needed to sound strong.

But still, the risk to Ava made her keep quiet after that. Leaving her daughter without a mother wasn't an option. She couldn't do that.

If she didn't help the animals Marco kept, they could die.

There seemed to be more reasons to cooperate than not.

At least for now.

But she didn't want to. She wanted to rage against his entire... whatever on earth this was. "Tell me what the 'business' is."

"Just a little country fun for locals," Marco said. "You'd be surprised how much money can be made around dog fighting. Booze, bets. There's some overhead, like a good vet. But not that much."

She wanted to spit in his face. If she thought the car door would open, she might try pulling the handle and making a run for it.

After she hit the street and injured herself.

"That's despicable." She couldn't even articulate how disgusting dog fighting was. He should be ashamed, but clearly, he had no functioning conscience.

"What can I say?" Marco shrugged. "I'm a despicable guy."

"I'm not being a part of this. Not even if you..." Threaten her. Kill Ava.

She couldn't say that. She wasn't strong enough to stand up to that.

Morgan couldn't lose her daughter.

"The sooner you accept you have no choice, the happier everyone will be." Marco reached over and ran his finger along the outside of her pant leg. "Or I can force you to accept it. Which I'll enjoy very much."

She pressed her lips together and looked out the front window, trying to memorize where they were going so she could tell the police where it was located. Just as soon as she was free to, she'd go to the cops and tell them everything.

No way was she just going to accept this.

A stream of cars passed going in the opposite direction. Overhead a helicopter passed by with its light on, the bright beam sweeping the treetops.

"Boss?"

"Pull over at the inlet," Marco said, "and we'll see what's happening."

They eased into the turn lane where a stream of vehicles turned from a side street—what looked like a single-track road, or barely wider—onto the highway.

The driver of this vehicle, Mr. Bar Mugger, honked his horn and pulled onto the lane. People eased over to the side. He pretty much laid on his horn all the way along the winding lane, up an incline, around several switchback corners and over a ridgeline. The car slid down a dip, and Morgan yelped.

One of the guys in front chuckled.

They entered a wooded area of tall pines that blocked out the sky. She realized she could smell burning. Hopefully, someone had set fire to everything, but in a way that didn't hurt any of the dogs on the premises.

A few minutes later, they pulled over onto the side and the two men in front jumped out. The driver dipped his head back in. "We'll call with news."

Marco lifted his chin. As soon as they were out of sight, he shifted.

She flinched.

"So tense. Good thing I like the taste of fear." He grabbed her arm, just above her elbow, and opened the door with his other hand. The hand on her arm squeezed so hard it took her breath away, and he whipped her out of the car.

Morgan yelped, and okay, it was more like a scream. She landed on the ground by the open car door.

He kicked her stomach. "Get up."

After that? She gasped, unable to speak.

He grabbed her arm and hauled her to her feet like she weighed nothing.

"Okay." Morgan tried to catch her breath. "Okay."

The helicopter circled again.

"Let's go." He pulled her along, into the trees. From the "inlet" he'd ordered the car stopped in, away from the road, to a thin path. Maybe a deer trail. It wound between the trees up a hill.

Morgan dragged her legs along, wondering if this day was ever going to end. "What is the point of dragging me up there...wherever we're going?"

"Leverage."

She didn't want to look at him. She was focused on not falling over. "You don't seem like the kind of guy who gets his hands dirty. Why would you need leverage?"

He didn't respond.

For about half a mile, they just trudged along the thin trail—her arms prickling with the cold and her breath puffing out in front of her face, her core warming from the exertion.

Finally, Marco stopped where they could see a few structures, one of which was blowing smoke up into the air. The helicopter circled overhead here now, illuminating the clearing. Looking for somewhere to set down?

Two men ran from one building to another, one leading a woman and the other carrying a dog.

Marco let out a rough expletive from under his breath.

Morgan thought that might mean he recognized the men as Jay and Caleb. Or he knew the threat they represented.

She turned to confront him and swung right into his punch.

Morgan collapsed to the ground.

"They're dead. I'll kill them for this."

She tried to blink against the pounding pain in her face, just about able to focus in time to see his boot slam down and kick her.

Everything went black.

CHAPTER EIGHT

Jay laid the dog on the ground. The female didn't even lift her head. He looked at his watch. "How much longer until animal control can get here?"

Caleb was within earshot, walking back from where he'd helped the woman into her car. "No idea, but the state police will be able to tell us as soon as they land."

Every time the helicopter circled, Caleb lifted his hand. A couple of times he used hand motions, signals they would hopefully understand—probably from his days as a DEA agent.

"Looks like they found a clearing." Jay needed to get back in there and secure any other dogs that were vulnerable. The ones in their cages should be all right until animal control came, but the dog he'd pulled out had been in the open in an area quickly filling with smoke.

Too many of the dogs had scars from fighting other dogs and being mistreated, and most were far too skinny. They all needed love and treats from someone who understood how dogs rehabbed from a situation like this.

A side door opened, and two men ran out carrying bundles of cash. One stumbled and nearly went down. His buddy kept going.

"Should we stop them?" Caleb asked.

"Leave it to the police," Jay replied. "Or whoever they just stole that money from. My guess is that their victory won't last long."

He'd rather look around—or ask around—for Marco. That was who they'd come here looking for. Instead, what they discovered was nothing but a giant mess.

"We need to find this Marco guy," he added.

"Anthony Montbatten." Caleb glanced over.

"Right. Maybe then the sheriff and his people will believe he's here." Jay had researched the guy plenty. It was why he and Caleb were here tonight. But separating that guy—international criminal Anthony Montbatten—from the man Jay had seen shoot Whitman, who'd then shot Jay in the back as he ran after his dog...

That guy was the one he wanted to find.

Jay continued, "Tell me again what Tessa said about Morgan."

Caleb squeezed the back of his neck. "They called the vet office and got hold of the tech working. The day person went home, and the night shift guy took over. They figure at some point Morgan left. But her purse and jacket, and her phone, are still there. They have no idea what happened to her."

"Security cameras?"

Caleb shook his head. "They're really worried. She took Ava home and managed to get her to sleep, but said the kid is pretty restless."

Jay nodded, even though they had no idea where to even start looking for Morgan. "Let's get this done and get out of here."

A man ran out of the barn and nearly collided with Jay.

"You." Jay grabbed him. It was Knife Guy from the bathroom. "Guess you ran the right way."

The guy yelled in his face, blood running down his forehead.

Jay spun him, swiped his legs out from under him, and laid him on the ground, holding down his arms so he didn't hurt himself or anyone else. Knife Guy smelled like smoke, and something more pungent. Burned flesh. Not an odor Jay had wanted to smell again, ever. But here it was.

The guy did look shellshocked. What had he seen? The memory of it was bright behind that glassy gaze.

"Where is Marco?"

The guy's gaze darted around, his eyes not focusing on anything.

Jay lifted him and slammed him back down on the ground. "Listen!" He yelled the word in the man's face. "Anthony Montbatten. Where is he?"

Caleb rooted around in the guy's pockets and found a wallet. "Eric Nellis."

"Eric!" Jay yelled. That got the guy to focus to an extent. But not much. "Where's Marco?"

The guy seemed to come out of his shock a little more. "It's over. Who cares?"

"Where is he?" Jay was going to keep repeating the question until he wore the guy down and Eric answered. "Where's Marco?"

Whatever he'd seen in the barn, whoever was dead, Jay didn't care. He wasn't going to waste any empathy on a man who took advantage of people.

Cops swarmed onto the parking lot, racing between what vehicles were left—which wasn't many. The dog Jay had rescued whined.

He spotted about half a dozen cops. But he needed answers before they got here and took over. He curled Eric's fingers into a fist and squeezed, applying pressure until the man almost cried out. Then he backed off, but not much.

"Where is Marco?" Jay demanded.

Eric gritted his teeth. "Drove him here myself."

Jay tensed.

Caleb looked around. "We'll need to search the whole place."

Eric started to laugh. "You'll never find him."

"He's the boss. He should be here." Jay needed Eric to talk more, and open up. Not that he thought a guy like Marco would want to "go down with the ship" so to speak.

"We left him back in the car with the doctor lady. His new vet." Eric grimaced. "She was all over him, wanting to do whatever he said."

Jay's stomach churned. "Morgan Lawson?"

Eric struggled against Jay's hold. "Get off me. I'm gonna kill you."

"You're gonna tell the police everything. Including where to find Marco." Jay tightened his grip. "Be sure to call him Anthony Montbatten so they know who they're dealing with."

"Sir!" An officer ran over. "We'll take over from here."

Caleb pulled the officer aside and spoke with him.

The dog whined. Another officer ran up and took custody of the man on the ground. When Jay shifted his weight and rose to standing, the officer said, "Don't go anywhere."

"I know the drill." Jay wanted to point out that he was one of the good guys, but explaining he was the one who had started the fire might not go down well.

A neon yellow rural fire department vehicle with thick tread tires pulled to a stop in front of the barn, and firefighters jumped out.

Morgan was missing.

Jay turned, looking everywhere within his view. As if she would simply be standing there, waiting for him to notice her. Eric whatever-his-name-was needed to tell him more.

But when he turned back to the officer, Eric had already been escorted away.

Jay strode back to Caleb. "If Morgan was kidnapped and she's here, in the area, we need to find her. Especially if Anthony Montbatten has her."

That got the officer's attention. "Seriously, you really just said Montbatten?" He frowned. "Why would he be here in the middle of a dog fighting ring we've been trying to locate for months?"

Jay wasn't going to get into that. "We found it because of a connection to Montbatten. Who knows. Maybe he gets his jollies with this particular form of entertainment. Maybe he's all about extracurriculars."

The officer folded his arms, making the gear he wore—tactical clothing like this was a SWAT raid—creak and groan. "He's here?"

Jay nodded. "No question."

"I'll inform the lieutenant." The officer jogged away.

Jay turned to face Caleb, doing a visual sweep of the dog as he did. "I need Cass if I'm gonna find Morgan in this mess."

"You need a sample of her scent?"

"If he can get one, it'll help." He'd done a little work teaching Cass Morgan and Ava's names, but wasn't sure if it was enough to seal the skill in. After all, it had been one afternoon at her parents' house.

But he couldn't worry about that.

He needed to pray, to allow God to give him wisdom, and let Him do the leading in finding her.

Caleb nodded. "You start the search. I'll call Pops."

Jay felt bad that they'd probably be waking up the old man, but he answered the phone quickly. Probably waiting to hear about Morgan, or their operation.

Lord, help me find her.

In this haystack, he could walk right by and never even notice her.

"Thanks, Pops. See you soon."

Jay set off walking. However long it took Pops to get here, Jay wasn't going to wait.

He wasn't the guy that sat around doing nothing, waiting for God to drop the answer in his lap. He was going to pray.

And he was going to move.

🐾

Morgan regained consciousness, first feeling breath on her face. She sniffed, which hurt a whole lot. Plus, it smelled like dog breath. She groaned out a sound that didn't seem like a word—if it was even a human sound at all.

"Good girl. Good seek." That was a man's voice. "Good girl. Morgan, oh shoot." He touched her shoulders and turned her face one way, then the other.

Light shone against her face.

"I need a medic!"

She flinched at the volume of his shout.

He touched her cheek. "Sorry. I'm sorry." Hands ran over her arms and legs. Palpating. It didn't feel good—everything was kind of swimming around her. She also didn't know what he wanted from her.

"That looks bad." She recognized Caleb's voice.

Turned her head toward it.

Pain flared to life, mostly around her nose.

"Move out of the way, sir!"

She heard the low growl of an animal, then, "Cass, come!"

Morgan's head swam through the jostling, and whatever cold thing that was that touched her chest. She opened her eyes and looked around. Everything was blurry, but she blinked and tried to focus anyway. "Caleb."

"I'm here. Jay is here. Cass found you in the woods." She saw his face for a moment, then it was gone and someone else swam into view.

A guy in a high-vis jacket. "Ma'am, can you tell me your name?"

"M-Morgan Lawson."

"She's the vet," Jay said.

Cass had really found her?

Morgan's mind struggled to assimilate what had happened. Why she was lying on the ground, and her nose felt thick. What had happened to her?

"Morgan, we're going to get you to the hospital so we can get you checked out by a doctor, all right?" The EMT continued, not missing a beat, "On her side, and we'll get her on the backboard."

The world shifted, then she was on her back again a second later. They lifted her, and everything rotated. Morgan nearly rolled to the side so she could throw up, but she'd probably have rolled off the backboard.

The pace they set was quick but steady. She didn't even know where she was. Aside from that, the air smelled like fire and smoke, and animals. The scent of pine trees underneath everything, along with dirt.

They slid her into the back of an ambulance.

Morgan immediately pushed up off the bed they put the backboard on. She leaned too far forward and reached out a hand to brace herself.

"Whoa." The EMT caught her by the shoulder. "Easy, Tiger."

"Jay!" She couldn't speak around her lips. Not well enough. She reached up toward her mouth. "What's wrong with me?"

The EMT touched her hand. "We're going to let the doctor assess the damage and tell us the answer to that, okay? Let's put some ice on it, though. I need you to lay back down so I can take some vitals."

Jay and Caleb stood at the open back doors of the van. Both just stared at her. Not saying anything. She even saw Ian Rourke, Caleb's grandpa.

Tears fell down her cheeks, the salt stinging her skin.

Jay grabbed the edge of the door and climbed in. "I'm coming with you." He turned back. "Cass—"

"No dogs!" The EMT held up a hand. "One passenger only. That's final."

Caleb said, "I'll take Cass to Morgan's house so she can be with Tessa and Ava. We'll come and see you first thing. Okay, Morgan?"

She tried to nod, but it hurt a whole lot.

Caleb shut the doors and hammered twice on the back of the ambulance.

The EMT leaned over and slid open a partition. "Ready when you are."

The driver up front said, "Got it."

Jay sat huddled on the bench, watching her. "I'm glad we found you."

Tears kept rolling down her face, and she was pretty sure her nose was running. She reached up to rub it.

"Don't rub." The EMT grabbed her wrist again, holding it gently but firm. "Put this ice pack over your nose and your top lip if you can." He helped her lie back.

"Jay." She couldn't see him. The questions in her mind threatened to overwhelm her, but she didn't have the strength to voice any of them aloud.

The EMT said, "Switch with me."

Then Jay came into view. He touched her shoulder, a blank look on his face.

"Am I okay?" Maybe she was going to die and they didn't want to tell her.

Jay's expression softened. "My guess is he did a number on your face, probably with the heel of his shoe. But you'll be all right."

Kicked in the face? It had never happened to her before, but with how she felt, it wasn't so surprising. She probably looked hideous.

What was Ava going to think? She would no doubt frighten her own daughter!

She closed her eyes, and nightmare images of being dragged through the woods dissolved into the back of the car, sitting beside that man. The two guys burying that body.

A dead man, staring at her with unseeing eyes.

She choked on a sob and opened her eyes, trying to anchor herself. She was here. Jay was here. She was safe.

"It's okay," he whispered. "You're safe now."

As if he knew exactly what she was thinking.

He put his hand on her shoulder, then ran his fingers through her hair. Smoothing it back.

She drifted for a while as Jay talked to the EMT, but she couldn't make out what they said. Then she heard that man's voice in her mind. Felt his punishing grip on her arm. He'd threatened her family —her daughter.

Morgan gasped.

Jay looked at her and leaned down. "What is it, honey?" He helped her right the ice pack back on her nose.

She spoke from underneath it, still able to taste blood in her mouth. Her lips thick and swollen. "He said he would hurt Ava."

"She's safe with Tessa. Caleb and Cass will be here. No one is going to allow anything to happen to her."

"He knows where I live." She wasn't sure how she knew that, but she was certain of it.

"She is safe, I promise." He showed her a picture on his phone. "Is this the man?"

Morgan looked away from the screen. "Yes." She never wanted anything to do with him in the first place. Now she never wanted to see his face ever again.

"That's good, Morgan. It's witness testimony. And witness testimony sways judges. It gets results."

She didn't want to talk about that. Right now, she never wanted to think about any of this ever again. Though they would need to know about the dead man and where he was buried.

"I don't care about that." She didn't intend to say it aloud, but it was out now, and she needed to clarify. "I only care about Ava."

"I promise you she's safe," Jay said.

"He knows about her."

"Morgan, I do need to know what Marco said to you."

"That's all you care about right now? Intel?" She noticed blood on his shoulder. "You reopened your wound. If you want information from me, you have to let a doctor stitch you up."

He muttered something about Tessa's cousin, though what that had to do with anything she wasn't sure. "If you want me to see a doctor, I will."

"For information."

Jay shook his head. "No, for you."

She stared at him, her head far too dizzy for whatever this conversation was. That little bit of bravado, demanding an agreement, was all she'd had in her. Now she was spent.

"I've lost people before," he continued. "They're gone because of me, and I'm not living through that again. I don't know Ava well, but I know I'm not going to let *anything* happen to her." The ambulance came to a stop, and he swayed on his seat. "I promise, Morgan."

She closed her eyes for a second, offering it as a nod. "I trust you."

CHAPTER NINE

Jay stepped out of the elevator wearing a snazzy new sling. He was supposed to keep his arm in it for a month. As if that was going to happen. First chance he got, he was ditching this thing. Which meant as soon as he got Morgan back to her house.

He couldn't believe he'd told her even as much as he did about losing people. Kids, in fact. Sure, it was the reason he'd come here to recover. But that didn't mean he had to face it, or some such nonsense.

No one cared about his actual feelings. People just wanted to know if he was good to go.

He spotted Tessa, Ava, and Cass walking into the ER and decided he was definitely not mission ready. Not seeing the fear on the little girl's face.

Cass had her VETERAN military dog vest on, walking proudly. Turning heads everywhere she went—and getting unquestioned access to the hospital.

Jay bent and scratched her chin. "Hey, gorgeous."

Tessa chuckled. "Hey, yourself."

He straightened. "Ladies." Then crouched in front of Ava. "How are you doing?"

She sniffed, looking younger than eight years. And tired from a restless night. "O-kay."

He touched her shoulder, and she looked at his sling. "Your mom needed to rest. But I heard she gets to go home soon."

Ava nodded.

He straightened, and Cass leaned against his leg, facing behind him. Watching his six.

"Have you seen her since they admitted her?" Tessa asked.

"No, but the doctor who treated me checked, and they said she was sleeping." He glanced down at Ava, then said to Tessa, "The damage was mostly superficial, but she's got a broken nose."

Tessa nodded, sniffing. Looking like she was about to cry if he was honest with himself. Not something he was used to dealing with —especially not twice in a twenty-four-hour period.

He asked Ava, "What's your favorite way to wake up your mom?"

Her eyes lit with a tiny bit of excitement. "I made her pancakes on her birthday! Grandma helped me cook them."

"Do you think Tessa should go get your mom some pancakes?" Jay suggested. "We can wake her up gently and see if she's hungry."

"She will be. She always is." Her little hand slid into his. "But then she always just has cheese and crackers and calls it 'girl dinner.' But I like mac and cheese better."

"I like mac and cheese, too."

She smiled up at him.

Tessa squeezed his shoulder and handed him Cass's leash. "Coffee?"

"Yes, please." He tried not to sound too desperate and heard her chuckle. To Ava he said, "Ready?"

"I hope she's awake. Sometimes she gets mad when I wake her up."

Jay squeezed her hand. "We can go in real quiet and check first."

"Okay."

He held the dog leash with the sling hand, and Ava's hand with the other. It hit him then, where he was. What he was doing. The fact he'd never in a million years have guessed this was where he'd be right now.

Almost like there was some other plan going on right now, aside from what he had figured this trip would be. Recovering in the barn with Cass. Getting their collective heads straight. He hadn't had a nightmare in days, so it was working.

He needed about three weeks of walks with Cass to figure it out, but protecting Morgan and Ava were the first priority. And finding Montbatten was the second.

Straightening himself out was so far down the list he had no idea when he would get to it.

A nurse pointed them to the curtained bay and pulled it open.

Jay spotted a chair beside the bed and clicked his tongue, indicating the chair.

Cass hopped up and curled her legs under her, which made her look small and less like a tough military dog. Better in a place like this, where she could be in the way, underfoot, in a split second.

He lifted Ava and set her on the end of Morgan's hospital bed. "It looks worse than it is. The doctor told me that." He whispered the words like a secret. "And the doctor probably gave your mom some medicine so it doesn't hurt."

Ava looked at him with tears in her eyes. He stood close by the bedside, and she leaned against the outside of his arm.

Jay whispered, "Everything is going to be okay. Your mom is going to feel better soon."

"What if the bad man comes back?"

Jay wondered what Tessa had said that the kid had overheard, or what she'd explained to Ava about what happened. "Uncle Caleb told me he's going to stop the bad man, and I'm going to help him. We're going to protect you."

"Uncle Caleb told me that Uncle Noah is a superhero, but he made me swear not to tell anyone. Can Uncle Noah help Mommy?"

Jay shifted and pulled out his phone. He found a group picture from a team barbecue that he wasn't supposed to have kept, but he saved it on a secure app Marina had designed that was unhackable. Mostly they used it to send memes back and forth, but it could come in handy one day.

"See this?" He pointed. "Who do you know?"

Ava peered at the picture. "That's Uncle Noah!"

How she could tell it wasn't Caleb, he didn't know. The twins were basically identical. Most people couldn't tell them apart easily. Except the team, and family.

"And that's you!"

"All my friends are superheroes," Jay said. "That's how I know your mom will be safe."

"I knew Cass was special. Not like other dogs."

"That is definitely true."

The dog laid her head on her paws.

Jay told Ava, "There's a command I can give her. It means 'guard,' and I use it when I want her to protect someone. I can ask Cass to guard your mom."

Ava nodded.

"And I'm going to call Uncle Noah, and we'll make sure you and your mom are safe. Okay?"

"Okay."

She sounded so small and fragile that Jay wanted to scoop her up and protect her forever. His heart was melting toward this little family. In a way he'd never expected.

He'd never even had a family. Not in the sense of loving, and being loved. He'd had parents, but they had never been a family.

Morgan exhaled, drawing his attention to her. She blinked with awareness. "Hey, baby."

"Hi, Mommy." Ava shifted on the covers. "Your face looks smashed."

Morgan's eyes, swollen a little but not as much as last night, glinted with humor. "Guess I'm too early for a Halloween costume."

"You would be very scary."

Jay let out a laugh before he could keep it from escaping. "Sorry." He cleared his throat.

"Auntie Tessa is getting pancakes for your breakfast."

"Great. After that, maybe I'll be able to go home."

"Cass needs to come with us so she can guard." Ava nodded, very matter-of-fact about it.

Morgan looked at Jay.

He nodded. "Caleb and Noah will be doing their superhero thing. I'll be with Cass, on protection detail. Until we know for sure that the situation is under wraps."

She stared at him.

He knew how scared she'd been. He'd seen it on her face in the ambulance. Never in his life was he going to forget the tears rolling down that face.

If he could help her...

Maybe it would make up a little for the things he had done, protecting this woman and her child. Their only crimes had been living normal lives in this town. Maybe crossing paths with him. But it wasn't about making amends to them for putting them in danger —if that was what he'd done.

No, it was far more than that. Much deeper than remorse.

He wanted to protect them because they meant something to him.

Tessa swept into the bay. "Pancakes, and coffee," she announced, taking over the conversation. A good thing, so he could begin the work of protecting the mother-daughter duo.

He stepped to the curtain and surveyed the hall outside the bay while they chattered behind him. Then he pulled out his phone and dialed Noah's number, his back to Morgan's bed.

As soon as his boss picked up, Jay said, "Is your thing done?"

"You need the team?"

"I need something."

"Whatever it is, you got it. Email me the details?"

Jay said, "Yep," and hung up, knowing Noah would be on the phone with Caleb getting the lowdown right now.

The fact Jay had actually reached out and asked for help? What he should have done was quit, given the way he and Noah had left it. But it couldn't be denied that the team would be a benefit in this instance.

When the lives of innocent civilians were on the line, Jay would take all the help he could get.

A doctor who used too much gel in his blond hair and smelled like—was that cologne?—stepped in front of him. "I'd like to see the patient, if you'll permit me entry."

Jay didn't like the guy immediately, but stepped aside.

Morgan looked like she was about to throw up. "Jared?"

Tessa didn't look much better. Actually, she looked angry more than anything.

Ava looked at the doctor. "Daddy?"

"Hi, munchkin. I wasn't sure you'd remember me." The doctor stepped toward the kid, but she didn't reach for him. "I'm glad you do."

"What are you doing here?" Morgan asked her ex-husband.

❀

As Jared stared at her, Morgan tried to see anything she'd ever thought was commendable about him. Sure, he was handsome enough. He'd always been enigmatic.

Now, standing so near to...

Where was Jay?

A second ago, he'd been standing there like a bodyguard. As if she were someone important—or someone important to him. He'd made a phone call. Things had been really nice for a second. Her meds were starting to wear off, but Jay had been there. Being sweet with Ava, sweet with her. Talking about superheroes, and protecting them.

Now she was face-to-face with her ex-husband, and Jay had slunk off like a coward.

Okay, maybe not. But what was she supposed to think? The guy disappeared the moment Jared showed up.

The doctor who now cleared his throat.

"Seriously…" Morgan eyed him. "Why are you here, Jared?"

"I'm not going to treat you." He lifted his hands. "Not since you're family. I disclosed that when I got a job here, and when I came on shift this morning, they told me you were here."

She wanted to shake her head, but bad idea. "That still doesn't explain why you're here. Last I knew, you were gunning for the head of cardiology job in Salt Lake City. Now you're working here?"

"It's only been a couple of months. I wanted to get settled before I…came to see you." He glanced at their daughter. "And Ava, of course."

She wanted to find fault in him, but she'd been blindsided, and now everything was majorly out of whack.

After the night she'd had, she didn't need this. But she didn't know how to say it in such a way that Ava wouldn't draw a wrong conclusion. This whole thing was too messy, too complicated. Especially considering she'd been kicked in the face and a guy she felt safe with, and maybe really liked, was out in the hall.

Cass lifted her head and sniffed in Jared's direction.

Tessa glanced at Jared. "Maybe you can find out if Morgan is going to be released. She's hoping to go home soon. You guys can have this conversation later, when she feels better."

Morgan knew that meant when she was firing on all cylinders—able to fight back against whatever Jared brought against her.

"I'll do that." Jared nodded. "I just… I'm here because I want to have the conversation. I know there's a lot to say, but I just want you to know." He seemed almost nervous. "I miss you, and I'm working at this hospital now because I want to be here. In Breckenrow."

Morgan stared at his back as he left the bay.

She couldn't believe he'd just said that. It was like someone else stole Jared's body, because there was zero chance her ex-husband would have ever said something like that.

She looked at Tessa. "What just happened?"

Her cousin shook her head. "I have no idea. That was like *Invasion of the Body Snatchers*."

"Wasn't that a book? Or was it a TV show?"

Jay leaned around the curtain into view. "It was a movie."

Ava watched them all, tension in her body.

Morgan said, "Honey? You good?"

Ava shrugged.

Morgan reached for her daughter's hand. "Whatever happens, you get to decide what you want. If you don't like something, you don't have to do it."

"I like Cass."

Morgan smiled. "I do, too."

She wanted to say, *If we ask nicely, maybe she'll stay forever.* But that kind of question was a whole lot more of the everything overwhelming Morgan right now.

She should be lying here alone, her eyes closed, thinking about that scary man kicking her in the face. Instead, she was trying to figure out how to deal with her ex-husband being back in her life.

In her town, looking like he wanted to...

What?

She had no idea, and asking sounded like a terrifying proposition.

What she wanted was to go home, watch a ridiculous movie with Ava and Cass—the three of them snuggled up together on the couch —and know that Jay was making them safe.

Tessa's phone rang. She looked at the screen. "It's Caleb. I'll be back in a second."

Morgan nodded.

Jay stepped back into the room. "It's a little less crowded now."

She wanted to hear his story, talk to him with the lights low, speaking in whispers. Not something Jared inspired—it had to be noted. What she wanted was a hug. A snugglefest with the dog, because asking Jay to hold her was too dangerous.

"Can we go home?" she asked.

His eyes flared. "Soon as the doctor says you're good, I'll take you home."

"And you'll stay, right? You'll protect us?"

He reached out and laid his hand over hers. "Of course. For as long as you want me around, I'll be there."

"I'm going to hold you to that."

Ava said, "Me, too."

Morgan was pretty sure she had no idea what she meant, but it was still adorable.

Jay's expression softened on the girl. He let go of her hand and touched Ava's cheeks, laying a kiss on her forehead. "Ready to go home as well?"

She wanted to keep watching them, but she noticed Jared in the hall outside the bay, over by the nurse's station. Staring at them, and looking wrecked by the sight of another man being sweet to his daughter.

She wanted to write off this too little, too late attempt, whatever it was. But she had to give her ex-husband a shot, even if it was only about Ava spending time with her father. Just because Jared was here didn't mean anything was going to happen between them.

"I'm very ready to leave here and get some real rest at home." Morgan nudged Ava's leg. "Did Auntie Tessa call the school and tell them you'd be absent today?"

Ava nodded. "I wanna stay home tomorrow, too."

"We'll see."

Ava looked at Jay. "That means no."

He smiled at her. "We'll talk about it."

Ava looked at Morgan. "He agrees with you."

"Okay, smarty pants." Morgan chuckled. "You're so smart you can choose what we have for dinner."

"Yay! I love the soup at the Chinese place."

It was Thai, but Morgan wasn't going to correct her.

All the way home, she kept the good feelings close, the camaraderie of the three of them and the way Jay made her feel safe close to her heart. She even drifted off in the car, not worrying about how she looked, because they didn't seem to care. She almost lowered the visor to see her face but wasn't sure that would be a good idea.

Jay pulled into her drive.

Morgan looked around. "I have no idea where my purse is, or my keys, or anything."

Jay turned off the engine. "Caleb swung by your office on orders from Tessa. They closed up and told your techs to call everyone with appointments this week to reschedule."

"Doctor—" She wanted to say Dr. Shelton would cover for her. But he was dead.

She'd seen him buried in the woods.

Tears filled Morgan's eyes.

Jay pushed out his door and came around, letting Ava out and telling her what command to use to get Cass to pee in the front yard.

"Okay, Jay!" The girl hopped out, followed by the dog who loved her.

Jay opened Morgan's door. "You good?"

She tried to get her belt unlatched, but he did it for her.

"Morgan?"

She grabbed his arm before he could pull it back, holding on like she needed him. "Thanks."

"You don't have to thank me."

"I mean it." She tugged him a little closer. "Thanks."

The skin around his eyes flexed. "You're welcome."

"I want to hear your stories. I want to watch a movie, and I want to take an epic nap. Unfortunately, I can't do all three at the same time."

He patted her hand. "I want to walk through the house before you and Ava step inside. I want to order my dog to work on protecting you guys and ruin a little girl's doggy playtime. And I want to make you my famous peanut butter smoothie."

Morgan let him help her out of the car.

Whatever was going on with Jared, she wasn't going to worry about it right now. She was going to set it all aside and focus on being safe, and healing. Because who knew what might happen next. Whatever it was, she figured she needed to be on her A game.

For her sake, for Ava, and for whatever developed between her and Jay.

Lord willing, whatever He had next would be a blessing. The life she'd been asking Him for. The answers to her questions.

The desires of her heart.

CHAPTER TEN

J ay took the empty plates from the coffee table to the kitchen, then rinsed them and loaded the dishwasher. Morgan and Ava were curled up together on the couch, watching their second movie in a row. Morgan's eyes had grown heavy, so he'd laid a blanket over her and given Ava a wave.

Both of them were probably thinking about the doctor showing up.

That's how he'd decided to think about the guy. Jared. Not as Morgan's ex-husband, or Ava's father. But as The Doctor.

Didn't help.

Jay was here to protect Morgan and Ava from Montbatten. That was all.

Because he wasn't about to get in the way of a guy who wanted his family back.

He'd done what he said he would do and made the peanut butter smoothie, which turned into soup and grilled cheese for lunch. If Morgan wasn't in too much pain later, he was thinking they could order pizza for dinner.

Jay's phone buzzed in his pocket. He checked it and saw that Caleb was outside.

He went to the front door and let his friend in. "Hey."

"All good here?" Caleb looked around and saw the girls on the couch. He waved at Ava, who waved back.

"Let's go in the kitchen." Jay led Caleb in there and poured them both a cup of coffee. "It's been quiet here."

"That's good."

"Have you talked to Noah?"

Caleb nodded. "They're filing reports on the plane, headed here."

"We need to find Montbatten before he does whatever he's going to do next."

"Considering the cops didn't even know he was here, we can't rely on their intel to gauge where he might be." Caleb sipped his coffee. "We need to find him ourselves."

"Great. Where is he gonna be? Because aside from finding a trail somehow, and having a sample of his scent, there's no way to know where he went after he…" Jay couldn't even say it.

That dirty coward had stomped on Morgan's face before he walked away.

Jay had to put the mug down to keep from throwing it at the wall. The anger burned in him like a fire that wouldn't go out. Like a volcano about to erupt. He curled his hands into fists.

Cass scratched at the back door.

Jay let her in, running his hands along her sides. As always, she had a calming effect on him. He soaked her presence in like a balm.

"Tessa told me the ex showed up at the hospital," Caleb said. "Working there."

Jay straightened. "So?" It wasn't anything to do with him.

Caleb came over to the back door, probably so he'd be farther out of earshot of Ava. Not that Jay even wanted to have this conversation. Still, Caleb asked, "What do you think of him?"

Jay wasn't about to say that he thought the guy used too much product in his hair. "He wants them back. Probably woke up and realized how much of an idiot he was letting them go and moved back here, took a job, and set about figuring out how to get them back."

"Not that you've given it any thought." Caleb put down his coffee mug.

Jay would never have let them go in the first place. "If he's here to be part of their lives, that should be a good thing, right?"

"Maybe." Caleb shrugged. "Tessa doesn't hold the guy in particularly high esteem. Sounds like he gave them up pretty easily. Didn't agree with Morgan about what she wanted her life to be. Didn't fight to see Ava."

"So he's a moron."

Caleb clapped a hand on Jay's shoulder. "She gave him up once."

"Ava needs a father."

"Everyone does, but fathers come in all shapes and sizes. It isn't always about blood. And no one ever said a person can't have two father figures in their life."

Jay shook his head. "I'm here to protect them. That's all."

"Throw your hat in the ring and let Morgan choose. That's all I'm saying." Caleb backed up, palms facing up.

"I don't live here," Jay countered. "I don't work here." What exactly could he offer Morgan, even if he wanted to throw his hat in the ring? Which, he wasn't sure he actually...

Fine, he was curious what it would be like to have something like what Caleb and Tessa had. Add Ava, and it was a family.

"I don't know how to do this." Jay waved his hand. "I have no clue what I'm doing."

"Seems like you're doing fine to me."

"This is protection detail. I know how to do this. The family thing?" Jay shook his head. "I have no clue."

"You think I do?" Caleb folded his arms across his chest. "My parents dumped us off with Pops whenever they felt like it to run off and do...whatever it is they did. Noah thinks they were CIA, but the bottom line is, they didn't want us."

"They showed up to help you guys get Kessler, though. Didn't they?"

"I have no idea who that message was from. Might've been them, but why help me and then go back to no contact? They're obviously not interested in us being a family, so I'm making my own. Pops won't be around forever, and Tessa's dad is getting up there in age. I need to figure out how to hang on to whatever family I can get for as long as it's available to me. Then I'll be building my own, with Tessa. Life will move on."

"Is there a point to this?" Jay scoffed.

Caleb shot him a look. "No one feels equipped to do this. I've been reading marriage books, and Tessa and I are going to premarital counseling. These are skills you learn. It won't be perfect. No one has a perfect example of how to be a husband and a father. Even a good situation will have had drawbacks, or things that could have been better. The point is, you go into it admitting what you need to learn and willing to try."

Jay crossed his arms. "'Cart before the horse' in my case."

It wasn't like he and Morgan had actually committed to each other. Nothing like where Caleb and Tessa were at. It wasn't a given, or a sure thing. It was a wish.

One he didn't want to bank any hope on. Because when had hope ever paid off for him once in his life?

"It won't be anything if you don't at least let her know how you feel about her." That was a whole lot of assumption on Caleb's part. Reading into Jay's behavior with Morgan.

"You know I'd be protecting her regardless." Jay had to say that, because Caleb didn't need to think that this was only about him being attracted to Morgan, and her being hurt.

"Yeah, but you'd have me in the rotation. Not taking care of it single-handedly, making lunch and taking care of Ava."

Jay ran a hand through his hair. "Can we talk about Montbatten already?"

"If we can't find him, maybe there's a way to get him to come to us."

Jay shook his head. "Only if no one else is in the crossfire." Still, he was interested in the idea. "I need to call Marina. See if she has anything on him that'll help us find him."

Caleb lifted his chin, indicating behind Jay. "I'll do that outside."

Jay found Ava behind him. "Hey. Everything all right?"

She nodded. "The movie ended." She wandered to the fridge and pulled out a juice, tugging off the straw.

"I always had trouble with those pouches when I was a kid," Jay told her. "One time, I punched the straw through both sides."

"Really?" She smiled wide, amused by his story.

"I could show you, but I'll make a mess." He smiled. "How is your mom?"

"She started snoring. I'm gonna get my book and read."

"Great idea."

She trailed off down the hall as Caleb came in through the back door.

Cass was curled up on the recliner chair, like she was supposed to be on the furniture in someone else's house. He let her be, though. She was closer to the front door than Morgan and would raise the alarm if necessary.

"Anything?" Jay asked.

Caleb nodded. "Marina has a phone number for him, and it has pinged in the area recently. But it's off right now."

How she could tell all that, Jay had no clue. Probably some kind of deep hack, NSA-style. He knew better than to ask.

For now, they were going to have to wait and see what happened. Which meant he would be here, playing happy families—the protection detail expansion pack—and trying not to be lured in by the idea of a home. A wife, and a daughter. Bottom line was, they were someone else's family.

Not his.

Morgan woke from a bad dream without startling herself. Alone in the living room. At peace with the deep knowledge that she was protected.

The house wasn't silent. Ava was in her room, and Jay and Caleb cleaning up the kitchen. Cass moved her paws in her sleep, chuffing quietly.

Morgan's phone vibrated, tucked under her in her pocket. The second she shifted, the same nagging pain flared in her face. Her nose had a butterfly strip across it, securing the part where the skin had split. She could feel the cut on the inside of her lip where it had smashed into the edge of her teeth.

It would be a while until she felt good, or presentable, again. And yet, Jay didn't seem to notice.

She dragged out her phone and saw Jared's name on the screen. Not thinking too much about why he might be calling, she slid her thumb across the screen and put it to her ear. "Yeah?" She then closed her eyes, trying to preserve some energy, even though she had just woken up.

"Did I wake you?"

"It's fine." Though that was conditional on whatever he was about to say.

"I had a break between patients, so I wanted to see how you were doing."

Jared had moved his life to Breckenrow and taken a job in the town hospital without telling her. She didn't want to be suspicious of an ulterior motive, but how could she not be? Even if the motive wasn't bad, it didn't mean there would be no upset in her life—or Ava's.

Morgan groaned. "I feel like I got kicked in the face."

"Maybe after I get off shift, I could bring you some soup," he suggested. "It's strange working eight to six and having an evening."

A small chuckle followed his words. "But I'm getting used to working normal hours and having time for a life."

"How long have you been in Breckenrow?" She didn't want the question to sound suspicious, but it was what it was.

"Three weeks," he replied. "There's probably a pool going at the hospital in Salt Lake for how long I'll last, and when I'm likely to show back up with my tail between my legs."

"So it isn't just me who thinks this might be an uncharacteristic change."

"It might not be normal for me, but I had to do it." He paused. "Do you want to hear the story right now, or maybe over dinner?"

"Ava would probably like to hear it as well."

"I was thinking maybe just you and me?" Jared said. "I'd like to spend time with her as well. But maybe...separately?"

Morgan frowned. "I haven't had a chance to talk to her about you."

"We have time. I'm not in a hurry," he said. "That's part of why I wanted to move here first. Get settled and get my life together. I actually saw you guys at church the other day, but I didn't want to ambush you and catch you off guard."

"I appreciate that." But however it might have happened, it would have been a story. "Tell me what made you want to make the change."

Giving up his life in a huge hospital, on track to be a department chair. The Jared she'd known and married wasn't the guy who would have given up that life for anything.

Not even a family.

"I got the job," Jared said. "Eight months ago, they announced I was the new head of cardiology."

"Congratulations?"

He chuckled. "I had everything I'd been working toward for years. I was the definition of my own success. But after a few weeks, I realized I hadn't changed. I felt empty, and nothing I did helped to fill that hole. I tried everything and wound up getting pulled over and breathalyzed. Thankfully, I was within the legal limit—but only barely. Still, it was a wake-up call."

"Wow."

"A few days later, this couple comes in, and the wife isn't going to make it. I'm looking at her, and I just know. But they're talking, and both of them have so much…peace. That's the only way I can describe it. They're good. Not in denial. They know it's going to be a hard road."

"Did they tell you what gave them that peace?" she wondered.

"The husband told me all of it. Sat me down and gave me the whole gospel. It just made so much sense. I realized all the things I'd done wrong, and how it stemmed from having so much pride. I was… *broken* is a good word."

"I understand." Trouble was, being broken was what had happened to her because of Jared and the end of their marriage.

She'd had to grieve the life she thought she would have and build a new one. These days, she had to remember to thank God for it and not fall into pride thinking any of it was because she was so great. God had been so, so good to her.

"My whole life changed," he went on. "I got in a Bible study and started talking to the leader afterward about how to make amends. Sounds like I'm in recovery, but the truth is, it does sort of feel like that. I need to be better. But at the same time, I know I'm a new creation. I just have to live it. Be humble, do what's just and right. Be merciful to people. It's kind of foreign, but I'm learning."

"That's so great, Jared." Morgan spotted movement in the doorway and found Jay watching her. She smiled at him.

"Thanks, Morgan. It feels a little bit like it's too late, but I'd like to spend time together. And I want to get to know Ava. Be part of both of your lives, however that happens. If you'll allow me to be part of your life."

She ducked her head. Little girls needed their dad in their life, and she didn't think it was ever too late to fix that. Especially not when Ava was eight, not eighteen or older. There was so much to her daughter that was still soft. She would have to trust that Jared wasn't going to hurt her. But some pain was part of life. Her thoughts and feelings were all mixed up about it.

He continued, "One of the nurses here told me about the dog fighting ring, and why that guy kidnapped you."

"It was pretty scary."

"I can imagine," he said. "Sounds like being a vet might be a dangerous choice."

"I didn't do anything to invite what that guy did."

"But if you'd been at home with Ava, it never would've happened. Right?"

By that logic, she should never leave her house. And yet, there were plenty of ways a person could get hurt at home. Physically and emotionally.

"Did I lose you?"

She shook her head, even though he couldn't see her. There was no way she would apologize for being silent. "I'm just processing. Let's talk more. And plan to do something together. You, me, and Ava."

"Great. And maybe on Sunday at church I could...sit by you guys?"

"I'll be back at church when my face doesn't look hideous, but that sounds nice." Not just because she wanted to see him worshipping and listening to the Word being preached with her own eyes. Yes, to see if it was genuine. But also to be able to thank God for the change in Jared's life.

She wasn't perfect, and everyone had room to grow. But Morgan wanted to see the version of her ex-husband who had been made new by Christ.

"I'll let you go," he said. "I should get back to work."

"Thanks for calling."

"Anytime, Morgan." His voice was soft, and it sparked more memories than she needed right then. With another man in her kitchen—one that she liked a whole lot.

It was all so new. She didn't need Jared showing up, muddling things when Jay wasn't going to be here for long.

But life was life, and it almost never went as planned.

She set the phone on the coffee table and stood, putting the blanket on the back of the couch. "Ava?"

Jay appeared at the doorway again, Caleb behind him.

"I should take more pain pills." She wanted to touch her nose and feel the swelling but knew that wasn't going to feel good. "What's for dinner?"

Ava skipped down the hall. "Mommy, the movie finished, and now I'm done with my book as well."

"The joy of skipping school, I guess." She smiled at Ava, who came over for a hug.

"I'll call Tessa," Caleb said. "If you're up for it, maybe we could go to the ranch and Pops can fire up the grill. We'll have a cookout."

"Great idea." Morgan felt energized just thinking about it.

The questions surrounding Jared's arrival in town faded into the background of her mind, and she found she could focus on this. The here and now.

After Ava let her go, Morgan wandered over to go in the kitchen.

Jay stood there still, unmoving.

"Everything okay?" she asked.

"I don't know, is it?"

She didn't think it through. Just slid her arms around his shoulders and pulled him in for a hug. He really was huge, but she made it work. "Thanks for being here."

His arms came around her back. "You're welcome."

She moved to pull away, and he stiffened.

Cass started barking.

Jay spun Morgan behind him as Cass sprang to attention. He yelled, "Caleb!" and ran to Ava, scooping her into his arms.

The front window shattered as an object on fire flew through the living room, landing on the couch right where she'd been sitting.

The blanket whooshed into flame.

CHAPTER ELEVEN

Jay spun Ava toward the kitchen. "Caleb!"

His friend caught the young girl. "Got her!" He swooped Ava into the kitchen out of sight. Away from the flames.

Jay shut the acknowledgement of the screams from his mind. "Fuss!"

Cass bounded over the couch and stood beside his leg.

"Morgan!"

She seemed frozen. Not quite staring at the flames. But she hadn't moved in a few seconds.

"Morgan!" He went to her.

The back door slid open, and air whipped in from outside, fanning the flames so they flared higher.

He dragged Morgan against him. The back door, the way Caleb had gone with Ava, was their best route. "Come on. We need to—"

The front door flung open and bounced off the wall. Men with bandanas tied over the lower half of their faces rushed in, guns pointed at them.

"Cass, find Caleb!"

The dog ran out the back door.

Jay shoved Morgan behind him at the same time, pushing her toward the kitchen. "Run!" He turned back to face the threat single-handedly.

One of the men fired in her direction.

Morgan screamed and froze again.

Close enough for him to touch her. She'd barely made it a step away.

He tucked her behind him, holding on to her. Defending her from the threat coming at them fast. Too fast for him to draw his gun.

The first guy pointed the pistol right at his face. "You're coming with us."

"She stays here." Jay wasn't arguing with them about that. It was a fact.

"She goes where we tell her to go."

Morgan's hands tightened on his jacket.

"Then we're all going to burn to death in here, I guess." As long as Ava was all right, Jay could protect Morgan.

Caleb would've already called 911, so firefighters and police would be here soon. He could hold out until then—standing fast through anything. Insurgents. Warlords. Montana thugs. Fire. Ex-husband phone calls.

All of it.

The guy pressed the barrel of his gun against Jay's forehead, then lifted his arm to slam it down. Jay swung his hands up to block the blow, but the butt of the pistol slammed into his injured shoulder instead of his head.

Thanks to the sling advertising he was hurt.

That thought rolled through his mind while he stared at the floor, on his hands and knees.

Morgan yelped. Then she yelled, "Jay!"

He looked up and saw her being dragged through the living room to the front door. He got up.

The thug shoved him forward and pressed the barrel of the gun to his back. "Walk!"

He followed Morgan to the door, stepping into the smoke-filled air.

A van was parked at the curb. Jay spotted Montbatten—Anthony, Marco, whatever his name was—in the front seat.

Morgan did as well, because she visibly reacted.

"Get them inside," Montbatten ordered.

Morgan stumbled through the open door of the van, and Jay climbed in behind her. He sat close and put his arms around her. Holding on, as much for him as it was for her.

The van driver hit the gas, and they swayed. Everything, including them, smelled like smoke.

Jay didn't like the look of the guy still holding his gun pointed at them. "You can put that down."

"Can I?" He didn't, though.

Morgan held on to him all the way to...wherever they were going.

Why take them both? Aside from the fact they'd been inside the house when these men ran in.

He took a second and thanked God that Ava and Caleb had fled out the back, along with Cass.

"What do you want with us?" He looked toward the front, figuring Montbatten was the one in charge.

"Cost me a lot of money."

"I'm bad for business? It's what I do." Jay wasn't going to apologize for it.

"Don't worry," Montbatten said. "You'll pay, and so will she."

Morgan stiffened against him.

"You can leave her out of it. This is between us." Jay paused. "But I have to admit, I'm surprised. Figured you'd be busy running from the feds. Too busy to waste your time with a small-town dog fighting ring."

The thug in front of him with the gun said, "You mean his biggest money maker?"

"Shut your mouth," Montbatten said. "All of you."

Jay wanted to smirk at the thug but kept his opinions off his face.

After about half an hour of the van shifting up and down, they came to a stop. Morgan still huddled against him, her face carefully tucked against him. The pain in his shoulder was the least of his worries right now.

When the door slid open, fresh but cold air rushed in, chilling his body. Adrenaline had left his system, so he'd be slower. Shaky. Jay surveyed the men as he moved.

No way he'd be able to take on all of them.

Two men stood back, holding weapons.

Montbatten, who seemed to have an endless supply of local thugs to do his bidding, appeared at the open van door. "Get out. Both of you."

Morgan braced a hand on Jay's abdomen. "I don't want to do that," she whispered.

"We don't have a choice."

He wanted to promise her that nothing would happen to her. That he wouldn't let her get hurt. But he couldn't, could he? All Jay could do was pray.

Good thing that was the most powerful tool at his disposal.

He shifted to the edge of the van and set his feet on the ground, Morgan behind him again. He reached back with his good hand, and she took hold of it. Which left him with only the injured side to protect himself—both of them, actually.

Lord...

More prayers roiled through his mind.

In the past, he'd often rushed into dangerous situations with no thought, and no prayers. Now, it seemed far wiser to trust that God had this in hand. Because for once it wasn't about him. It was about Morgan getting home to her daughter.

Montbatten stepped back. "Get them inside."

Morgan walked close to his side, her head ducked against his shoulder. Protecting her face—and not wanting to look at anyone else.

Jay needed intel, so he scanned the whole area. Whatever side of town this was, the houses were set farther apart. Trees between, and fenced-off fields with livestock. Goats. A horse or two. One cow.

Families who raised most of their food, trying to live off the land.

They certainly didn't need a federal fugitive causing trouble in their neighborhood. But if something kicked off, they could be the kind of people who stepped in and showed up—armed and ready to defend themselves and others.

The gunmen took Jay and Morgan to a barn with a hole in the roof. Inside was freezing. No animals had lived in here for a long time.

They were shoved into a room at the back, more like an oversize cage.

"Hey!" Jay turned, and the door slammed in his face. He pounded on the door with a closed fist. "Montbatten, I wanna talk to you!"

A lock snapped into place.

Jay swayed the whole door, but it didn't budge. What now? Whatever Montbatten wanted, he should just get it over with. Jay didn't like things to be dragged out. He didn't like being trapped in here.

It was entirely too much like...

Don't think about that.

He grabbed the door again and tried to bring the whole building down. It didn't work so well for Samson—he wound up killing himself and everyone else. But Jay could certainly understand the sentiment.

These people were going to make them suffer, then kill them. All because they ruined the money-making scheme.

"Montbatten!" Jay's yell echoed back at him.

He got no answer.

Jay squeezed his eyes shut, and all he could see were the walls of another dark room, far away from here. He could hear the cries of those children.

Saw them running, chasing him to the exit. To freedom.

Heard the rat-tat of gunfire.

Watched them fall.

🐾

"Jay." Morgan wasn't sure if touching him was a good idea.

Not right now.

"Jay." She moved beside him, but kept some space between them.

He'd protected her. Physically. Supported her emotionally.

Now she got the feeling he was the one who needed support.

"Jay." She touched his sleeve. It was freezing in here, and she hadn't been wearing a sweater under the blanket in her house. She didn't even have shoes on. Just socks, sweatpants, and a long-sleeved sleep T-shirt.

He looked at her, his expression definitely somewhere else.

Morgan shuddered because she couldn't help it. "It's freezing in here."

He looked down at her feet, then back up. "Come here." He opened his jacket, and she took the invitation, sliding her arms in and around his back.

She moaned. "You're so warm."

He chuckled.

"When did they take your gun?" She must have missed that, so focused on not drawing attention to herself.

"Back at the house, I guess. I still have weapons on me. They didn't completely pat me down."

She leaned back just far enough to look at him. "You do?"

"There's a knife in my boot."

"I thought you were going to say something cool and manly like" —she lowered her voice, trying to sound like a tough guy—"I *am* the weapon.'"

Some of the tension in him evaporated. "You seem okay."

"I'm not. But I'd like to know what you were thinking about just now." She rubbed a hand up and down his back. "Will you tell me about it?"

They weren't doing anything else right now, and she needed the distraction.

She had no idea what "making them pay" meant, or what would happen next.

Jay let out a long breath, as if he had to relieve the tension somehow. "It was my last operation. It's what got me here, recovering."

"What happened?"

"Cass was having surgery. I took a job because I was ordered to, not because I wanted to. There was nothing to do but sit around waiting to hear if she pulled through the surgery and what the prognosis was. But Noah thought I needed something to do, so he ordered me to sneak into this compound in Libya and do some recon. No one had any idea there was a bunch of girls being held there. Most were younger than twelve, but there were some older ones who took care of the rest."

Morgan didn't ask what they were for. She could guess, and hearing him say it out loud would make the whole thing so much more real.

"I wasn't going to leave them there." He paused. "I couldn't contact the team, so I made an executive decision."

"You saved them?"

Grief flashed across his face. "I tried. I should've gone back out, left the area, and got the whole team to go in and save them. It wasn't the mission, but sometimes we do things just because it's right. But I didn't go get backup. I couldn't stand to think what would be happening while I wasn't there."

She held on to Jay, wondering if her being so close helped.

"I started a fire—like I did in the barn. A couple of the men there died when it caught too fast and a whole room went up in flames. The whole place went into chaos. I took the chance and got the girls out of the room where they lived. Told them all to run with me, toward one of the side gates."

His breaths were coming hard now.

"We were just through the gate when someone yelled," he continued. "They opened fire at all the fleeing girls. Mowed most of them down like they were nothing. Just for having the audacity to want to be free. Only one or two got out. They were screaming. I carried a girl for two miles, and the team picked us up. She was dead by the time I reached them. She'd been shot in the leg and bled out fast. I carried her all that way, and she was already gone."

"You tried," Morgan said. "That counts for something." She needed him to know there was honor just in the attempt.

"They were all killed. Because of me."

"No, they were killed because their captors took their lives." She searched his eyes. "Should you have left them to their fate? Trapped in that horrible situation." In some circumstances, death might be preferable, but the choice was never a good one. And she didn't want the kind of power that dictated a person's fate.

Morgan lived a small-town life, raising her daughter, building her business. And she did it for a reason—because this was the life she wanted.

The scale Jay worked on was a whole lot different.

"You gave them the chance to live." She squeezed his sides, feeling warmer than before. "And if I'm going to be someone's captive, I'm glad it's you here with me. No matter what happens."

"I'm not going to let Ava lose you."

Morgan wasn't sure that was a promise he had the power to make. She had a will in place, and Tessa and Caleb had agreed to raise Ava if anything happened to her. Jared would be in the mix, somewhere. Though hopefully, he could keep his opinions about her job to himself.

"What's that expression?" he asked.

Morgan didn't want to talk about it. "My face hurts."

"I bet it does, but I don't think that's what's going on in your head right now." Jay rubbed warmth into her back. "I shared. Now it's your turn."

She shook her head, amused at him. "Is that how it works?"

"No. This isn't some tit-for-tat thing. But I would like to know."

She sighed. "Jared made a snide remark on the phone, that's all. Something about how if I'd been home with Ava, being a mom and not a vet, I'd never have been in this situation."

Jay shook his head. "As if that needed to be said?"

"It's an old argument. I'm the woman, so I should give up the dream I've had since I was eight years old and be a stay-at-home mom. Nothing wrong with that. It's a valuable calling. It's just not *my* calling. It never has been, and he knew that."

Did she really want to get into this with Jay? Maybe he didn't want to know.

Before she could ask, he said, "Tell me the rest."

"I felt about being a vet the way he felt about being a doctor. But just because I'm the one capable of carrying and delivering a baby, it means I should be happy to set my dreams aside so he can conveniently still have his. Not with both of us pulling our weight and parenting equally, but with me shouldering all the responsibility and taking care of everything. He thought my dreams would get in the way of me being the housekeeper and parenting our child so he could work long hospital shifts and not have to worry about any of it."

"But he's here now. In town. Seems like he wants you guys back."

"We don't always get what we want." Morgan shrugged.

She wasn't about to be miserable again—undermined and devalued—just because the father of her child seemed interested. Thankfully, her relationship with him was separate from Ava's. Her daughter could have her father in her life, while Morgan simply worked on a friendship. Or at least being cordial co-parents for Ava's sake.

Morgan didn't know what was happening between her and Jay, but it seemed like they'd always been more than acquaintances.

She lifted her chin, which put their faces close together. "What's best for Ava, and what's best for me, can be two different things. But sometimes it isn't. We both want to be loved for who we are, not who someone thinks we should be."

"I've never been loved like that," Jay said. "Maybe by my teammates, but that's different."

"It's good, though."

"I've never met a woman like you. You're strong. You stand up for yourself, and you love the people around you without asking for anything in return."

"I don't feel very strong right now." Morgan had to admit that. So it would come as no surprise when she fell apart at what happened next.

"I'm glad I get to be here with you," he whispered. "Because you deserve to have someone in your life who will do whatever it takes to make sure you have the freedom to be whoever you want to be."

She tightened her grasp on him, stepping closer.

He dipped his head. Hesitated.

Morgan touched her lips to his, being careful of the swelling and the damage to her nose.

The kiss wasn't much to speak of, just a gentle touch. A brief statement—but loud in what it declared.

Almost as if, with that one moment, everything changed.

CHAPTER TWELVE

There were times when a kiss was the most terrifying thing in the world.

On missions, Jay usually worried about Cass. Maybe his teammates. He worked solo. He saved who he could, and usually only sent information back and waited for his team.

Two things were true right now that weren't normally true.

He wasn't alone.

No one was coming to help him save Morgan.

At least, he needed to proceed as if no one was coming. If someone did? Bonus. Otherwise, it was up to him.

"Everything okay?" Her finger slipped into his, entwining them in that small way.

Nothing like the kiss they'd just shared. Boy, it had been a while since he'd done that. Good to know she still wanted to hold his hand afterward—not that it was something a person forgot how to do.

"Just focusing." He squeezed her hand. "We aren't out of the woods. Far from it, actually."

"It was a nice distraction," she said. "Thanks for sharing your story with me."

He leaned over and touched his lips to hers, trying not to even think about it. Just do it. "You're welcome."

She'd opened up about Jared. Whatever happened, she got to choose how things proceeded. Jay had learned plenty that life didn't usually work out as planned. But the point was that Ava was safe and happy, knowing she was loved, and that Morgan experienced the same in her relationships. Whether that was Jay, or if she eventually got back together with Jared.

Jay didn't want to pray that the guy never grew in his faith far enough to quit being a turd, but he should. He wanted to pray the guy messed up and Morgan chose Jay instead, but that wasn't fair.

He decided to sit on his prayers and let God do what He wanted to do.

Your will, Lord. Whatever it is.

The door swung open with no warning.

Morgan jumped back, tugging on his hand. He ignored how much that hurt his shoulder. The pain meds they'd given him at the hospital were wearing off, and all the poking and prodding they'd done—and the stitches—were starting to seriously hurt.

Two men pushed their way in, guns pointed at Morgan.

The first said, "One wrong move, and she gets her brains splattered on the wall. Got it?"

Jay squeezed down on his molars. He nodded.

The gunman dragged out Morgan.

Jay followed her, and the second man shoved his gun in Jay's back. "That's getting old."

"Give me a reason to pull this trigger, and we'll be done with this whole charade."

Anthony Montbatten stood in the middle of the barn. "Neither of you will do that until I get what I want." He spoke as if he had all the authority. And more surprisingly, the local thugs obeyed him.

Jay glanced over his shoulder. "He pays pretty well, huh."

"Now that you ruined the business, gotta earn money somehow." He sneered at Jay.

Montbatten unfolded the newspaper under his arm.

Dressed like the locals, he could fit in here in Breckenrow just fine. Unless a person looked too closely and realized the labels were designer. The clothes were a little too...clean. Not quite lived in. His entire demeanor was as stiff as the starch in his checkered shirt.

Montbatten shoved the newspaper at Jay, hitting his shoulder in the process. "Smile for the camera."

Jay didn't look at it.

Someone wanted proof of life—or he was going to back up what he said with photo evidence. And he was going to use Jay's phone to send it.

"Now, which of these contacts is your boss, huh?" He showed Jay the screen.

As if Jay didn't know that every contact in his cell was a number or lettered code, and he needed to see it for himself.

"Unless you're prepared to tell me where to find Nathan Kessler."

Here it was. Jay wasn't sure, in the heat of the moment, how to play this. "Who?"

Montbatten smirked. "Sure. You have no idea."

Jay shrugged. "Above my paygrade."

"I'm sure it is. That's why you're going to call your boss."

Jay didn't glance around. He didn't look at Morgan, or the man still pointing a gun at her face. He stared down Anthony Montbatten.

Morgan probably had no idea what this was. But he couldn't let her feelings affect him, or his judgment about what to do here. She didn't live in his world. But she was the kind of woman who made him want to live in hers. It would gamble everything he was to make it work, but he had a feeling it would be worth it.

"I give you his number"—he motioned toward Morgan but still didn't look at her—"you let her go."

"A big tough guy like you, I figured you'd need to be persuaded." Montbatten ducked his head toward the phone, typing.

"You could just give me what I want," Jay said. "Let her go."

"You just hope your boss is in the mood to give me what I want."

Montbatten lifted his chin. "Or you both die, and none of us get what we want."

That was why he wanted this guy to let Morgan go. He'd still have all the leverage he needed to get Noah to find Kessler and release him. This had to be about freeing the man they'd captured a few months back.

Too bad Noah knew there was a bigger plan in the works. Whoever Kessler worked for, it wasn't Montbatten. It was definitely someone else. Senator Chalmers, perhaps? They'd had intel about him along with evidence Kessler was involved.

But who was the tip of this spear?

And what did they want?

Jay prayed that Morgan didn't have to lose her life in order for the world to find out.

The phone rang.

"Guess he cares about you after all."

Jay stared at Montbatten, who put the phone to his ear.

"You know who I am."

Jay clenched his teeth and prayed. God hadn't given him a spirit of fear. Power. Love. A sound mind.

The power came from God.

Love sacrificed all.

He needed a sound mind, and thankfully, it was perfectly clear right now.

It was up to him to get Morgan out of here. No matter what, she had to be protected.

"To whom am I speaking?" Montbatten asked. A second later, he said, "Noah Rourke." His eyes flared.

Yep. He recognized the name of Jay's boss.

And Jay knew then that the guy had sense but no brains. If he was smart, he'd have hung up the phone right away and walked out the door. Called it quits on this entire situation.

He clearly wanted Nathan Kessler badly enough that he ignored that the stakes were now so much higher.

Jay worked on the team because if he didn't, he might one day find himself on the opposite side from Noah. And that was a bad place to be—with a short life expectancy.

"Is that right?" Montbatten said.

He crossed the distance to Jay and jabbed out with his fist. A knife went into Jay's shoulder, and Montbatten pulled it out before Jay even realized what had happened.

He sucked in a breath, his knee gave out, and he caught himself with a hand on the floor. Breathing hard.

Listening to Morgan scream.

"Explain." Montbatten put the phone to his ear.

Jay was supposed to tell his boss that he just got stabbed? "Albuquerque," he managed.

Montbatten moved the phone away and kicked Jay in the chest. "Your man is going to die for that. And so is the woman."

The man holding Morgan dragged her back to the storage room while she screamed and struggled against him.

Jay started to stand.

And got kicked in the stomach.

He rolled with the momentum, farther away than they'd be expecting. Used his legs and got his feet under him. Stood up.

Determined to face these guys on his feet.

His shoulder was a mess, but that didn't count him out.

The gunman came at Jay, who kicked out and caught the guy's knee—not taking him down, but that blow from Jay's boot would hurt.

"Stop playing around," Montbatten said, shifting the phone away from his ear. "Take care of him already."

The guy rushed Jay, who planted his feet and grappled with his good arm. Turning his body so that his messed-up shoulder wasn't facing his attacker.

Still hurt.

He cried out.

The guy stomped on the back of his leg.

Montbatten said, "Very well. We have an agreement." Then, "Put him with the woman."

Something hard hit the side of Jay's face, and he collapsed.

🐾

Morgan didn't have a lot of self-defense skills in her arsenal. But she'd used as many as she could, and thrown in some random ones, making things up and getting creative purely out of self-preservation.

After all, the situation called for it.

The man who'd dragged her in here stumbled back, crying out. Touching his eye where she'd jabbed him as hard as she could. He cursed at her, calling her a horrible name.

"How rude. I'm not attacking you, I'm just defending myself."

Before he could counter her argument, the door opened and another man dragged Jay inside the room. "Quit playing around."

They both left, shutting and locking the door.

Jay lay still on the ground.

Was he dead?

Morgan rushed to him. "Please, please."

He rolled to his back, his eyes closed. She leaned down and listened to his nose and mouth, looking at his chest. She saw the steady rise, then fall. "Thank You, God."

She wanted to be selfless, but she also didn't want to be here alone. She needed Jay. Not only because he knew what he was doing —and understood the gravity of the situation. But also because she needed *him*.

There had to be a reason God had brought him into her life. Maybe because without him, she would've been forced to work for Marco—Montbatten. Whatever his name was. She'd have been co-opted into being his veterinarian and given no choice but to comply. She'd have seen the previous vet buried in a shallow grave, then threatened into keeping her mouth shut.

She would've protected her family and done whatever they asked.

Instead, thanks to the fact that God had intervened, she was with Jay and her daughter had Caleb and the best dog in the world looking out for her.

She reached for Jay and started to shake his shoulder, but stopped.

He was unconscious, and would be in far greater pain if she woke him up. Yes, she might need him, but it was better if he woke up on his own.

Morgan prayed through the quiet moments, scooting to the door to try to see...something through a crack. Anything. She found a knot in the wood that had created a natural hole and peered out.

In the main area of the barn, Montbatten gave orders to his two guys. The one who'd decided he was going to get handsy with her and the man who had hurt Jay. Of course, the boss had no intention of getting his hands dirty.

She had realized when he was talking to Jay that something about this was beyond what she knew. Even Jay had said it was, *Above his paygrade.* She figured he'd been trying to play dumb, to an extent. Not giving Montbatten what he wanted.

To her it had seemed like a conversation where so much more was said without words.

Then again, if any of them were in an emergency situation with her and any of her vet techs, they wouldn't understand any of it.

"I want my life back," she whispered to herself.

She watched Montbatten lift his chin, and one of the men strode out. All of them disgusted her with their actions, victimizing animals to make a profit. Doing it with no care for the pain they caused.

The fact it was going on in her town was worse. She didn't want this anywhere near where her daughter grew up.

When the police had cleaned it all up, she could do something to help the dogs heal and rehabilitate. Morgan wanted to discuss it with Jay, realizing after the thought that she had considered him before anyone else.

Because you've fallen for him.

Who wouldn't? And not just because she was in danger and he was a trained guy who could protect both of them—if he was conscious. It was because the guy was both strong and gentle. He cared, but he would stand fast and protect the people he considered worth dying for.

He encouraged her instead of tearing her down. He'd known outside the hardware store that Ava needed the reassurance of feeling safe and had told his dog to "guard" her. Morgan had been hurt, and he'd taken care of her in a way that no one ever had.

She wanted to know if it could last forever, but was still too scared to voice it aloud. To ask for what she wanted.

The desire of her heart.

Montbatten turned and left the barn, leaving the wide doors open at the far end.

A cool air blew through the big room and dried her eyes.

Morgan sat back, blinking, and looked around. Another way out of here would be great, but she didn't usually see miracles in her regular life.

Maybe she would today, because things were life-or-death right now.

At least Ava was all right.

Morgan got up and stretched the stiffness out of her limbs. Jay was stirring. When he woke up, she could have a plan of action. Probably not, but optimism was a whole lot less depressing.

He moaned. She left him to it and traced her way around the outside of the storage room, feeling the wood boards on the walls. Pushing against them at intervals. Working her way around the perimeter.

"Morgan."

"I'm finding a way out," she said. "How are you feeling?"

He only groaned.

"Yeah, I figured." This wood board gave a little under the pressure of her push. "Hello."

She pushed some more, and it gave at the bottom. Not enough to crawl through.

She knelt and pushed against it with her shoulder, shoving the vertical board as hard as she could. The wood groaned, and she felt it give a little more. Probably prying nails out. "Come on. I need a hole big enough for a big guy to crawl out."

Jay eased over, dragging his weight across the floor with his legs and one arm.

"You should've stayed over there. That looked like it took far too much effort."

"If I stand up, I'll fall over." Jay motioned her to the side. "Let me try."

Morgan wasn't so sure, but shifted herself back.

He pulled his knees to his chest and hammered his boots into the wall. Once, then higher up the vertical panel. The wood splintered and didn't come back to its starting position—it stuck out now.

"You did it!"

"Don't get too excited. Getting out this way might get you in more trouble."

"You mean *us*. And I'm not going to sit here and not even try to escape. If something happens to me, it'll be because I was making a run for it and got in trouble."

"You think I'm going to watch that happen again?"

Morgan couldn't argue. He didn't want to watch her get shot in the back, trying to escape. "I don't want to be shot either. But I'm not being a victim. I'll sneak out instead of running. I'll bide my time and be smart instead of scared."

Jay stared at her with an odd look on his face.

"And I won't be alone. You'll be there to be smart and escapey with me."

His lips curled up, almost like he wanted to laugh. Seeing that was worth it. More than anything she'd been given in a long time, the gift of getting him to relax enough to be amused.

Jared had seen her as…she didn't know what. Fulfilling a role. Housekeeper, plus mother—which to him meant doing most of the parenting. She was doing that now, but without the hassle of resenting him for not helping out.

She doubted he had ever delighted in her. He'd only been concerned with what she could do *for* him. Not who she was.

She lifted her hand and touched Jay's cheek. "Wanna get out of here?"

When she did, she probably needed some therapy. Or Christian counseling at least. A way to get rid of the resentment of her failed first marriage. If she didn't let go of the hurt, it would poison everything in her future, and any relationship Ava might have with Jared.

"Everything okay?" Jay asked, scanning her face.

"Most things, sure. Everything? No," she replied, just needing to get back to her life. "I don't like being kidnapped."

"I don't like you being kidnapped either."

Morgan frowned. "But it's your job?"

"Let's talk about that later. Maybe over dinner."

"Maybe at my house, since we both look like our faces went a few rounds with someone's boot."

Jay chuckled. "Can you get out the gap between the boards?"

"I think so."

He pushed it open, and she found she could wiggle between. Out into the dark night. With no idea where she was. Surrounded by guys with guns.

Maybe this was a bad idea.

She turned back and grabbed the board. "Come on. See if you can squeeze through." She held the edges, ignoring the way it made her broken nose feel. Jay was hurt a lot more than her, and he wasn't complaining. He just quietly bled all over everything.

"Hey!" The muffled shout came from inside the storage room.

Jay yelled, "Go! Run!"

He was dragged back from the panel, crying out in pain.

Morgan didn't want to leave him, but she had to get him help. Or she had to fight for him, the way he fought for her.

She spotted a two-by-four against the outside wall. Beside that was a crowbar.

She winced. "I'm gonna get shot."

But there was no way she could leave him. Not when it might take hours to get help.

Morgan grabbed the crowbar. "Here goes nothin'." Then ran around the barn.

As she reached the open front doors, a gunshot rang out.

CHAPTER THIRTEEN

Jay was dragged by the legs back into the main room, then tossed around, and when he tried to kick out at the guy hauling him into the center of the room, that was when they shot him.

He'd never liked being shot.

Cue rolling to the side. And thankfully, God had given him some insight in his training, or he would never have seen it coming in time.

The bullet snapped past his ear.

That was too close.

But the point was that Morgan would be safe. She was making a run for it, leaving this place. Free. Alive.

"Are you deaf as well as stupid?" Montbatten roared. He shoved the guy who'd shot at Jay to the side, pulled out his own gun from the back of his belt, and pulled the trigger.

The local thug dropped to the ground, dead.

Thug number two just stared, not happy but unwilling to voice his opinion for fear of being shot like his friend. Brother. Cousin. Whoever they were to each other.

Montbatten said to the other guy, "Go find the woman. There are animals to take care of. As soon as my business with him is done, I want the vet working on the dogs we have left."

So the state police hadn't managed to get all of them. Montbatten still had a business, and he wanted to get it back up and running.

Jay lifted his chin. "She won't work for you."

Thug number two headed for the door, got two steps outside, and walked right into a piece of wood. Someone out of sight swung it around and slammed it into his head like it was a baseball bat.

The guy dropped.

Montbatten turned his back to Jay, who launched up and tackled him.

The element of surprise was always the best way to attack. It caught Montbatten off guard and gave Jay the edge he'd die without.

He punched Montbatten in the small of his back while the guy whipped around.

Montbatten slammed his hand back, holding his gun.

Jay grabbed the guy's wrist, even though that was his injured shoulder. Pain lanced through his arm, firing nerve endings in his fingers until he felt himself almost black out.

Morgan ran in. "Jay!"

Montbatten tried to aim the gun at her. Jay yelled, "No!"

She scrambled to the side and ducked out of sight.

Montbatten chased her with his gun, firing off shots trying to hit her as she ran.

Jay yelled, "No!" again as Morgan screamed.

Cass bounded into the barn, raced over, and jumped at Montbatten. Then multiple people rushed in the door, yelling words Jay's mind couldn't understand.

Montbatten shoved at Cass, but she chomped down on his arm. Jay hit the ground.

A gun went off.

Then another.

Then so many the sound swirled around him.

Familiar faces washed in front of his face. "Hey, buddy. Nice vacation?"

Jay stared at his team leader, Nix.

Where was Noah? Seemed like everyone was here.

Jay looked around.

"I don't think he's glad to see us." Ice glanced at Kai. "Probably interrupted his good time."

"Cass." He managed to croak the word.

"Seems like she cares more about that woman than she cares about you." He tore open a bandage and pressed it against Jay's shoulder. "Geez, you're a mess, buddy."

Jay's eyes rolled back in his head, but he managed to keep from passing out.

He turned his head and looked at Morgan, holding on to Cass like she was a lifeline. The dog almost completely in her lap.

Jay looked at the ceiling again.

Kai glanced back over his shoulder. "Do we have the helicopter?" After a pause, he said, "Then we may need a transfusion on route."

Kai and Ice strapped him up with so many bandages Jay's shoulder wound up twice the size it should be.

When they lifted him up to sitting, he got a look at Montbatten, covered in blood and bullet holes. Staring up at the ceiling with unseeing eyes. "Cover him up. Morgan doesn't need to see that."

She had buried her head in Cass's fur, and Jay didn't blame her. It was a good place to be.

Ice got a foil emergency blanket, shook it out, and covered the dead man.

"How did you guys know where I was?" Jay asked.

"Followed your GPS signal, dummy," Kai replied. "Montbatten is an idiot if he was trying to hide you. Seems more like he wanted to be found."

"He wanted Kessler," Jay said.

Ice shot him a frown, then looked away. "Noah!"

Caleb's twin broke off from a conversation with Jay's team leader—Nix—and strode over.

Ice said, "Repeat your last."

Jay was ready to pass out, but pushed the feeling to one side. "Montbatten wanted to know where Kessler was."

Noah frowned. "None of us know where Kessler is. That's the point."

"Probably thought you could get to him." Jay looked at Morgan, still curled around Cass. "Morgan needs to get out of here so she can see Ava."

Kai said, "Who's Ava?"

"Her daughter."

"Dude," Kai said, dragging the word out. "She has a kid?"

"Can we go?" Jay said.

Ice chuckled. "Your ride is almost here. They're doing cleanup outside."

That meant more gunmen who weren't taken out yet. If the rest of the team had "cleanup," the situation wasn't safe.

His team was here, though. They were making it safe.

He'd told Morgan to run. She could've been killed, but he'd done it anyway. He'd done what was right in spite of his fears.

Thank You, Lord.

God had kept them safe.

Somewhere in the distance, gunfire rang out.

Ice and Kai both got distant looks at the same time, their heads turning slightly to listen to the comms channel in their earbuds.

All Jay could hear was ringing.

"Morgan." His voice sounded gruff, but there was nothing he could do about it.

She lifted her head from Cass's fur and looked at him.

"You okay?"

She nodded, a shell-shocked look on her face.

Jay tried to get up, and Kai and Ice both pushed him down.

"Bro." Ice shook his head.

"What are you doing?" Kai said.

Morgan sat beside him with her legs crossed. Facing him. "Are you okay?"

"Nothing that time won't mend." He shot Kai and Ice a look, telling them to get lost.

Neither of them moved. In fact, they just sat where they were. Grinning at him like this was the funniest situation they'd ever been in.

"Get Caleb on the phone." He didn't care who responded to his order, so long as Morgan got to talk to Ava.

Cass got up, shaking off from head to tail. She wandered to him, a distinct limp in her stride.

"Oh, girl. What did they do to you?" Jay scooped her one-armed onto his lap. His dog curled up, partly on him and partly on Morgan.

She ran a hand down Cass's side, slowing when the dog reacted to the injury. "Okay, baby." She palpated the area a little, but not too much. Still, she said, "I'm sorry. I know it hurts." She looked at Jay. "I need to get her to the office and examine her. She could be hurt."

"As soon as it's clear, we can go."

"No-go, dude." Ice sounded adamant. "You need surgery. Morgan can take care of Cass. Kai will go with her."

"I'm going." Jay wasn't going to take no for an answer.

Ice shook his head. "I'm going to update Noah. Only place you're going is the hospital."

Kai got up, too, going with them. Finally leaving Jay alone with his dog and the woman he...

Yeah.

That was a revelation on its own. He loved her. That was all there was too it.

"Are you really okay, Morgan?"

She leaned forward and put her head on his shoulder.

Jay kissed her hair.

"It was scary," she said, "but I didn't run. I faced them, and I did what I had to do."

The full force of what she'd done would hit her later, but she would be in a safe place when she fell apart. Surrounded by people who cared about her.

"You're safe," he said. "And you did amazing."

Morgan lifted her face. "I'm worried about Cass."

"Did he hit her?" Jay scanned his dog for injuries. "I didn't see."

"I don't know. But she shouldn't be this lethargic." Morgan paused. "Maybe something happened before she ran in."

Jay leaned over and touched his lips to hers, even though more than one of his teammates was watching. Then he yelled, "Someone get me Caleb!"

Finally, the guy strode in, parting the team like he was Israel in the Red Sea. "What is it? Life Flight is almost here to get you."

Jay didn't care about a chopper for himself. "Morgan needs to get Cass to her clinic."

Caleb nodded. "I'll have Tessa and Ava meet you there."

Morgan said, "We need to hurry. I think something might be wrong."

Cass stuck her tongue out and started to pant.

Caleb turned to the others. "Get them up. We're rolling out."

🐾

Six hours later, Morgan was beyond dead on her feet. But she was finished. She leaned down and kissed Cass on the forehead. "Sleep well."

She backed up from the dog and didn't bother locking the enclosure.

She found Tessa and Ava mopping the floor in her surgical suite, finishing up the cleaning. They were both singing a worship song, acting like the mop was a microphone stand.

Morgan leaned against the wall and watched them for a moment.

Ava spotted her. "Mommy!"

As if she hadn't seen her just a few minutes before, when she'd gone to transfer Cass to the enclosure where she would recover.

Morgan gave her daughter a hug. "Thank you for helping me today. You did a big job, and I think you should get paid for it."

Tessa wrung out the mop, smiling.

She didn't know that Morgan was going to treat her to a girls-only spa day. But for Ava? "I think we could get you those fancy sneakers you were asking for."

"Really? You said they were too expensive."

They were. "You earned them."

Ava beamed. "Yes!" She ran back to Tessa.

Morgan said, "I'm going to update everyone in the waiting room."

Tessa nodded.

Morgan stopped by the bathroom, as if slashing water on her face and smoothing back her hair would help fix the fact she still had a broken nose and puffy eyes.

She took off her lab coat and switched it out for the sweater she kept in her office, bundling up because it was chilly in here.

The waiting room was full of people. Most of them big guys who needed the maximum amount of strength they could comfortably maintain to do their jobs.

Her receptionist looked a bit nervous, but smiled at her. "Hey, Doc. How is she?"

Over by the seats, Jay stood. Pops did the same beside him. Both twins were here, Caleb and Noah. The rest of Jay's team. The ones who sent him out ahead of them so he could get intel. But they'd shown up when Jay needed them and saved both of their lives.

He wove between the other men and came to her.

Before he could ask, Morgan said, "She's okay. She must've been hit somehow, at some point. Her gallbladder ruptured, and it looked like it was trauma rather than infection. I fixed her up, and once she's awake, she'll be on the mend."

Jay let out a breath that visibly relaxed him.

"You can see her whenever you want, but she won't be awake for a few hours." She glanced at Caleb. "You can go help Tessa and Ava if you want."

Caleb headed to the back, followed by Noah and Pops.

The rest of the guys went outside to mill around, and her receptionist suddenly had copies to make.

Now that Morgan was alone in the waiting area, she found she was self-conscious. "Are you all right?" she asked Jay.

He had his arm in a sling again, and when he moved it was stiff. He led her to the chairs and she sat turned toward him.

"Jay?"

"I'm better hearing that Cass will be okay. But I'm not really all right."

Morgan shook her head, silently asking the question.

"The doctor took a look at my shoulder and said I need surgery," he continued. "The knife did serious damage to my subscapularis tendon. It's part of the rotator cuff. They need to put it back together."

"What does that mean for your work?" Surely, he wouldn't want a long healing period. Jay wasn't the kind of guy who sat around doing nothing. Though, that was precisely what Cass needed.

"It means I need a year before I'm fully operational. Months of physical therapy. If I want to get back to peak performance, it'll be a long road."

She touched his knee. "I'm sorry."

"Thanks." He laid his good hand over hers, his arm across his body. "I'm still grasping what it means." He glanced at the glass front doors.

"What?"

"The guys think it's a sign from God that I should stay here. That both Cass and I should recover under your 'watchful eye.'"

Morgan smiled. "But you'd rather go home, I'm guessing."

"I have an apartment. I wouldn't call it a home." He looked at her. "I don't want to bombard you with something huge after the past few days. But the truth is, I'd like nothing more than to be here in Breckenrow for a while. Under your 'watchful eye.'"

Morgan raised her eyebrows. "I'd like that as well. And you promised me a dinner."

"I did."

She wanted a whole lot more than that as far as promises went. But he was right—it was too soon after the past few days, and everything that had happened.

"How is Ava doing?" Jay asked.

"She was safe with Caleb, and he took her to Tessa," Morgan replied. "Now she's getting to do her favorite thing—pitch in here at the clinic. I promised her the shoes she's been asking me for as a thanks for helping out."

"What is Jared going to say when he finds out you've got her cleaning up here?"

Morgan winced. "I don't want to know. But I also don't want to borrow problems from the future."

"Right. Sorry."

She shook her head. "Whatever happens, she deserves to have a relationship with her father. I just hope he doesn't mess it up."

"We can pray that her heart is protected, no matter what. But the world isn't a safe place."

Morgan looked at him. "Sitting next to you is the safest place I can be. At least, that's how it feels."

"Good."

And if her daughter came to feel the same way about having Jay around, and his dog, that would be a blessing. If she got the same feeling from Jared—all the more blessing for Ava. She wanted only love and warmth for her child, but Jay was right. Protecting her from everything and everyone that might hurt her, just in case, wasn't going to help her grow up with strength.

"I want so much for Ava," Morgan said. "I want her to be strong in the Lord, and go to Him when she needs safety. But I also know that He puts people in our lives that help us. Stand with us. Who are willing to give everything to help us feel safe."

She almost wanted to apologize that her life wasn't simple. She came with baggage—an ex-husband, and issues she needed to work through. But the reality was, no one in the world could be completely free of the past.

"I fell in love with you back there."

She twisted to look at Jay and gasped. There in his expression was the truth of his words.

"I wanted to give you everything," he continued. "The good and the bad. And I knew you were someone the Lord brought into my life to help me. To reassure me. To settle me. To give me confidence, and a reason to keep going. To be the man God wants me to be." He paused. "And in return I could give you all the love you're looking for. Someone to shoulder the load you carry. To help you feel settled, and confident. Reassured."

Tears rolled down her face.

This man was all the things she hadn't dared dream she might find. Part of her didn't even believe it was possible. But he was here, and if she trusted what he offered, she might gain everything she'd been looking for.

"Jay..." She hardly knew what to say.

He let go of her hand to swipe away a tear. "Thank you. For everything."

"I want you to recover here." She winced. "My house is probably toast from that fire, but I'll sell it or rebuild."

His mouth softened into a smile.

"I don't want you to leave."

"Maybe I'll enjoy recovery so much I'll get a job here. I could help dogs who need it. Train them. Rehab them."

Morgan smiled. "I was thinking the same thing in that barn. They need us."

But getting ahead of herself wasn't going to help her take it slow.

"However it works out, I'm glad you came here, Jay."

"So am I."

"Because you're an amazing man. The kind any woman would be an idiot not to fall in love with." She leaned into his touch on her cheek. "And the rest of them can back off. Because you're mine."

His eyes flared.

Morgan leaned in and kissed him. "For however long we can make it last. Hopefully forever."

"Count on it."

She liked the idea of putting the work in, making it good between them. She liked that a lot. "You've got yourself a deal, Mister."

Jay tugged her toward him and kissed her, which hurt, but she didn't care. He leaned his forehead against hers. "Thank you for taking care of my dog."

"Mommy, can I have—" Ava skidded to a stop and looked at them. "Is Jay your boyfriend now?"

Behind her, Caleb, Noah, and Tessa looked on as if this was the funniest thing they'd ever seen.

"If I say yes, how would you feel about that?"

Ava rushed over and hugged Jay. "Can I adopt Cass? Can she be my dog now?"

He looked down at her, so much love in his eyes it blew Morgan away. "She can be *our* dog."

"Yes!" Ava jumped up and down and clapped. "I'm gonna go draw her a picture."

Morgan laid her head gently on his shoulder. "Get used to that tornado coming around."

He kissed her hair. "Sounds like an adventure."

ABOUT LISA PHILLIPS

Find out more about Lisa Phillips at her website, where you'll discover more romantic suspense fan-favorite series and heart-pounding thriller novels.
https://authorlisaphillips.com/

Signup for Lisa's newsletter by scanning the QR code below to stay updated on sales, new releases, and recommendations for your TBR pile. New Subscribers even get a FREE book!

Find Lisa on Social Media!

facebook.com/authorlisaphillips

instagram.com/lisaphillipsbks

bookbub.com/authors/lisa-phillips

amazon.com/stores/Lisa-Phillips/author/B00HZSOSOO

BOUND BY EVIDENCE

KARI TRUMBO

CHAPTER ONE

Sherlock sat at Chris Johnstone's feet, his German shepherd energy like a coiled spring. He didn't have to give the dog any orders to sit still. Sherlock would do exactly what was expected until given the order to work. Sergeant Leo Colder steepled his fingers in front of him and took a deep breath. His dark brown eyes bored into Chris with more seriousness than he'd shown to this point. He'd begun to believe Leo had asked him here just to meet the dog.

"You can't say a word about this. If Marin finds out we found this, she'll spiral and we'll never find out who killed Alyssa. If Marin ends up finding you, because she's out there looking right now, you need to convince her Sherlock is on a search and rescue mission. That's it."

While Sherlock was dual-trained for both searches and bodies, the way the dog acted during those searches was totally different. It didn't even take a trained eye to tell the difference. "You're sure her sister is dead? How?" He'd understood he was there for rescue, not recovery.

Generally speaking, his dog was rare. Either dogs looked for the dead or the living, not both. Some dogs were both drug sniffers and search and rescue. Some dogs that were dual-trained were bomb and drug sniffers. Sherlock was uniquely trained to search for both the living and the dead. He'd won awards for being equally good at search and rescue as he was at recovery.

The room seemed to shrink as the sergeant took a plastic bag from his desk. Sherlock leaned subtly forward, as if he sensed it too. The bag held a blue jean shirt, stiff and stained in blood. Through the clear plastic, he saw the embroidered name on the front placket, the name *Alyssa* in scrolling gold lettering stood out against the deep blue denim.

"We're fairly certain with the gunshot hole placed where it is and the amount of blood on this shirt, she's dead. There are no other missing women with that name. I've sent a sample of the blood off for testing. We'll confirm our suspicions soon enough. We don't know the motive and Marin is convinced Alyssa had no enemies. Unfortunately, we can't disregard this evidence." He put the bag on the desk in front of Chris.

While a monogrammed shirt might seem like a great clue, those ended up at thrift stores all the time. Plausibility didn't equate to fact. This suddenly felt like he'd been called in to 'accidentally' tell her about the death of her sister. He was not the guy to inform someone they'd lost a close family member, and he didn't want to be the guy who told someone incorrectly their sister was dead. His job usually came into play when people already knew their family member had passed or when they were missing and needed to be found. Most people in his position never had that choice.

"I don't work with detectives. I work with Sherlock, that's it. If I see her, I won't be working with her. That's what we agreed to when you called me." He glanced down at his trusty partner. He'd worked with human partners before. No, thank you. Never again.

Leo laughed. "Sherlock, huh?" He leaned forward, his face melting to the look of a father about to make a decision he knew would hurt. "Look, you and I both know Marin shouldn't be anywhere near this case. It's a conflict of interest and it's going to gut her when she finds out the truth. That's partly why you're here. If we can get this over quickly, all the better. Then I can give her a little time off to grieve.

"If I had any other detectives, she wouldn't be working this case. But there's the issue. I don't. She's the only investigator I have. The moment her sister came up missing, she's been unstoppable, working around the clock. So, I know you think I'm rotten for not telling her, but she'll actively be looking for clues while you're hunting for a body."

Great. They'd be at odds from the start, and he'd end up being the one to break the news to her. Yup, this was a pass the buck mission.

"Are you telling me she's going to be shadowing me and making things difficult for me and the dog? These dogs have a ninety-five percent success rate. If Alyssa is out there in the area we search, we'll find her. Is that *really* where you want Marin to be? Isn't there something she can be doing here in the office, at least for today? It's why I work alone."

"She's out there right now, looking. If I intervene and stop her, she'll know something is up. I can't do that to her." His gaze fell on Chris's ear and stayed there.

He didn't want to know how Leo understood that to be a fact or that the shirt absolutely belonged to Alyssa Bayless. That wasn't his department. He had to rely on the work done before he was called in on the case. Hopefully, the lab would have answers soon. In a usual case, he didn't deal with evidence. Even having the shirt could make finding the body more difficult, not less. Especially if they weren't certain it was hers.

Sherlock had been through four years of intense training to sniff out the scent of human decay. That was how they differentiated a recovery from a rescue. In rescues, he often tried to use scents the living left behind. With a body, the dog looked for the scent released by decay.

"That shirt is all well and good, but I won't use it. Where was she last seen and how long has she been missing?"

Leo rolled his eyes. "You say missing as if you don't believe me. We found the shirt yesterday. It was still . . . damp. She went missing a week prior to that."

Just because he wasn't an officer under this sergeant didn't mean he had to be treated like he was squeamish. Calling the shirt 'damp' was an understatement. "And location?"

"One of my patrol officers found it in the park. Clearly, she was assaulted and then the body was moved because he saw nothing there besides the shirt. No blood or any other evidence. She went missing from the local bowling alley where she worked."

The deep blue denim looked crunchy within the bag, like it had been drenched and was now drying. The sergeant was right about one thing: if that was Alyssa's shirt, she likely hadn't survived the attack.

"I assume you've already searched the rest of the park visually?"

Sergeant Colder leaned back in his chair. "Yes, I had the uniformed officer who found the shirt walk around the perimeter and do a search. You understand I have to be careful here. If Marin finds out what I'm doing, I'm out a detective, my *only* detective."

Obviously, Leo worried about being without Marin. Meaning he probably heaped a lot of cases on her. She would end up feeling too guilty about missing work to take the time off she would need to process the loss of her sister. That illustrated the life of an LEO.

He wasn't about to disrupt another department, but his own sergeant wouldn't break protocol and trick one of his investigators into working a case. If Marin's sister was deceased, she deserved the time off to deal with the loss. She absolutely shouldn't be working on it.

He made no promises he couldn't keep. "I'll leave that in your possession, so you don't have to worry about the evidentiary chain of command. We'll get to work, and I'll let you know what he finds." He glanced down at Sherlock. "Hopefully quickly." He stood and Sherlock immediately stood in tandem with him.

"Godspeed." Leo held a finger to his forehead in a lazy salute.

Sherlock stayed at Chris's side as they walked through the building. It was quite a bit smaller than his own. He lived and worked in Cheyenne, WY, which was about three hours north of Poplar Bend, where he was now, helping a force that had no K9 officers.

"What are *you* doing here?" A woman's sharp voice drew him up short.

He paused, since he'd seen no one else in the hallway. "Me?" He wasn't used to being talked to in that tone by anyone on the force.

"Yeah, you. What are you doing here?"

A petite woman stepped out of the shadows of a doorway. She wore dark blue jeans similar in color to the shirt in Sergeant Colder's office along with a white tee and a blazer with ¾ sleeves. She crossed her arms, and he noticed her clipped-on security badge to access the building. It read *Bayless*. He'd hoped to get out into the park and start working before he had to talk to Marin. Could this day get any worse?

He kept his voice low in case any other officers listened in behind closed doors. "I've been asked by Sergeant Colder to do a search."

Likely, she hadn't heard of him or his dog, and she wouldn't realize he wasn't on a search and rescue mission. Since many officers, even investigators, didn't know the ins and outs of handling a K9, she might not know what was going on. He could hope, anyway.

"You're here to find Alyssa? Leo said he wasn't going to waste resources to find her. I'm so glad he relented. I'm leaving in ten minutes to do a search of the area around her apartment. You can come with me."

"Wait, no. I don't work with anyone else, and I'm not headed to her apartment." He held up his hand to stop her in her tracks. The likelihood of finding her there after she'd been missing for over a week was none. If Marin went with him, she'd know within minutes

Sherlock wasn't looking for an injured woman who needed to be found. This interaction alone was far above his pay grade.

"What do you mean? I have all the information on the case. We've already done grid searches throughout town. You can't just open your car door and let your dog run all over town, hunting for a stray scent. What if he finds something and destroys other evidence in the process?"

Little did she know he was generally given a search perimeter and stuck to it. Sherlock did exactly that, and he was very good at it. He never touched anything besides marking where the living or the dead could be found.

"I still work alone. I'm sorry. I'll let you know whatever I find." That had to be the end of talking to this woman. He turned to walk away.

"Not in my town and not on my case." She reached in her pocket and drew out a large set of keys then caught up to him. "I'll get my car and show you what I know. I'm Marin, by the way." She held out her hand as she kept pace with him.

"Chris," he said as his stomach twisted. This day looked to be one of the worst in his life. For once, he prayed his dog failed at this job.

❧

Why did Leo have to ask *that* handler to look for her sister? Marin peered down at the massive German shepherd with his black tactical vest marking him as an officer. She'd wanted to work with a K9 so badly when she'd started that she'd researched all the dogs and their handlers in Wyoming, hoping to eventually be one of them. This one was about as famous a pair as Wyoming could have.

Leo couldn't have asked Chris to use Sherlock as a cadaver dog. No, this was a search and rescue mission until she was told otherwise. Unless he had information he wasn't passing on to her. . . She pressed the button on her keyring to unlock her cruiser. If Leo had hidden facts from her, she would soon find out.

"I don't think you told me. Where were you planning to search?" All he'd told her so far was that he wasn't looking at Alyssa's apartment.

"The park. Generally. No specific area." He didn't turn his face to look at her. His profile was strong, his jaw clear of any stubble. He had a deep scar down his right cheek. She forced herself to quit staring and watch her steps.

"Well, what area of the park would you like to start your search? There's the picnic side, the area for skateboards, not to mention the walking trails. . ." The answer to that question might give her insight into what Chris knew.

"The whole park," he answered, sharing nothing more with her and sounding annoyed she spoke to him.

He opened the back door and patted the bench seat. Sherlock stepped into her vehicle without the slightest hint of a jump and sat, looking bored like this happened all the time. Chris affixed a lead to Sherlock's vest and clicked it into the seatbelt buckle. Safely locking him in.

She bit her lip and tried to make her voice sound like when she spoke to her sister, not a fellow officer. One who was increasingly annoyed by her presence. "What do you hope to find? I know there was a uniformed officer searching the perimeter early this morning. His car was out there when I drove by on my way to work. I didn't think it had to do with this case, but Leo informed me they'd received a tip and were following through with it."

And that's where the information had ended. Leo refused to share what the officer had found with her, if anything. He'd always been good to her as a boss, but this case had her wondering if he was on her side at all.

"Did the officer find something? Is that why you're here?" If she could make herself humble and let him know she hadn't been given the information, he might share it. Then again, she'd told him she had all the evidence for *her* case . . . The more she thought about it, the more sure she was he hadn't been called in that morning. The drive from Cheyenne was three hours. He had to have been called the day before.

"It's just a hunch. Nothing more." He closed the back door and came around to the passenger side.

As soon as he settled in, she started the car and ambled it toward the town park. Alyssa had to be alive. She had to. Her sister was all she had left. Their parents had separated from them the moment Alyssa graduated high school. It had been like a divorce. They'd stopped communicating with their daughters and after a year of silence, Alyssa and Marin had assumed they wanted nothing to do with their children anymore. They had no other family nearby.

She pulled into a sunny parking spot, glad for the warmth. The late-May sunshine could be balmy one minute and frigid the next. Wyoming was like that in the spring. She watched Chris get out of the car and head back around for his dog. He was tall and rangy, like he might have been a cowboy when he was younger. Then again, that could be the cowboy hat giving her that clue. His sandy brown hair barely brushed his ears. If there were more officers like him, she might agree to having a partner.

A hot jolt ran through her brain, stopping her thoughts. She refused to think of him in that way. He was just a guy from far away who would help her find her sister. End of story. She gathered her evidence collection kit from the trunk and met Chris in front of the car.

He frowned as he glanced around the park. "I work alone. I feel like I've said that one hundred times today, and it keeps getting ignored."

She couldn't help grinning. "That's small-town police work for you. We always need more help. We're so used to offering assistance to everyone else that we don't take no for an answer anymore."

He turned away from her, clearly not warmed by her attempt at joviality. "That's great. I'm sure it makes for fun holiday parties, but that's not why I'm here. I need space, and so does Sherlock. If you want me to find your sister, you'll need to follow my rules."

Her spine stiffened at his words. She'd worked hard for a lot of years to get where she was. Women didn't generally make it into the role of investigator at all. In such a small jurisdiction, it was almost unheard of. How dare he strip her of all credibility? This was her case.

"Are you insinuating I can't do my job or that I'm not needed? I would beg to differ on both counts." She crossed her arms and waited for him to answer.

Instead of giving her the satisfaction of a good argument, he headed off into the park with his dog so close to his side she was sure they'd trip over each other. She held tight to her kit as she jogged after him.

"Hold on. Are you looking at the whole park or one specific place? Remind me again?"

He glanced over his shoulder. "Alone."

She wanted to like this guy if she had to work with him, but he wasn't helping matters. "Yeah, I get it. Do you wear a mask and appear when a light shows up in the sky, too?"

He glanced over his shoulder and narrowed his eyes at her. "For a woman who wants to get her sister back, you certainly aren't acting as if this is urgent."

Cold like ice water fell down her neck and back. He was right. Blast him for pointing it out. She'd been so sure exactly what she needed to do that she hadn't counted on the disruption of a K9 and his handler.

"Fine. I've got a few leads to check on at her apartment, where I was headed in the first place. I'll be back in an hour." She glanced at her watch.

How could she leave when he might find something? No, he wouldn't. If he found anything in the park, that would mean Alyssa was gone. She couldn't be dead. Alyssa was closer than a sister. They were like twins. They finished each other's sentences. Hot tears that she hadn't allowed herself to shed collected in her eyes. She wouldn't wipe them until she was safely in her car, away from this man's sight. He's probably assume that was typical behavior from a woman officer.

She unlocked her cruiser and sat in the driver's seat for a second, waiting for her eyes to clear and watching Sherlock pace around between a few trees with his nose to the ground. Nothing seemed to slow him down. He was clearly working, but there wasn't anything in that area to make him point.

In the next instant, the dog froze, nose to the ground, perfectly still, like a living arrow stuck to the ground. She'd never seen a dog stand so motionless. Even his tail stayed on point. Chris glanced over at her for a long moment, his face guarded, but she could see the worry there. Then, he headed out to check on what the dog had found.

Lord, please. Please, not Alyssa. I don't mean to be selfish, but I can't lose my sister. I don't feel like she's gone. I know you don't work that way.

A bark brought her out of her prayers. Sherlock was now bounding toward the car, obviously happy with himself. Chris held a paper evidence bag in one hand and had his phone in the other. As soon as he opened the back door, she had to know.

"What did you find?"

He frowned. "Before we get into that, can I use your evidence kit? I had plastic bags, gloves, paper bags, and my phone to document the scene before touching anything but I didn't have the ability to mark the bags."

"Sure. More talking while you're writing," she encouraged him to share.

He snorted. "Give me a minute. I'm a one thing at a time kind of guy."

She wasn't sure how she'd known that, but it had been evident when she'd noticed him in the hall back at the station. He had purpose. Drive. Meaning he probably lived the same way, with singular focus.

The moment he finished marking the evidence and putting it in her collection kit to bring back to the station, he put Sherlock in the rear seat. He came around and buckled himself in. By then, Marin was ready to wrap her fingers around his neck and shake the truth out of him.

"So?"

He let out a soft breath. "So, I'll have to come back out with a CSI team. This kind of thing is outside Sherlock's scope. It wasn't your sister. At least, there was no body there in the park. But I did find a bloodied shirt very similar to the one in your boss's office. Does the name Cami mean anything to you?"

Cami was Alyssa's best friend. They both worked together, but what he'd said first choked her words. "Yeah, I know her. Why? And what do you mean, 'similar to the one in my boss's office'?"

He frowned and closed his eyes for a second. "First, just know that a piece of clothing doesn't mean anything. It isn't a body."

Why was he saying this? Dark shadows rimmed her vision, making her blink quickly, and take deep breaths of air to keep from passing out. She reached for her phone and pressed Cami's number. It rang six times before the voicemail kicked in. Cami was one of those people who brought her phone into the bathroom. She set it next to her pillow. Cami didn't miss a phone call. Ever.

"We need to go check on her."

"I think that's a great place to start."

CHAPTER TWO

Chris stared straight ahead as Marin drove. She seemed to finally understand that he didn't want to talk. It wasn't that he didn't like her or even that he didn't think she was capable. He didn't want to have to tell her what her boss should have. Leo's avoidance was grossly negligent and frankly made Chris angry. Marin gave and gave to her department, and they thanked her like this?

Marin pulled to a stop in the spot she'd left not twenty minutes before. She turned the key toward her and let her hands fall into her lap. "I know there's something you're not telling me. I'm not a betting person, but I'm guessing you're here because my boss believes my sister is dead. Can you at least tell me if that much is true?"

He refused to lie to her face. That wasn't his way. "That is what he believes. I haven't seen evidence that would convince me of the same, but he seems sure."

She bowed her head and closed her eyes in what looked like prayer. He'd done his fair share of that on the way to the park. He never let himself get close to cases. His chest constricted as memories assaulted him. There were good reasons to avoid conflicts of interest in law enforcement. He'd gotten burned in every way.

"Can you tell me what he found? Was it that shirt you mentioned?" Her voice was strong, but there was a quality to it that made him want to be as gentle as possible.

Sherlock whined from the back seat and nosed Marin's elbow. Marin jumped, then looked at Chris. He knew that look, the one that asked without words if it was okay to pet the K9. He looked at Sherlock, who had done such a good job. He deserved a little break and some attention. If he wanted to support Marin right now, who was he to stop the dog?

"Rest."

The moment he gave the command, Sherlock gave a full-on whine and nosed her elbow enough to jostle it off the armrest.

She unbuckled, then turned in her seat to scratch Sherlock's neck. In the next instant, the dog had climbed up on the center console, like he did in Chris's car, and pressed his fuzzy head into Marin's chest. He heard the soft, controlled breaths that said she was trying to sob quietly enough he wouldn't hear. She probably thought he'd think she was weak. On the contrary, the fact that she could still have emotions after working on the force that long spoke volumes about her fortitude.

"If it helps, I don't believe his theory until I see more proof. I'm going to wait until we hear back from the lab. One of his officers found a shirt identical to the one I found, except it had the name Alyssa on it. According to Leo, it was found at seven this morning, and I was called in immediately. Likely, I was called in to shorten this case because you're too close to it. This could destroy you."

She didn't respond right away and closed her eyes. He hated waiting and wanted to get the evidence into Leo's custody right away, but this was important too. This was a fellow officer who was about to go through something very similar to what he had. He wanted to offer help or a listening ear . . . or maybe just a dog who was safe.

"I appreciate that you've held out hope." She reached into the small front pocket of her blazer and dabbed at her eyes with a tissue that had clearly been used for the same purpose earlier.

"I wouldn't call it hope as much as instinct. I've been wrong before, but this feels off. It's too blatant. Too in your face. Plus, why leave the shirt there and not the body? Whoever is doing this knows you're on the case and they want you out. They want you to believe she's dead, so you'll walk away to grieve. There are two things I can't figure out. Why didn't the officer see this when he looked this morning? The second is, why the coworker?"

Marin shrugged a shoulder. "Officers miss things. Just like everyone else. As to Cami, they were best friends. Cami tagged along when Alyssa and I would go places, but I didn't know her that well. I understand why you want to drop off that evidence first, but I will be heading over to her apartment next. I was given a key and told I could go in at any time, so that's what I'm going to do."

"Don't you think we should get a warrant first? What if you find something, then can't admit it in court because you didn't follow the proper protocols?"

Jules' voice mocked him from within with a pointedness only a former partner could. *You're such a legalist. You don't have to follow rules every minute of your life.*

"I'll talk to Leo, though he's got a lot of explaining to do and I'm not so sure I want to even hear his voice right now." She got out of the car and slammed her door.

Chris glanced back at the dog. "Let's work."

Sherlock immediately sat in the seat and waited for Chris to come back around and get him. While Marin gathered the evidence kit, he got the dog, and they both headed inside. The office was now bustling with officers, people in handcuffs going to the jail or to rooms to be questioned, and various others. Where the building had been quiet, now it was a dull roar of activity.

Marin didn't seem to notice as she pushed through the crowd and shoved open Leo's door without knocking. "How dare you?"

Leo shifted his focus from her to Chris.

She stopped him before he could say anything. "No, don't you dare blame him. This is between you and me. If you had evidence in my sister's case and you kept it from me," she jabbed her finger into her chest, "I'll quit and go somewhere else. Is that clear?"

He narrowed his eyes. "I understand you're under a lot of pressure right now, so I'll ignore your tone . . . for now. Sit down." He pointed at the chair nearest her.

Chris wanted to back out of the room, but he was still holding the evidence Sherlock found in the park, which had to be properly handed off to Leo. He stepped forward and left the bag on Leo's desk. "I think you should glove up and look at that."

Marin glared at her boss from her chair but remained silent. Leo put on gloves as fast as most nurses he knew and unsealed the paper bag with a flick of his finger. He opened the top and gently lifted out the plastic, sealed bag. Marin held her breath. He wanted to rest a hand on her shoulder, but she was so angry with Leo she would likely take his action the wrong way.

Better to stay in his lane than make an enemy.

Bright red smears covered the inside of the heavy-duty plastic. For a split-second, Leo glanced at Marin, then he set the sealed bag on his desk. He drew out Alyssa's bag that looked almost the same and laid it next to the other.

"I think it's safe to say we have an issue."

Chris held up his hand to stop Leo from going further and making assumptions like he had earlier. "Did you get any results back from the tests performed on that shirt this morning?"

Leo shook his head. "They've only had the evidence for a few hours. Give them some time. We're a small department in a small jurisdiction. The big city crimes will be considered more important."

"The test to determine if that blood is human or animal takes seconds, and it's likely the first test they would do. You don't even have that back?" A CSI team would've done that in the field.

He assumed the blood was human, judging by the fact that Sherlock had pointed to the second shirt instead of ignoring it, but he still had to ask. Sherlock hadn't sniffed the first shirt at all, so he refused to believe anything until they offered more information.

Leo frowned. "Tell me you come from the big city without telling me you come from the big city. We don't have the resources you do. We don't have the test kits you do. I have a few patrol cars, a few officers, a detective, and a coroner who was a nurse at one point. That's it."

Frustration forced his spine into a rigidity he couldn't hide. "Murder is murder. No matter where it happens."

Marin made a small gasp beside him. He realized he'd done exactly what he'd planned to avoid, saying out loud that—while he wasn't sure Alyssa was dead—there was a very good possibility.

She stood and headed for the door.

"Bayless, sit down," Colder ordered.

She continued walking from the room, slamming the door behind her.

Leo turned his attention to Chris. "Why did you do that? You made me look bad."

"I didn't do anything. You should've told her what you had and worked from a theory of evidence instead of assumption. If you had brought her your evidence and said, 'This doesn't prove anything until we know whose blood this is or until we find a body. Let's keep working.' You would've had an ally. Instead, you kept information from her and assumed it meant her sister was dead. This is on you." He stood and headed out of the room.

He couldn't find Marin in the hallway, and he didn't want to look for her when she was likely dealing with a lot of emotion. He was sorry for making a statement that sounded like he believed Alyssa was dead. Sherlock sat and looked up at him, then chomped his jaw twice, his signal that Chris had stood motionless for too long and it was time to move. Sherlock liked getting things done and stillness was not his friend.

"Alright, boy. Let's take Marin's lead and check out that apartment. But first, I need to find out which one it is . . ." He glanced around and noticed the door Marin had come out of when they'd met in the same hall an hour before. It just happened to be hers.

❧

Marin was one of only three female officers in the entire force of Poplar Bend. She could sit in the nursing mother's chair in the corner and not be bothered since the other two women were not on duty and there were no nursing mothers on staff.

The chair had been placed in that restroom when a man who was repeatedly arrested for drunk and disorderly conduct had a long stint in the jail. His wife had been thirty weeks pregnant when he was arrested, and the baby was three months old by the time he was released. But in that time, they'd found this comfortable chair to give her a private place to nurse her infant. While the bathroom was a horrible place to feed anyone, they'd reasoned that it was rarely in use. Marin had to admit, the chair was nice to have right now.

She let her bobbed dark hair fall forward and hide her face. Officers didn't cry. Hadn't her father told her that repeatedly when he was a teacher at the law enforcement academy? Female or not, officers were supposed to suck up their feelings, press them down into the recesses of their souls, and deal with them after retirement. Not now.

All her pep-talk did was make her feel guilty for the overwhelming hurt and anger threatening to spill out and down her cheeks. How dare he? Leo had been behind her every step of the way. When she was a green patrol officer, getting in her hours and learning the ropes, she'd told him her intentions. From that point on, he'd helped her grow, rise up the ranks, and get her ultimate goal. This felt like a stab in the heart after assisting her all this time.

After a quick glance at her watch, she stood and headed for the sink. Sitting here in the bathroom and wallowing in her grief wasn't going to find Alyssa. No matter how much she didn't want to believe

Alyssa was gone, she had to admit the possibility. She splashed cold water on her hot cheeks and looked into the mirror.

Olive green stalls lined the wall behind her with old toilets peeking out from partially opened doors. The scent of disinfectant and pungent lemon air freshener never quite went away. A line of fluorescent lights lined the top of the mirror above the sinks, casting a bluish glow over her face. She was too pale, too tired, too ready to give up.

She dried her hands and checked the hallway before leaving the quiet protection of the bathroom. The only noise that revealed her presence in the hall was the slight brush of her clothing. As she passed Leo's door, she was thankful it was closed. He was the last person she wanted to see right now. He was probably still talking to Chris.

A burning spike of pain pierced her chest. Leo had trusted Chris, a stranger, with the evidence about Alyssa. Not her. She hurried her steps to her office, just down the hall. As she touched the knob, Officer Coulter waved at her.

"Bayless! Wait." Parker held up his hand and jogged toward her.

"Can this wait? I'm kind of busy." Not a lie, but she wanted to duck into her office to avoid anyone seeing emotion on her face. If anything, she had to remain professional.

"I was the one out in the park this morning. I thought you'd want this. I know. I should've handed it in." He glanced over her shoulder, down the hall, then back to her eyes. His warm brown stare told her he had her back.

He handed her half of Alyssa's driver's license, the half with her image. The other half, with all of her details, had been cut away.

"Wait, this is evidence." She hated to give up something tied to her sister, but if this would help find her . . . "You weren't even wearing gloves." She looked up at him again.

"I tested it first. It was clean. There's nothing on there to further the investigation, so I thought you'd want it." He smiled sheepishly at her. "I'm sorry, for what it's worth."

She clutched the image of her sister in her palm. "Thanks."

Officer Coulter strode past her, as if he'd been heading in that direction to begin with. She glanced to where he'd come from. Why had he been in the coroner's office? Had he gotten the card from there? She rushed toward Flynn's office and barged in without knocking, half expecting to see Alyssa's report displayed all over his desk.

"Good morning, Marin." He barely looked up as he gathered specific pages off his desk and put them in a folder. "How can I help you?"

"Has my sister come in? You'd tell me if she had, right?" She sounded too emotional to her own ears. Marin swallowed hard and started over. "Colder told me Alyssa is dead. I just need to know if you've seen her or anything having to do with her."

Flynn Barnard's face softened. "You know I would've told you immediately if that were the case. Leo sent over a shirt as if that would seal the deal on this case. While it doesn't look good, a shirt is not a body. I'm in the business of bodies, not guessing."

Somehow, the older man's words gave her a little hope. The same hope Chris's words had dashed when he'd talked about murder. "Thank you."

"On that note, go back to searching. I'm praying you find her." He reached for her hand with both of his own and patted the back as he shook the other. It was an old gesture of support that seemed to be fading with time, but she was thankful in that moment that this particular gentleman hadn't let it slip away.

"Thank you. I'll take all the prayer I can get. Alyssa too." She stood and gave a brief nod of goodbye, then headed for her office.

At her door, she heard sounds coming from within. There was no way to look inside without opening it, so she palmed her Glock and pushed the door as quickly as possible. Of all the people she thought she'd find looking through her paperwork, the last one she expected to find was Chris.

"You have ten seconds to tell me what you're doing. Starting now."

Her tone must have set off Sherlock because he immediately put his burly self between her and Chris.

"Stand down," he told the dog.

Sherlock sat, but the look in his eyes said he was far from mentally obeying the order and the one who needed to stand down was her. "I'm only going to say this once more. Explain yourself."

Chris moved from behind her desk, not looking sheepish in the slightest. He picked up Sherlock's lead and strode to her chair on the opposite side of the desk, leaving her to wonder what he'd been up to.

"First you come here and completely disrupt my case, then you break into my office. You tell me in the field you're not sure my sister is dead, but in my boss's office you admit she was murdered. Whose side are you on?"

Sherlock gave a low *woof* of a warning. Marin went around her desk and sat to put a little space between herself and the dog. She stared at the handsome SAR officer and waited for his response. He wasn't going anywhere until he spoke up.

"I'm sorry for going into your office. I felt bad for making it sound like I thought your sister is dead. I still don't believe that completely, though with the evidence I'd be stupid to say there was no chance. She obviously could be. But the fact is, the moment she was abducted, she could've been killed. I still haven't seen any concrete evidence to prove that either she or Cami are actually dead."

Marin took a deep breath. "Okay, then we're on the same page. But why were you in here, looking through my files?"

He still didn't look guilty, and she wished he would. Her desk was none of his business.

"I wanted to see where your sister's apartment was, so I could take Sherlock out there and see what I can find. Likely nothing, but if anyone can scent a trail, it's him." He thumbed toward the dog.

Marin wanted to believe that a K9 could do the impossible, that he could find her sister. "All you had to do was ask, and I'd have taken you there."

"I didn't want to bother you. I did enough damage to you today." He looked down at the dog as if to avoid Marin's gaze.

Maybe he did feel a little guilt. She took a deep breath. "You're forgiven. I appreciate your willingness to help. I can take you to my sister's apartment if you want to go." She'd planned to head back there anyway before the day had gotten away from her.

"I make no promises, but Sherlock is pretty good." He grinned.

His handler was pretty good too. She mentally took back the things she'd said in her head about him when she first saw him that morning. If he hadn't been called in, she'd still be in the dark about the bloody shirt belonging to Cami and the apparent matching one belonging to Alyssa. "Let's go."

CHAPTER THREE

After getting settled back into Marin's car, Chris took out his phone to check emails. At the top, he'd received a surprise.

Christian, I need to talk to you. I've realized you were right. We can't work together and try to have a relationship. I'm so sorry about what happened. Can we please meet up and talk? I miss you. Jules

Even reading her name made his eye twitch, the one he'd almost lost because he'd been protecting her instead of getting out of a risky situation. He'd asked their boss at the time to split them up because they were dating and he didn't want the hazard of putting her safety above anyone else's. He knew himself. He would absolutely do that and had.

He stared at the phone for a full minute until the screen blacked out to the home screen. Later. He'd think about Jules later. A soft muzzle pressed against his shoulder, then Sherlock whined before he licked Chris's ear.

"It's okay, boy." He scratched the extra soft fur right behind Sherlock's ears.

"Everything okay?" Marin glanced over at him as she turned into the parking lot of a large, brick two-story building.

"Yeah, fine." He hated sharing even more than he hated working with other people. Internally, he repeated his mantra. *I work alone. Except for Sherlock, I work alone . . .*

"Okay. Um . . ." She bit her lip. "Do you want to see her apartment first or just do your thing outside?" She chose a parking spot right near the front door.

With Sherlock trained as an SAR dog, getting a good scent might give him a place to start. "I wouldn't mind looking in her apartment as long as it's already been cleared. I don't want to mess up anything having to do with the investigation."

She turned off the car and dropped the keys into her purse. "You won't. Leo sent two guys over there right away to see if there was any hint as to where she might be the first day she went missing. They found nothing, so he released the apartment back to me." She reached over and brushed his knee with her arm as she reached for the glove compartment.

The unexpected connection felt far more intimate than it should've. *Get a grip, Chris. It's because you just thought about Jules and what working with a partner can do. Stop thinking about all things attraction and get your head in the game.*

She pulled a keychain from the compartment and closed the door, then got out of the car. As soon as he'd taken Sherlock from the back seat, she locked it. He realized she hadn't done that in the park. "Any reason for locking here?"

Mainly, he wanted to know what kind of environment Alyssa lived in. Did she worry about her own safety? Did he need to worry about others in the apartment, or were there possible suspects here?

Marin turned a light pink shade that gave her an innocence she didn't usually show. "This is the side of town that has the most crime, mostly drugs. Granted, it's not much. We're small potatoes. It's enough that I don't leave my car unlocked though."

"Got it." So, if he could read what she wasn't saying, the neighborhood probably had a petty crime issue with small-time theft like bicycles or things left unattended in garages, and drugs like she'd mentioned. Murder wasn't on that list. At least, not yet.

She opened the front door to a large, open lobby with a wall of mailbox slots, similar to what he'd seen in old post offices. Little dials for combination locks stuck out along the wall, some small, others medium, and four of them were large, clearly meant for renters who got packages often.

Marin glanced at the wall, then went to one on the top row, three from the right. She spun the dial, quickly turning it to the combination like she'd done it a million times. The door burst open as soon as she freed the lock mechanism, sending mail all over the floor. Marin stood staring at the letters scattered all over the floor.

"I take it she hadn't checked her mail in a while?"

Marin shook her head, her mouth hanging slightly open in bewilderment. "I checked it two days after her disappearance, hoping to find something sent by her abductor."

He glanced over the floor and at the cubby. There were probably over a hundred letters. "Did she have a lot of friends?" Even so, who sent actual letters anymore? He'd been told by Jules, when she'd thought they were headed for marriage, that even wedding invites were being sent by email now.

"No, just Cami and me. We're both loners. We like our privacy." She crouched but didn't touch any of the envelopes. "They're blank. No addresses. How did they end up here?"

"I think you need to call Leo and have him send over a team to gather evidence. There's no way to know what those are until they look at them."

"I'm going outside to grab my kit. I'm the closest thing we have to a CSI." She handed him the key. "Her apartment is 215. Go on ahead and take a look. Open anything you want. Get clothing for a scent if you need to . Whatever you need, do it. I'll be here for a while."

He watched her head back outside and took a few pictures with his phone, then stood off to the side to prevent any renters from accidentally 'helping' by cleaning up the mess. Marin didn't need any more work.

Her movements were clean and decisive. No one looking at her from outside the situation would ever know she was dealing with a personal crisis. He wanted to tell her to stop. Get out of this if she could. He'd been hurt by doing the same thing. While Alyssa wasn't an officer, Marin would put herself in danger—even if that danger was to her heart and soul—to find her sister or heaven forbid, her body. That was why rules existed about conflicts of interest.

She opened the door once again and gave him a strange look. "Done already?"

He didn't answer her question, instead saying, "I thought I'd stand guard over the evidence while you gather what you need. Chain of command and all that."

She heaved a quick breath. "Thank you. Sometimes I forget there are perks to having a partner." Her head whipped around quickly to look him in the eyes. "Not that we're partners. I know how you feel about working alone."

He held up a hand to let her know he hadn't taken her words as critical. "You're welcome. Here's my number in case you need anything quickly. Like, too quickly for anyone else to show up." He drew his card from his chest pocket and handed it to her.

"Thanks. I really hope I don't need it. Thankfully, there are only two people here right now, both elderly, so hopefully I can avoid blocking off the apartment building with police tape."

He gave a nod and waited a few seconds to see if she would want him to stay. There was something about her, sensitive but not needy, vulnerable but not a push-over. She had strengths Jules craved, strengths that made working with Marin much easier than Jules.

He unlocked the security door and headed for apartment 215. Sherlock took the stairs at a trot, ready to work. He seemed to sense the tension in the air. When he reached the door, he said a quick prayer for Alyssa's safety and that Sherlock would find something to help them.

He unlocked the door, then put on a set of gloves and turned the knob. The apartment wasn't at all what he'd been expecting.

🐾

Crouching low on the floor to get the best camera angle, Marin documented every last letter on the floor. She took pictures of the whole scene, starting in each corner with the camera held high, then individual letters. Even though every one of them looked identical. All of them had deep waves along the glued edge, meaning whoever had sealed these likely used a water stamper, not their tongue. There was too much liquid used for it not to be a mechanical solution.

She prayed they'd find a fingerprint or fibers, anything to further the investigation. The longer this went on, the odder it became. First, Alyssa had disappeared without a trace. She'd been at work, stayed for her entire shift, then disappeared before she'd made it to her car that night. Strictly speaking, her apartment was the last place that should have any clues to her whereabouts, unless she'd been doing things she shouldn't and hadn't told Marin about it.

No. She wouldn't ruminate on things she could do nothing about. Yes, Alyssa and Cami had both acted weird in the weeks before they disappeared. Cami had been inconsolable, having to actually go to her doctor to get a prescription to help her sleep afterward. Acting weird and disappearing were two different things. Both girls were good, trustworthy people with no enemies that Marin knew of. None of this made sense.

One of the envelopes slipped from her nitrile-gloved finger and landed on the floor, revealing a long hair. It was dark with silver at the root. She dug a pair of tweezers from her kit and gently picked it up off the flap of the envelope. Bullseye. It had the root attached. She quickly deposited it in a small, clear cylinder tube and capped it, then tagged it.

Next, she had to deal with all the letters still in the mailbox. Oddly, it looked like they'd been packed in there as a stack, but the box hadn't been quite wide enough, so some of them had been shoved to the front. Each envelope was light, almost feeling empty. When she held one up to the light, she could see a small rectangle inside, about the size of a business card.

Was this connected to Alyssa's disappearance? Should she go to Cami's apartment and check for the same thing? If both were missing and both had their names on bloody shirts found in the park, then it would stand to reason their cases were connected. She tugged off one glove and reached for her phone, dialing the bowling alley from memory.

"Spike, who do you need?"

She frowned. Spike was the last person she wanted to talk to. "Spike, this is Marin. Other than Alyssa and Cami, have any other workers gone missing today?" She had to make sure the connection wasn't employment. If it was friendship or proximity, then Alyssa and Cami were probably where this spree ended. But if anyone else at the alley hadn't shown up for work, she needed to find out right away if they were missing.

"Nope, all present and accounted for." His tone suggested he wasn't paying much attention and didn't care if anyone called in.

"Have you seen or heard anything? Has anyone made any odd requests or threats that I should know about?"

Spike was silent for a moment. "You do realize we deal with alcohol and competition, right? Two things that almost always lead to some kind of smack talk or worse. I didn't see anything weird going on with Alyssa or Cami before they disappeared. No one has said anything. If you need anything else from me, you'll need to get a warrant. I have work to do." He hung up.

She held the phone away from her head. "Thanks for caring."

"Everything okay, dear?" Mrs. Bloomenthal held open the security door, looking like it could crush her with its weight at any moment.

"Yes, sorry." She shoved her phone back into her pocket and grabbed a new glove.

"So, you're not doing something for the police, and it's okay if I go over and check my mail?" The older woman's voice pitched high, then cracked.

"If you could wait about ten more minutes, I'd appreciate it." Surely she could wrap up all the envelopes in that amount of time.

"That's fine, dear. Take your time. I'm going to have a seat here on the bench. This door weighs more than my husband when I married him." She hurled a cackle from her throat.

Mrs. Bloomenthal had married years before Marin was even born, and her husband had been dead for over a decade. Long enough that, Marin guessed, Mrs. Bloomenthal could joke about it. "It is heavy." She went back to gathering the envelopes with tweezers from the small mail slot.

"I don't think I've ever seen so many letters in one box. Popular girl. Haven't seen her in three days." Mrs. Bloomenthal's right eyebrow inched up in a question Marin didn't want to answer.

That couldn't be right. She'd been missing for nine. "Are you certain you saw her on that day? It could've been more days, right?"

"No, I'm certain. We talked for about a minute while she waited upstairs. She wore a hood though, and kept it up the whole time. I almost didn't recognize her. Why? Did something happen to her?"

And there it was. She hadn't actually seen Alyssa at all. "You know I can't talk about work."

The woman gasped. "Are you telling me something happened to her? Or are you saying she made something happen to someone else?"

Marin froze mid-grab. Had Alyssa been up to something? Was the fact that she was missing part of a cover-up? She hated to admit Alyssa could've committed a crime, but everyone had parts they didn't want anyone else to see. She herself hid the hurt of being abandoned by her parents, even though they hadn't done it until she was an adult. The pain was still there. Clearly, she'd done something to hurt them, or they wouldn't have stopped communicating.

"I don't know. Right now, we're in the discovery phase of this case. All we know is that something happened to Alyssa. We don't know what yet."

Mrs. Bloomenthal whistled out one side of her mouth and rubbed her knee like it pained her. "That's a heavy burden. You be sure to talk to someone. Don't bear this alone. No, you shouldn't. No matter what, find someone you can lean on."

She'd leaned on herself, her sister, and God all this time. She was pretty sure she could keep that up. "Thanks." She bagged the last envelope after looking for visual evidence on it.

Most of them had been completely clean and identical. All the paper rectangles inside were stuck in the same spot in every envelope, like they'd been glued there. That was another thing she couldn't figure out. The more a criminal had to handle evidence, the more likely they'd leave evidence of themselves behind.

"There. Let me move my bag and camera out of your way, and you can have your lobby back." She slowly rose from a crouching position on the floor. Her knees now ached too. Unfortunately, she wasn't twenty-five anymore. Thirty had passed her by a few years ago. Various parts were starting to hurt consistently, and she didn't like it. She'd always figured she'd grow old next to someone else going through the same thing. Yet, she was still alone.

"Thank you, dear. I'll pray you find Alyssa. I assume she's missing or left based on what you're doing."

There was no point in lying. "Thank you. If you see anything, think of anything that happened recently, or see her . . . please call me."

"I will, dear." She hobbled over to her own mail slot, slowly turned the dial, and opened the door. She had one envelope inside, and Mrs. Bloomenthal let her breath out slowly. "Just a bill. I have to admit, I was worried about what I'd find after watching you."

Marin nodded. She'd cleaned up slowly because she was curious to see if the envelopes had only been left for Alyssa or if everyone had them.

She waited for Mrs. Bloomenthal to head back through the security door and went inside so she didn't have to call Chris and ask him to let her in. She jogged up the stairs, leaving Mrs. Bloomenthal on the first floor. Chris had left the door ajar.

She approached, not sure why it bothered her that he'd left Alyssa's home open to anyone who walked by. That was her privacy. What if she returned and found out he'd treated her home like a guided tour?

As she pushed the door open further, the sight took the steam right out of her argument. Chris was to her in a second, and she realized her knees had lost all their strength. He braced her from falling, and he smelled of Old Spice. Original, not all the new varieties.

"I didn't realize you'd come up here after you finished. I thought I'd be done before you. I didn't want you to see this." He held her steady as he walked her to the sofa, helping her around broken picture frames and décor smashed on the floor.

She'd been in this apartment five days before and it had been in the same condition as when Alyssa had lived in it. What had happened? She slowly sat on the sofa, taking in the utter destruction around her. Sherlock lay on the rug in front of the sofa, pouting at being ordered to sit this search out.

"I . . . It wasn't like this before. I promise. She didn't live this way." Marin swallowed hard. None of this made sense. The letters and the mess had to have happened before the shirt was found. "Wait, the shirt! Check her room. If there's a work shirt hanging up, then there's still a chance she's alive. She had two of them and always kept one clean if she was wearing the other."

He gave her a look of compassion. "All of her clothes are gone." Chris came from the bathroom and handed her a sealed clear bag with three pill bottles in it. "Recognize these?"

All three were for depression with Alyssa's name on them, but Marin had never seen her sister depressed, nor had she mentioned taking anything. "I'm so confused. It's like I'm finding out my sister wasn't at all who I thought she was." She bit her lip, considering what Mrs. Bloomenthal had unknowingly suggested. "I'm beginning to wonder if my sister was less a victim and more of an accomplice."

"How so?" Chris sat next to her.

The entire couch seemed to shift toward him, and she scooted a few inches away to keep from getting pulled into his gravity. She wouldn't allow herself to think of anything but this case. Not how handsome he was, or how much she appreciated his help . . .

She told him about the conversation downstairs and how things didn't feel right, ending with, "Why would anything change in this apartment after it had been cleared?"

"Those are good questions. I was able to find a hairbrush in the bathroom that I'm pretty sure was hers. If you can confirm it, I think it's time to let Sherlock do a little sniffing."

She stood to check it out. Thank God, they might finally get to the bottom of all these clues.

CHAPTER FOUR

Within a plastic bag, Chris held the hairbrush Marin had given to Alyssa as a gift. It was specially made from seashells. She'd gone on a trip to Mexico on a whim and found it at a vendor near the shore. He'd had many varieties, but this one looked like Alyssa would love it. That had been the only vacation she'd ever gone on.

Chris glanced at her. "Do you want to wait here? Sherlock races all over the place for a while until he finds a scent. He can be a little hard to follow."

She paused for a moment, not sure what her answer should be. He'd told her a handful of times that he worked alone. Was this yet another way to remind her? Or was he genuinely warning her away from a situation that would be difficult? Would she end up holding Sherlock back or forcing him to slow down for her? "I . . ."

"It's okay. I won't do anything behind your back. I'm not Leo. I don't have any ulterior motives to keep things from you."

That wasn't it, but she nodded her thanks as if that was exactly what she'd thought. "I don't want to hold you back. It means a lot to me to find out what happened to Alyssa. She's the only family I have.

The only friend I have." Why hadn't Alyssa told her if something was going on?

"Can I ask you something before I race all over and probably get sweaty and tired?"

She swallowed hard as the image of Chris with sweat glistening off his forehead, hair damp with curling ends by his ears, and his well-fitting tee molded to tired muscles passed through her mind.

"Um, sure."

"Did your sister say or do anything in the days before her disappearance that made you pause for a second? I'm not saying off the wall. Those things people remember easily. I mean something offhand, like she mentioned traveling, but never traveled. Or maybe a friend you'd never heard of? I'll give Sherlock the scent and we'll see where it takes us, but if clues lead us somewhere else, I'd rather use Sherlock's excitement first instead of here where her trail should be days old."

"Should be?" What did he mean by that?

"Someone came in here and trashed her apartment, looking for something. You said she wasn't wealthy. She worked at a bowling alley. It's likely she lived paycheck to paycheck. Am I wrong?"

"No," though, now that she thought about it, she wished she'd helped Alyssa more. She wasn't wealthy either, but if she and Alyssa had pooled their resources as they'd done when they were younger, she wouldn't have had to worry so much.

"Wait, you really do think she's not only alive but that she's the one responsible? What about all the letters in her mailbox? I suppose she left those too?" She wanted to punch him in the nose, but Sherlock would probably eat her. His head was as big as her face.

He slowly shook his head. "I'm not saying that, though it's possible she was kidnapped and forced back to her apartment. Someone might think she had something important. So, I'll ask you. Do you know of anything she had that someone else might want?"

Now there was a question she hadn't asked anyone and hadn't

been asked by Leo. Did Alyssa have anything? Alyssa was broke, just as Chris had said.

"Not that I know of, but I'm beginning to realize there were things I didn't know about her. I wish I could tell you, but I don't know. I guess she was better friends with Cami than with me. I can't tell you how badly that betrayal hurts." She'd been the one to stand by Alyssa when their parents left. Why hadn't Alyssa remained as faithful as Marin?

"I think, instead of starting here, I want to go to the bowling alley."

She slowly shook her head and recounted the conversation with Spike. "He won't let us on the property without a warrant."

"I suppose he owns the lot. Is her car still sitting there? Or is it in impound?"

She hadn't had a chance to pay to get it out yet. It was still across town at the lot where both the city and dealerships took cars people had to pay for to get back. "It's across town."

"And was it searched?"

She assumed so, but she hadn't been the one to do it and as far as she was aware, none of the lab work had come back yet. "Likely."

"That wasn't a yes." He laughed.

"It's as close as I can get and still be honest with you."

He grinned at her, gentle but warm. It wasn't a smile that made her feel like he was laughing at her. He empathized with her situation, and that tore at her heart. How could he unless he'd lost someone super close to him?

"Need directions?" she asked, only then realizing he'd helped her into the passenger seat of her own car.

"Nope, that's what my phone is for. You can just relax for a few minutes."

She closed her eyes and rested her head against the seat. "Why, do I look like I need it? Don't answer that."

He laughed as he pulled out onto the road. The entire population of Poplar Bend was only about sixty-five hundred people. Small, yet large enough to have a few amenities. Even so, Chris had driven to the lot and parked before Marin could get properly comfortable in the seat. So much for a rest.

He gave Sherlock the command to work, knowing the dog would follow along at his heels with no other command needed. He pocketed the keys then led her to the only building near the lot. She reached for the handle, but he got to it first and held it open for her.

She went inside and headed to the man at the counter. "Mick, I'd like to see Alyssa's car. I'm sorry I haven't had the chance to come and get it out of your lot."

He looked confused for a moment. "It's not here."

Chris held her elbow, and she realized the starch had gone out of her knees once again. When was the rollercoaster going to stop?

"What do you mean?" Chris asked. "I was told the car was impounded after Alyssa's abduction. Who paid to get it out?"

"Do you have a warrant? I can't just give out private information like that." Mick stood straighter and looked down his nose at Chris, even though Mick was a good two inches shorter.

Pressure pounded against her temples. Whoever had taken Alyssa had done everything to cover their tracks. There had been no evidence left behind at the bowling alley, nothing in her apartment, nothing with Cami, who was now missing too.

"Let me call Leo and see if he looked at the car when it was in the bowling alley lot. I can't imagine they would've missed it if they'd had it towed." She pulled her phone from her pocket and dialed the top number.

She glanced at her list of calls made recently, sad that the person she called the most was her boss. Not her sister, no other friend, just her boss. And she didn't even like him all that much right now.

"Calling to apologize?" Leo's voice instantly made her clench her teeth.

"No, actually I wanted to ask—because I don't recall seeing any photos in my case file—did you check Alyssa's car when she went missing?"

"We weren't told there was a car. Not sure what to tell you."

"You mean someone called in a missing person and you didn't check the parking lot of the last place she was seen?" Her chest ached with the pounding of her heart. She'd assumed he'd taken pictures but hidden them from her.

"That sounds like your job. Not mine. You're our only investigator, and this is your case. Go check it out at the impound lot. I'm sure it's there."

She modulated her voice to a reasonable tone and volume. If she didn't, she'd scream at him, and that would get her nowhere. "That's where we are, and it's gone. I can't get them to tell me anything without a warrant."

"So, call the judge and get one." He hung up the phone.

Marin closed her eyes and gave herself a moment to think. This day had already felt like five. She wanted to find her sister so she could rest. This pace wasn't sustainable.

"Everything okay?" Chris touched her shoulder.

She jolted out of her own thoughts. "I have to call to get a warrant. Leo seems angry about what I said in his office. He's not helping."

Chris gently took her arm and pulled her far enough away Mick couldn't hear. "Getting that warrant will take some time. I need to find a hotel room if I'm going to stay and help you, and I'd like to. You need some rest. Today has taken everything out of you. Seeing that shirt drained all your reserves."

"There are no hotels within an hour of here. There's a little bed-and-breakfast above a café in Basil Butte, but she doesn't allow animals, not even service animals."

Sherlock seemed to understand her words and sat down with a *humph*.

"I mean no disrespect, Sherlock."

Chris looked at his watch. "Well, it's almost three hours back home, so I'll need to leave shortly. I don't like driving in the dark when I'm tired."

She gave a nod of understanding because she didn't either. She allowed herself to drive in town, where the speed limit was only 25 since the roads were narrow, but never in the country if she was too tired.

"You can crash in my spare room. It used to be Alyssa's, but it hasn't been used in years." She shrugged, only then realizing she was opening herself up to rejection. She never allowed that. Maybe he was right, she was too tired to be making any decisions.

"As long as you're okay with that? I clean up after myself and my dog. You won't even know we're there."

She doubted that. There was no way to be around this man and not know instantly that he was close by. "Then it's a plan."

She turned to Mick. "I'll come back tomorrow with a warrant. Might as well have what I need pulled up and ready in the morning."

He heaved a breath that sounded a little like a challenge and waved them off.

"That was weird," Chris whispered as he led her toward the door.

"You caught that too? I thought I was just tired and over-sensitive."

He reached for Sherlock's lead before opening the door, then held it open for her. "No, that was definitely a deflection. I wonder what he knows."

She took a deep breath, then let it out. "I don't know. I'm beginning to feel like everyone in town knows more than I do about this case. Like everyone has a small piece of the puzzle, but they aren't willing to share them. Usually, it takes only one small clue to break open a case. In this one, the puzzle has been thrown in the trash."

She held out her hand for her keys. This time, she wasn't going to let him drive. He dug in his pocket and handed her the keyring. She glanced around the parking area out of habit. Situational awareness was a good way to stay alive as an officer and even more important as a woman. Something about the lot felt off.

"Wait." She held out her arm to stop him. "Who's that?" She

pointed to a car sitting in the lot with its lights on. The car was so far away, she couldn't make out the color or anything distinctive.

"I don't know. Might be someone waiting for us to leave?"

He didn't sound convincing. "I think you're thinking the same way I am. That car wasn't there when we pulled in, and now it's waiting here. Like they expected us to come. I'm going to follow them."

He followed her to the car, and she unlocked it so he could get the dog in quickly. Marin buckled in while Chris took care of Sherlock. He closed his door, and she took off toward the car. When she started moving, it quickly raced from the lot.

"I know every car in this town. I wave at just about everyone. I've never seen that car."

❧

Chris got himself buckled in as Marin raced after the car. While running off was a little suspicious, this wasn't a choice he would've made. He wasn't going to tell her how to do her job—she could clearly handle her position, and it wasn't one he shared—but there wasn't enough evidence or suspicion to give chase.

"Where do you think they're going?" Marin asked as she got close to the car. "Can you write down the license and call it in?"

He wrote it down on a notepad from his pocket. "Are you sure this car has done enough to warrant more attention than what we are already giving?"

She slowed the car and glanced at him. "You don't think we should follow him? You don't think it's weird that he left the moment he saw us moving?"

"Wouldn't you?" He took a deep breath and waited for her to get angry with him. He wasn't supposed to question the jobs of 'real cops'. Hadn't he been told that in his own department?

"I . . ." She swallowed hard. "Maybe you're right. I'm just so frustrated that every lead seems to dry up before I can do anything with it. Every. Last. One. I'm never going to find my sister. Do you have any idea how hard this is for me?"

He glanced at the window. Losing someone he thought was going to be a spouse wasn't the same as losing a sister. And Jules hadn't died. She'd only turned on him after he'd finally set work boundaries.

"Only vaguely. Look, this isn't about comparisons. If you want to follow them, that's fine. Exhaust every single lead. But let's wait until they commit a crime to call in the cavalry."

She gave a short, single burst of laughter that was clearly snarky. "At least you have the license plate for when that happens."

She followed the car as it roved the streets for about twenty minutes. He noticed the same decorations in front of a certain house the third time they'd driven past it. "We're going in circles. I think they know you're there and are seeing how long you'll follow them."

Marin took a defeated breath. "You're right." She flipped on the turn signal, the first she'd used it since she'd begun following the car, and headed right instead of tracking them further. "I'd like that page you wrote down the plate number on. I can look myself in the office tomorrow. I'd like to know who I was following."

He nodded, knowing he shouldn't say anything more. Marin directed the car to a small house on the edge of town. The grass needed to be mowed out front, but not badly. The gutters had leaves peeking out at odd intervals. Cracks in the paint around the windows looked like webbing even from the street. Marin was too busy to keep up with things that weren't on the top of her list, and she had no one to help her.

The fact hit him right in the chest. She worked, came home tired, and rested just enough to go right back and give this town more than she had the very next day. He suspected she gave just as much when the hunt was for someone other than her sister too.

"Sorry, it's not perfect, but it's mine. I had to save up for three years to have enough for a down payment, but she's mine." Marin stifled a yawn as she tucked her keys into her purse.

"I'll take Sherlock around back so he can take care of what he needs to. Should I knock in back or come around to the front?" He didn't know if she had carpet right inside the front door. Some people didn't want pets walking across the carpet.

"Either one is fine. There's a patio door back there. You can come right in through that. I'll unlock it for you." She got out of the car.

Chris hooked Sherlock on his leash and headed for the backyard. Things were in slightly worse shape back there where no one could see. It was fenced in, and the grass was up almost to his knees, still brown and broken from last fall. He couldn't really blame her. He had an apartment, so he didn't have to do anything with a yard, knowing that his job could take him away for days at a time. Since May marked what Chris called 'tentative spring' weather, he doubted she'd had time to do any lawn maintenance yet.

As soon as Sherlock had raced around the perimeter a few times getting his zoomies out, then finished his business, he came back to Chris so they could go inside. A warm glow came from the sliding glass door, but she hadn't turned on the security light above it. He wondered briefly if the bulb had burned out. It was possible she was simply too tired to think about turning it on.

He slid open the door, and the subtle scent of an oven preheating tickled his nose. He hadn't thought about what they would do for supper, but she clearly had. Maybe she was more awake and aware than he'd given her credit for.

She came into the kitchen in flared leggings that hugged her subtle curves and a loose-fitting light sweatshirt that somehow made her even more attractive than the cut of the blazer she'd been wearing all day. Her dark bobbed hair was pulled back into a messy ponytail, at least the hair that would reach. She looked comfortable.

"I'm preheating the oven. I had a lasagna in the freezer. It will take an hour to bake, but it should be filling. I've never had to feed a guy before, so I wasn't sure how much to cook." Her cheeks turned slightly pink.

For some reason, the idea that she hadn't dated anyone long

enough to feed them was attractive. "Thanks. I promise I won't eat everything in your house. I need to think about what to do for Sherlock though, and I didn't ask you to go back to the station so I could get my own car."

She closed her eyes in defeat. "I thought I'd thought of everything. I'm sorry. Here." She headed for her purse. "You've already driven my car. It's no big deal. There's a Dollar Store that carries small bags of pet food. It's on First Street."

"I saw it when you were showing me around town by following that guy." He grinned, hoping she wouldn't think his teasing was meant to be harsh. She wanted to find her sister alive. He wanted the same.

"Go, I'll stay here with Sherlock. I'll have him eating out of my palm by the time you get back."

He laughed. "I doubt that. He's a good dog, but completely loyal to me. He'll be friendly, though. Does that store have any clothes, by chance?" He hadn't brought a thing, thinking this was a one-day job.

"They have some sleep pants, socks and the like, tees . . . You won't find jeans there, but if you get a pair of the sleep pants, we can throw your jeans in the washer tonight."

That would work. He wasn't one of those people who wore jeans more than once without washing them. Lots of people did it. He was aware of that, but that just wasn't like him. "Sounds good. I'll be back as quickly as possible. Anything I can pick up for you? They probably have some garlic bread if you want that with your lasagna?"

"Nothing for me, thank you. If you want something other than coffee or water, you should grab that though."

"Noted. I'll be back shortly." He took the keys from her but didn't go out the front door. instead, he went back to the sliding door and went out that way.

The security bulb was frosted and old. It was likely burned out. He touched it and noticed a slight wobble with pressure. With a quick twist, it turned back on. Why had it been loose? What was the purpose? Had she turned it off for some reason?

Marin slid the door open. "You got it to turn back on? I flipped it on and off a few nights ago and assumed it was burned out. How did you fix it?"

❧

Marin watched the quick emotions play over Chris's face. He wanted to ask her more, but something held him back.

"That bulb has been in there since I bought the house. I assumed it had burned out. But it didn't. Or could it be a short in the wiring?" She tugged on her sweatshirt. Why didn't he say anything?

"I twisted it back in and it lit right up."

His words sent a chill down her spine. Her light had gone out the same day Alyssa had gone missing. Coincidence?

"Oh." She stepped back into the house.

He followed her and slid the door closed. "Look. I don't want to alarm you, but I'm glad Sherlock will be here with you while I'm gone. I don't like that your backyard would be easy to hide in with no light and lots of places to hide. If someone can get into your backyard, they can get into your house without being seen."

She shivered at the idea. Her job came with risks. She'd known that from the start. But this was the first calculated attack against her. "Okay. I'll keep Sherlock nearby while you're gone."

"Good." He headed for the front door. "Lock this. I'll knock when I get back."

She nodded and followed him, locking and dead-bolting the door. As soon as she heard her car back out of the driveway, tension skittered and twisted through her, binding her like rope until she couldn't move.

"This is silly. No one is after me. There would be no reason." She headed for her room to grab slippers from her closet. Even though the weather was warm, she'd been cold since arriving home.

She opened her closet door and flipped on the light. A dark denim jean shirt with her name embroidered on the front placket hung from the light fixture. It was just like the ones from the bowling alley where Alyssa and Cami had worked before they disappeared.

She reached for her pocket, only then realizing she'd changed and didn't have her gloves or anything else at her disposal. When this was catalogued and bagged, then she could freak out. Until then, compartmentalize. She closed her eyes for a moment and said a prayer. Someone was after her, meaning the only one who could keep her safe was God.

She backed out of the closet and called in the crime. Someone had been in her home while she'd been gone. She recalled the slow chase earlier. Had that been a way to make sure she didn't arrive to find someone in her house? They hadn't done anything explicitly wrong, but it had detained her.

Leo hadn't answered his phone, but she left a message with the duty officer detailing everything and what she would do. Since her kit was in the back of her car and she couldn't get to it, she had to wait until Chris returned.

What would he think of this? She didn't really want him in her bedroom, looking at all her personal things, but she would need help to gather any possible evidence because this hit far too close. He had training to do that sort of thing. She remembered he'd gone through standard police training to be on the force. Though, some departments hired sub-contractors as their K9s. He was a trained LEO.

While she waited for him, she documented everything with her phone. Unfortunately, she'd already touched the light switch, which might have smudged or removed any prints left by whoever had hung the shirt there.

She took a second to look at the shirt. At first glance, it was identical to the others, but the brand tag at the collar was different from the first two. The denim wasn't as heavy and not quite as dark. The stitching was yellow, not gold. While it was a good facsimile, it wasn't from the same place the bowling alley got their uniforms.

Chris knocked on the front door, jolting her from her task. She put down her phone and rushed to let him in. He carried three bags and set them down on her small kitchen table. As soon as he turned to look at her in the light, he stopped short.

"What's wrong?"

"I'm going to need my evidence kit from the trunk. Someone got into my house while I was out today."

He looked at her, studying her for a few seconds. "I'll go get it. Be right back."

She waited while he retrieved the equipment. How did she fit into this equation? And how could she fight it if she had no clue what the motive was or even who the prime suspect might be?

He came back inside and handed her the kit. "What would you like me to do?"

"I'm going to need your help." After losing her parents to whatever had turned them on their children, asking for help was one of the hardest things for her to do.

"Then I'll help you. Let's look for evidence. Maybe they left something behind we can finally use. They can't take away anything from here. For once, they may have overplayed their hand."

She hated to agree with that assessment, but he could be right. It could also mean that, like Alyssa, her home was about to be ransacked. "I don't understand how all this fits together. I thought the two missing girls sort of led back to the bowling alley, but Spike allowed two uniformed officers to look that first day. He didn't act like he had anything to hide. It wasn't until after you found Cami's shirt that he refused to cooperate further."

"Letting you look there when he knew you wouldn't find anything isn't honesty. It's manipulation. He's the closest thing to a suspect we have right now. All clues point to the bowling alley, which points to Spike."

She couldn't disagree, but she'd have to ask for yet another warrant to do another search there. They'd found nothing in the last search, so the likelihood of being able to get one was slim. "I don't know where he lives."

She'd never thought about it, but Spike was a fixture at the alley. Some people simply existed to others in the only places they were seen. Like seeing a coworker at the store, sometimes she didn't recognize them until she'd already passed by.

"Well, that's probably another thing you'll want to look up when you get to work tomorrow."

She gave a nod and opened the kit. Her house was older, and her closet was little more than a hallway with shelves along one wall. The space was tight for a tall, broad guy and her, even without his cowboy hat. She kept brushing against him without intending to.

After about thirty minutes, she needed a breath of fresh air and more than a few inches of space to herself. "I'll be right back." She left the room without waiting for him to say anything.

Would she be able to sleep in her bedroom tonight, knowing someone had been in there? Had they touched anything else? Not that she could tell. How had they gotten in? The front door had been locked. She didn't lock the fence, but her sliding door had been locked when she'd arrived home.

Did someone have a key she didn't know about? Was that what someone had ransacked Alyssa's apartment to find? She hadn't looked for the key her sister kept because it hadn't occurred to her when they were there. She rushed back into the room.

"I need to go back to Alyssa's. I think someone looked through her apartment to get the key to my house."

CHAPTER FIVE

Chris wasn't sure what he should do. Part of him wanted to go with her. The other part of him knew someone had to stay here to watch the oven. He also didn't want to leave Sherlock alone in a house he didn't know.

"What would you like me to do? I can stay here and wait, or go with you."

She clipped a holster onto the waistband of her leggings and tucked her gun inside. "I'll go. It will only take a few minutes. If the oven alarm goes off, pull it out. I'll be back before it's cooled enough to cut."

He hoped that was the case. "Want to bring Sherlock with you? He's not trained to protect, but he's still a typical shepherd."

She shook her head and held up a hand. "No. I don't know his commands, and I'd rather he have a chance to rest a little. We might need him tomorrow if we find any other clues. It's not like I can have you let him loose to run all over the town. It likely wouldn't do any good."

A bolt of lightning flashed across the sky. Thunder followed a few seconds later. Rain pelted against the window.

"Are you sure you want to go now? Nothing in that apartment, or rather, *not* in that apartment, is worth putting yourself in danger. We can go look together tomorrow. If the key isn't there, I can see if Sherlock can sniff out anything in the apartment that doesn't belong. It's not a science by any means and not admissible in court, but if he can find something and you can attest that it didn't belong to Alyssa, we might be able to get DNA or trace evidence from it that will lead us to a name."

She slowly nodded. Going out in the storm likely wasn't on her list of things she wanted to do. While she'd been absolutely ready to go alone, he hoped she'd choose to stay and eat supper, get some rest, and tackle this problem in the morning when it was light.

"I hate admitting you're right, you know that?" She pulled the gun from her holster and returned it to the drawer where she'd hidden it.

Only then did he realize she'd removed it and put it there when he'd been in the backyard. "I think that's a good idea. If you've had someone break into your home, gun or not, you should play it a little safe right now. At least until we catch this guy."

She nodded, though she didn't look completely convinced. "I've always done this on my own. This feels wrong. I don't rest."

"Maybe it's time to. Resting is important. I'm not asking you to start taking a whole day of rest or anything, but a few hours will give you clarity." He prayed she didn't take his advice as putting her down.

"I've always wished I could take a Sabbath. I just don't feel like I can. If I take a day off, something might happen. I might miss something. Someone might not get closure." She shook her head. "I know. I'm not powerful enough to really make that much of a difference, but I'm scared."

Only believers in the One True God spoke of taking a Sabbath. Unbelievers talked about sabbaticals. "You aren't God. I know you know that, but letting go will help you feel more successful and even let you get more done. I know it's crazy. I didn't believe it either."

She gave a sheepish smile as she unclipped her holster from her waistband and put it back in the drawer with the weapon. "I know. I also know that free will makes it easy to think you're 'not bugging God' with the trivial while just doing things your own way."

"Hey, no judgement here." He held out his hands to show her he'd been guilty of the same. "Police, Fire, Rescue, and anyone in the medical fields all have the same issue. We're so used to being called to help, protect, defend, and save that we sometimes forget we have little to no power over situations. Any control we have is God given." He reached down, and Sherlock pressed his forehead into his palm. The soft fur reminded him that the world might be a shadow of heaven, but even shadows could be enjoyable if they were created by God.

"Thank you." She massaged the bridge of her nose, leaving a red spot. "I'm lost. If I'm being honest. This case is getting to me. And why target me? Was that shirt a way to tell me to back off? Was it a genuine threat? Since I have no clue who I'm after, I don't know. It's infuriating."

He couldn't explain why he wanted to reach out and hug her, but he didn't. He hardly knew her. Nothing but encouragement would be welcome. "I'm sure it is. While we eat that lasagna—that smells amazing, by the way—you can tell me about what you know and all that happened. Maybe if we put our heads together, we can think of something others missed."

She nodded her agreement and headed for the kitchen. She put her phone on the counter, and it buzzed as she released it.

"Oh, that's the lab. I wonder if they have the results from the shirt?" She looked over at him, and her eyes welled with emotion. "I don't want to know. What if it is her blood? If it is, she's dead."

"While the amount of blood on the shirt indicates she couldn't have survived, we still don't know everything. Until the ME rules she's dead, she's not."

He pressed the icon to answer her phone and picked it up. "Officer Johnstone, Marin is away from her phone right now."

"This is LeRoy Evenson of the Basil Butte lab. We have the results from Alyssa's shirt. They are confusing at best. We're likely going to have to send this to the FBI office in Cheyenne."

Alarm bells went off in his head, and he could see Marin had heard what was said even though he hadn't put the phone call on speaker. "Okay, why is that?"

"Well, we tested three areas, hoping to find if she was the victim and maybe have the DNA of the killer as well. We have four distinct blood signatures on this shirt and only one of them is Alyssa's. Since I don't know how much of the blood is Alyssa's, I can't make a guess as to if she is alive or dead."

❀

Marin reached for the nearest chair and fell into it. Four blood types? Had she gotten into something ritualistic? Was she killed by a gang of people? The shirt showed a gunshot wound. Was that where they had found Alyssa's blood?

"Wait!" She reached for the phone and took it out of Chris's hand. "LeRoy, this is Marin. I need to know if the swab you took that found Alyssa's blood was from the area of the gunshot or was it somewhere else?" If it weren't near the hole, Alyssa might still be alive.

"That's the odd part. I found her DNA near the collar of the shirt, and while it was her blood, not sweat based on the methylation patterns, it still tells us almost nothing. I need to find out who the other donors were on the sample."

The 'donors' would be those who helped kill her, those who tried to, or possibly other victims. "Okay. As soon as I get a few good suspects, I'll aim to get DNA samples from all of them."

"If it helps, only one sample was male. Alyssa's is obviously female, and there were two other female donors."

Her arms went cold. Numb. "Can you please test to see if one set of DNA matches the other shirt we just submitted? Cami's?" She suspected it would be on there, fully connecting the two cases.

"Absolutely. I'll get back to you as soon as we have the data available. Also, the blood sample submitted yesterday was also Alyssa's." LeRoy hung up.

Chris lowered to a crouch in front of her, and Sherlock pushed to nuzzle her hand. "You okay? That was a lot to take in. I'm sorry you heard what he said through the phone. I had hoped to hear it and relay it to you in a less clinical manner."

She waved away his concern even while still appreciating it. "It's okay. I needed clinical. If he had tried to be my friend and offer condolences and false hopes, then I would be crushed." She touched his arm, immediately noticing the corded muscles in his shoulder and upper arm. "Thank you for trying to shield me, though. No one ever does that."

Investigators had to be tough as nails, able to handle anything. She had a special budget just for her counselor because this job could take a lot out of anyone, and she wasn't about to become a horrible statistic. At least, not intentionally.

"I don't even know how to process the information he gave. Four sets? Only one was Alyssa and in a weird spot? More women than men? And I didn't even know about the earlier sample sent in. What was that from? What is going on?" She'd trained to stop her mind from wandering where it shouldn't. The key to solving crimes required focus, but this case seemed to change by the second. There was no plausible way to put the pieces together.

"I've never seen anything like it." He slowly rose and sat on the other side of the table.

Marin forced herself to stand and pulled the food from the oven, then slowly cut it into servings. She plated two pieces along with a slice of garlic bread from Chris's trip to the store and put one in front of Chris.

"For now, let's eat. We can talk about the case after we refuel a bit. The goal was to rest, and we haven't exactly done that."

He laughed. "You got me. I try, but I'm not perfect by any stretch." He reached out his hand to her.

She slipped her fingers through his. They were warm, strong, and covered hers completely. She rarely felt small or petite. Being an officer often meant putting aside anything feminine or girly. Even the desire to be that way felt a little foreign.

"Lord, we ask you to bless this food and the hands that prepared it. We ask for help solving this case. You know what's going on where we can't . . ."

She let him continue to pray for a moment while she added her own thoughts. *Grant me some peace, Lord. I don't know if my sister—my only real family—is alive. This is tearing me apart inside.*

Chris finished the prayer and released her. She immediately tucked her hands under the table to give herself a second to gather a little composure. She'd been a mess from literally the first moment they'd met.

"Thank you. I often say a quick prayer in my head. Sometimes I don't even close my eyes." She wanted to change the subject to something other than work. "So, what is your life like? You live in the big city. Being out here must feel a little weird." She picked up her fork, hoping for a few minutes to relax and talk.

The side of his mouth crept up slightly. "It is. I grew up in a small town on a big ranch, so I'm thankful I understand how things work, and the differences from living in Cheyenne, but it's still an adjustment. I haven't lived in a small town since I was eighteen. Quite a few years ago." He took his first bite.

The utter happiness on his face as he let the lasagna sit on his tongue sent a giddiness through her she had to mentally tamp down. This was crazy. Why did this guy make her feel things she had no business feeling? He lived three hours away. Even if they decided to pursue a relationship, nothing would come of it without one of them moving.

If Alyssa is dead, would you want to stay?

The thought made her choke and cough. She pounded on her

sternum for a moment until the food came loose and she could swallow. Chris looked at her with deep concern lining his forehead. "You okay? This is just really not your day."

For some reason, his little joke made her laugh, and that was the best medicine she'd had. "Thanks. I guess eating and thinking at the same time is not an option tonight."

Someone pounded on her door. "Police! Open up."

CHAPTER SIX

Chris stood to answer the police request. He and Marin had finally had a moment to talk, and he was looking forward to getting to know her better when chaos erupted at the door. Sherlock barked since the order sounded like a threat.

He grabbed the dog as Marin slowly opened the door. "Leo, what's going on?" She brushed hair out of her face, making the whole loose ponytail fall out.

"I'm sorry to have to do this to you, Marin, but you're under arrest. Your blood was found on your sister's and Cami's shirts. None of the other DNA samples were in our system. You'll need to come in right now for questioning."

Marin went immediately pale. "What? I didn't kill her. I have nothing to do with this. Leo, you have to believe me. I've done everything to catch whoever took Alyssa. I don't know what this is about, but it's a mistake."

"I have to go by the evidence. I think it's interesting that you're our only detective and you're the prime suspect. You probably thought you could get away with this because you could cover up evidence. This won't go well for you. Cops don't get good treatment in prison."

She shivered. "Innocent until proven guilty."

She was innocent. He'd never had a doubt.

"Chris, I didn't do this."

"I believe you. We'll get this figured out." He turned his attention to Leo. "We talked to LeRoy not twenty minutes ago. He said nothing about the blood matching Marin's. Why wouldn't he say something? Better yet, why even call her if she was a suspect?"

Leo reached for Marin's arm, but Chris pulled her out of reach. "Answer my questions first."

"I don't have to answer anything. I outrank you. You're little more than a civilian here. What I hired you to do is finished. Go home." He yanked Marin away.

"He has a point, Leo. What's wrong with you? You've never been this combative. If I didn't know any better, I'd think you were trying to keep the truth as far away as possible."

Leo slapped the cuffs on her wrist, then wrenched her arm behind her and pushed her against the wall, knocking her cheek against a corner.

"Hey, cool it. She isn't fighting you." Chris stepped in Leo's way.

Leo pulled back his fist. Sherlock lunged at Leo, nipping at his shirtsleeve.

"Call off your dog or I'll have him shot." Leo grimaced, holding still so Sherlock wouldn't rip his shirt.

"Answer my questions. You shoot my dog, and you'll lose your position. You know that."

Leo growled, making Sherlock growl back. He gave Leo's arm a quick shake, ripping the shirt. Instantly, Sherlock gripped him tighter, this time around his arm.

"Fine. I'll let her go. But if she turns out to be our killer, this is on you." He pointed at Chris. "She's the only suspect we have, and you'd better have a good explanation as to why her DNA is on that shirt. In fact, you'd better have a good reason for the fact that blood from all three women have DNA evidence on Alyssa's."

Three shirts. Three blood traces. Three women. So, who was the man represented? Was he another potential victim, or the killer? How had someone found enough of Marin's blood to make it look like she was part of this case and why?

"She won't be found guilty. I will find out what is going on. Release her."

He generally wasn't that bold. His office didn't treat him like a sworn officer, and he wasn't included in precinct camaraderie. He was an outsider who knew his place.

"Sherlock, drop."

The dog immediately let go and sat, staring at Leo as if he expected the man to do something else that warranted protection. He'd never seen Sherlock act like that, and he wondered if it was less for him and more for Marin. Had the dog decided she was one of his people?

Leo shook his arm and stared at the dog while he spoke to Chris. "If I find a single additional thread of evidence against her, she's coming in. I will find Alyssa and Cami's killer. I don't know how they do things in Cheyenne, but around here, we get justice." He unlocked the cuff around Marin's wrist and strode out the door.

The other officer along with him glanced at Marin. Chris expected him to say something threatening. Officers usually sided with their sergeant.

He took a deep breath. "I don't think you had anything to do with it, but he's so frustrated by the lack of evidence in this case. I hope you can still trust him when all this blows over, and we catch who did this."

Instead of answering, Marin rubbed her wrist where the shackle had been. The officer gave a nod like he understood her silence, then walked out, closing the door behind him. The entire house felt eerily silent. He might have jumped at a pin drop.

Sherlock took that moment to bark loudly, making Marin scream then laugh at herself. She shook her head quickly then smiled as if the noise reset her emotions. "Thanks, buddy." She scratched Sherlock behind the ears.

"You're welcome," Chris said, knowing she meant the dog, but still hoping she'd appreciate him too. Why did the K9 always get all the attention?

She smiled at him. "I'm glad you were here or I'd be in the back of a patrol car, headed for jail. I'm so confused about what he could possibly be thinking. Anyway, why didn't LeRoy tell me one of the samples was mine?"

He led her back to the table and pulled her chair out slightly, then sat in his seat. "Are we sure it was? You seemed to have a pretty good working relationship with LeRoy. It's weird. It seems like everyone you used to be able to trust is turning on you. I know, in any other situation, you wouldn't be on this case at all. I wonder if they aren't purposely treating you differently because they don't want to cross a line. But in so doing, they are reaching for shadows that aren't there."

"Maybe." She didn't sound convinced. "I had nothing to do with my sister's disappearance. Whatever they try to pin on me, they won't find the most important detail, motive. I have none. I love Alyssa, and I always will. I didn't know Cami except superficially, so I have no reason to do anything to her either."

"We both know motive can be made up by looking at a situation in different ways. While motive is important, it's not what makes cases anymore." He didn't want her thinking she was in the clear just because she knew she didn't do it. Innocent people went to jail.

"Yeah, I know." She glanced down at her plate. "Go ahead and eat. I'm not hungry anymore." She stood and headed into the living room. Even though it was warm outside, she grabbed a blanket that looked like it had been knit or crocheted years ago. The edges showed wear, and the color had faded.

He couldn't ignore his appetite, so he quickly finished his plate, washed it, and put it on the drying rack next to the sink. He put away the leftovers and covered Marin's plate, then put everything in the fridge. She'd get hungry later, and it would be easier to simply reheat the plate.

He sat down on the opposite end of the sofa, and Sherlock laid his head between them, his soft brown eyes begging permission. She patted the space, so the dog jumped up, curled in a ball, and lay pressed between the two of them. Marin rested her hand on his back, burying her fingers in the thick fur. Sherlock hadn't released his winter undercoat yet, and he was still soft. In a month he'd look like he had a case of the mange and need a blowout.

"Do you want me to hang out here with you, or would you like to be alone?"

She didn't know him. His presence might not offer the comfort he hoped it would. If she needed time or space, he'd try to avoid intruding.

"I'm okay if you want to sit out here." She scrunched up her face. "LeRoy didn't mention Cami's shirt, meaning he either didn't know anything yet or he hadn't finished. He usually waits to tell me what's going on until he has a reasonably complete picture, which is why it took him all day to get back to me. Since he usually doesn't have results that fast, he must have rushed as much as possible. I know Leo is the boss and gets information before I do, but showing up to make an arrest with no evidence?"

He'd disliked Leo from the start, so that feeling could cloud his judgement. Hiding material information from Marin had been the first indication he was untrustworthy. Whether or not he thought he was helping her, keeping evidence from her had made the situation worse. What had tripped his con-meter was that he wanted her to still work on the case and figure it out *while* withholding that information.

"I'm not saying he's a bad guy, but he kept the knowledge of that shirt from you. He didn't want me to tell you he thought Alyssa was dead because he was sure you'd need time to grieve instead of finding her killer. That doesn't scream trust to me."

"That's just Leo. He's never worked anywhere but here. The rules that apply in the city don't apply out here. He likely meant well. I'm used to it, though I've never had him try to arrest someone on his own team before."

"So, I'll ask again. Are we sure he knew anything, or is he grasping at straws? You know this man better than I do. Help me trust him."

She closed her eyes. "I'm not so sure I can do that."

❖

Sleep. That's what she desperately needed, but having company in her house was the opposite of helping. If anything, she'd be listening all night for him walking around or the dog, or... She closed her eyes and saw the image of the shirt hanging in her closet and shivered, pulling the blanket her mom had crocheted years ago tighter around her. The blanket reminded her of a time her mother had cared. A time she would love to have back. She settled into the comfort of her couch beneath her. Maybe she could stay out here.

"If you can't trust your boss, this isn't a safe environment for you. What makes you stay here?" Chris turned slightly so he faced her instead of turning to look at her.

"Until now, it was Alyssa. She had Cami and her job. She knew everyone and was friendly. I didn't have those things, but that was okay. I had Alyssa and didn't need anyone else." She shrugged.

What would she do now? If Alyssa had been killed, she'd be so lonely. If she were arrested and found guilty of her murder, she'd never work as an investigator again. This one case could take everything from her. "By the way, thanks again for going to bat for me with Leo. No one ever stands up to him."

"You did earlier." Chris grinned. "The look on his face told a whole story of surprise." He laughed.

She had, hadn't she? Could that be part of why he'd focused on her? He could be vindictive, but wasn't often wrong. He had an uncanny way of knowing what people did and thought. In this case, he was totally wrong, though. She hadn't had contact with her sister the entire day she'd gone missing.

"I guess I did. Next time, I'll know better," she joked. "This just makes me want to find out who did this even more. I have to clear my own name and hopefully find Alyssa. I have to admit it. I'm losing hope. She's been gone for over a week now. The likelihood of finding her alive is almost none."

"Don't think that way. Until you know for sure, hold on to hope. If you don't, and you find her, you'll feel guilty for giving up."

She ducked her head, giving herself a moment to gather her thoughts. No one on the force was friendly with her. There was camaraderie for sure, but not friendship. All the officers but Leo were married, so they kept her out of any friendship beyond work out of respect for their wives. She'd never questioned it or complained. Good for them. The other female officers had their own friends.

"I don't know why you're sticking up for me and why you're friendlier than anyone on my own force. I certainly wasn't nice to you to begin with . . . but I appreciate it. I'd be so alone right now if not for you."

❖

Chris swallowed hard and glanced away. How could he answer that? And why did she have to sound like Jules being vulnerable? That alone should send up all sorts of warning bells in his head. Would he listen? Weren't warnings meant to protect him from what he'd already been through?

Marin wasn't ever going to give up being an investigator. While they likely wouldn't work together if they were on the same force, they could. That alone should make him run in the other direction. The scar on his face pulsed though he couldn't say whether that was his imagination or if his face visibly twitched. Feeling anything for

Marin was dangerous. Even a friendship could lead to something he didn't want. Another work relationship.

Hadn't one swipe to the face been enough?

"I should head for bed and get some sleep. Where do you want Sherlock to stay? His hair vacuums up fairly easily if you want him on the floor."

Her brow furrowed at his change in the conversation. She didn't answer him for a few seconds and looked visibly uncomfortable that he'd ignored her vulnerability. The same vulnerability that was both attractive and too close to what had happened in the past.

"Um, sure. The bed is made. I keep it that way in case my sister ever wants to crash here. The quilt is microfiber, so it won't stain or hold on to the hair. If you want Sherlock on the bed, let him lie there." She shrugged a delicate shoulder, and the wide collar of her sweatshirt slid down, exposing her delicate collarbone.

No, he wouldn't look at her. He wouldn't allow himself to say or feel anything. This was a case. She lived three hours away from him. She was an officer. This situation was literally a list of all his red flags.

"Okay, I'll see you in the morning. Unless you'd rather sleep in the guest bed and I can stay on the couch. I can't imagine you'd want to sleep in the room where someone had been earlier. I don't blame you, and I don't mind."

She looked away and gathered the blanket closer around her, covering her completely in a cocoon. "I'll take the couch. I'll sleep better if I'm closer to the door, knowing I'll hear it the moment anyone even touches the knob. Since I don't ever sleep in that room, I probably wouldn't rest anyway. It's better this way."

He wasn't so sure he believed her. "I can leave Sherlock out here. He sleeps pretty hard but also wakes up fast. He won't bother you." And then she might sleep better, knowing the dog would respond to any sounds before she even heard them.

"He can sleep where he'd like to. I imagine he'd want to stay with you."

Chris chuckled. Sherlock was sleeping with his head resting on Marin's feet, clearly comfortable with her. Why were he and his dog so at ease with this woman? It was like they'd known her for years, not less than a day.

"Okay then, I'll leave him to decide. Thank you for being so open with your home." He waved goodnight and headed for the spare bedroom.

With the light off, he could see into the backyard. The state of the house and grass struck him again. She'd worked hard to have this place. That she was unmarried, in her thirties, and had her own home was a testament to how hard she worked. She was a rare case. Most people couldn't buy homes without the safety net of a second full-time income.

He grabbed his phone and looked at the email from Jules. Why had she contacted him now? Of all the times to reach out and remind him of his past mistakes and all the reasons he refused to date anyone he worked with, why now? Was this God trying to warn him away from making the same mistake twice?

If he were honest, he could picture himself getting to know Marin better. If she didn't work for the PD, she would tick all of his boxes. She was a woman of faith. She had a strong work ethic. Her humor made him laugh and complemented her intelligence. Yup, honestly, he was falling too hard and too fast for a woman who was all wrong for him.

"I'm listening, God. I won't go further into this."

He pulled out his phone and sent off an email to Jules letting her know he still wasn't ready to talk to her. After all they had been through, she had ignored the few absolute issues he'd had with their relationship. Instead of helping the situation, she'd dug her heels in and forced him to adjust instead of working on a compromise. A relationship couldn't be that way. Both parties had to give, or he would become a doormat.

Would Marin be that way? Would she work with him or work against him? He'd watched her stand up to Leo earlier in the day. She was fierce about what she believed to be right and wouldn't let others take advantage of her. It wasn't until she was almost arrested that she showed any weakness. That was mainly because she couldn't do anything else.

He heard her shuffle around the kitchen, her bare feet making soft noises on the linoleum. He waited, keeping as silent as possible to hear what she was doing. He hoped that since he wasn't a stranger sitting there in her living room, she might finally be comfortable enough to eat supper. She'd looked so tired all evening. This case got to her. Who wouldn't be affected by it? This case showed the obvious reason officers weren't allowed to work on cases where family members were the victims.

The fridge door opened and closed. He heard the microwave rev into action then beep a few minutes later. He waited, hearing nothing but silence after. She didn't clatter her silverware against the plate or scrape it against the ceramic as she cut portions off. He wasn't sure how anyone could eat so quietly, but hopefully she did.

Sherlock released a huff of breath at his door, startling him from his focus. "Need to go out again, big guy?"

Generally, he didn't have to this late in the evening, but they weren't in their usual home, he hadn't had his usual dog food, and the yard had been a challenge all its own.

Sherlock turned and headed for the door. Chris grabbed his phone as a flashlight and found Sherlock sitting by the sliding glass door where they'd come in before. Marin stood at the sink, washing her plate. She glanced over her shoulder at him.

"I'm sorry. I saw him sitting there. I was going to let him out in a minute. I figured it was safe for me to do that, since the yard is fenced in. He would come back in for me eventually, right?" Her sad eyes made him want to make promises he shouldn't.

"I'm sure he would've come back in for you. He seems to like you more than most other people. Shepherds are good dogs, but they often choose one person they like. They rarely care about others. If they're part of a family, they'll enjoy the company of the family, but one of them will be the dog's clear favorite. I wasn't expecting him to immediately decide you're on his good list."

"He knows I'd never do anything to him. Or maybe he knows I wanted to be a K9 officer at one point in my life."

The same alarm bells that had gone off in his head earlier doubled in volume. If Marin became a K9 officer, then there was no chance they could ever date. His chest clenched. Why was it so hard to let that idea go? He had to, but it was hard.

"I think you would've made a good handler." And that's as much as he'd say.

"I don't think so, but thank you. It's not my goal anymore. I'm an investigator through and through. You're the first K9 handler I've ever worked with and, I'll be honest, I can see I would've felt like I was in the wrong position."

Being a handler was one of the few jobs where there wasn't much advancement. He did what he was trained to do because the dog worked with him. If he chose to advance, he had to let the dog go, and Sherlock likely wouldn't work as well with a new handler as he had with his original. So, for the sake of his partner and for the entire police force he worked for, he'd never considered advancement.

"You seem to have chosen the right path." He slid open the door and followed Sherlock outside. A thin haze of fog hung over the tall grass, collecting in density near the bushes along the back. Sherlock sniffed around, looking for the perfect spot. He nosed his way to the far-right corner of the yard and disappeared for a few seconds.

Chris concentrated on the place Sherlock had disappeared and waited for the dog to come out. "Sherlock, come."

Nothing. Sherlock never ignored an order.

"Sherlock, touch." He dug a treat from the pouch at his waist and held it between his fingers, waiting for his dog to push his cold nose into Chris's hand.

When a few seconds went by, he grabbed a flashlight from his belt and headed for the back of the yard. Wet grass brushed against his jeans, chilling him as the damp clung to the fabric.

"Sherlock." He didn't want to yell in a residential area when it was late enough for people to be in bed, but where was his dog?

Sherlock lay in the back of the yard next to a plate of raw meat left by someone. His one-hundred-pound dog didn't move. "No," he rasped. He dropped to his knees and held his phone screen up to Sherlock's nose. The warm breath temporarily clouded the screen.

"Thank you, God." He carefully lifted Sherlock into a fireman's carry and brought him back to the house.

Marin gasped as she rushed to slide the door closed behind him. "What in the world?" She ran to the living room and gathered a blanket from a cabinet. She laid the folded blanket on the kitchen floor as a bed for Sherlock.

"What can I do?" she asked.

"Do you have the number of an emergency vet? I don't know who left a trap for my dog out in your yard, but we need to find out what's wrong. Right away."

He was breathing. That was a good sign, but he wanted to know Sherlock would be okay. Whoever had done this just poked the wrong bear.

CHAPTER SEVEN

"I'm glad you called me when you did." The veterinarian adjusted his position on the floor next to Sherlock. He'd even brought knee pads, probably knowing he'd have to treat the dog from the floor.

"Thank you, Mark." Marin sat on a kitchen chair but had folded herself almost in half to keep an eye on Sherlock, allowing herself to pet him every few seconds.

"It's not a problem, Marrie. Thankfully, it looks like Sherlock didn't do more than sniff whatever compound was in the meat. It was enough to knock him out, but not hurt him. If he'd eaten it . . . I don't know." He shrugged.

Once the vet had arrived, Chris had gone back to where he'd found Sherlock and he'd bagged the evidence. When the doctor had finished and Sherlock was naturally snoozing instead of medically knocked out, Chris followed the doctor outside to pay him.

"Thank you for coming over so late and so quickly." He pulled out his wallet and started counting his cash.

Dr. Blakely held up his hand. "I owed Marin a few favors. This one is on the house. She's always looking out for everyone else and never asks for anything in return. I was happy to come and finally be able to repay her a kindness."

His answer helped fight a little of the raw tension in his throat, both from Sherlock's reaction to whatever was in the meat and from how comfortable the vet seemed with Marin. "You friends?" he asked.

Dr. Blakely chuckled before answering. "I wouldn't call us friends. Acquaintances who attend the same church would be a better description. I think Marin is afraid of making deep connections. Her parents did a number on her and Alyssa. Town gossip is that both were adopted when their parents wanted to raise children but couldn't have any of their own. When the cute stage of matching outfits and proms was over, they bailed, leaving town completely and heading for California. Marin and Alyssa had to figure things out alone."

He didn't know the whole story by any means, but what Dr. Blakely said matched with the little he'd heard so far. "That's really sad. I can't imagine living life without deep friendships. I'm sure she doesn't really trust anyone."

The doctor loaded his bag into the passenger seat of his pickup. "Likely. I'm not sure. She doesn't talk about it openly, and it's never an appropriate time to ask, which is probably why gossip flies about it. If people knew the truth, they could stop speculating."

He wished he had the resources to look up her parents and find out what had happened. They would likely want to know one of their daughters was missing and possibly dead. "Know of anyone who might know how to reach them? If they lived here their entire lives, someone has to."

Dr. Blakely slowly nodded. "The owner of the bowling alley, Spike, his parents were good friends with Marin's way back when. As far as I know though, they haven't been in contact since they left."

Chris immediately wondered if that had something to do with Spike's insistence that they get a warrant if they wanted to talk any more about the case? If he had nothing to hide, why try to block

Marin from asking questions? Had Spike and the sisters grown up talking to each other? Was there more to all of this than it looked like on the surface?

"Thank you again. You've given me a lot to think about."

The doctor slowly nodded as he leaned against the passenger door. "Be careful. Things are always pretty quiet in a small town. Lately, things have been different. Everyone is locking their doors. People are scared to talk. Even the old farmers who used to sit at the café and jabber about life have stopped. Until this gets figured out, it's like there's a cloud hanging over Poplar Bend."

"We'll do our best." He waved at the doctor and headed back inside.

He closed the door and gave his eyes a moment to adjust to the dim light. Though it was dark outside, the lamp inside created an instant impression on his vision that he had to blink away.

"He's doing better," Marin said from the kitchen.

"Good. Thanks again for knowing exactly who to call. Not sure what I'd do without my partner," he said as he entered the kitchen.

Marin tilted her head down and slowly ran her fingers down Sherlock's back. "You figure it out. We who are expected to solve the world's problems always do."

He lowered himself down to the floor so he wasn't standing over her and talking down to her. "The vet talked to me for a few minutes outside and what he said got me thinking . . ."

"Oh?" she asked with no enthusiasm.

He pressed ahead. "He told me your parents were best friends with Spike's parents. Have you talked to them to see if your parents could be reached? They might want to know about Alyssa. They may even know something about the case. Who knows?"

She shook her head. "I want this finished, but there are things I will not do. Spike's family sided with my parents, saying they'd given all they could and now it was time for them to spread their wings. They even said they'd lived without children for so long that having us was too much of a shock for them."

"Having?" Hadn't the doctor said Alyssa and Marin were adopted?

"My parents tried for a long time before Mom got pregnant with me. She was so sick she didn't allow anyone to take her picture. All the duties of having an infant were so overwhelming she didn't create a baby book or anything. The earliest photos I have of myself are from when I was three."

"Do you remember your mom being pregnant with Alyssa?" Lots of families didn't tell their children they were adopted, hoping to give them a normal family life, but wouldn't Marin recall Alyssa coming into the home?

"Mom told me she got pregnant with Alyssa within a week of coming home with me, which is also part of the reason why she was so overwhelmed. I can't blame her for that. Infants aren't easy. She did the best she could."

"So, Alyssa is less than a year younger than you?" He hoped his questions only sounded curious. The story was plausible except the picture he'd seen of Alyssa looked younger than Marin, though guessing from a photo didn't make his guess a fact.

"Yes, though Mom and Dad usually planned our birthdays on the same day." She absentmindedly scratched Sherlock's neck. "It is odd, though. When I went to the DMV to get my driver's license last year, I wanted to get a Real ID, but the county records office couldn't find my birth certificate. They said they'd get back to me, but they didn't. I got my regular license and kind of forgot all about it."

"You know there's a rumor going around that you and Alyssa were adopted, right?" He had to know how much or how little she knew.

"That's impossible. I always lived with my parents. I don't recall any other time without them."

He reached across the distance between them. "If LeRoy has Alyssa's DNA, and they know it's hers, then I think you should give a sample for him to test against it. First, it could squash the rumors surrounding your childhood and it might eliminate you as a suspect in her murder."

She tilted her head slightly. "I hadn't thought about that. Honestly, I wasn't sure where he got the sample to make sure the blood was hers, and I certainly don't know how they determined the other donor was me, if that was even true."

He stood and helped her up off the floor. "I'll carry Sherlock back to the bedroom where he can get a good night's sleep. Tomorrow, first thing, let's go talk to LeRoy and exonerate you."

She smiled, making something warm deep within him. He wanted to see that look on her face more. Relaxation, or at least the hint of it. She deserved a rest. "Sounds good. Maybe I can sleep knowing there's a plan of action for tomorrow. One thing I don't know is, whose blood is on that shirt? This case is weird. Beyond weird."

Unique cases usually thrilled him. Something that wasn't cut and dried created a challenge his brain loved, even though he wasn't usually the one puzzling it out. "Good. Get some rest. I'll see you in the morning."

He listened as she headed back to the sofa. He gathered Sherlock as gently as he could. Carrying a dog that heavy wasn't an easy task, especially when he was trying to avoid waking the dog. After a few minutes, he managed to get Sherlock onto the end of the bed. The dog took up about a quarter of the space, but he didn't mind. At least his partner was safe.

Thank you, Lord, for protecting Sherlock. Please put a hedge of protection around Marin and help her clear her name. Give us clues to help us find her sister or her sister's killer if she's dead. Help us find her body for closure if it can be found.

He lay on the bed, wide awake. So many things about this puzzle didn't fit together, yet none of them stood out as completely out of place either. Someone had clearly done something to Alyssa and Cami, but who and why? Only two men had acted suspiciously, Spike and the man at the impound lot. Both had asked Marin to get warrants before they would talk. Were they scared Marin would find something in a quick look around? Were they afraid she'd ask the wrong questions?

One of them had to know something, even if that something was small. It was enough that they were scared to talk without being forced to. Asking for a warrant didn't make them guilty, but it made him suspicious.

❦

Marin dressed the next morning with little care. She wouldn't go into the office today anyway. The closest she would come to it would be to call in a warrant for the impound lot so she could find out what happened to Alyssa's car. They'd go to the lab so she could give a sample of blood to prove she wasn't represented on that shirt.

Would LeRoy even allow her to do that? He hadn't said a word to her about potentially being a suspect, which seemed way out of character for him. LeRoy was as straight as an arrow. She threaded her belt through the belt loops of her jeans, then holstered her weapon.

She'd heard Chris take Sherlock outside for a morning walk, leaving her alone for a few minutes in her house. She headed to the spare room to make the bed and found he'd cleaned up everything. The bed was made with military precision, and she didn't see a hair from the dog anywhere on the covers. How had he managed that?

She ran her hand over the blanket but couldn't find any hint that he'd even slept there. If she hadn't heard his deep breathing in the middle of the night, she'd be convinced he hadn't been there at all.

Her phone buzzed so she headed for the kitchen to sit while she took the call. Taking notes was easier there, and no one ever called for fun. She sat and set her phone down on the table. The number was listed as restricted, but she answered it anyway.

"Officer Bayless," she answered.

"Marin?" Alyssa's voice sounded confused as it came through the speaker.

"Alyssa? Where are you?" she spoke quickly, clearly, hoping Alyssa could answer.

"I don't know. It's cold. Dark. I'm not alone. There are three of us here. You've got to help me."

Marin bit the inside of her cheeks. "Did they hurt you? Are you injured?" The blood on the shirt had been Alyssa's. LeRoy had said so.

"Whoever took me sliced my palm the first night. He brings food but won't talk to me."

Her mind whirred. If Alyssa was truly being held, how had she gotten a phone? "Whose phone are you calling from?"

Alyssa didn't answer.

"How are you calling me?" She wanted to keep Alyssa on the line as long as possible, but she wasn't sure it would matter.

"Alyssa?"

The line went dead. Marin slammed her hand on the table. At least she knew Alyssa was alive. That was all that mattered. Now, she needed to find her. Chris walked in the front door and took off his shoes.

"Morning."

She waved away his greeting. "Alyssa just called me from a restricted number."

"What?" He strode toward her.

As he bent over to look over her shoulder at her phone screen, his scent curled into her nose, making her want to breathe deeply. She couldn't name the scent, but it wasn't like flowery detergent or overly manly body spray. He smelled clean and fresh, which was far too attractive.

She unlocked her phone and showed him the call data. "See? I heard her voice. I need to track this number. I'll have to call my carrier and find out where it came from. Restricted doesn't tell me anything."

"I hope they can help you. They might be able to at least tell you which cell tower she was nearest when she made the call." He looked around the kitchen. "You ready to go? Might as well get done what we planned, and you can make that call in the car. I really feel like there will be a break in this case today."

She took in a deep breath. As much as she wanted to call the phone carrier immediately and ask about that call, that had to be something for later. Right now, she needed to get rolling on the warrant for the impound lot, turn in the evidence from her home invasion since Leo hadn't taken it the night before, and go see LeRoy who worked forty-five minutes away at a bio-lab.

She took him out to the car with Sherlock trailing behind. Chris opened the door, then hesitated before telling the dog to get in. "We should go back to the station and get my car. The compartment Sherlock rides in is safer than the clip I have. Not to mention he's going to leave so much fur in your back seat you'll never find it all."

She appreciated his concern about the condition of her car. It didn't belong to her. Though she wasn't the one who detailed it, she doubted Leo would keep quiet about having to pay extra because she'd had a dog in her car for hours. "Thanks, we'll stop there first."

She drove to the station. That early in the morning, only four cars sat in the lot. She recognized Chris's car, one dispatcher, and two officers who worked overnight. Despite Leo's appearance at her house after hours the night before, he wasn't there. That suited her fine. She didn't want to see him after what he'd done. Accusing her of killing her sister with little to no evidence wouldn't go under the radar. She would report it once this was done.

"Is it possible the voice I heard wasn't Alyssa's?" She'd wanted it to be. The voice had sounded tired and frightened, but there had been a quality to it that didn't ring true. More than just the questions she'd asked Alyssa, something about the call didn't sit right.

"I suppose it could be. AI is growing bigger by the day. If someone had a recording of her voice, that's all it would take to spoof a phone call from her." Chris got out of the car and unhooked Sherlock.

The poor dog had looked tired that morning, as if sleep hadn't refreshed him at all. She was so thankful he was fine and nothing lasting had happened to him. Who would ever target a dog? People did cruel things to make others mad. Murder couldn't be justified away, but she could understand why someone would get angry. A dog did nothing to deserve being attacked.

He clipped the lead onto Sherlock's collar. "Is that why you didn't want to call the phone company right away? Are you worried that will be yet another dead end?"

She hadn't had much time to consider the reasons she hadn't pushed. She simply knew that she wasn't supposed to do it immediately. "I'm not sure. The voice sounded afraid, but not as afraid as I would expect someone to sound who'd been held for a week. She couldn't tell me how she got a phone. If she was being held in a dark and lonely place as she said, how did she get her hands on a phone? It makes no sense. I feel like—and this is complete speculation—that call was meant to throw me off course."

Chris slowly nodded. "I agree. I think a lot of things lately have been to get you off track. If you don't know real evidence from things that are being planted, then you can't ever figure out what happened. Someone wants to see this become a cold case. Fast."

"And that's why they tried to take out Sherlock. He's the key. There must be something they're worried about him finding."

Chris grinned. "I like where your mind is running. Let's get the warrant started, then go talk to LeRoy. We might have it by the time we return." He commanded Sherlock into the small kennel in the back seat of his car. The dog immediately went inside, and Chris slid the door closed.

She'd imagined working with a dog in much the same way. Her K9 was going to be her best friend, the one who kept her from loneliness and from feeling like she needed to fit in on the force. Then she'd gone to a seminar offered in Cheyenne where Chris's trainer had offered a class. He seemed mean to the dog with all the orders and expectations. After that one class, she'd hung up her dreams of ever being a handler. He'd also told a story about his first K9 and how the force he'd worked with had retired the dog without letting him adopt her. The dog had been put down before he could convince them otherwise.

She couldn't handle that. Law enforcement should make sense, but it didn't always. There were rules and red tape. Different departments did things in unique ways. She hated the idea of losing a dog outside her control. Just like her parents had left.

She bit her lip. "I know you're right about calling my parents, but I don't want to. Let's wait until I've donated a blood sample, then I'll call them."

Chris pulled out of the parking lot and headed out of town toward the highway heading north to Cheyenne. The lab was at a small college. He'd worked there as long as Marin had been on the force. He was thorough and intelligent. She picked up her phone and pressed the screen to return his call from last night. He answered on the third ring.

"I didn't expect to hear from you today," he said.

"I'm headed your way, actually. I wanted to ask you something strange. Leo came to my house last night and tried to arrest me. He said my blood was found on the shirt."

LeRoy was silent for a moment. "No, I didn't find that. Leo came in yesterday afternoon and brought the other shirt. The odd thing is that the blood on the shirts doesn't make sense. It's like they were lying flat on the floor, and the blood was spilled onto them, then spread. There are no splatter patterns, which would've helped me delineate where the various blood signatures started and stopped."

"You think the shirt was a plant? A distraction?" she asked.

"I'm not sure what to make of it. I'm not even sure the hole in it is a bullet hole."

She had one last question, and it was the one she didn't want to ask at all. "How did you know the blood was Alyssa's?"

He went silent again. She heard him massage his jaw as if he needed to think. "Well, I assumed you already knew this, but Alyssa had a prior conviction. She assaulted a woman at the bowling alley. The charges were later dropped, but she was arrested and, at that time, they collected a DNA sample from her because the victim said it was two women who attacked her, but what they found was that the other aggressor was to blame."

"And who was that?" She suspected she knew.

"Oddly, that person's DNA was found on the shirt as well. Cami Cambridge."

CHAPTER EIGHT

J ust inside the entry to the lab, Marin reached for Chris's arm. She didn't want to hold his hand—that would be weird since he hardly knew her—but she needed support. She'd had the entire ride there to think about what LeRoy had said. Cami and Alyssa had assaulted someone and now they were both missing.

The blood sample on the shirt confirmed the connection, but it wasn't a connection Marin could understand. She breathed in deeply.

"I don't get it. I thought I knew Alyssa, but she never told me about getting arrested."

Chris gave her an understanding look. "Don't take it to heart. She was likely embarrassed and assumed you'd find out. She probably thought you never said anything about it because you were disappointed in her, when the truth was that you simply didn't know."

While that made total sense, it didn't release the guilt weighing her down. If she'd known Alyssa was getting into trouble, she might have helped in some way. Alyssa was night to Marin's day, but their love of difference had always made their relationship stronger.

"I never saw her as someone capable of attacking another

person. I'm embarrassed my colleagues likely knew and I didn't. There must not have been any investigation needed, or I would've found out. As it is, I don't hear about regular crimes investigated by the responding officer. If I did, I'd never get any sleep at all."

"Yeah, let's not push for that." Chris directed her to the man sitting at the front desk.

He wore business casual clothes and a friendly smile. The entire front office felt a little like a biology classroom. Pictures of cells magnified by thousands hung on the walls. There was a fragrance coming from some vent or system, and it was both pungent and fruity. Marin fought the urge to cover her nose.

"We're here to see LeRoy Mason. Is he available?" Chris said to the man at the desk.

He smiled. "He sent up a message almost an hour ago saying you'd be stopping by. Here are your temporary security badges. You can go on back. His office is the third on the right." He pointed to the door they should use.

"Thank you," Marin said as she choked on the fragrance.

Chris headed over to the door and opened it, then held it for her. As soon as they got into the hallway, the scent disappeared, and she took a deep breath. "How in the world does he stand that?"

Chris nodded. "I'm glad Sherlock stayed out in his kennel. That would've been overwhelming for his nose."

She wondered what in the world the fragrance was covering up. Three doors down, she knocked and opened the door as soon as LeRoy responded.

"Good morning, Marin. How are you?" He stood and held out his hand for her to shake.

While he wasn't exactly like a grandfather figure to her, since they'd only met in person a few times and they had a work relationship, he was like a professor whose class she'd utterly enjoyed. "I'm doing as well as can be expected. I came today at Chris's suggestion. Leo insisted my blood was found on Alyssa's shirt and that was enough evidence to arrest me and bring me in for questioning."

LeRoy shook his head. "I think Leo just wants this case to be finished. He's been pestering me hourly to get everything squared away. He even came to my office yesterday, claiming he needed to see the first shirt again. When I showed it to him, he was angry at the holes I'd cut in it to pull out samples."

Chris tilted his head. "Why would he be angry if he's been pressuring you to finish? Does he know how samples are taken?"

LeRoy sat back down and folded his hands in front of him. "Some samples can be pulled with a cotton swab. Others, I have to cut a small piece of the fabric out and drop it in solution. I started with the swabs but got results that made no sense. When that happens, we need to move on to more sensitive means, even if I destroy a small portion of the evidence to get it."

Marin's mind whirled. Leo shouldn't have been allowed to get his hands on it if LeRoy was in possession of the evidence. Paperwork needed to be filled out for a change in who had possession of evidence so there could be no disputes in court as to who handled what and when. Leo knew this.

"Did he fill out the proper paperwork to see evidence in your possession?"

LeRoy's brow rose. "It was a quick look, and I was in the room. Do you think that's necessary?"

Sometimes old-timers could be sticklers for rules. Other times, they hated change. LeRoy was obviously one who didn't stick to newer rules. "I think it's important to have documentation. Anyway, let's get this sample taken care of."

He gave a nod and dug in his desk, pulling out a box about the size of a book. He unwrapped it and pulled out a long swab, dipped it into a solution within a tube, then had her open her mouth. He rubbed the swab along her cheek, then put it into a clean vial and snapped off the long portion of the swab so the vial could close.

"There," he said with a smile. "Now we can get you declared innocent. I'll be working on Cami's shirt today. Let me show you something interesting though." He stood and went to a binder behind him, then brought it back to his desk. "Look at this."

He opened the binder to a page near the back. In the image, both Alyssa and Cami's shirts were next to each other. The blood areas looked exactly the same.

"What in the world?" Marin squinted, sure she wasn't seeing the image correctly. "How is that possible?"

"Oh, I'm sure there's a smidgeon of probability that two shirts found at two separate times could have the exact same staining. It would be minuscule, of course, but I deal in the minuscule."

"Have you ever seen it happen before?" She never had, though her career was still fairly young as far as officers went.

"No. Never. Which is why I pointed it out. May I tell you my hunch?"

Chris answered, "By all means."

Marin nodded her agreement.

"I think these shirts are little more than a report that something has happened. We don't know what that something is, but it was meant to start an investigation. Other than that, I think they mean nothing. I've done some preliminary swabs on Cami's shirt, or rather, the one with Cami's name on it, and the staining is exactly the same. The preliminary results are exactly like Alyssa's shirt."

"Wait," Marin held up a finger to pause the conversation. "You said, 'the one with Cami's name on it'. You don't think it was actually hers?"

He slowly shook his head. "No more than the Alyssa shirt was hers. There was nothing in the collar or armpits of those shirts. Those are places where people notoriously deposit DNA, and there was none. As far as I can tell, those shirts were new, and someone dumped blood on them. Not just any, but a mixture of four people. I don't know how the blood was taken, either by donation or force, but I can tell you these shirts look like a set-up. A distraction."

"It's odd that those two shirts look like they came from the bowling alley. They are identical except for the names embroidered on them. The shirt left in my home is different. What do you think it means?" She wanted his opinion since he was working the case from a different angle.

"They left a shirt in your home? That's horrible. I'm sure I'll get that later today. It's possible they started out having a connection to the bowling alley but then lost it. So, instead of being able to get a shirt matching the first two, they had to find a look-alike. They must have planned this in advance, though. Shirts like that take time to make and order."

"I checked the brand of the one left in my house, and it takes them two weeks to turn around a shirt. So, this had been in the planning for a while."

Chris leaned forward in his seat. "We should contact the company and find out who ordered it."

"I'll do that." She wanted to rest more, to think more, to decipher all the variables in this case. Every time she did, it got more convoluted.

"When will we have confirmed proof that her blood is not on the shirts?" Chris asked.

"Give me a day. I'm swamped with evidence right now. Apparently, spring is criminals' busy season. They were pent up all winter and now have to make sure everyone pays for it."

LeRoy pressed his fingertips to the desk and rose from his chair. "If you want to leave the shirt in my custody, we can get that paperwork started. It will save Leo from having one of his guys drive it back to me. If he wants to see it, I can send photos."

"I left it with Leo earlier. I'm glad there isn't blood on it, but doesn't it seem odd that there isn't any?"

"Honestly, yes. With as careful as this person is to make everything look right and cover up evidence against them, it's odd that your shirt flips the script."

Chris touched her arm, sending an immediate calm through her. Her shoulders relaxed slightly, and she hadn't realized she was as tense as she'd become.

"Marin got a call early this morning from someone claiming to be Alyssa. We're going to call her phone provider and see if they'll tell us anything, though I'm sure we'll need a warrant for that too. Have you dealt with any evidence of that nature?"

LeRoy shook his head. "This office is as technical as I get. I barely touch my smartphone. I wish you luck in finding out where it came from, and I hope it means Alyssa is alive. You always spoke so highly of her." He reached out and shook her hand once again.

"One more quick question that has nothing to do with the case. What is that fragrance up front? It's really potent," Chris asked.

Marin glanced at him in horror. Why would he offend LeRoy like that?

LeRoy laughed. "This is a college. Occasionally we get cadavers. It takes a lot of fragrance to make sure the scent of dissection doesn't make it anywhere the public can smell it."

In the hall, Chris slowed his steps. "Let's move on to the phone call. We can worry about warrants later today when we'll likely need to pull three. That way, we only need to bug the judge once."

She nodded and let him take the wheel on the case for a little while. Finding out all these things about her sister had taken a toll, one she wasn't sure she'd ever get over if Alyssa was dead.

🐾

Chris drove toward Poplar Bend, leaving the radio off and the windows open a crack. The fresh air seemed to help Marin. She'd had a headache after going to the lab, and he suspected it was from the fragrance in the front office.

He'd been thankful for the reason given, glad it wasn't anything as bad as where his mind had gone and glad he didn't smell of death, since his dog was trained to seek out that scent. Still, it seemed odd that they'd have bodies anywhere near the front of the school. This was a distraction, and he needed to stop worrying about it.

There were enough facets to this case. He didn't need to be

adding more. They'd decided to go back to her house to make the call to the phone company and attempt to get the information. He hoped, since it was her own number, they might relent and give her anything she wanted. She wasn't asking for the phone records of the president, only who had called her this morning and where they were from.

Marin laid her head against the window and let out a soft groan. He was pretty sure she didn't even realize she'd made. He reached across her and opened the glove compartment. Inside, he kept various pain medications to help with muscle aches, headaches, and whatever else he could think of. "Help yourself."

She looked through the bottles and settled on an antihistamine. She popped the cap and shook two pills into her palm. He'd assumed she had a headache, so the choice surprised him.

"Allergies bothering you?"

She shook her head as she took the pills and swallowed without water. "I don't know why, but I never get headache relief from the things people usually take. Not even migraine meds help. But for whatever reason, about a half hour after taking certain allergy meds, I feel better. Thanks for offering your pharmacy." She closed the door of the compartment.

"No problem. That's interesting. Is your sister that way too?" He tapped the wheel, hoping to sound curious. He really wanted her to think about the possible differences between her and Alyssa. Finding out there might not be any blood relation there would hurt. Especially if she felt like Alyssa was the only family she had.

"No . . . Alyssa rarely gets headaches at all. Then again, she's one of those people who drink a gallon of water every day. She's probably perfectly hydrated and healthy. I'm not." Marin shrugged.

This wasn't his battle. He shouldn't feel like he had to fight it. Yet he also didn't want to leave when this was all done, knowing Marin had no one. Her life was about to be turned upside down even more than before he got there.

"What will you do if you get the results of the DNA test back and you find out Alyssa isn't your sister?" He gripped the wheel and prayed she wouldn't get angry.

"Not my sister? That's not possible. It's just rumors. People can be cruel. When no one could figure out why my parents left, they made up what they thought was a plausible excuse. The adoption theory was the one that panned out for those who talk. It's nothing. Alyssa is my sister. End of story."

He wondered if Leo knew the truth. Was that why he'd allowed Marin to work on the case? Had he realized she would find out what had been hidden from her all these years? Was he doing it out of the goodness of his heart, believing she should know, or was it meant to hurt her?

After the long drive, he pulled into the police lot so she could get her car. They'd planned to meet back at her house. Leo stood outside, smoking a cigarette by the side door. He waved both of them over.

Marin seemed hesitant, but there was no good reason to avoid Leo. Chris stationed himself just slightly in front of Marin, hoping to protect her from Leo if he tried manhandling her again.

"Leo," she said stiffly.

"Marin. Look, I'm sorry. I got a call from LeRoy about half an hour ago asking me what I was doing. He claimed I was assuming things and saying things that had no basis in reality. He was angry I tried to arrest you."

"I gave a sample of my DNA. I have nothing to hide."

Chris said a prayer, hoping no one had planted her DNA at any of the scenes or on the evidence. She was good at what she did, and he'd never worried for a moment about evidence contamination.

"I told him to recheck Alyssa's shirt once he's done with Cami's. If there were four blood signatures on that shirt, there could be five. You're the only one with a motive for either death."

Marin gasped at his side. "Oh? Funny. I feel like I'm the only one who *doesn't* have a motive to kill. We're talking about my sister, the only family I have. I love her."

"Do you? She's turned into a bit of a problem child over the past year. With an assault, a drunk driving conviction, and Spike says she was about to lose her job at the alley because of the way she treated customers. Would you still be so supportive if she had to move back in with you?" He let out a quick puff that blew away quickly but left a stink in its wake.

"I would've gladly taken her back in. Why would you believe I wouldn't?"

He touched her arm, reminding her she wasn't talking to a friend. This was not only her boss, but the one who could lie to her to get her to admit something by asking a question in a backhanded way. Marin knew that. He was certain, but this was an emotional situation.

"If you had taken her in, you would've lost your position as an investigator. You can't do your job with a walking parole hearing living with you. This job means everything to you. More than your parents. More than your sister."

"You don't know that. You don't know anything about me," she said through clenched teeth.

"Oh? Your sister has been missing for over a week. Yet your parents hadn't been told yet when I contacted them before I came out here. They're worried. They'll be coming to town later today. I also had to tell them you were our prime suspect. They didn't seem surprised." He tossed the cigarette butt onto the ground and shoved his hands into his pockets. "It's funny that not a single person except LeRoy thinks you're innocent. Maybe there's a reason for that." He swiped his key card in front of the door and headed inside.

Marin stood frozen for a few seconds, obviously processing all he'd said. "My parents are coming back? I tried countless times to get them to speak to me after they left, and they wouldn't return a call. Nothing. It was worse than abandonment. At least, at the time, I thought it was the worst thing they could do. I was wrong. This is worse. How could they believe I have anything to do with Alyssa's disappearance? How did I become the bad guy in all this?"

He turned her back toward the vehicles and led her to her car. "I don't know. Things are falling into place, but they seem stomped into position, not fit there like puzzle pieces. I don't know who's pulling the strings, but we're going to find out. Let's meet back at your house and call the phone company from there. For all we know, the phone call is the one thing in this whole case that is accurate."

She let out a long breath and closed her eyes as she leaned against her car. "Wouldn't that be interesting? I was sure the voice was AI, but what if Alyssa and Cami have slowly found themselves on the bad side of Poplar Bend? What if they started with small-time drugs and steadily got worse?"

Chris nodded, then added, "Then, they needed to disappear because people found out who they were. They could do that by disappearing, leaving clues pointing to nowhere, and then pin their deaths on you when there isn't any other explanation. Evidence would be flimsy, but just enough to convict you. They could move on and do as they please with the only person who really knows them in prison."

"You think this is all about me? You think my sister is trying to get me arrested?"

He felt her pulling away from him. "That was a guess, a theory, nothing more. If your sister's voice was the only thing about this case that was accurate, it's an option."

She shook her head, then wiped her eyes. "Except my sister asked for my help in that call. She wouldn't have done that if she had been trying to pin this whole mess on me."

He had to admit she had a point. "So, if you had to go with your gut, where do you see all the pieces fitting together?"

She ducked her head, then pushed away from the car and strode around to the driver's side. "If I knew that, I'd have a better plan."

CHAPTER NINE

While the cell phone provider had offered a lot more help than Marin thought they would, she wasn't any closer to understanding how the new information fit with what little they already knew. She scratched out a few notes on a pad of paper from a nearby junk drawer.

Chris came in fresh from the shower with Sherlock at his heels. She'd assumed the dog would stick close to her while Chris was busy, but apparently the dog was used to being with him no matter what. Droplets of water clung to his forehead from his untamed curls. Once it dried, it would calm down a little, like it had been before. Or maybe his cowboy hat had tamed them. Now, his look reminded her of Dean Cain as Superman, strength and all. She'd watched the show on a streaming service after learning it had come out around the time she was born.

"Find out anything?" he asked as he lowered into the chair across from her.

"The call came from a rural area an hour north of Cheyenne." She drummed her fingers and tried to lasso her brain back to where it needed to be.

"That's about a couple hours from here. Did they say anything about the phone number?" He eyed the leftover lasagna she'd warmed up while he was in the shower.

She pushed the serving spatula toward him as an offer. "The phone is linked to an FBI agent who went missing over a month ago, Ben Sterns." She released her breath, trying to keep the frustration at bay. Why couldn't there be a break in any of this?

"it is that anyone you've heard of? Might be connected to an old case of yours," Chris offered as he lifted a large square of lasagna onto a plate.

At least the man liked her cooking. There was no denying that. She often had to freeze leftover lasagna because she'd be sick of it before finishing the entire thing. With him here, they'd almost finished it together.

"That's a great idea, but I don't recognize his name. When I called the field office right after the phone company, they divulged that he'd been working on a case in this area when he went missing."

"I think LeRoy should ask if they have a record of his DNA. We might have the male contributor to the DNA on the shirt." He cut off a corner and slowly lifted it to his mouth.

Could the missing FBI agent be the one behind all of this? If Leo had known there was an FBI connection, that would explain his actions. He hated the idea of the feds being asked to advise any case. If he'd gotten wind of FBI involvement, he'd do anything to make sure they got what they needed immediately so they would leave.

"That's a thought. Either way, I think we're going to need to head toward Cheyenne and talk to a few people. Maybe this guy had a partner who knows about his last case? Maybe there are notes they'd be willing to share to help me out?"

He puckered his lips slightly in a frown. "They won't help you. In fact, if they find out you're working a case involving your sister, they may try to take it over. Especially if they think it's connected to a missing agent."

He wasn't wrong, but she didn't want to say that out loud. "Well, what do you suggest?"

"I'm not saying your idea wasn't good, just that it could lead to more problems. I think you're right. We should talk to his partner first. See what we can find. Did you get a name?"

She pushed her notepad toward him and helped herself to some lasagna. If they ended up driving all over, she might not have a chance to eat again for a while. "Alyssa didn't travel. She didn't make trips to Cheyenne. She didn't leave town. Her idea of a good time—as far as I knew—was disco night at the bowling alley. The more I get into this case, the more I'm sure I didn't know my sister."

Her phone rang and she pulled it close enough to see the screen. LeRoy's name traveled from left to right across the screen. "I wonder if he found anything?" She bit her lip as she touched the screen to answer the call. "This is Marin."

"Are you sitting down?" LeRoy avoided a greeting.

". . . Yes, why?" She glanced at the phone, then at him, wishing she hadn't turned on the speakerphone now. What if he said something she wasn't ready to hear?

"Marin, I'm very sorry to be the one to tell you this. Alyssa is not your sister, not your half-sister, not your blood relative at all."

She glanced at Chris for a moment to make sure she'd heard what she thought she had. He didn't look the slightest bit surprised. She closed her eyes, trying to remember as far back as she possibly could. All memories included Alyssa. She couldn't remember a time without her.

"Marin? Are you there?" LeRoy asked.

"Yes, sorry. This is a huge surprise." She tried to hold back the tears fighting to free themselves.

"I'm sure it is. Chris asked me when you both were here what my working theory is. It's changed since we talked. It only takes about an hour and a half for me to run the buccal swab test if it's at the top of my list. Knowing your DNA profile allowed me to look at all the DNA samples on the shirt. I compared the shirt to the pictures I took, and I realized something had changed between when I tested it and when I looked at it today. Someone added a sample of your blood to the shirt, and I know it was added after because the new spot was in an area I had already tested."

"Leo . . ." She didn't want to believe it. What could he have to do with this?

"He's the only person who had time and opportunity to do anything. It also means this shirt is no longer valid evidence in court."

Why would he do that unless he was involved? "Thank you, LeRoy. Is there anything else I should know?" Not that what he'd said hadn't packed a punch already.

"As a man who works with blood every single day and can say it's critically important, it also isn't the period at the end of any sentence. Your genes don't determine who you love like family. Your actions do."

If she didn't share any genes with her sister, did that mean one or both of them were adopted? She massaged her brow. "Okay, I'll need to confront Leo before I head for Cheyenne again to try to figure out what the connection is between my sister and a missing FBI agent."

"Agent Sterns?" LeRoy asked.

She paused for a moment. Of course LeRoy would know. He was close to the halfway point between Poplar Bend and Cheyenne. The field office probably used him when they were swamped. "Yes."

"Interesting. This case has more facets than a radiant cut diamond and not nearly as pretty."

"That seems to be the case. Thank you for looking at that shirt one more time. I think Chris was suspicious of Leo starting yesterday, but I was too close to see it."

"That Chris seems like a good guy."

She glanced at him and stifled a chuckle at his darting eyes. He clearly didn't believe the compliment.

"Yeah, he seems like a good one. I'm sure you'll hear through the grapevine how my talk with Leo goes. It's frustrating that we've now lost the biggest piece of evidence in the case."

"I suspect once Leo is taken to task for this, the rest of the case will fall into place. Not sure why I believe that, but I do. If I find anything else, I'll call you." He hung up without any other sign-off.

"You were right," she said as she turned her phone over.

"About?" His brows shot up in question.

"Suspecting Leo." She hadn't imagined that. He had asked the question, and she'd ignored it out of hand.

"Yes. I also suspected you were adopted and, yes, I do think that is material to this case. Both of you have been hunting for family and meaning since your parents walked away from you. It seems like she went on a search of her own and found herself in the wrong crowd."

🐾

Sherlock nudged Chris's leg with his large, wet nose, then clacked his jaws twice. He reached for the dog and scratched him behind his huge ears. Marin stared at him as if she'd never truly seen him before. He'd been honest. Abundantly clear. More than he probably should have been, and now she was in shock.

"I'm sorry. I shouldn't have said anything." He stood and Sherlock followed him to the door.

After letting him outside, Chris stayed by the sliding door to watch him. Not only because he'd been injured by someone already but also because he didn't want to see the hurt on Marin's face. How could he have used his words like a battering ram? That hadn't been fair to her.

"It's okay. You're right." Her words were quiet and—if he had to guess—she still sat in the same spot he'd left her in.

"Am I? Sometimes I'm so convinced I am that I don't think about how my words will come across. That was pretty rude, considering you let me stay here and fed me . . ."

Sherlock bounded back toward the door. He didn't have room to run around like this back in Chris's apartment. Granted, he got a lot of exercise all day, but once the job was done, he had no room to roam.

"It wasn't rude. It was honest, and I can take it. Look, I know this isn't your case, so I appreciate you've stayed on to help me. Especially since the first handful of words you spoke to me was that you work alone. I think you may have even said it multiple times. So, I know this isn't your usual."

It absolutely wasn't. He slid the door open and let Sherlock back in. "Is this where we part ways? That kind of sounded like a goodbye. I'm willing to stay and help, but if that's not what you want or need, I'll be on my way." And he'd be praying for her safety the entire time.

If Leo was behind this and there was some tie to the FBI, there was no way Marin would ever get to the bottom of it. She'd wind up missing just like the others, and no one would ever put two and two together. They'd make it look like a grieving sister couldn't take the pain.

"I'm not asking you to leave. In fact, I think you might be the one who finds what we need to figure out this case, or your dog." She bobbed her chin toward Sherlock.

Sherlock could do a lot of things, but could he find a trace of her scent in the middle of nowhere with only GPS coordinates of the nearest cell tower to guide them? He hoped so, but Sherlock had never been tested like that.

"We can try. We still have the hairbrush."

"I need to get this question out before we go any further. How are they so far away, yet stuff keeps happening here?"

He sat back down across from her and drummed his fingers on the table. "Not sure unless there's a few people who are doing this. I think Leo might be one of them. Not sure if the FBI guy is the other or what. Someone is holding Alyssa and Cami, probably wherever she called from, but someone here is orchestrating evidence, stirring up issues with Spike and the impound lot, and even drawing us away from your house with a car."

Her eyes widened. "So much happened last night, with Leo coming over to arrest me, I forgot to get that license plate from you and have it run. Can I have that?"

Her excitement brought him back into the case. They could do this. "Sure." He reached into his pocket and drew the little sheet of paper from his wallet, then slid it across to her.

She called dispatch and gave them the information to add to the case and asked her to let Marin know what they found as soon as possible. She ended the call and set her phone down. "That shouldn't take long, then we'll know."

She stood and headed for the fridge. Chris went back to the bathroom to get his unruly hair under control. He'd have to deal with curly hair until he returned to his own apartment. Washing it with no product to put in it for control left him with unruly curls.

He opened the door and walked into the hall just as Marin walked by. He ran right into her, making her squeal momentarily. Instinctively, he roped an arm around her waist, so she wouldn't lose her balance or fall.

She felt good in his arms. Too good. Her gaze met his and they stared for what must have been a few seconds, but he couldn't say for sure. She was so pretty. Jules had been too, but irresponsible, reckless, unable to adjust course. Not like Marin. His brain screamed that he'd only known her for a day and a half. He had no business feeling anything at all.

But tell that to his heart. It beat like they'd been dating for years. Fool thing.

He bent, lowering slowly to allow her time to stop him or dash off. Instead, she leaned in, tilting her face to him. Accepting him. He brushed his lips over hers slowly. Letting his touch be his request. She wrapped her arms around his neck, pressing closer to him, raising on her toes.

He hadn't expected her to return his kiss, and he certainly hadn't expected her to take charge, but he should've. That's who she was. He held her tight, letting the kiss extend longer, running his hands up and down her back slowly. Never pushing too far. There was no way this could work with them living so far away and on the same career path. That didn't mean they couldn't enjoy the time together they had.

He finally broke the kiss when he started to feel the urge to take the kiss deeper. That wasn't the trajectory he wanted to take, and he was certain she didn't either. Her kiss was intoxicating though, and he'd have to be careful about indulging.

She ducked her head. "I don't know what to say. I don't usually do that with houseguests. Just so you know." She brushed a hank of hair from in front of her eyes back behind her ear.

"I didn't think so." He gently tipped her face back up to look at him. "I don't know where this is headed, but I won't let this become a stumbling block for either of us." He pointed at the deep scar on his cheek. "This is what happened when I let my partner get too close. It's why I usually only work with Sherlock. You don't have to worry about me pushing you. Ever."

She rested a hand on his chest, and he resisted the urge to grab it and kiss it. He wanted to touch her skin, even if it was only her fingers.

"I won't either. I don't allow myself to get into relationships. My parents were in love. Look what they did to Alyssa and me. They put themselves first, not only first but last. Only. No one else was important. I can't do that in my job. I can't let myself ever fall in love because it would hurt my career. I can't investigate like I do if I put myself or someone I love above those I'm trying to help."

Which meant she was the perfect person to be in a relationship with. They could enjoy each other's company and never have to worry about the future or where they would go from here. Their relationship would never be deeper than a kiss.

No matter how good that kiss had been.

"Did you want to wait for your parents to arrive, or do you want to go see if we can find that cell tower?"

He wasn't sure what he wanted to do, though staying there in the house with nothing to do seemed like the worst idea. He needed to get out, move, find something, use his sudden burst of energy for good.

"I don't want to see them. Not right now. Why didn't they tell me? Why did they let me believe I was their biological child this entire time? I wish I would've asked LeRoy if Alyssa was theirs or if she was adopted too."

He brushed his hands up and down her arms, trying to infuse her with strength. "I think it's safe to say, since they have treated you the same, you were both adopted. I can't explain why they abandoned you. I wish I knew. Maybe it's time to ask them."

She frowned as she stepped back one pace. "You're probably right. I'm not doing any growing without knowing. All this time, I assumed we had done something unforgivable. We had to. What other reason would they have for running off?" She gently wiped under her nose with her finger.

"We won't know until we ask. Until then, let's see if Sherlock can find something. Do you have the coordinates of the cell tower that the call from Alyssa bounced off of?"

She nodded. "I want to go to Alyssa's first, then I'll put that point in my phone and we'll head there."

He agreed and they went to his car. Traveling with Sherlock was much easier when they had a safe and comfortable place for him to ride. He got Sherlock put into the kennel, though he left the door open. Sherlock wouldn't come out while the car was in motion anyway.

At Alyssa's apartment, Marin daintily stepped over all the items on the floor as she headed for the bathroom. When she returned, she carried a pair of flannel PJs in a plastic bag. "I didn't touch them with my hands. Her other clothes are gone, but these were in the dirty clothes in the bathroom. Alyssa had a thing about her jammies. She's been that way since childhood. She hated when anyone else touched them. Anything she slept in was personal. No touch. She wouldn't even let Mom fold them after age 8. I don't know what the reason was, but for now, it works in our favor."

He nodded and took the bag, then sealed it. If she'd worn them multiple days, as some people did with the clothes they slept in, the fabric would be infused with her scent. Sherlock would have an easier time finding her with a good sample.

They headed for the door then Marin's phone rang. She stopped short and looked at the screen, then flinched. She swiped and held the phone to her ear.

"Hey Mom, what's up?"

He heard some kind of yelling on the other end but couldn't hear the exact words.

"I'm doing my best to get her back. You'll have to trust me. In the meantime, you might want to find a hotel."

More screaming. Chris reached out and threaded his fingers through her free ones and squeezed. She took a deep breath as if his presence helped.

"No, I don't have room at my house."

Her mother said something short. Definitive.

"Well, I can't visit you there. Spike told me that the next time I talk to him, I'd better have a warrant."

He couldn't blame them for wanting to stay with friends when the nearest hotel was so far away, but would they choose to once they heard Spike could be involved? He tried hard to hear Marin's mom.

Marin let out a long breath. "Well, that's fine. It's not like I've seen you in years. Why change now?" She ended the call.

CHAPTER TEN

Marin cleared her throat but knew she wasn't really choking. Her body wanted her to cry, to give in, to expel all the bad feelings stuck inside her. Now was not the time. She'd allow herself to cry later. Preferably next to Chris on a couch where she could curl into his strength and be weak for just a few minutes.

Why had she picked a job where she had to be superwoman all the time? Never a break. Never a day off. Not even when her own sister was abducted. She refused to believe Alyssa was dead. Even if the evidence pointed in that direction. So far, the evidence hadn't been good. No smoking gun. Nothing that would allow her to make an arrest.

Her phone rang again, and she almost didn't answer it. After the call with her mother, she wasn't in the mood. LeRoy's number scrolled across her screen. She answered, "Marin."

"I've completed the testing on Cami's shirt. I expected to find the same results as I did on the first, since the staining is identical. It's not though. With the amount of blood that was clearly Cami's, it is my determination that she is deceased. This is now an official murder investigation."

Marin's stomach twisted. "But Alyssa said on the phone she wasn't the only one there. If Cami is dead, it can't be her."

"I'm not sure what to tell you. The male DNA is still unknown, as is the third female donor. Hopefully, if we figure out who they are, we'll know who killed her. Have you reached out to the FBI agent who worked with Ben?"

"Not yet. I wanted to see if we could find Alyssa by using our search and rescue dog. Since someone tried to kill him, we think he'll be the one to solve this. Evidence can be manipulated, but Sherlock can't."

"Good. I'll keep you posted if I find anything else."

She hung up and set her phone face down on her lap. *Lord, please let me have a few minutes of peace before I get another call. This has been such a tiring day, and it's still morning . . .*

"I'm sorry to hear about Cami," Chris offered from the driver's seat.

She'd allowed herself to check out into her own world for a moment and had forgotten momentarily that he might want to talk about what he'd heard.

"Thanks. I knew her superficially, only as Alyssa's friend honestly, but I was hoping we'd find her." She closed her eyes. "I don't want to be hurtful, but I wonder if Cami was the reason for this change in Alyssa? My sister didn't beat people up. She didn't get into trouble. If I'd known Cami was that kind of person, I'd have tried to get Alyssa to back off from her without completely cutting her off. I wonder if she's the reason Alyssa stopped going to church? I may never know."

"That's true. You may not. But let's hope we find Alyssa. If she's in trouble like that call suggested, then we have to work quickly."

Marin only responded in her head, and Chris didn't push her for more. She appreciated that she could talk with him and be real, but he didn't force her to feel or do anything. Just like he'd promised. He wanted her to think, which was why he'd asked so many questions about her parents and Alyssa, but he'd remained respectful of her feelings the whole time.

Chris followed the directions on her phone until they found the cell tower. It truly was in the middle of nowhere. The chances of Alyssa walking close by were none. Especially if she was being held against her will.

"Thoughts?" She shaded her eyes from the sun and slowly did a circle to look at the wide-open space all around them.

"I think we should start by working our way slowly out in a grid square from this point. At every place, I'll have Sherlock sniff the inside of the bag. When we knock on doors, we'll know if she's inside the house or not."

"That's a good plan." Marin pocketed her phone and made sure her gun was on her belt. While Chris headed back to the car, she took a look around the area. The grass was cut like people came weekly to take care of it, meaning there weren't any areas of long grass that had been trampled.

She walked the perimeter, letting her gaze fall on anything that caught her eye. If they were going to start right here, then it only made sense to do a thorough visual search first. Her sister had disappeared ten days ago and clearly someone had been here since then to mow. If—for some reason she couldn't fathom—Alyssa had been here, evidence of her presence would've been bagged up and hauled away with the clippings.

Finding nothing, she headed for the car. Chris had already started the engine, and Sherlock whined from his kennel in the back. He seemed to know it was time to work, and he was done being locked up. She buckled in. "Which way do you want to go first?"

"The land is distributed in sections. Let's start with that one. If you pull up a 3D map, we can see where houses are and keep track of them as we go."

She got out a pen and paper, then opened an app on her phone to track where they were and all the details of the surrounding area. So much of it was farmland with only a few houses. "Let's stop there first." She pointed to a house on their left.

Chris nodded and turned down the lane. A big cracker-box style house stood in the middle of scattered large trees and looked to have been built in the forties. The owners had taken good care of it. The paint was fresh. The lawn mowed. Even the fences were in great condition.

"Someone cares about this place," she commented. The outbuildings all looked new because they were well-maintained. There wasn't equipment sitting out, nor any projects sitting out.

"I've never seen such a clean farm." His brow furrowed.

"I'm going to make a prediction that this isn't the place." Marin stepped out of the car and closed the door quietly. The whole place was so peaceful she didn't want to disturb it with the noise of slamming a door.

Chris brought Sherlock around and let him take a scent from the bag. While he sniffed the area, he wasn't engaged. Nothing about the front walk made him point like he had before. She'd seen him be more energetic in her own backyard. Disappointment weighed heavily on her shoulders.

She'd known this place would yield nothing from the moment they saw the house, so why was the confirmation so sad? With each house they checked off, they eliminated one more place Alyssa could be. Then again, what if they ran out of places?

Chris knocked on the front door and waited. An older woman answered in a pair of mended overalls and a straw hat. "Afternoon! Fine dog you've got there."

"Thank you," Chris said. He pulled out his wallet and showed his badge. "I'm here looking for a missing person. Can I ask a few questions?"

Her smile faltered slightly. "Want to come inside? Or we can sit out on the porch so your dog can run."

He motioned for the seats on her porch. "After such a long ride,

I'm sure he'd like to stretch. Do you have any chickens or anything he might get into?"

She waved away his concern. "The chickens are all cooped. I used to let them run free, but we've had some theft around here lately. I don't like having to buy new ones."

"I don't blame you." He unhooked Sherlock and turned him loose. "Have you noticed any new neighbors who moved in recently?"

Her happy face morphed into a frown momentarily. "Only the city-boy. He's been making trouble around here. We've all had to keep on our toes. I've caught him in my backyard. Our woods connect, starting right there." She pointed in the distance.

She wasn't sure whether or not that information was worthwhile. Rural people tended to stick together and help each other. They often didn't like outsiders. But trespassing would be a good way to turn any neighbors off on the newbie.

"Where's he from?" Marin asked.

The woman shook her head. "Cheyenne. Said he was some kind of police officer or something. He said he was looking for a missing woman. That's what he was doing in my backyard. As if I would kidnap anyone." She rolled her eyes. "I told him to get off my property straight away. My husband and I are the only people here, and he wasn't welcome."

She glanced up at the house and waved. Marin glanced over in time to see an elderly man at the window. She nodded in his direction.

"He didn't push the issue and left. I've seen him in town since then, but not out here."

The door swung open, and the older man hobbled out onto the porch. "Can I help you folks?"

"We were just asking about any newcomers to the area," Chris said as he peeked over Marin's head to look for Sherlock.

"Trouble. That's what he is. No one needs to be snooping on land that's not theirs." He pounded his fist on the table, making him cough deeply.

"Can you tell us what he looks like?" She kept her voice steady.

"Absolutely. That one has dark hair, like yours." He pointed at Marin. "He wears designer duds like he comes from California. Not local."

Chris whistled softly and Sherlock gave a quick bark before running over to join them. "Any distinguishing marks? Anything that would let us know, 'yup, that's the guy they saw'?"

"He has no eyebrows," the woman said, casting a glance at her husband. "Or maybe they are painted on or some such."

"You don't know that," the husband said. "That's what you thought you saw. You might be wrong."

"I'm not. I know what I saw. That man had no real eyebrows. I'd swear on it."

The older man shook his head and walked back to the house.

"Thank you. That gives us something to look for." Chris stood and clipped Sherlock's lead to his collar.

"Thank you." Marin stood and said, "You've been very helpful." She followed Chris and waited for him to load Sherlock into the car before she got in.

The moment she sat, Chris looked over at her. "You thinking what I'm thinking?"

"The fed ain't dead?" She'd seen the missing man's image and, though the image showed eyebrows, they looked drawn on.

"Precisely."

🐾

Chris started the car. "I didn't specifically ask, and maybe I should have, but I noticed neither of them mentioned a car. I suspect if this guy has one, it would be one they don't approve of."

Marin nodded. "I agree. I think if he had driven to their house, they would've mentioned the type of car. It would've given them more to complain about. Not that they weren't justified. Knowing I had someone messing around in my own backyard was stressful."

Chris dipped his chin in agreement as he headed for the next house. "These guys act like they have complete immunity or maybe impunity. They don't think they'll ever get caught. If they do, they fully believe they won't be convicted."

"Leo is highly trusted. The town likes him. He even mentioned running for office in the future because people like him so much." Marin looked out the window. "I know nothing about the FBI agent. Maybe people trusted him too. What I can't wrap my brain around is Leo working with Ben, an FBI agent, when I know how he felt about them."

"He doesn't even like to share the spotlight in your little office. I can't imagine him taking a backseat to someone who might be perceived as someone more important. A federal agent would definitely have seniority, depending on the case."

He pulled into the next driveway. "I hope you're up for what could amount to days of work. Using Sherlock like this isn't guaranteed and might be a waste of our time."

"I can't think of any other way to use him, and why would they try to get rid of him if he wasn't the way we'd find answers? Is there any other way?" Marin finally turned to look at him. Her eyes were deep pools of concern, probably worried he'd give up. He wasn't, but that's probably what it sounded like.

"No, that's not what I mean. I wanted you to know that if each house takes an hour, we could be here for days. Some houses aren't going to let us get near their doors. They'll see the big scary dog and not answer."

"Let's just pray we find her quickly and keep going. I don't have any other leads to follow until I hear back about that license plate."

The only other evidence they had was the shirt that had been left at her house. "Marin, hear me out here. I know you'll be furious with me, but we have to exhaust all options. Is it possible that the destruction at Alyssa's apartment was her doing ? I know you talked about Mrs. Bloomenthal being wrong about the number of days since she'd seen Alyssa. Maybe she wasn't. If she got that right, it could've been Alyssa looking for something or trying to make it appear her home had been ransacked. Maybe to throw you off the trail. She may have left all those envelopes herself."

Marin's mouth fell open slightly, and she didn't say anything for a charged minute. He could feel the tension building between them in the car like a thunderhead. This wasn't his place. He shouldn't be working with her. He shouldn't be allowing himself to get closer to her. Officers were off-limits to him.

"I hadn't considered that. I just assumed, since Alyssa was missing and I thought everyone local knew the date she went missing, that she was mistaken. She had to be. If Alyssa weren't missing, she would've contacted me."

"She did . . ." he pointed out. "She called you. The more I think about all of this, the more I think there's only one missing person, Cami. So, what did Cami do to make herself a target to Leo, Ben, and Alyssa? Did she do something that threatened them, and how are they connected?"

Marin looked uncomfortable for a moment. "Leo mentioned a few months ago that he was seeing someone new, someone I would be surprised by. He dropped the subject after that, and I was glad. I don't like bringing personal-life stuff into the office. The guys can talk all they want. I don't want to hear it." She scrunched up her face. "Office gossip is the worst."

He tried to follow her train of thought. "So, you think he may have been talking about Alyssa? Since he mentioned it, but didn't tell you who?"

She paused. "I think so now. I didn't then. It would also make sense why I never heard about her assault charge, because he would've taken care of it for her. It makes sense if that's how she ended up getting off without any charges, but Cami wasn't so lucky. Maybe—and this is all speculation—Cami started to complain about the relationship, making herself a threat to Leo. I believe this. If they took a DNA sample when they arrested Alyssa to have one on hand, whoever arrested her thought they would need solid evidence to convict her."

Those ideas had not only bite but plausibility. "Okay, so *if* that's the case, how does her disappearance help them stay together and how does the fed fit in? I'm not discounting your idea. I think it's a great start. I'm saying, let's start adding more of the puzzle pieces and see if they still fit."

She grinned, making his chest squeeze. She was gorgeous when she looked happy. The kind of gorgeous that made a man crave things Chris usually didn't, like making pancakes on a Sunday morning or going for a drive just to talk. He didn't know a single guy who wanted to do those things with other guys. But the perfect girl . . .

No, he put the brakes on his thoughts. She wasn't perfect. Not by a long shot. He had to stop putting her up on a pedestal because he'd start forgetting all his reasons for avoiding this exact situation.

"Well, like I said, I can't figure out the fed connection. Leo doesn't like them. Never has. If he had his way, he'd never let a fed into an investigation of his. He likes being small town, so he doesn't have to deal with them."

So, what would make a man work with someone he considered an enemy? "He probably had to. I didn't like Leo from the moment I met him, so I know I'm coming at this with bias. So, that being said, correct me if I'm out of line."

"I will. You know it." She grinned again.

"I think the only reason he would work with Ben was if he'd found something that would've gotten Leo not only removed from office, but arrested. Maybe he hid drug trafficking or prostitution in Poplar Bend, and Ben figured it out. Instead of telling him he'd go to jail, he gave Leo an ultimatum. 'You let me in on it and I won't turn you in.' Leo's not happy, but he doesn't have much choice."

Marin blinked twice quickly. "I don't know. He's always been such a straight and narrow kind of guy."

Usually, Chris could pick those out of a crowd, since he was one. "Was he? Or did he appear to be? He lied to you to get you to investigate this case. In fact, his lies make more sense in that light. Most sergeants would've wanted you on leave, not hunting for your missing sister. But if you're out looking for someone he knows you can't find, you won't put the dots together about what he's doing behind closed doors. You won't even look at him. He's playing Oz while you're playing Columbo."

She shook her head, but her smile said she agreed with him. "I don't know. It will be really hard to convince his team, much less a jury, that he's anything but honest and hardworking." She glanced ahead at the house. "We'd better go up. They're looking out the blinds, probably wondering why we're sitting here."

"We could kiss and really make them wonder." He wasn't sure why he'd said it. This was absolutely the wrong time to be flirting with her, but he couldn't keep his mind off her for long at any given time. Keeping his attraction at bay had because a daunting task.

She laughed and opened her car door. "You'll have to ask me later, when I'm not on duty."

He was pretty sure that being paid to kiss her would be even better than kissing for free. "I'll take you up on that."

She looked back at him, and he couldn't miss the look of expectation in her eyes. He took the plastic bag from the center console, opened it partway, and let Sherlock get a good sniff of the inside of the bag.

Sherlock shot out of the car without a command and ran off into the woods. Two men slammed open their front door, hollering for him to get his dog.

"Sherlock, come!" he said in a tone that Sherlock would definitely ignore.

Marin reached for her weapon and stood to the side, keeping track of him and the two men by the door.

"You need to get your dog. This is private property. Didn't you see the signs at the end of the driveway?" the older of the two men growled.

Chris pulled out his badge and held it up. "That's Officer Sherlock in your woods. He's a search and rescue dog. Care to explain why he might race off into your forest?"

The two men glanced at each other then ran back inside the house, slamming the door behind them.

Marin lowered her weapon. "Now what? Do we follow Sherlock? I can't call in for backup because we're too far from my jurisdiction, and it'll give away what we're doing to Leo," she said quietly enough for only him to hear.

"Right now, I want to find Alyssa. If she's alive, she's the key to understanding everything that's going on."

Marin ducked her head as she turned toward the woods. "Up until two days ago, I would've assumed the same thing. Now, I wouldn't be surprised if she was part of the whole thing."

CHAPTER ELEVEN

Aching shoulders always came at the worst time. Marin tried to gently massage out the knot forming between her neck and shoulder. They'd been walking through the woods for about an hour, and the men hadn't come back out of the house. She'd been listening for any sounds that would indicate they were coming the whole time. She wasn't going to get shot at because she wasn't paying attention.

"Did Sherlock make a mistake?" She hated asking, but he'd worked so quickly in the park that she'd assumed he'd find Alyssa within the first ten minutes. They'd rescue her and bring her back to Poplar Bend. The end of that story would be the beginning of the one where Alyssa told everything and the bad guys would get arrested.

But nothing about this case had been what she'd expected. Why start now? She looked ahead at Chris's back. He was a man's man, the kind that protected those he loved and did the hard work, no matter how tired he was. He wasn't perfect, but he was stable, and that's what most women wanted.

"I don't think so. He's following a trail. We'll see where it leads.

Clearly, they walked her around this forest. Possibly making her believe she was farther from the house than she really was."

That made sense and was cruel in its own way. If she'd been blindfolded, she wouldn't have any idea they'd been walking in ever-tightening circles, and they never got more than a half mile away from the house.

Ahead, Sherlock froze in what she now knew to be his point stance. He'd let Chris know exactly where to look.

"Marin, stay back."

"Why? Did you find her?" Marin pushed forward, a branch scraping her cheek in her haste.

"Yes, but this is not how you want to remember your sister."

Marin froze. He could see her. She wasn't in some sort of shelter under the ground, held against her will. She was in the forest alone and waiting for Marin to find her. In all the hunting for clues, she'd allowed herself to forget Sherlock was also a cadaver dog. That's why they'd tried to kill Sherlock. He could find Alyssa's body.

"I'm sorry, Marin. She's here, and so is another girl. Probably Cami." He moved slightly, shifting to stand in front of her view and protecting her from seeing whatever lay in front of him.

"Do you want me to ID Cami?" Her mind immediately went into work mode. She could get through this if she shut off every emotion and pushed through. Grief could happen when this was all done. And she *would* find who did this.

He glanced back at her. "Just stay where you are for right now. I'll get an image of her face, and you can tell me if it's Cami. We'll need to call in the locals and get a medical examiner out here." He drew his phone from his pocket.

"Why are you protecting me? You don't need to. I'm an adult and an investigator. I can handle this. You act like I haven't seen death before." Part of her raged at the idea he thought she wasn't capable of doing her job. Another part wanted to walk away and say never again. He was right in part, but allowing him to think she wasn't strong would set her back.

"It isn't that at all. You're an amazing officer and investigator. The trouble is that your immediate reaction will be to touch her, and she can't be touched right now. You can't help her. The only thing we can do is find who did this."

He was right, but she didn't want to admit it. Maybe he had a good idea when he told people he worked alone. If she did, she wouldn't have to deal with others telling her to stay back, hold on, we'll do this for you, you can't handle it . . .

He strode toward her, compassion all over his face. "I'm sorry, Marin. I thought we'd be finding her today. Not this."

He handed over his phone, and Cami's splotchy face made her stomach revolt. "It's Cami," she muttered.

A text message popped up at the top of his screen.

> Chris, why haven't you answered me? We
> need to talk. This isn't cool. It's like you don't
> love me anymore.

Cold dread washed over her. He'd kissed her while he was still with another woman. Hearts couldn't be trusted. Ever. She'd thought her parents loved her, but they walked out. They had imitated love her entire life, but when it wasn't convenient anymore, they'd walked away. Just like Chris. He'd acted interested in her because she was there and letting him stay with her, but he'd walk away the moment the case was finished. He'd even made up a story so she wouldn't question why he didn't want commitment.

She turned around and strode toward the edge of the forest, still clutching his phone. Tears burned her face. A tree stump near the edge of the woods seemed like the best place to put it. She couldn't leave him stranded, and couldn't take his car.

Leaning against the stump and keeping the large farmhouse in sight, she called dispatch.

"Hey Duke, this is Marin, badge number 034. We've found Alyssa Bayless and Cami Cambridge. I need you to call the local PD to this address to send out a few uniforms and the ME." She rattled off the address from the map on her phone.

"10-04, should I let Leo know?"

Marin swallowed hard. Leo wasn't here, but that didn't mean he wasn't involved. Neither of the two men had been Ben either, but they could be scapegoats. They might have no knowledge at all. "No, not yet. I'll tell him when I find out more."

"Sounds good. I wanted to let you know that the warrant for the impound lot is ready. You've got forty-eight hours to execute it. The judge wouldn't give you one for the bowling alley. He didn't feel there was enough reason for it."

Interesting. The place where Alyssa disappeared didn't get one, but the place her car disappeared did. "Thank you. I'll be back as soon as I can."

The loud crack of someone engaging the hammer of a pistol startled her, and she almost fell off the stump. A pistol muzzle shoved against the back of her head. "Stand up."

The male voice wasn't familiar and wasn't old enough to be either of the men in the house. This voice sounded like a man between 25 and 40. It didn't have the subtle rasp and depth of age.

"I said, stand up." He jabbed the gun into the back of her head once again.

She stood and slowly raised her hands. He grabbed her phone from her palm, and she heard him tuck it away somewhere in his clothes, he then grabbed her gun from her holster. He wrenched her hands down behind her back.

"Thanks for giving my friends enough time to call me and let me know some cops were too close."

"I already reported the bodies. The police will be here any minute."

"That's fine. They won't be able to tie them to me. They'll continue to believe it was you. Leo will help plant more evidence to make it appear you found your sister and were so distraught by what you found you couldn't stand to live anymore."

He planned to kill her. In that instant, she saw an image in her mind of her own bludgeoned face with splotches of green coming in at her hairline. Death was an equalizer. No matter how pretty a person was, death made everyone equally ugly.

She turned her face slightly to look back at him, and he hit her with the back of his hand. "Don't you dare look at me. You don't need to know who has you. I have to be careful in case you escape. You won't, but I will make sure I'm protected no matter what."

"Okay, Ben." She wanted to know if this was the missing FBI agent.

He smacked her again. "Don't you dare speak that name. Not out loud. Not in your head. Not ever."

He grabbed her arm and dragged her into the house. She put up as much of a fight as she could, hoping Chris would hear or come looking for her or his phone. Where was he? He wasn't an investigator, so he didn't need to do anything with the bodies.

She closed her eyes and tried to be rational. He had to stay there until police arrived. An officer had to stay at the scene until it was handed over to the medical examiners. Standard procedure. Why hadn't she stayed with him? One kiss didn't make them a thing. That's likely why he hadn't mentioned he was dating someone else.

The thought turned her stomach. She could never be with two people at once. Even dating one was a stretch. She was too busy and had too much baggage to have a healthy relationship. She should've known better.

Ben shoved her through the house, then opened a squeaky basement door. He reached over her shoulder to pull on a thin string, turning on a bare lightbulb. A milky shaft of light spread down the stairs, offering just enough light to show where to put her feet and not much else. She had no way of holding onto the rail with her hands bound behind her back, and the stairs were all narrower than her foot.

He held onto her wrist and nudged her down each step. Her knees wanted to give out under the stress. What if she fell? She'd go headfirst down the steps with no way to stop until she hit the basement. She breathed a deep sigh when her foot touched the cold cement floor at the bottom.

He pulled another string, and an equally weak light bathed the small cellar in light. Along three of the walls, old shelves held food that might have been canned about a decade before. The smell of mustiness clung to the air. A single folding chair sat right under the light, and he pushed her down into it.

Within seconds, she was bound to the chair, and he shoved a damp sock into her mouth.

"I don't know when you'll get out of here. That really depends on how long the police take to finish up the task out in the forest. When they're cleared out. We'll go hunting. Will you be good prey for me? I guess we'll find out." He laughed as he pulled the string and the room went dark.

❖

Sherlock barked at him for the third time in under a minute. Chris glanced at his watch. The trees seemed to close in around him. Why hadn't Marin come back? She'd taken his phone with her when she'd walked off, and he couldn't leave the scene, putting him in a bad situation. If he left, anyone could tamper with the evidence if they came upon it. He didn't have his phone to take pictures anymore.

All that and Sherlock wanted to leave the area, which wasn't like him at all. The waiting was part of the job, and he was used to doing it. Then again, Sherlock might be reading his body language and knew Chris wanted to go after Marin and see if he could help her. He'd tried to be a wall between her and Alyssa, but maybe she'd managed to look anyway.

"Marin?" he called quietly, in case anyone from the house had come out. He'd been listening at first for any noises coming from there, but had let his focus go completely on the task of cataloguing as much as he could without any resources.

Men's voices came from a distance, and he caught sight of a few officers and two men who were clearly with the medical examiner's office. They carried with them large tackle box style evidence collection kits and body bags. This was the side of police work he didn't enjoy. Medical examiners and their investigators had to have a special skill set he didn't possess. Even though he worked with a partner who could be used as a cadaver dog, death was the least favorite part of his job.

"Hey, thanks for getting here so quickly." Even though it had felt like a long time, they'd had to come from about half an hour away. It had seemed longer because he was worried about Marin.

"No problem. Where's Marin? I thought she was with you? She's the one who called it in, but she said you and Sherlock were here."

"I don't know. She walked off about thirty minutes ago. I'll brief you on the scene, then go find her. I didn't let her approach anyway because one of our vics is her sister."

One of the medical examiners flinched slightly. "I can't blame her for avoiding the scene. Thanks for taping it off."

He'd brought crime scene tape and a few evidence bags and gloves on Sherlock's tactical vest. Good thing because Marin hadn't brought hers along. Without her at the scene, he wouldn't have been able to document anything.

In a rapid look through the scene, he pointed out to all four men why he thought this was the site where the two were murdered, likely at the same time. He explained how Sherlock followed the trail of their scent in circles all the way to this spot.

"I knew the moment the scent Sherlock took in was no longer the scent of the woman, but of decay." He hated explaining this part and had been glad Marin hadn't noticed the change. "He acts differently, depending on what he's searching for."

The officers thanked him as they suited up for scene preservation. He showed them where he'd been standing, since his footprints were there, and also confirmed there had been no footprints there before he stood on that spot.

"Sherlock, come." He glanced around.

Now that they could leave, Sherlock was nowhere to be found. He never left a scene. Ever. "Sherlock?" He didn't yell because he didn't need to. The dog could hear him from over a mile away. Where had his partner run off to? Could he be in the car? Breakfast had been hours ago, but that was completely unlike Sherlock.

He avoided going back the same way he'd come. Instead, he took a straight path based on where the sun was so he could get back to the house. When he got close, he found Sherlock sitting on a large stump within sight of the house. As he stood, Sherlock revealed Chris's phone.

"What?" Why would Marin leave his phone out on a stump in the middle of nowhere?

He opened it, hoping whatever she'd been doing would give him some clue as to where she was or why she'd left. The text from Jules popped up first, making him groan. He'd dealt with her. Why hadn't she listened? He didn't want anything to do with her. They'd broken up, and he didn't want another chance. Some decisions were final.

As soon as he found Marin, he'd deal with Jules in no uncertain terms. There were very few things in life he wouldn't compromise. The first was his faith, and the second was his reputation. Working with Jules had ruined his reputation since he'd been so focused on her protection that someone had died. He had to live with that.

What if Marin died because of him?

His stomach twisted. Someone had already threatened her by leaving the same shirt in her home as the two missing girls. Just because it didn't have blood on it yet didn't make it any less of a threat. The other two women were dead. Marin had walked off alone, and the men inside the house were now suspects in a double homicide.

Sherlock gave a high-pitched bark, the kind that usually meant he wanted Chris to follow. "Okay, if you know where she is, take me there."

Sherlock leapt off the stump and put his nose to the ground, weaving in the grass until he reached the front door. Not just the stoop where she'd stood while they were questioning the two men, but the actual doorjamb. Sherlock pushed his forehead against the door and growled.

"Call off your dog!" one of the older men yelled from behind the window near the front door. "You've got no reason to come in here. I won't allow a search."

"I'm sure a warrant is coming. You can't avoid it." Not with what they discovered on the property.

He glanced over at his car and noticed a new Cadillac DTS parked next to it. It was black with darkly tinted windows. The car hadn't been there before. He headed for it, and Sherlock sat at the front door, guarding the spot. The car had a thin coating of dust on it, probably from coming to this house, but it was still mostly clean, meaning it likely didn't drive these rural roads often.

Who could afford a car like that out here? He grabbed his phone and pressed the number for his boss. He wouldn't call Leo and potentially clue him in to the fact that they were close to him and his little scheme.

"Fletch, glad I caught you. I need a little help with the case I'm helping with over in Greenville. Can you run a set of plates for me?"

"Sure. Go ahead."

Chris rattled off the place number while listening to his boss plug in the information. After a minute, his boss cleared his throat. "That car is registered to Ben Sterns, FBI agent for the Cheyenne field office."

"Missing . . ."

"Yeah, he's been reported missing. Did you find his car?" his boss probed.

"More than that. I may have found him." Chris tried to see into the car but the tint on the windows was too deep. If anyone sat inside, he wouldn't know.

"Is he alive?" Fletch said.

"Not sure." Just because he had the car and just because the car had been moved didn't mean Ben was still alive. Someone drove his car, but it might not be him. "I need to do more looking around."

He didn't have a reason to break in, but if he could, Sherlock could figure out where he'd gone. The likely spot was in the house. The one place he couldn't go until local law enforcement got a warrant to look at the house.

He whistled for Sherlock and jogged back to the officers as fast as he could through the downed branches and undergrowth. Twigs snapped and leaves crackled under his feet. He got there just as the two investigators zipped up the first of the two victims.

He went to the officer closest to him, knowing they were now there to protect the examiners while they documented the scene and the bodies before transport. "Can I ask you a question?"

The officer glanced over at the other as if to ask permission.

The other nodded.

"Sure, what's up?"

He glanced at the scene, unable to look away. "Did they find any evidence that links to the nearest house? I have reason to believe they are hiding other potential victims and possibly our killer."

The officer shook his head. "We let those guys go first, then we'll look at the evidence left. They get the bodies. We get shell casings and anything else that's left behind."

He knew that much, but they likely didn't know how often he'd had to be around for scenes like this. "When will you be calling in a warrant to search that house?"

The second officer spoke up this time. "When we've had a chance to see what we have. While the people who own the house could have something to do with this, it's also possible someone dumped these two out here thinking no one would ever find them. We can't assume anything."

And in the meantime, Ben might get away. He headed for the clearing and opened his car door. Sherlock went right inside his kennel and *harumphed* as he rested his head on his paws. As much as Sherlock was a K9 to the core, he still didn't understand rules. They couldn't break the door down and look for Marin without cause. Even if he wanted to.

"I don't know what you expect me to do, boy. They haven't kicked me off the property yet, so I can sit here until they try to leave, but that's about all I can do." He glanced at his watch.

There was literally nowhere else on the property Marin could be, but if she wasn't in there and he went up to the door and barged inside, he could ruin any case they might build against the men inside the house. If they killed Alyssa and he ruined any chance of getting a warrant because he busted inside, Marin would never forgive him.

Just like he'd done with Jules, he'd tried to make decisions to protect Marin, not the victims in this case. He couldn't make the same mistake twice.

CHAPTER TWELVE

Somewhere in the dark, something dripped. Marin closed her eyes and fidgeted against the tingling pain of her arms tied behind her back. Another drip. Was a pipe leaking or had something happened? Had it been dripping the whole time or had it just started?

Her mind raced into overdrive. What if they'd left the water running above her so it dripped on her as she sat in the pitch dark unable to do anything? The high-pitched chitter of a mouse came from her right, then skittered across the floor. Had it touched the toe of her shoes or was she imagining that?

The dark had never bothered her until now. She had no control over her surroundings. No control over what happened to her. Almost worst of all, she couldn't scream with the wadded-up fabric in her mouth. The longer it was there, the more it absorbed all the moisture from her tongue. Her throat ached for a drink.

That was it. The cause of the drip. It was psychological. He'd known what would happen to her, how she would crave a sip of water, but not that water. The drip was to remind her she couldn't get free, couldn't drink anything. She was completely under his control.

Footsteps slowly came down the stairs, and a fragile beam of light danced around her feet. Ben stood behind her, and a phone rang as if he'd called someone.

"Hello?" Chris's voice came over the line.

She squirmed in her seat, bouncing the chair to make as much noise as possible. She moaned as loudly as the fabric stuffed in her mouth would allow.

Her voice filled the room, but not with what she would ever say. "Chris, where are you? I caught a ride back to town. I need you to come get me. I'm stranded in Leo's office."

That would confuse him. They'd left her car there. He had to question that. They'd discussed someone using AI to clone Alyssa's voice. Now she was sure that was exactly what Ben had done.

"Marin? There's no way. No one came to pick you up and your car is sitting in the lot at the station. Who is this and where is Marin?"

She heard Ben typing on his phone behind her, frantically typing. Her voice answered him, "Of course someone came to get me. Where else do you think I could be? I'm at the office, and my car is not here. Come get me. I need you."

Please, Lord, don't let him believe that. He would know I would never ask for help that way. I wouldn't react like that. Please . . .

"I'll be there in forty-five minutes," he answered, but sounding frustrated, like he was sure this was a mistake, and he'd pay for it.

She flung as much energy as she could into making the chair hop or scrape. Maybe the noises would make him question the truth of the call. It sounded exactly like her voice. If she were in his shoes, she'd believe it too.

"Marin, wait . . ." he paused for a moment. "I'm really sorry about what you likely saw on my phone. As you can tell, I found where you left it. The text you saw was a lie. I just wanted you to know I'm sorry. I'm sorry you saw it. I'm sorry it likely hurt you when you didn't need an ounce more hurt. I thought the relationship with Jules was over a long time ago. It's her confusion. Not mine. As far as I'm concerned, we're through. I just needed you to know that."

Marin froze, taking in the words. He hadn't kissed her to mess with her emotions. That woman had texted him to start something he didn't want restarted. She should've gone and confronted him right away, but that would've meant going back to the scene where her sister lay.

I forgive you. She couldn't say the words out loud, but God knew her heart. God would let him know if she didn't make it through this. Somehow. God always had a way.

Ben typed out what he wanted the voice to say, and it answered, "I don't care about that. You're a lone wolf, right? After you come pick me up, you can go back to Cheyenne. Thanks for helping me find my sister. We'll take it from here."

No. Please, no. If Chris left, she would be totally alone. They'd get away with everything. He likely wouldn't even hear she'd been killed because rural news never made it to Cheyenne. He'd go home and do his job, never thinking about her again.

"Um, okay. I'll see you in a bit and we can talk." She heard the muffled, scratchy sound of him ending the call.

"Don't think for a second he cares about you. I did a little research on him. He used to have a partner, you know?" Ben touched the back of her head, and she immediately flinched away from his touch.

"He was in the middle of a hostage situation. His dog had led them to a house where an officer was being held for ransom. They busted in to retrieve him, and a couple people opened fire on them upon entry. Instead of getting into a safe position to fire their way farther into the house, he decided to be a hero and protect his partner. He ended up getting cut on the face and having to go on leave for a month and was under investigation. The cop they went in after was shot. Dead. He's to blame."

The realization hit her. That's why he never wanted to work with her or anyone else. He'd made a mistake. Who would ever want to repeat a history like that? Ben had used psychology again on Chris. He'd played to Chris's weakness of wanting to help his partner since she was in danger, overlooking the obvious issue of safety.

"Now I don't have to worry about him. As soon as the police leave the woods, you and I are going to play. You'll enjoy it. At least for a few minutes. Though, I guess I don't really need to fool you like I did Alyssa and Cami."

She wanted to ask him why. Why had he killed Alyssa if she'd been dating Leo? How did Cami fit into all of this? Motive was always the driving factor of a case, and there didn't seem to be one. Knowing why Ben wanted them dead would give her what she needed to know in order to solve the case. Assuming she ever got away to tell anyone.

Ben grabbed a chair from along the wall and flipped it around facing her, then straddled it. She could see now that the eyebrows she'd thought were drawn on were likely tattoos. There was no depth to them at all, and they were a little too perfect to be penciled on. He also had one down his neck, hidden mostly by his collar. His smirk made her flinch for a second before he shined the phone flashlight in her eyes.

She blinked, finally giving up and closing her eyes against the glare. What did he hope to accomplish by torturing her?

"Tell me about Leo. I need to know his weaknesses. If you help me, I might be persuaded to let you go."

She knew better. She'd seen his face, knew who he was, and was aware of his crimes. Not only that, she had the authority to arrest him. He wasn't going to let her go. He yanked the sock from her mouth, and the damp air forced a cough from her dry throat.

"Give me even one thing and I'll get you a drink."

She swallowed, trying to force her saliva ducts to work so she wouldn't crave what he offered. "You were a profiler, weren't you?"

He laughed. "No. Not hardly. You can't work for the FBI and not learn who criminals are. A lot of us do the job to end the desires of people the public sees as bad. Some of us see their plans and understand what they want. I can't blame them. Take your boss, for example . . ." He paused and chuckled shortly.

"Your boss thought it would be a good idea to use his office as a drug-smuggling warehouse. He arrested people for drug use, waited until after court, then sold the drugs to certain buyers. He used your sister as bait for drug cartel leaders because she made one stupid mistake, and she couldn't bear for you to hear about it. So, she offered herself as collateral for him to hide what she'd done from you."

Pain sliced through her chest. The assault had happened months ago, meaning the changes in her sister were all due to the fact that she had turned into a forced prostitute for the sake of pride. She closed her eyes. Instead of seeing her sister, she saw the envelope from Alyssa's with the long dark hair in the flap. Very similar to Ben's hair, tied in a low pony at his neck.

"You have nothing to say? Leo likes to talk. He told me all about her. How she was perfect for the job because no one would ever suspect her of doing something like this." He laughed. "Then Leo fell for her, and her usefulness turned into a liability. Couldn't have that." He made the squishy sound people make when joking about cutting off a head.

Marin refused to cry. She had to maintain control if she hoped to get free.

A squeak from above sounded like an opening door, and she wondered why she hadn't heard it before Ben had come down.

"Boss? He's not leaving. I know you said he'd pack up and go in the next few minutes, but he ain't leaving."

Ben cut loose with a string of profanity. He stood and tossed the wooden chair against the shelves. Jars fell, shattering all over the floor. She waited for the stench to hit her, but nothing came. She hoped it never would.

He gripped her chin. "He will go. There is no help for you. You haven't given me what I want yet, and that's the only thing keeping you alive. I won't wait long. Consider this your only shot at revenge against the man who made sure your sister would die. Your last thought can be that you got justice for her. How fitting, since that's all you wanted anyway."

He trudged up the stairs, and the room plunged back into darkness. The drip her only companion.

❧

An AI voice had to be what he'd heard. Chris sat in his car and stared at the door to the farmhouse, waiting for someone to emerge. They couldn't stay in there forever. When they came out, he'd confront them. He was even more sure now Marin was inside.

If they tried to trick him into leaving, then they had her, so how could he get her free? Not an ounce of his being believed what had been said over the phone. He'd hoped she'd been listening, but there was no way to know. Perhaps knowing he hadn't betrayed her would give her some motivation after losing her sister. She had to feel completely alone.

Sherlock clacked his teeth from the back, a reminder the dog didn't like to sit still and wait.

"I know, buddy. We have to be ready for the moment they open that door."

Leo's number came across his screen. Would he try to trick Chris like the call that looked like it had come from Marin? He pressed the screen to answer the call.

"Chris here."

"Where's Marin? I have some information for her. She's not picking up."

Should he tell Leo and risk greater danger because it might make whoever had her angrier? "She's being held at a farmhouse outside of Greenville. As far as I know, she was taken inside a little over an hour ago. I'm waiting for someone to come out so I can question them. Oh, and she found Alyssa and Cami."

"Are they okay?" Leo sounded far too needy. He couldn't possibly know.

"Not hardly. I thought you assumed she was dead. Wasn't that the whole reason you asked me to come?"

Leo faltered, the noises in his throat giving him away. "Well, of course, but Marin believed there was hope the whole time. Are you saying she was wrong?"

"I'm saying your question doesn't make sense given the reason you asked me to help you. Marin isn't with me on the call, so your story doesn't hold water."

"You're saying she's dead." His voice held an accusing chill.

"For at least a few days," he answered.

"Where are you? I'll be there as soon as I can."

Chris gave him the address and let him know about the team already back in the woods doing their jobs. "If you have any idea who has Marin, you need to tell them to release her. Two murders on their hands is bad, one more puts them in serial killer territory."

"You're assuming you know about all of their crimes," Leo snarled.

"So you know who I'm talking about?"

Leo ended the call, and Chris set down the phone. Sherlock growled right behind his ear, making him realize the dog had gotten up from his spot and now stared at an approaching man. A man who looked very familiar and had tattooed eyebrows.

If he stayed in the car and waited for Ben to do anything, Sherlock would protect the car with everything in him. He didn't want to see Sherlock get hurt, but he had to play this situation correctly. Ben likely wasn't afraid of Leo, but he might worry about what information Leo left to be found by someone else.

"Who are you and why are you sitting by my house?" he yelled through the closed window.

He rolled down the window an inch. "I'm with the team removing the victims in the woods," he lied.

"You're blocking our driveway. Why are you here and not with them? I don't appreciate your presence here. We aren't guilty of any crime and haven't been accused of anything. Get off my land." He pointed down the drive.

"First, it's not yours. I checked. The homeowner is probably twice your age. Second, I was told by Sergeant Leo Colder to stay right where I am until he gets here."

His eyes narrowed. "I don't know that name. Who is Leo Colder? He's not a local."

"No, he's the officer in charge of the murder case that's ongoing with the victims in the woods. I'm sure someone will be in to question all three of you shortly."

"Three?" He scrunched his forehead like he was confused, but his eyes told a completely different tale.

"Yes, you and the two older men who came to the door earlier. Last I checked, that equaled three."

Ben flushed, and his right hand clenched into a fist. "You're out of your jurisdiction, Chris Johnstone. All I have to do is call your superior to get you off my property. You can leave now of your own free will or you can get written up and be put on administrative leave for not following directions. Your choice."

"If you knew who I was, why did you act like you didn't?" He was through playing these games.

"Leave. Now."

"Give me Marin's phone. I know she's inside that house. When Leo arrives, hopefully with a warrant, we'll be coming inside to get her. Even if I drive off, I won't go far. As soon as you so much as breathe wrong, I'll be on you like stink on a skunk."

Ben narrowed his eyes, and his smile turned pure evil. "Funny thing about skunks, they only stink when provoked." He turned around and headed back for the house.

Lord, keep Marin safe. Give me a way to get to her to help. I know I shouldn't want to, but I don't know what I'll do if I let her down.

He picked up his phone and opened the text from Jules. She was certainly tenacious. He'd give her that. But she wasn't the woman for him. He needed someone who knew when to take their own path and when to be a team. She wasn't that person. Maybe Marin was, but she couldn't be if he didn't find her and get her back.

The examiners, one on each end, carried out the first bag and put it carefully in the back of their van. In under an hour, he would have no excuse to stay parked there. Without reason or evidence, he'd have to leave.

He wrote out a text that he hoped would end the situation with Jules.

[Jules, I'm sorry you thought I'd want to restart a relationship after breaking off the first one. I hope you find what you're looking for but it's not with me. Please don't contact me again.]

He left it at that. There was no reason to be more cruel than necessary. He simply wanted the past to stay in his past. After about twenty-five more minutes, the crew brought out the other bag and put it in the van. They got inside and drove off, leaving the officers in the woods.

Leo pulled up in an unmarked car and parked on the other side of Chris. He'd either sped far above the speed limit, or he'd been halfway there. He got out of the car and slammed the door. His first glance was to the house, then he headed for Chris.

"Where is she?"

He wasn't sure whether Leo meant Alyssa or Marin. "Who?"

Leo scowled. "Marin, of course."

"I'm certain she's inside. As certain as I can be without seeing her." He dipped his head toward the house. "You know the place?"

Leo rolled his eyes. "Why would I? Do you think I know every rural piece of land between Poplar Bend and Cheyenne? It's hard enough to learn all the areas within my own jurisdiction."

He didn't want to give up all the knowledge he had just yet. Maybe there was a way to trick Leo into helping. Which meant he had to play dumb.

"I didn't. I was only asking if you were familiar with this place. It didn't take as long for you to get here as I thought it would. Wasn't sure if you sped or if you knew the place."

"Let's go to the front door." Leo turned away and walked off in a rush.

Chris got out, and Sherlock followed. They met at the front door. He waited for a moment, listening for any sounds from inside that might clue him in to anything happening inside. Though he'd hoped to hear some noise, nothing made it beyond the threshold.

Leo knocked, the noise sounding loud and hollow in the clearing. Sherlock sat at his feet, his front legs twitching. With as aggressive as he'd been at that door earlier, he'd be surprised if Sherlock didn't run into the house the moment they opened the door. He just hoped no one shot at his partner.

The door opened a crack, barely enough to see the eye of one of the older men. Not Ben. Would Leo know either of these two? He was certain Leo and Ben knew each other and likely worked together to commit crimes. There was no way of knowing how much this man knew.

"What?" he said, his eye darting between the two of them.

"We're missing an officer, and we suspect she's inside. I'd like to come in and take a look around." Leo flashed his badge.

The man at the door moved back slightly, perhaps to shut the door. They'd never find out what he meant to do. Sherlock took a calculated leap at the door and shoved the man off his feet, landing on his rear.

"Get your dog before he ruins everything!" Leo screamed. "I never should've brought you onto this case."

Sherlock raced for the kitchen to the left of the door, only visible because he'd knocked it fully open. The older man sat in a daze, looking up at them.

"Oh, he's not going to like that."

Scuffling in the back of the house made Chris draw his weapon. "Go after them!" He hoped Leo would at least act like an officer.

Leo drew his pistol and headed for the back door. It slammed a few seconds later. He spun to find Sherlock. The sounds of sniffing drew him to the kitchen where Sherlock stood in front of a hidden doorway. It looked like a floor-to-ceiling mirror, but the stains on the floor gave away that it was a doorway.

He pulled the mirror toward himself and found the recessed hole where a knob had been at one point. He pushed it open, and a narrow staircase appeared. Sherlock raced down the steps without a hint of hesitation. Chris tugged on the string just above his head as a female scream came from downstairs.

CHAPTER THIRTEEN

Something cold shoved into the palm of Marin's numb hand. She'd lost track of time after Ben had gone back upstairs. The darkness and dripping water invaded her head. The only way to disassociate was to close her eyes and imagine herself somewhere else far away.

"Marin?" Chris's voice came from the stairs behind her.

"I'm here!" Her voice was hoarse and quiet, but if she could hear it, he certainly could.

"We found you." He took hold of her hand in his warm one and cut the tie binding her wrists.

She fell forward as her body slumped, and he caught her, lifting her off the chair. She reached for him, her sobs clogging her throat. "Chris?" Was she imagining this? Ben had said she was as good as dead. How had he gotten into the house?

Something acrid stung her nose. She breathed deeply, trying to place the smell. "Is that . . . fire?"

She couldn't see Chris's face. In his hurry, he hadn't turned on the light once he'd gotten down there. The distant bulb at the top of the staircase didn't reach. She heard sloshing and realized Sherlock had found the puddle in the back of the room.

"We'd better go up and see what that is." Chris draped a strong arm around her waist and helped her toward the stairs. When they got there, she realized her knees weren't working the way they should and there wasn't enough room to go up the stairs side-by-side.

The pungent smell hit her again, and she glanced up the stairway. Dancing light licked along the top of the door. Dark smoke billowed through the doorway and collected along the ceiling. She held tight to Chris.

"We've got to get out of here." She reached for her leg to lift it. Why weren't her knees working? She'd never had trouble with them before. "I need help. I can't move."

Chris stood in front of her and wrapped her arms around his neck, then held her tightly right above her elbows. "Sherlock, up," he commanded.

The dog bounded up the stairs and through the doorway into the blazing house. He trusted his partner. If Chris told him to go, he would. She held tight to his neck and tried not to kick him as he navigated the stairs. There wasn't enough room for him to carry her any other way. When they neared the landing, he lowered himself as much as possible and gripped the doorway to pull himself through so they could both avoid the fire.

He raced outside and laid her on the grass next to Sherlock, who'd waited about twenty yards from the house. She reached over and hugged the dog. She wasn't sure how she knew, but innately, she knew Sherlock had been a big part of her rescue.

"Good boy," she said as she scratched him behind the ears.

Chris lowered himself to the ground and dug his phone out of his shirt pocket. He poked the screen three times and the phone rang.

"911, what is your emergency?"

He coughed as he rattled off the address and told them about the fire. He also warned them the fire was close to an ongoing homicide investigation, and they may want additional officers in the area.

"Do you need an ambulance?" she asked.

"No," Marin answered at the same time Chris said, "Yes."

The dispatcher waited for a few seconds. "Was that a yes or a no?"

"I want them to look over both of us. Marin has some weakness in her knees. I'm not sure if it's from the way she was tied to the chair or if something else is wrong. I'm likely fine, but I had to breathe deeply as I was carrying her up the stairs. I think I inhaled more than I should've."

He'd saved her and hurt himself. Just like he'd done with Jules. The second he hung up the phone, she reached over and laid her hand on his. "I'm sorry."

"For what?" He tilted his head and looked at her.

"While I was downstairs, Ben tormented me. When he called you and used that text to talk voice that sounded like me, he told me your history. It seems he never gains a partner or an adversary that he doesn't research first."

"It's wise, if we can call anything he does wise."

She squeezed his hand. "He told me why you never work with anyone. Part of it was that you got injured while protecting your partner. I know we're not really partners on this case, but close and you got hurt again because of me. So, I'm sorry."

He slowly shook his head. "I needed to go in there to get you. It was driving me out of my mind to think about you being in that house, where Alyssa and Cami probably were before they died, and I couldn't get to you. I had to follow protocol, or I could ruin everything. Thankfully, Sherlock doesn't have the same rules I do."

"I'm surprised Ben didn't open fire on you the moment you stepped through the door. He's deep into drug trafficking. I don't think we're going to take him alive. Prisons aren't happy places for anyone, but law enforcement . . ." She sucked in her breath as she winced. "It's worse for anyone with a badge."

"Leo was here too," he said, as his shoulders slumped slightly. He drew his hand from her touch and rested his arms on his bent knees. "He called me, looking for you. I had to either bring him into the conversation or weasel my way out of talking to him. I chose to let him in. He went after Ben as soon as Sherlock ran through the door."

"He's been part of this the whole time." She clenched her teeth. "What did he say?"

Chris looked away. "Nothing, really. He did slip up when he was talking about Alyssa. He knows I'm aware there's a connection. We're not safe around him anymore than we are around Ben."

She gave a nod. "Noted. Thank you for coming in to get me. He told me my life was over the moment he had an opportunity to take me out to the woods. Every sound was torture. Minute after minute. I realized down there I don't have the faith I need. I used to read about missionaries who faced all sorts of hardships and never succumbed to the stress. They always looked to God for provision. I didn't. I crumbled."

Her chest ached in confessing her lack of faith. She wanted to be one of those people, but how could she get there? It wasn't as if she ever wanted to be in that position again to test it.

"No one is perfect. He'll forgive you. Especially since you literally repented as soon as you were safe again."

She allowed herself a half-smile. "I suppose you're right." She laid down and looked up at the trees, thankful for the sun, the air, the sky, and the man beside her.

"I know I should go and try to fight that fire. I should try to save evidence instead of letting it burn, but I also don't want to leave you alone out here, defenseless, when Ben and Leo are likely close by."

"I'd like it if you stayed. The firefighters and ambulance should be here soon. They will put it out faster than you could with only the well and the bucket next to the pump house."

She heard the sirens in the distance. "See, just like I told you."

"You sure like to tell me things." He grinned and leaned on his elbow, blocking the sun from her face.

He was so handsome, strong, capable, and smart, but all those things wouldn't matter if he didn't like her. He leaned closer, closer still, until he claimed a sweet, gentle kiss. Lying in the grass, feeling the breeze against the heat on her face, hearing the birds, and enjoying his kiss felt like a preview of her future.

And just that quickly, he ended it. His face scrunched in confusion. "That's not the face I expected to see. What's wrong?"

"Nothing," she lied.

Today had shown her she wanted more. Alyssa was gone. Her parents weren't her parents anymore in any sense of the word. She was alone. Chris would leave in a day, maybe less, and she would have no one. Her job might not even be there because Leo would get arrested once the facts of this case came out. He couldn't sell drugs and run a police force.

"I know you've had a horrible day. I shouldn't have pushed myself on you like that. I'm sorry."

He was sorry for kissing her. Nothing like adding insult to injury. "How long can you stay, or will you be heading back to your real life as soon as possible?"

Two fire engines pulled into the yard. People in bright yellow gear poured out from the doors. They pulled a hose from the side and hooked it up to the truck. She prayed they'd have enough water between the two trucks to get the fire put out. Maybe they had a tanker on the way.

"Do you want me to go? Is having me here too much? You've gone through a lot." He pushed himself upright.

How could she answer that truthfully and not sound like she needed him? He'd been totally honest from the start. He found her attractive, but there wouldn't be any depth to their relationship, just a little fun and flirtation. Unfortunately, now that she knew her sister was dead, she couldn't flirt and didn't want to have fun. She wanted to catch her killer or killers and see them face justice.

She watched the firefighters walk around the house and break open strategic windows for ventilation. Black smoke rolled out, bringing the burning stench with it. She took in a deep breath then regretted it. Even from this far away, the smell burned her throat.

"I'm not asking you to leave. You can stay if you want to. I just know you have a job back at home. Now that we know who we're after, it shouldn't take too long." At least, that was true with some cases. Others weren't so cut and dried.

"You really think Leo and Ben are going to let you walk up and arrest them?" Chris's eyebrows arched high.

"I do. That's why I said you can stay or go. It's up to you."

🐾

Chris couldn't swallow. What had just happened? He shouldn't have kissed her there in the grass, but he'd been so glad to see her alive and mostly unhurt. She'd been in the hands of killers and was now acting as if she didn't need him at all.

Maybe she didn't. He'd known from the start she was the kind of woman who ran her own life and did her own thing. She answered only to God and Leo, and Leo had let her down. She likely wouldn't trust anyone for a good long while. He'd even told her he wasn't looking for a partner or commitment, and that had been fine with her. Now, it was almost too fine with her. She seemed to want him gone.

"Maybe I misunderstood. It sounded like you wanted me to go. My boss knows where I am and hasn't asked me to come back yet, so I don't think Sherlock and I need to run off so soon. Plus, those guys are busy and if I leave, you're all alone again, facing two men who want to kill you. While I have no doubt about your ability, I wouldn't want two men trained in law enforcement and with who knows how many thugs at their disposal coming after me. I'm thinking you wouldn't want that either."

She shrugged a shoulder. "There's only so far they can run."

"Has it occurred to you that if they kill you, I'm the only other person who knows about our theory? We're the only people who can do anything about this. LeRoy is good, but he's not an officer. He'd have to convince someone else to investigate, and they could easily say no. Most of the force won't believe for a second that Leo is guilty. Even after he's convicted, they won't believe it, and some of them will blame you."

She sat up and looked down at the grass. He wanted to take her in his arms and hold her. He wanted to tell her it was okay to cry a little. Her sister was gone, and Marin hadn't had a second to grieve.

"I know they will. It won't be the first time either. As a woman in an office mostly full of men, I get blamed for a lot of things. I don't make the coffee, but the running joke is, if the coffee is cold, it's my fault. They call me the 'mom' in the office, though I don't think I act in a motherly way."

He hated that jobs with the closest-knit teams often had outsiders from the group, and Marin was an outsider. They'd never let her into the fold, either because she was a woman or they'd simply decided they didn't like her.

"I'm sorry. My boss wouldn't put up with that. Small town politics can be brutal."

A man from the ambulance approached them. "Can I have both of you come on over and get checked out? I want to make sure you're fine before we focus on being here if any of the firefighters need us. These old houses are full of chemicals and old insulation. There's going to be trouble before we're done."

Marin sat on the gurney first, and the EMT checked her over, listening to her heart and lungs, checking her oxygen saturation, and her pulse. Once they'd determined everything was normal, they let him sit down. It wasn't until they were halfway through looking at him before she laughed.

"I just remembered I was supposed to have you look at my knees. They're working now though."

The EMT glanced back at her. "Good. It was likely from sitting in a hard chair. It may have been your hip flexors got too tight. Be sure to do some stretches tonight and for the next few days."

Chris let him finish getting all his vitals. Other than a sore throat, he was fine and all his numbers supported that. As soon as he was off the gurney, he headed for Marin.

"Let's head back to the office. We can call up the Cheyenne FBI field office and tell them what happened. They can put out a BOLO for both of them. If they are selling drugs at the scale you indicated, plus two murders, this is definitely a case for the FBI."

"I suppose you're right. I'd hoped to finish this case, but it seems like I won't. As long as Alyssa's murderer gets justice, I'll be happy. But I wish it could've been me."

"I don't blame you." He whistled for Sherlock.

The dog scooted out from under his car where he'd been waiting out of the way. The poor boy was likely hungry after such a long day. "Let's go home, boy." He opened the back door and let him inside.

Marin sat and buckled in. She seemed weak and tired, like every ounce of energy had been completely drained from her. She leaned her head against the headrest. He closed his door quietly to avoid startling her.

"Feel free to rest on the way back."

She let out a forced breath. "I have to relax. I have no phone. They took it. I have no weapon. They took it. I have no sister. They killed her." She covered the side of her face with one hand, then wiped her eyes.

"We're close. Don't give up. I know it's not the same as chasing after Ben and Leo, but we have that warrant on the impound lot that we still need to get to before it expires. You never know what we'll find if we locate Alyssa's car."

Marin gave a nod. "You're right. It's spring, and you said it likely happened three days ago or so. Which means Alyssa was alive for quite some time. As soon as they abducted Cami, they decided to get rid of both women. Ben said Leo decided he wanted to remove Alyssa from . . . the position they'd given her. He wanted her to be his. Ben didn't like that idea because it put her on equal footing with both of them. The more people at the top, the more they'd have to share the money."

"I can't figure out Cami's role in this." As far as he could tell, she'd died for being friends with Alyssa. "She took the rap for the assault both of them committed. Maybe she was fed up and threatened to come forward?" he speculated.

"It's possible. Maybe, like you said, we'll figure out when we find her car. I doubt there's much, if anything, in it anymore. Whoever had their hands on it between the impound lot and where it went had plenty of time to scour it."

"Don't lose hope. We'll keep working." He put the car in reverse, glad they were finally leaving the farm.

They'd been there a lot longer than they'd planned, and the day was almost gone. Marin groaned loudly. "I forgot I have to deal with my parents when I get back. They don't know yet, and I don't want to tell them. I'm so angry at them for what they did. It's hard not to blame them, at least in part, for what happened. If they'd loved us like they promised to, Alyssa wouldn't have had to look all over in the unhealthiest of places to find belonging."

"She had you," he pointed out. "She had all the same opportunities you had. All this time, she could've leaned into you and grown. Instead, she chose a volatile friend who got her into a situation where she beat someone up. That put her in Leo's sights."

Marin closed her eyes. "I know you're right, but it's hard not to blame them. I've been doing it for so long. They deserve it. Why did they have to adopt us at all if they were only going to bother with us for a few years? It's not fair."

He knew this really had nothing to do with parenting at this point. It was the unconditional love a parent was supposed to give that she missed. Lots of people didn't have unconditional love, but that didn't make her need or her loss any less valid.

"I'm not going to nonchalantly tell you to forget about it. I know it's not that easy. I don't think you're going to change them without understanding why they did what they did, though. You've got the perfect opportunity to find out. And if they don't have a good reason, it's okay to cut them from your life. The Bible says to honor thy father and mother in the Lord, not 'even if they abuse you and steal every good breath from your lungs'."

"What about the part that promises it will go well with you if you do?" She looked out the window as if to block his view of her.

"I believe it's talking about listening to parents' instruction in the ways of God. If they are not teaching you God's ways, then this does not apply. God wants parents to bring up their children to follow Him, but He won't make them. I'm not a theologian, so pray about it, but if God is unwilling to force anyone into a relationship with Him, which is why He gives free will, then He's not going to force His children into an earthly relationship either. Especially one that could damage your walk."

She faced forward, and the corner of her mouth inched up. "That does make sense. I'd like to talk to my pastor, but that actually gives me some peace about talking to them. All this time, I've avoided them because I couldn't honor them. I couldn't show them mercy or grace. I was and am angry with them."

"Even Jesus flipped tables when the situation warranted it." He reached over and threaded his fingers through hers. "No one is perfect. We're all just out here trying to do what's right. The only way to know for sure is prayer. If you ask God to direct you in your steps or give you the words to avoid hurting your parents or yourself, He will."

She gave a quick nod. "Let's go take care of the impound lot . . . then we'll check in on my family."

CHAPTER FOURTEEN

"You're back?" Mick sat behind the counter at the impound lot as Marin slapped the warrant down on the counter.

"I need to know what happened to my sister's car. You can tell me, or I can start hunting through your files. This allows me to look through any transactions that occurred up to a month prior to my sister's car landing here. What am I going to find?"

Chris had informed her on the way of what he thought of the unfolding case, and she'd told him what Ben had said to her when he'd been sure she wouldn't live to see the next day. His bragging would help solve the case.

Chris and Sherlock stood behind her right now, her rear guard. They were strong and intimidating, meaning this might not take long if he caved and told her what she wanted to know.

"Who has my sister's car? Who came to take it?"

He glanced away and opened a drawer under the counter. Marin reached for her weapon, then remembered she didn't have it. Chris stepped in and drew his. "Hands where I can see them," he said.

Mick slowly raised them. "Am I under arrest?"

"Not yet. You weren't willing to help me the last time I was here.

Now, I've brought the paperwork that says you need to help me, or it won't go so well for you. This could've been handled more easily if you'd simply told me where my sister's car is. A car I co-own."

"Leo took it," he mumbled. "I don't know what he did with it, but he took it. He came in here the day it was towed here with paperwork saying it was evidence, then he had it towed away by a company I've never seen before. I didn't catch the name, but the truck was bright blue. That's all I've got."

"Do you have any video of the lot?" Chris asked. "Security?"

"Can I go get the video? I will bring it right back." He remained in place with his hands up.

"Chris will go with you. Last time we were close to catching our guys, they got away on a technicality."

"But I'm not under arrest, so I have no reason to run." His statement sounded more like a question to her.

"Unless you received a payment to look the other way, then you'll likely only be questioned and potentially be asked to take the stand at a trial. But if you took payment and you knew what the payment was for . . . then you're an accessory."

He turned slightly pale. If only reactions like that were evidence, but they weren't. She waited at the counter with Sherlock while Chris followed him back to his office. They returned a few minutes later with Chris holding a file.

He put it on the counter and opened it. Inside were stills taken from surveillance videos of the lot. Since the images were black and white, there was no way to see what shade of blue the tow truck was. The logo on the door was grainy and blurry.

"I've lived here all my life, and I've never heard of that company." He squinted at the image. "I'm sorry I don't remember the exact name. Maybe if you show these around, someone else will."

"Anything else we should know?" Chris crossed his arms and widened his stance behind her.

She held in a grin. The man knew exactly how to look even stronger and more intimidating than he was.

"I have nothing else. Except . . . this isn't the first time he's come in like this. It's the first time he's used that towing company. Usually, he has me take cars to a specific place. This time, he didn't want me involved. I don't know why." He quickly looked the other way.

His mannerisms gave him away. He knew exactly why Leo hadn't wanted him involved. Was it because this car had drugs in it that could be traced back to him? Or could it have held evidence that would've made her look at his doorstep when she'd been hunting for Alyssa?

"Can you give us the address where you usually take cars?" Chris asked.

He nodded and reached for a pad of paper on his right. Instead of writing down an address, he drew a map. "I don't know what the address is, and it's way out of the way. You'd never find it if you went out for a drive. It might be visible if you use satellite images or something."

She slid the map into the file with the pictures of the tow truck. He may not think he'd given her much, but he'd actually helped a lot. When they put all the dots together and found out who the tow truck company was, they would be able to show these images to a jury. Seeing the actual tow truck with a blurry image of the same truck is easier than trying to identify it with no information.

"Thank you for being helpful. If you think of anything else, give me a call." She slid her card across the counter. "You don't want to be on the wrong side of this one."

She didn't wait to see his reaction or hear if he responded. Now, she had to face her parents. Once she was done with that, she could let all her emotions come to the surface to deal with them. While Alyssa might not have been her sister by blood, she had been her sister for her entire life, and the feeling of loss was the same.

"You ready to talk to your parents?" Chris asked as he loaded Sherlock back into the car.

"Not really. I've put it off for so long. I tried getting in touch with them for literally years when they first separated from us. They went no-contact. Cold turkey. Nothing I said was important enough to warrant a response. I just can't fathom what they could say to make that okay." She didn't want to cry in front of him, but tears didn't always listen.

"Do you want me there? For case stuff, I will be there, but this is personal. I don't want to push my way into something that's already peak stress for you."

She held back a smile but sent him a look of gratitude. "I appreciate that. I'd like you to be there. Especially since I plan to invite them to my house. I don't want to see Spike's family any more than I want to see him. They picked sides. They might know more about all of this than I do. That makes this whole situation even worse."

"Then I'll be right there."

He hadn't balked at being in her house during what could be an emotional conversation. Most of the men she knew would actively run from a situation like this. "Thanks. I'll need all the support I can get."

"Don't forget, we don't know what's going on, and they'll be finding out about Alyssa too. If they aren't ready to have a conversation, then have it another time. Just don't let them leave town without getting your questions answered. You might not get another chance."

This felt like using Alyssa's death for her own gain. As much as Alyssa had always wanted to know why their parents had abandoned them, she likely wouldn't hold this against Marin, but there was no way to know. She could only go by her own feelings. "This doesn't feel right, using trauma and death to get answers."

He shook his head as he pulled into the police station parking lot and parked next to her car. "You're not. You're using their presence to get your questions answered. They finally came out of the woodwork, so you can do this."

He was right, but she still flinched at all the emotions this brought up. "I'll call them as I'm driving over. See you back at home." She leaned over and kissed his cheek.

While that might not have been the best kiss they'd shared, it felt comfortable. Right. Like she could kiss him for the rest of her life. She got out and closed the door, focusing on her car. Now was not the time to get wrapped up in a romance. She had to plan her sister's funeral and deal with the investigation. She had to deal with her parents, however long they were staying in town. Either one of those would've been too demanding to allow herself to take on a new relationship. Both made it impossible.

She reached for her phone as she got in her car and remembered she no longer had it. Her phone, with her ability to retrieve her parent's phone number, had been taken by Ben. Stark dread slithered down her neck. What if he used her parents to get her back?

She whipped around to wave at Chris to get his thoughts, but he'd already pulled to the back of the station, likely to give Sherlock a moment to burn off some energy before he brought the big dog into her little house. He'd been on duty all day and needed to race around and be a dog for a few minutes.

"I can handle this." She flexed her fingers and headed inside the building to get her spare keys. Ben had taken her purse and her gun, leaving her without her ID, her badge, her keys, wallet, and money. "There's another thing I'll have to do," she ticked off the list in her head of calling her credit card companies to cancel the missing cards.

Duke peered out from his office and grinned at her. "You're back? Leo was busting around here earlier asking everyone if they'd seen you. He was in a mood, that's for sure. He'll be glad to know you're alive."

She wasn't so sure about that. "Yup, I'm here." She waved as she avoided talking more and slipped into her office.

The building was small, and there was almost no privacy anywhere. Other officers often popped in if they needed something or wanted to talk. Duke stood in her doorway.

"I saw you got a warrant for the impound lot. Did you go over there already?"

He usually wasn't one to care what she was working on, and his curiosity made her wary, especially as a dispatcher. "I haven't had a chance yet, why?"

He looked away. "No reason. Just curious." He rested his hands on his belt at his sides.

"You keeping up with the case? If you are, you know Alyssa and Cami were found earlier today."

His mouth dropped open slightly. "I didn't know that. I'm assuming condolences are in order?" His eyes softened slightly.

She wasn't sure if his goal was information for Leo or if he was simply poking into a case out of curiosity. Either way, she didn't want to talk anymore.

"Sorry, Duke. I'm expected at home in five minutes. If I don't arrive, the K9 is going to come hunting for me. You know, they have a 95% success rate?" She hoped she sounded innocent, just giving facts. If he'd planned to stop her in any way, he had to know they would find her.

"Wow, that's pretty amazing. Do you want me to go run that warrant for you? I don't mind. If you're busy, you'll miss the window. I wouldn't want that . . ."

She held up her hand. "No, thanks. I think I've got this. I just need to get home. See you, Duke." She slipped past him and closed the door to her office. Unfortunately, she couldn't lock it until she was able to get a new copy of the key.

Duke brushed against her as he moved to back away. "Sorry." He held up his hands. "Clumsy me." He turned and strode off down the hall.

❖

His watch didn't lie. Chris looked at the face again. She'd been inside for fifteen minutes. He didn't want to stalk Marin, but what could she be doing inside the office when they were heading back to her house right away? He'd taken Sherlock out back, so he wouldn't leave such a mess in her backyard, but her car had still been there when he'd returned.

She came out of the building and glanced down at her watch. He waited next to her car since he wasn't sure if there was a spare key at her house and her keys were gone. He could've simply waited at her house, but then he would've had to deal with a whining dog. This had been the better choice.

Without noticing him that he could tell, she climbed into her car and drove off. The way she drove wasn't like she had when he'd ridden with her. She seemed distracted, so he hung back a few car lengths to give her space. He hoped that if she chose the quiet of her car to have a moment of grief, she'd pull over if she needed to.

When they arrived at her house, she slowly got out as she quickly wiped her eyes. Sherlock raced to catch up to her and nosed her hip so hard she stumbled slightly. He rushed to her side, not to catch her but to make sure she didn't fall off the step. He got to her, but she'd already gained her footing.

Her red-rimmed eyes were shiny, like she'd had a quick cry and now didn't want anyone to know. Strong women were tough for men to understand. He wanted to help her, to hold her if she wanted, but did she? Sometimes the toughness was a cover for hurt. They didn't want to be let down. That meant they had to do everything on their own to meet their standards. Others truly wanted no help because they didn't want to be seen as weak or hurt. So, which was Marin?

She moved aside a large planter that looked like it weighed fifty pounds and picked up a weathered key from beneath. She shoved it in the lock and turned, opening the door quickly and stepping inside. He followed, hoping she would turn back to him and allow him to comfort her. How could she deal with all that had happened and not take a little support?

Because she'd been taught she must. The realization hit him so hard he stopped in his tracks. The teenage years were just as formative as the younger years. Maybe more because they were more memorable. As a teen, her desires were labeled unimportant. She had to be strong because she couldn't turn her worries over to anyone else who cared. Her sister would listen but couldn't help.

"Marin?"

She headed for the kitchen and opened the fridge without turning back to look at him. "Yeah?"

"You want to talk about it?"

She grabbed a soda, popped the top, and took a long drink. When she looked at him again, the hurt on her face tore him to pieces. "I'm alone. Everyone I thought I knew is after me. I can't prove it, but I think the other officers on the team have been convinced I'm the issue. Leo had to have told them I'm the perp. I'm the one they need to watch. I'll never be able to work in that building after this." She wiped away another tear. "I've worked so hard. I gave this team everything I had, and they took it, chewed it up, and spit it out. Where do I go from here?"

He slowly closed the distance between them. "Come with me." He wasn't sure why he'd said it, but if he was the only friend she had anymore, why not?

"You don't work with partners, remember?" She looked away and took another drink from the can, then slammed it on the counter.

"No, I don't, but we wouldn't be working on the same team. You'd be in investigation. I'm just an officer. I have no way of moving from this position. My buddy here keeps me happy where I'm at." He pointed at Sherlock.

She reached down with both hands and framed the dog's face. "Thank you, Sherlock."

He wasn't sure if that was because of what he'd said or if the thank you was for busting in to rescue her. The dog likely didn't know or care which it was either. "He appreciates your thanks."

Marin leaned against the counter. "I know what I need to do, but I don't want to do it."

"Call Spike's parents to reach yours?"

She nodded. "I wonder if they knew about her? Did they know

what she'd gotten into? What did they tell my parents about us? Spike's family has lived here all their lives, and the town is small enough to keep up with everyone without much effort, especially since she worked for their son."

"I think it would depend on what your parents wanted to know. They can't find out if they don't ask." He didn't want her to walk into a talk with them assuming the absolute worst. It might be true, but making assumptions hurt all of them.

She picked up the cordless phone off the counter. He hadn't even noticed it was there earlier. She pressed in the numbers, and he heard the soft ring through the earpiece, but he knew he wouldn't hear their side of the conversation.

"Mrs. Ducet, this is Marin. Is my mother there?" she paused for a moment to hear the answer. "Thanks, I'll wait."

Marin looked at him and mouthed the words, "She's out back. It'll take a second." She looked away from him. "Hello? Mom?"

He heard mumblings on the line but couldn't hear what was said.

"Yes, I'm ready for you and Dad to come over and talk. I have a few important things I need to tell you."

More talking, this time longer. Marin's mouth slowly dropped open as she listened. He stepped forward, holding her elbows for support both physically and mentally. He hoped his presence helped her.

"I see," she said, her voice a register lower than usual. "If that's how you feel . . ."

The voice on the other end continued talking, and he resisted the urge to grab the phone and hang up, to stop the hurt written all over Marin's face. He was to blame. He'd been the one to push her toward closure. If she'd done as she planned and not spoken to them, she wouldn't be hurt now.

"Bye." The one word was so final. So dead. Like she never planned to speak to them again. She pressed a button and placed the phone back on its charger. She held herself around the waist, her focus far away.

He didn't push her to tell him anything. Instead, he opened his arms, and she stepped into them as a sob pierced his heart. Marin was the strongest woman he knew, and the last 48 hours had broken her. Healing would take a long time and maybe help. He hoped she trusted him to stand by her through it.

"She already knew about Alyssa. She spilled the whole story in, like, three minutes. In the late nineties, when I was born, my mom taught at a college. There was a young woman there who had come to the college on a student visa. She got pregnant with me and did her best to raise me, but couldn't take me back to her country. She convinced my mom that if she didn't abandon me, her family would kill her for sleeping with someone outside of marriage."

He held her close and let her relay the story. At least she knew the truth now. The truth would help her in the long run, even if it hurt now.

"My parents never wanted children, but they also felt like they couldn't put me up for adoption. What if I ended up in an abusive home? So, they raised me, dedicating themselves to doing the best they could. And they did, which is why the split hurt so badly. In all that time, they never came to love me. I was only a commitment."

He couldn't imagine the hurt and betrayal. "I'm not saying they did the right thing, but I see their thought process. I still can't imagine cutting off all contact with the person you raised. That's not something I would do to any living being, much less a person, but I can see why they kept you."

She pulled back slightly and nodded. "She didn't tell me Alyssa's story, just that it was similar and they don't want anything to do with the funeral or anything else. They would prefer to go back to being strangers. They feel like they dedicated eighteen years of their lives to making sure we had what we needed. Now, it's up to us." She swallowed hard. "I mean, now it's on me."

CHAPTER FIFTEEN

There weren't any tow trucks that matched the image in the impound lot footage. Chris scrolled to the next page of businesses on the web search. Not one company used blue trucks that he could find. He'd even widened his search to seventy-five miles away, thinking Leo had used an out-of-town tow so no one could ever make the connection.

He looked at the grainy image one more time, then back at the list in front of him. He squinted, trying to blur his vision just like the printout. That could be it, but those trucks were orange, not blue.

"Marin?" he called.

Sherlock jogged up first and laid his head on Chris's lap. "You're forgiven, buddy. She needs you. She can be your favorite for a while." He ruffled the dog's head.

"What is it?" Marin approached, back in her loungewear from the evening before. He loved seeing her in comfortable clothing. Her, relaxed, was beautiful.

"Take a look at this and tell me if I'm seeing things." He turned the screen so she could see, then held up the printout.

She squinted and bent at the waist to look head-on at the image instead of being above it. "That's the same shape for sure. Hard to tell if it's a match. Do they have blue trucks?"

He shook his head. "Only orange. I was thinking about calling them and asking if they've ever worked with law enforcement from Poplar Bend. There's only so many people Leo and Ben can pay before everyone knows they're drug dealers. Ben was able to disappear from his life, but Leo can't. I think they both need him in that position to collect free drugs to sell."

"When we're sure, we'll need to bring the FBI in on this. Especially since it's one of their own who's doing it."

He nodded. "Do you want to take a quick ride out to that lot he told us about? It won't be dark for another two hours, and it's the last thing we need to follow up on."

She shrugged a shoulder. "I want to. I'm just not sure I have the energy. This entire case has drained me. Like you said last night, there comes a point when you need to rest. I feel like I'm no help without my weapon. I'm not like most other officers. I don't have a spare."

"I still have Alyssa's clothes in the back of my car. Sherlock should be able to find it. I'm going to go and see what I can find."

"I don't want you to go alone."

People dealing with loss often struggled with goals that were opposites of each other, so her feelings didn't surprise him. "How about you come with me and wait in the car? You can be there for the hunt, so you're not left out, and you don't have to walk around all over and get worn out?" he offered.

She let out a long breath. "I can do that. Give me a minute." She turned for the bathroom.

He glanced around the small kitchen and dining area. The house had been built when homes often had very small cooking and eating areas because the goal was for families to be close while eating together, then relax in the living room. Bedrooms were smaller and fewer because families were reducing in number and children didn't use their bedrooms for things other than sleeping and doing homework.

"Okay, I'm ready." Marin had changed into a pair of jeans and a fitted, long-sleeved tee.

He gave a nod of appreciation, then headed for the car. Once all of them were inside, Marin took out the map and helped him navigate.

"This could be a trap. If he intentionally told us the wrong color of the tow truck, this place might not exist. It might be under massive security. We don't know."

He kept his gaze on the road ahead. "I know, but it's a chance we have to take. If the feds get involved, like you hoped, he won't be able to hide. They'll question him and his reasons for giving us false information."

"It seems to me, guilty people rarely have the foresight to see their own apprehension. If they did, it might stop a lot of crime. Odd how they can be completely self-aware, but not, all at the same time," she answered.

She pointed where he should turn, and the gravel road headed straight out of town and quickly became rural. He followed the road, noting that no one else seemed to be using it. No tractors. No pickup trucks. Not a single vehicle was on the road with them.

"I wonder who owns this," Marin said, again reaching for her phone, then sighing in frustration. "You'd think I'd remember I don't have a phone. I guess I was more addicted to that thing than I thought."

"You want to use mine?" he asked.

She shook her head. "Last time I borrowed your phone, I ended up angry with you. Maybe I'll let you keep your phone for now."

He wished he could laugh, but he understood. Jules had shown up in his texts out of the blue and with the worst possible request. "I meant what I said on the phone, and I'm glad you heard it. I don't want her in my life."

She reached across the space and touched his arm. "I know. I should've known even then, but I didn't. You were too new to me." She laughed. "It seems like I've known you twice as long now as I did then, but it's really only been a few hours ago."

Her math made him chuckle. "Yes, one plus one is still two except for extremely high values of one."

She snorted. "When you're talking about days, I don't think you can have high values of one, but nice try."

The banter with her was so fresh and fun. They didn't have to talk about serious things all the time, even though they were working a case. "I always try my best."

She laughed. "I know. And I'm so glad you do. Turn here." She pointed at a barely visible driveway between two large groups of trees. "Great. Another wooded area. My favorite."

"The better to hide the cars, my dear." He laughed.

She bit her lip. "We're not likely to find anything. Don't get your hopes up," she mumbled to herself.

He wanted her to continue having fun and not turn to the serious side yet. This trip had enough of a likelihood of being serious without adding more. "Having a talk with the boss?"

Her eyebrow rose and she smirked. "Yup, a meeting of the minds."

"There. There's her car." Marin pointed. "The white one . . . with the broken window."

He angled his car in front of it so they could look first from the safety of his car. "With that window broken, anyone could've gone in there. We don't know who knows about this lot. All we know is that Leo does. Maybe the rest of his officers do too. He's withheld information from you in the past."

She sucked in a deep breath. "I know you're right, but I'm going to look anyway. I don't have a warrant, but if this is a police lot, I shouldn't need one. I may not have my badge with me, but that doesn't make me any less of an investigator with the Poplar Bend PD." She got out of the car.

Sherlock immediately perked up.

"I know. You can go with her." Chris let Sherlock out of his kennel in the back, and the dog bounded after her.

She looked through the broken window, then walked around to the front of the car. Chris met her at the driver's side door. The car was in decent shape, if messy. The steering wheel had been used by someone who wore a lot of makeup. That much was clear. They liked stickers and the color pink. One of the seats had a bright pink fuzzy seat cover.

"That was her way of keeping men out of her car. The driver's side one is missing." She pointed to the very clean driver's seat. "Oh, and the seat is pushed back really far. She was shorter than me by half an inch."

"Tall enough for Leo or Ben to drive?" he speculated. Likely, there had been evidence in the car. After Leo had abducted her, he'd had to take the evidence and dump it somewhere else before she was reported missing. That way, when they looked through her car to see where she might be, they wouldn't find anything. Since he controlled the officers, he likely told them not to take fingerprints. He likely parked it right back where he'd found it in the lot at the alley.

He glanced in the empty backseat. "So, Leo took the seat to make sure no one would ever know he drove that car. That way, when they looked through the car the night she was reported missing, everything was still in place when you examined it. He wanted to make sure that part was done so he could claim all the evidence had been gathered when it hadn't, because no one knew the reason behind the abduction. Then, he disposed of it."

She tested the car door, and it opened. "Except I never looked at it that day, and he admitted none of his guys did either. I wondered why. Now I know."

He wasn't sure what she would do, so he stood back and let her. She was the investigator.

"This car has potentially been touched by who knows how many people. There's no way a judge would allow evidence found in here, especially since the alleged criminal is our sergeant. Everything we collect is going to have to be impeccable. No mistakes." She ran her fingers along the steering wheel. "Where would Alyssa have hidden something?"

"Wait." He took a step closer. "Are you saying you don't think that was Alyssa who looked through her apartment? You think she left evidence or a note or something in the car?" He hadn't considered that.

"I think it was her. She was seen. I can't dispute that. Judging by the hair I found on one envelope, Ben probably took her there to look for something or destroy evidence. She may have helped. She may have fought him off. We don't know. I know he had knowledge that Leo used to get her to willingly engage in prostitution. Even saying that breaks my heart. The fact that she was willing to do that instead of telling me she was in trouble, kills me. It's not like I would've judged her or abandoned her. She knew me better than that. Or I thought she did."

"Let's call LeRoy and see if he found anything in those envelopes. He may have tried to reach you on your phone since it was stolen," he offered.

"Ok. Quickly. I want to get out of here before it gets dark." She reached for his phone and dialed from memory.

He answered right away, and she turned it on speakerphone. "LeRoy? Do you have any updates on the envelopes I found at Alyssa's apartment?"

He cleared his throat. "Good of you to get back to me. I do have information. All of them were empty and free of any notable evidential debris with the exception of the hair you made note of. It appeared to have the hair follicle attached, but we haven't finished examining that yet. The most important aspect is what was inside the envelopes. Only one had writing on it, very tiny writing that said, *look in the compartment.* Do you know what it might be talking about?"

She reached over and opened the glove compartment. It was

separated into two sections, one with a separate door and the other larger one. It held the car's manual.

She gently depressed a button, and the door flipped open. An envelope lay inside.

"I know exactly what she meant."

❧

Marin cradled the precious letter in her hands. Alyssa had known. Somehow, she'd known Marin would search the car and find the letter. Likely because Marin was the investigator. She'd assumed from the start Marin would be the one to hunt for evidence in her apartment and in that car, so she'd left something in a spot where only Marin would know to look.

"It's still sealed, has my name on it, in Alyssa's handwriting. The only thing about this that breaks me is that I might have to give it up for trial." She held it to her chest.

Marin breathed deeply and caught the faintest hint of Alyssa's favorite perfume. Chris drove back to the house and they went inside, remaining quiet. He must have realized how much she needed simply to process that the letter existed.

She headed for the kitchen, and he let Sherlock in the backyard, then sat across from her.

"I'm curious, but if you want to be alone, I'll go in the living room. I don't want to intrude."

She reached over and laid her hand on his. How had she grown so close to him in such a short time? It wasn't love, but she definitely liked him. That respect and affection might be growing by the minute. "Stay. I'll read it out loud."

He headed for the fridge and brought out two sodas. He opened hers and put it in front of her, then sat and opened his. "Okay, let's hear what your sister had to say."

She took in a deep breath and let it out. "Dear Marin," her voice cracked.

"Take your time."

She nodded and pushed on. This was bound to hurt, but it was necessary. "I didn't want to write this. I am because I know I've managed to put myself on the wrong side of life. It started out simply enough. I wanted to party with Cami. She had lots of friends and had so much fun. Too much fun. You warned me about people like her, and I should've listened."

Marin reached for a tissue on the counter behind her and dabbed at her eyes. "At one party, a man in his thirties came up to me. I wasn't interested in him in the slightest, but he knew who I was. He said he worked with you. I assumed he was a good guy if he was a cop. I was wrong. I had too much to drink that night and ended up with him in the back of his car. I'm so ashamed of that. I wish I'd never gotten into this mess. I wish I had gone to you, but he told me he was your boss, and he would fire you if I left him. So, I stayed."

Hot tears burned her eyes, and she blinked to be able to see. She had to get through this letter. Would she list his actual name or just his title? If not, the letter might not pass the evidence phase.

"He asked me to beat up someone for him, someone who hadn't paid him. I asked Cami to help me, since she's so scrappy. Leo was furious with me for bringing someone else in on it. I didn't realize I couldn't. After that, his demands got worse. More degrading. I got to the point where I wanted out. So, I told him I didn't care anymore. I wasn't a pawn in his game. I was going to tell you. That was the night I disappeared."

Marin stopped reading. The letter was in Alyssa's handwriting, but how could she have written it after her abduction and still placed it in the car?

"Marin? Do you want me to finish it for you?" Chris asked so gently it almost broke her heart.

"No, sorry. I was just wondering how this fits together. I suppose I should read on and find out." She frowned and found her place again.

"I met Ben at a super-rural house where Leo took me to hide.

He's been working with Leo to sell any drugs Leo brings in, usually from criminals. He simply re-sells them. I didn't know about him until Leo took me out there. At that point, I knew something bad was up. They brought Cami in about a week after me because they assumed she knew more than she did after helping me. They kept her tied up. I begged them to let her go or at least to untie her. They didn't listen."

Marin bit her lip. There were only two paragraphs left of the letter. She knew she was in danger. How did the letter get into the car unless Leo had planted it there, but why would he do that?

"I told him I'd left some of his stash in a compartment in my car, which was the truth. That stash had always been my emergency exit. If I was in danger, I'd planned to call the police on myself and report the drugs. I'd get arrested and be surrounded by people at all times. He couldn't hurt me behind bars."

"He brought me to my car and, while he was removing the back bumper to get to the stash, I wrote and hid this letter in the compartment that only you and I know about. I hope you're well. I hope you understand. I doubt I'm alive if you found this, but know that I didn't blame you for anything and I love you. Your sister, Alyssa."

She set the letter down and closed her eyes. Deep anger welled up and dripped down her cheeks. "I can't let them get away with this."

"I know you want to keep it, and I think you should take a photograph, but this needs to be in evidence. It will have her fingerprints on it. It's her handwriting, which can be proven. This letter is exactly what we need to put Leo and Ben away for a very long time."

She slowly nodded. "You're right. But who do I trust? No one in the Poplar Bend department will believe for a hot second that Leo has done anything."

"It's time to call in Ben's partner. He'll have the resources."

She wanted to believe that, but Ben's partner could be just as big of an issue. "What if he doesn't believe Ben is alive, much less capable of all that he's done? And I do believe in my heart of hearts that it was Ben who killed Alyssa and Cami. He joked about hunting them down. Leo can be slimy, but he's no killer."

"Would you ever see him as a drug dealer? Because if you couldn't see that, then it's possible he could've fooled everyone about this too."

She shook her head. "No, I can actually understand the drugs. It didn't surprise me in the slightest. I'd be shocked if Spike wasn't in on that too. But murder is way different. He's not the kind of guy to get his hands dirty."

"Well, that leaves a few last questions. The shirts, trying to poison my dog and turning off your porch light, even bringing me on was a risk. She doesn't mention any of them. I still can't figure out why Leo would ask me to help you, knowing I would find the other shirt."

That had gotten to her too, but she had a theory. "I think that part was all Ben. He'd known about Alyssa long before she knew about him. I think he'd already planned to get rid of her as a witness to their plan. If she stayed around, he would have to share the earnings. That wasn't going to happen. He had to get rid of her. He planted the shirts, using Spike to get the first two, then he bought mine from somewhere else, way before you came to town. The only thing I think was Leo was the poison on the meat. He didn't want you on this case and thought that killing the dog would send you back home."

Chris nodded along. "I see where you're going with this. We don't know where he got the blood, but Alyssa said Leo asked her to do increasingly bad things. If they were doing any sort of rituals, they might have collected blood."

Marin nodded. "Alyssa said on the phone call that they made her cut her hand."

"It's all plausible. I think to find out anything more concrete, we have to find those two and bring them in. Tomorrow, we call the FBI office."

"I'd rather go and talk to him. I want to show him this letter and connect him with LeRoy who has the shirts, envelopes, everything. Then, they'll have all the same evidence we do."

"Except the bodies. They'll have to be transferred. I like your plan. It's a long drive, but we can head out in the morning. I'll call before we go and set up an appointment. Soon. Very soon. We'll catch Alyssa and Cami's killer and bring them to justice."

She stood and placed the letter on the counter. "Then I can sleep again."

He closed the gap between them and held her. "Sleep is important. Maybe now that you know her history, the reasons for all of it, you can get some rest." He kissed her forehead in the center, then once on each side.

Warmth spread over her. Chris was safety. He was security. He was all the things she'd known she needed but was afraid to ask for. Afraid she wasn't worthy or that anyone who said they'd stay would eventually leave anyway.

"Come, sit with me on the sofa." He let Sherlock back in, then went to the living room. He turned on the television to a movie channel and brought up a show about the weather. Mindless. No story. Just something she could stare at. He wrapped her in a blanket and tucked her against his side. She lay against his shoulder, letting herself feel everything and nothing.

She closed her eyes as an explosion lit up the front window.

CHAPTER SIXTEEN

Chris held tight to Marin as glass blasted across the room. Sherlock whined at Chris's left hip. Shards ripped hunks of flesh from his arms and face. Car alarms went off up and down the street. Marin pushed away from him, her mouth hanging open.

"My car . . ." Her fingertips slowly covered her mouth. "They destroyed my car."

"Those flames are too close to the house. We need to get out back." He helped her to her feet, glad that the blanket had mostly protected her.

Sherlock beat them to the sliding door and whined to get out. Chris grabbed his phone and called 911 as he opened the door. Marin gathered the quilt from the sofa and wrapped it around herself before following him outside.

He spoke to the dispatcher for a few minutes, letting them know what had happened and that they needed help immediately to protect the house. She assured him a crew was on the way. He hung up the phone and shoved it into his pocket.

"They won't stop until I'm dead, will they?"

"No," came a voice behind her.

He didn't recognize it, but she clearly did. She immediately hunched deeper into the blanket and screamed. Chris drew his weapon and swung it right to left. "Whoever you are, come out with your hands up."

"Nice try." Ben emerged from the shadows, wading through the long grass.

Sherlock barked at him, and Ben aimed his pistol at the dog.

"If you even think about shooting him, I will make life miserable for you." He put human life above animals, but Ben wouldn't die if Chris shot him. He might wish he were, but he wouldn't die.

"You're surrounded. Put your hands up. Marin Bayless, you're under arrest for the murder of Alyssa Bayless and Cami Cambridge. You have the right to remain silent," Leo said as he came from the opposite side of the dark yard.

Marin flipped the blanket down, draping it over her back instead of covering her head. "Alyssa hated you," she said. "She saw you as an abuser, and she left evidence against both of you. Evidence I've already turned in to the FBI. You can fake this arrest all you want. They're coming for both of you. There isn't a shred of evidence against me, but we've found a mountain against you."

Chris kept his weapon leveled at Ben. He'd told Marin not to discount Leo as a possible suspect for the murders. He believed she was right. They couldn't know for sure until the full investigation was finished, but he suspected Ben had done the killing. He seemed almost to enjoy being cruel.

Leo froze for a moment as if he wasn't sure how to proceed. Ben took a few steps closer. "You forget I'm with the FBI. I have friends who know I'm still alive and well. They'd tell me if anything had turned up to put my hiding place in danger."

Chris watched him carefully to see if he might be lying. He had a slightly self-deprecating smile that didn't move his eyes at all. It was the ultimate tell for a lie, especially if someone thought they were pulling the wool over your eyes.

"He's lying." In case she couldn't see it from her vantage point or was too emotionally hurt from the last few days to read his face, he didn't want her strength to wane based on what Ben said.

"Am I?" Ben sneered. "I don't think you know anything beyond what I told Marin when she was in my basement."

"We know Spike was involved, and now so does the FBI," Marin said.

They hadn't told anyone else yet, but he was certain Ben wasn't still in contact with anyone at the FBI. He'd talked to Ben's partner the day before to get information.

"We suspect you got the blood to put on the shirts from cutting Alyssa and Cami's hands when you first took them," Chris said so Marin didn't feel like she had to handle this by herself. Especially since she'd said she felt completely alone now.

Ben snorted. "They were into it. They both wanted so badly to belong to something. They wanted to believe in something, so I made up a ritual. They gladly cut themselves and didn't question one bit when I collected some."

"It's too bad you weren't smart enough to put the blood on the shirts randomly. If you had, the lab wouldn't have questioned the pattern. Leo made a huge mistake too. He tampered with Alyssa's shirt after it had been tested. That's when we started to suspect you." Marin dropped the blanket completely and crossed her arms. "Not only that, the car I followed after leaving the impound lot was registered to a man who died during a traffic stop. I noticed the car in the lot when Chris and I found Alyssa's car. The only one who had access was you." She pointed at Leo.

Sirens wailed as they pulled to a stop in front of the house.

"We need to get them out of here now." Leo glanced back and forth between Marin and Ben. "I can't get caught here. If I do, I'll lose everything. I can't go to prison."

"You should've thought of that before you became a drug dealer, a sex trafficker, and a murderer," Chris said.

Marin held up her hand. "You used my grief against me. The

night you came to my house to tell me what you'd done to look for my sister, you went out back to smoke and loosened the bulb, presumably so you could keep track of me by watching from my backyard. Did you plant the poison for Sherlock, too?"

Leo glanced at Sherlock sitting in the grass.

"I asked him to come here to find Cami's shirt, then go home. That shirt had your blood on it. I stole it from the blood drive last month. There's no way he couldn't have found it on Alyssa's shirt, but I dumped yours on Cami's."

Marin shook her head. "I don't know whose you took, but it wasn't mine. That was likely the third female donor LeRoy couldn't identify."

Chris maintained his focus on Sherlock. Most people would think he lay relaxed, not paying attention to the situation, but no one knew him better than Chris. He said a quick prayer Sherlock wouldn't be injured.

"Now!"

The only one who knew that command, in that tone, was Sherlock. He lunged for Ben's shoulder, his strong jaw clamping onto Ben's bicep. He pushed Ben to the ground. Chris lunged for Ben's gun so Sherlock wouldn't get shot. Ben screamed in pain, writhing to get free of the dog's powerful jaws.

"Hold!" He didn't want Sherlock to tear the man to pieces, but he wanted Ben contained when the police arrived.

He spun in time to see Leo race for Marin. She was completely unarmed but took up a fighting stance, ready to protect herself. Leo reached for her arm. She yanked back and thrust a fist into his face. The satisfying crack of Leo's nose made her smile even as she remained in a defensive position.

"Come at me again. I dare you." She held up both fists in front of herself, ready to take him on.

"Freeze! Hands up!" Parker said as he aimed at each one in turn.

"Arrest these two!" Leo stood, covering his face with one hand as blood dripped down his forearm.

"I'm sorry, sir." Parker frowned. "LeRoy contacted me about two hours ago telling me the male DNA found on Alyssa's shirt that was unaccounted for . . . was yours. You killed her, didn't you?"

Marin gasped and looked like she might collapse. Chris was to her in a moment, supporting her. "You? I was sure it was Ben. The way he talked about hunting . . . I was sure it was him. Not you. I didn't think you could do something that awful."

His smile was so cold, Chris held her tighter to protect her from it.

"No one suspected me of anything. I was just a lazy sergeant who told everyone else what to do and looked the other way when things happened."

"Sir, hands up," Parker stated clearly.

Ben whimpered on the ground. Chris gave a soft whistle, and Sherlock backed off but sat only a foot away. Ben wouldn't be running while Sherlock was on duty.

"I need an ambulance," Ben wailed.

Another officer arrived and headed immediately for Ben. On the way over, he glanced at Marin. "Your car is a total loss, but the crew got the fire contained before it could reach your house. You'll have a scorched area on your driveway, but your home is safe."

"Thanks, I appreciate it." She backed away a few steps and visibly let her guard down.

Parker returned to Marin, looking sheepish. "I have to apologize. Leo gave me that half of Alyssa's license to give to you. He told me not to tell you where I got it, to make up the story I told you. He claimed you were far too 'by the book' to take it if I didn't make up the story. I thought he was looking out for you, not hiding that he was the last one to handle her license."

She took in a deep breath. "What's done is done, and I know you didn't do it intending to throw me off. You were following orders."

Once Leo and Ben were both in custody, he picked up the blanket off the ground and draped it over her shoulders, giving her a squeeze in the process. "Let's go back inside."

If she'd looked tired before, she seemed worn out now. He supported her as much as he could back into the house. The sound of hammering caught him off guard. He headed to the front where they'd been relaxing when this had all started. A firefighter stood inside, holding a piece of Marin's trim in place so it wasn't damaged further while another hammered in a sheet of plywood to cover the open window.

"I know this isn't pretty, but Marin helps everyone. We weren't going to leave and let her deal with this so late at night. Sorry for the noise," the firefighter said.

Marin leaned into Chris. "Thank you so much. I didn't think I had anyone left I could count on. I'm glad to be wrong."

Her words hurt. Why wouldn't she trust him to be there for her? The answer came from his own words. He'd told her he wouldn't be. While he'd asked her just a few hours ago to come with him, he'd said from the beginning that theirs was a relationship that would never be more than on the surface. After only a couple days, he couldn't ask for any more than that either.

Within fifteen minutes, all the people, cars, and trucks were gone, leaving a mess and silence behind. Chris wasn't sure what to say. He wanted to talk to Marin, to tell her she could believe in him and trust him. He wouldn't walk away from her unless she asked him to, but she looked too tired for such a conversation.

He got her settled on the sofa and sent Sherlock to the spare bedroom. He wasn't sure what he would be doing tomorrow, but likely, he'd be driving home. For some reason, he felt like this was leaving home, not returning.

"Chris?" Her sleepy words held him with more force than any chains.

"Yes?"

"I know this is silly, but would you sleep out here in the recliner tonight? I don't want to be alone."

She could've asked Sherlock to lay beside the sofa, but she didn't.

She asked for *him*. Maybe there was more hope than he'd thought. "Of course. Let me grab a blanket. I'll be right back."

In the spare room, he grabbed what he needed plus brought Sherlock back into the living room. Once he got Sherlock settled by her feet on the sofa so she would feel his weight and warmth, he sank into the comfortable chair.

He wasn't sure how to deal with tomorrow, but God did. He'd have to pay extra attention to make sure he listened.

CHAPTER SEVENTEEN

Stiffness threaded through Marin's shoulders as she pushed herself up from her pillow. Sherlock rested his large head on her knee, forcing her to stay lying down. She'd heard people joke about 'puppy paralysis' to explain how a person couldn't move if a dog was using them as a pillow because they didn't want to disturb the animal. She got the distinct impression Sherlock knew exactly what he was doing, and he didn't want her to rise quite yet.

"I need to get up, big guy." She leaned as far as she could and scratched him behind the ears.

He made little grunting noises as he leaned into her. She could get used to this. She'd assumed K9s were aloof and all work, but Sherlock was a regular dog when he wasn't working. "I owe you a big debt." She moved to the other ear, forcing her to stretch more than her body wanted to.

He leaned back and licked her fingers, then jumped off the sofa and headed for the kitchen. Apparently, he'd decided she could get up now as requested. After freshening up, she found Chris in the kitchen on the phone. As she poured herself a cup of coffee from the pot Chris had started, she listened to him.

"The evidence will get there later today. They are both in custody with the Poplar Bend police. I know there's a conflict of interest with both the force here and your office, but someone needs to take this on."

She couldn't hear what was said on the other end but knew Chris would tell her. She grabbed a stale doughnut from the fridge. She'd picked them up days before, but hunger made her ignore the dryness.

"Sounds good. That's acceptable. We'll be there a little after noon." He hung up the phone and smiled at her. "Good morning."

She felt differently about him this morning. Without the case between them, she was free to examine exactly what she wanted, and more time with Chris was exactly what the doctor ordered. She sat down across from him. "I finally got a little sleep. It felt good."

He nodded. "I'm glad. You were starting to get a little restless about half hour ago, so I got up, started the coffee, and called the field office."

"I heard. What's the plan?" She took a tentative sip of the coffee and let the brew work its wonders.

"I need to gather everything from your house and get it packed up. Then, we need to contact your insurance company and get a car for you. Finally, we need to go to Cheyenne and deliver all the evidence from this case."

"Which means I'll also need to go into the office briefly. What is your plan now that the case is all but finished?" She wanted him to stay, but there was no reason for him to. He'd lose his job if he did. The department here was too small for a K9 officer.

He sipped his coffee. "I need to get back home. They've been waiting for me. I was only supposed to be here for a day. No rest for the weary." He laughed.

"What about us?" She prayed she didn't sound demanding. The last thing she wanted him to believe was that she was like his ex.

"I want to continue seeing you. If we can make it work. You've become special to me, and I'd like to see where that leads." He reached for her hand.

Warmth from his coffee mug made his fingers toasty where he rested them over hers. "I never thought I'd feel the same. I've rejected the whole idea of dating with any kind of seriousness, until now. Can we make it work, three hours away from each other?"

Her phone rang, and Chris reached back and retrieved it for her. She answered without looking at the caller ID. So few people ever used her landline that it had to be someone she knew. "Hello?"

"Marin, this is Chief Lohan. I was just made aware of the situation over there in Poplar Bend. Everyone I spoke to in that office said you're the most likely candidate to replace Sargeant Colder. He may be found innocent, but he'll be held in jail until his hearing. The judge has already denied bail to both of them early this morning."

"Oh . . ." She wasn't sure she wanted that position. With her discomfort the last time she set foot in the office, she didn't think she wanted to work for this police force after today. "Can I have time to think about it? I really need to take bereavement leave. My sister was one of those allegedly killed by Leo and Ben."

"I hadn't heard that part, and I didn't assume it was the case since your name was on the case notes. What in the world was he doing over there? Don't answer that. It was hyperbole. Yes, you can contact me after your leave. You have my condolences."

They ended the call, and she set the phone down, letting the stress of the conversation settle over her. When would all the stress end? When would life go back to normal?

"What was that about?" Chris asked.

"They want me to take Leo's position."

Chris tilted his head slightly in a look that reminded her of Sherlock and made her chuckle.

"And you don't want it?"

She shook her head. "I don't know for sure, but the way I'm feeling right now, the answer is no."

He bowed his head for a moment, then looked at her. "I know

this might sound crazy, but I'm going to say it anyway. I have a really good friend on the force in Cheyenne. He's an investigator, and he needs a partner. Everyone who's tried to get into the position hasn't fit the need. I know you would fit perfectly. I wouldn't tell you about this if I didn't think you were capable."

He thought she did such a good job that she would be better than the previous candidates? "What if he decides my work is trash too? Then I'll be in Cheyenne with no future."

"You'll always have a future. And you'll have me close by."

She couldn't hold back a grin. "I'd like to meet your friend when we're in Cheyenne. If he thinks I should apply, I will." Now that she had no ties to Poplar Bend, there was no point in staying. Her house would sell. That was the only reservation.

"Then let's get started."

🐾

After gathering everything they'd needed from Marin's office and deciding she'd get a rental car in Cheyenne where they had more than one car to choose from, they dropped off the evidence with Ben's partner at the FBI field office.

Leaving the evidence there lifted a weight off her shoulders. He'd even given her a photocopy of the letter from Alyssa. She couldn't keep the original, but he was glad she'd been able to keep that. Now, Chris had to take her over to meet Stephen Bund, Chief Investigator for the Cheyenne PD.

He brought her into the office and felt the eyes of every cop in the room follow Marin as they made their way through the building and back to the large room with the desks of the six investigators. Stephen rose the moment they walked in.

"Chris, good to see you back. I was worried when you weren't around for a few days. Who's this?" He eyed her with slight suspicion.

Chris gave Marin a grin he hoped would alleviate any stress.

"This is my friend Marin Bayless. She worked as the investigator for Poplar Bend up until today, though she hasn't given her official resignation quite yet. She may be looking for a position here in Cheyenne."

Stephen's brows rose slowly. "I'd be willing to talk to you, hear about how you handle cases, and what kind of things you've done. I can't guarantee a job, but there is an opening."

"Thank you," she said as she reached out and shook his hand.

Stephen was a workaholic who'd driven away the only woman who had enough patience to put up with him. Like, New York, far away. Chris knew what Stephen meant when others couldn't read him. Most thought he was insensitive and cold. He wasn't, he gave far too much to his career and not enough to himself or anyone else.

"Sounds good. I'll be in touch," she said.

He handed her a business card, and they left the building. She turned to face him. "What do we do now? I can't stay here until I sell my house and find an apartment, but I don't want to leave. I don't want to be there without you."

He gently drew her close. "I know. My apartment is going to feel so weird after the last few days. Promise me you'll call and let me know you made it home?"

She nodded. "I will, and I've decided to take my two weeks of time that they owe me and put in my two weeks' notice at the same time. I'll clean out my desk on the way out. If Stephen doesn't think I qualify, I'll find another job. I'm ready for a fresh start."

He kissed the top of her head. "I'm ready for that too. With you."

She stepped back far enough to look him in the eyes. "I'm ready, and I can't wait to see what God has in store for the both of us."

MINI TESTIMONY

I didn't really believe in earthly angels until . . .

I was newly married and right in the middle of my college education. Since I'd lived on campus the first two years of my education, then got married, I wasn't properly initiated into driving in Minnesota in the winter. The snow had been coming down for a few hours, and I was coming off of a six-hour shift after a day at the U of M campus.

My husband got off work at the same time I did, and we both left at the same time. He was right behind me as I pulled out of the parking lot and onto a short road before we had to turn onto a street that was fairly busy all the time. In good weather, you still had to lay on the gas to make a left-hand turn.

I waited and waited for a spot where there was more than a few seconds to blast through because I knew it was icy. I had slid to a stop at the stop sign and knew it would take a few seconds for my tires to grip. I didn't want to get broadsided by a car that couldn't stop. Did I mention this was on a hill? Once I crossed traffic and turned, I would be heading down a sharp hill, meaning oncoming traffic was going up a hill (and they were struggling). It was clearly icy, and everyone just wanted to get home.

Someone behind me honked. I know it wasn't my husband, but by then there was a line of cars waiting. I saw what I hoped would be adequate time and hit the gas. My tires spun. I prayed. I inched across the lane as a car barreled toward me. There was no escaping it. I was going to get hit. I didn't have enough traction.

My rear tires slid as I turned the wheel, praying to avoid a crash. In that same instant, the man in the car coming at me hit the same patch of ice and we spun in tandem, then separated. He ended up going in the opposite direction in his lane. I ended up going in the opposite direction in mine.

I was so shaken up that I couldn't move. I cried. I shook. One of my coworkers rushed to my car and banged on the window to see if I was okay. I still don't know how he made it across that road without slipping. He told me there were only inches between our cars. If he'd seen it anywhere else, he would've thought it was staged.

Daniel 10 talks about an angel fighting the spirit of Persia to answer Daniel's prayer. He'd been fasting for three weeks, and the Lord sent an angel to tell him he was precious to God, that angels assist in fighting the powers and spirits of darkness around us, is comforting. I was comforted after that, knowing that I was protected that day. It was nothing I did.

I can't answer why the Lord heard that urgent prayer and answered immediately and sometimes He doesn't. I can't even speculate. But I will say some experiences leave you knowing there is a God who sees YOU.

For my full testimony, visit www.karitrumbo.com/testimony.

READY FOR MORE?

Don't miss the next anthology collection from Two Dogs Publishing, coming in April 2026!

Four stories of sweet Christian romantic adventure! Featuring authors Megan Besing, Tabitha Bouldin, Andrea Christenson and Rebecca Reed, you're not going to want to miss this.

Scan the QR code below to learn more.

Do you love anthologies?

Sign up for the Two Dogs Newsletter to stay up-to-date on upcoming collections and releases, as well as news from our partner authors that have been included in previous releases! Scan or tap the QR code below.